MURDER

is against the

L A W

BUT....

MURDER

is against the

LAW

BUT . . . .

PATRICIA GRAVES

MURDER IS AGAINST THE L A W BUT . . .

iUniverse books may be ordered through booksellers or by contacting:

iUniverse
1663 Liberty Drive
Bloomington, IN 47403
www.iuniverse.com
1-800-Authors (1-800-288-4677)

Because of the dynamic nature of the Internet, any web addresses or links contained in this book may have changed since publication and may no longer be valid. The views expressed in this work are solely those of the author and do not necessarily reflect the views of the publisher, and the publisher hereby disclaims any responsibility for them.

Any people depicted in stock imagery provided by Thinkstock are models, and such images are being used for illustrative purposes only.
Certain stock imagery © Thinkstock.

ISBN: 978-1-5320-3097-0 (sc)
ISBN: 978-1-5320-3096-3 (e)

Library of Congress Control Number: 2017912625

Print information available on the last page.

iUniverse rev. date: 09/22/2017

Dedicated in loving memory of Kenny and David my brothers forever and Hilda and Joe Evans best beloved aunt and uncle ever, rest in peace.

Shameeka and khaseem Thomas, Ebbin Herring, Daryl Graves and God-daughter Khadijah Williams.

Special thanks to Joann Laughlin History and Law Professor at Salem Community College. Who gave the toughest assignments and critiqued them with a vengeance. Dr. Edmar Lacay and Dr. Manish DaDhania Cooper Physicians, whose medical knowledge and encouragement proved invaluable.

And Kenneth Ritter the first reader of this story who concluded that I was Wile E. Coyote – Super genius.

One

Murder is against the law, but some people need to die. And not only die-they first need to be tortured in the worst conceivable manner consistent with their crimes against humanity in order to perceive an understanding of how their actions hurt, abused and destroyed their victims. The guilty should not be spared from looking into the eyes of their executioner so they're forced to become aware of the what, where and why of their death. They should be fully aware that the eyes their own eyes were drowning in belong to a human being whose livelihood they attempted to or perhaps did destroy simply because those bosses possessed the arrogance and power to undo another person's life, employment and in some cases their sanity. It's just a game to them, the powerful bosses, Chapter 11, Page 112, in 'THE GREAT BOOK OF DIRTY TRICKS' Recommended reading for bullies, dictators, sadomasochist, ego maniacs and tyrannical employers who need instructions for flexing their muscles on subordinates who had no choice but to bow to their persecutors. These tyrants are the powerful bosses at the top who answer to no one and specialize in the terrorizing and intimidation of their employees. They teach abject lessons in tyranny, constantly reminding their victims of just who is the boss and when it comes to employee sabotage, they are equal opportunity saboteurs; their way or the highway.

The persecuted individual could probably visualize the execution or death of their evil, tyrannical boss at their hands. The desire is continuously fueled by ongoing abuse and unfair treatment which in most cases result in retaliatory termination of the employee. The abused employee relishes the vision of the tips of their fingers meeting each other around that wrinkled, scrawny, worn out neck with its multiple layers of desiccated hanging flesh. It would snap like a brittle twig. How many times has the abused and bullied employee fought the temptation to just reach out and shake the neck of their bosses until the head boggles back and forth

1

like a leaf blowing helplessly in a hurricane? Just imagining it would be an overwhelming temptation for the employee. Thumbs crushing that protruding Adams Apple that bobbed up and down when the boss spoke. Only it couldn't bob now because the abused victim's thumbs were pressing it down into the back of their boss's throat, squeezing harder and harder. The abused person would watch as their persecutor's eyes grew larger and larger; while their mind gleefully laughs singing, "Pop goes the weasel!" The tormented person can see their face reflected back at them and in that reflection their eyes are calm, reassured and satisfyingly happy. There is a certain maniacal hilarity mingled with the tenebrous connection of insanity in the employee's mind. They are finally killing their boss whom they felt deserved to die and that was just fine. They are putting an end to the abuse. The victims of the oppressors would feel no remorse at what they are doing, would accept no pleading. The employee's ears have drowned out the strangled, gurgling sounds of trapped oxygen in their persecutor's throat because no air is allowed to escape. This could be the scenario of an employee who has had enough of daily terrorism from the boss. The employee whose day ended with the boss informing them with a smile on their face, that they are fired! It could be if every day normal people were capable of murder.

Exactly, what is the mindset of the irrational, abusive boss? I'm not speaking about the mean boss who wants you to work overtime without compensation or refuses lunches or breaks. I'm speaking about the evil boss who is an expert at manipulation, a huge narcissist, isn't familiar with the term empathy; has psychopathic tendencies, compulsive-obsessive behavior disorders with just a touch of madness. These types of bosses are nurtured by high positions that they feel they are entitled to and when achieved they simply don't know how to act. Their entire personality changes and they become strangers to their previous peers. The once easy going peer is now caught up in their own power over others, and they use that power to make life difficult and impossible for their subordinates. Where there is no problem; this type of boss creates them and is never satisfied no matter what corrections the employee make. The fear and anxiety these bosses invoke in their employees is like a drug to them. They are addicted and required several 'fixes' daily. These types of bosses might commit suicide rather than accept a demotion or termination. It is completely unacceptable that they aren't running the show. What is remarkable about this type of boss is that they never consider the possibility that an employee will retaliate against them because of abusive treatment or unfair termination; yet it does happen as in the case of the archetypal postal worker who appeared at work armed and killed everyone in the office.

Most abused employees seek retaliation but only in their minds. They realize that they are incapable of acts of violence or revenge. They are unable to shoot, stab or strangle their boss and so they accept their lot in life. Then there is the employee who can kill but are hindered by thoughts of going to jail. Finally there is the employee who can do the deed; who plots and plans to commit murder. This particular employee doesn't attack blindly but plans what they are going to do to the boss and has no intention of getting caught. This employee determines that the boss can be killed without the spilling of blood or the use of bullets, knives or blunt objects. Are there methods of murder that are undetectable, can't be attached to a perpetrator and won't involve the law because there's no actual crime committed against a victim or victims? No, murder is murder and is a crime no matter how it's done or whether or not it's detected. It's not against the law to desire to murder someone because it's a mental longing, only thought about in the mind. But if it's carried out physically; it is murder and it is a crime with detectability, in most cases, being only a matter of time. What's unacceptable by society is the actual act of murder, the method is secondary. Will the world crumble to a fine powder, the economy come crashing down, planes fall from the skies and frogs leave the waters if some particular person or persons disappear or are murdered? There're billions of people in the world and hundreds of them disappear every day on their own or through foul play. Who is going to miss another four or five of them? They'd just drop from sight; sort of like entering a Raid Roach Motel: 'Roaches check in but they don't check out' Oh there are the slight exceptions of skeletons found buried in basements or half decomposed bodies growing moss and maggots after hasty burials deep in the woods. Most are found in the case of physical murder, but physical murder is not what the abused employee is concerned with here today. This particular employee is contemplating symbolic, imaginative murder

3

that leaves the victim alive, uninjured (sort of) and confused about what has happened. Trying to figure out how the subordinate managed to fire the boss!

In the meantime, what exactly is going on in the mind of the tormented and later terminated employee? Why has the employee decided that the boss must die? Could it be the seeking of some form of justice or is it simply revenge for the way they were treated that will bring them satisfaction? When the seeds of revenge are planted they will take root, because they have been so lovingly fertilized with abuse and tyranny. These seeds won't be concerned with reaching sun light; their purpose is not to bear fruit or flowers. The sole purpose is revenge. The employee has mentally crossed over to the dark side and couldn't find their way back with a map, compass and flashlight. The only sane thoughts going on in that mind, along with the decision to commit murder, is that there should be no room for error, mercy or remorse. The victim must never be seen again with the only trace of them remaining being in the fond memories of those who knew them well and those too would gradually dim with time. Is the motivation revenge? Of course, what else could it be in all honesty that is, when you plan a murder to exact payment for an injustice? It's of course premeditated, but being that it's not a physical murder what's the harm? There's no need to involve the law. When the injustices won't leave the employee's waking mind, invading their sleep like a swarm of mosquitoes incessantly drawing blood from punctured wounds; only to return again for more blood. Constant reminders of what has hurt them to the point of teeth grinding, insomnia and cries for retribution. Their nightmares are huge panoramic ventures where they are trapped running down endless corridors that bend back on themselves and worst of all is the huge specter of their employer's face suspended dreamlike over their head screaming like some deranged banshee. The employee would be snatched from these nightmares covered with sweat, confusion and fear until sleep becomes unbearable and in the reality of the morning they are still in the same position, fired.

Never mind that old saying that revenge is best served cold. If you're going to serve anybody anything other than a tennis ball, it should be smoking hot and steaming fresh from an oven preferably set at broil, or else why bother. A person must know themselves as well as their adversary when seeking revenge; because it's never a straight path. Instead it's a dangerous winding road fought with peril through dense forest with very little light to guide one to civility or sanity. It's easy to become lost in that forest, forget where you came in and become forgotten among the foliage. The victims of workplace abuse and bullying enters into the forest of revenge by way of their minds, dreams, depression and the decision that they just weren't going to take it anymore. Janet Nelson entered the forest through the doors of the administrative building of the Sawyer Developmental Center, following the path to the Human Resources Office where she applied for her first job as a virginal, naïve, shy and quiet nineteen year old book worm with no close friends or ambitions. She had the kind of open, innocent, fearful, demeanor that proclaimed to the world, victim. Everyday panhandlers ignored all the people passing them until they spied Janet Nelson and they hit her up for money and she always gave it to them. Something about her screamed, "If you ask me, I'll give it to you." Due to early childhood experiences she'd morphed, over the years, into a woman who was intelligent, manipulative, calculating, and treacherous. And in her there was no room for mercy or remorse...

There was something inside of the young child that was Janet that would years later be comparable to biting on tin foil. This thing or perhaps it was an instinct of self-preservation, was buried deep inside of her and would make its initial debut in the kitchen of her home and years later in high school it would resurface again. She wasn't aware of any inner strength existing inside of her; if it was there it was buried deep where it slept. This sleeping beast wasn't another personality, it was just the part of her that hadn't awaken but when it did, it would likened itself as a sort of protector, an avenger of sorts who would turn her into an angry, bitter, soulless street fighter who had very little or more appropriately no fear. There would be no meekness or weakness in that part of her and it would do whatever was necessary, by any means necessary, without looking back. That part of her would never back down from anybody or anything that affected negatively in her world, nor would it concern itself with the power or stature of her enemies. This thing in her wouldn't believe in the credo

5

that you can't fight City Hall. People believed this only because they'd heard it so repetitively. What they essentially believed was a propagated, unfounded lie spread by people who were afraid or unable to fight because they lacked courage, tenacity and anger. The meek are intimidated by power and simply give up, accepting the consequences. The only thing Janet Nelson would recognize when the fight came to her door step was that absolute power; corrupted absolutely. Sure there would be battles she'd lose; but the losses would not be due to giving up and failures were lessons to be learned. There would be those who would reluctantly give up in a fight against her, give her the respect she was due and wisely back off; as well as those too arrogant, self-important and too stupid to do so. Whomever she faced in battle would more sooner than later recognize her as a burning, itching hemorrhoid in their ass that no amount of cold compresses could soothe and the pharmacist was out of Preparation 'H' Enemies had best fasten their seat belts and hold on because it was going to be a bumpy ride.

In the silent, dark, twisting corridors of Janet's brain a sort of life had begun. That life might have been called a tumor. No one actually knows why tumors develop on the brain, they just do; beginning as a mass of tissue that's formed and enlarged by an accumulation of more abnormal cells. Janet's tumor began from the accumulation of mental, physical and sexual abuse at home and bullying in high school. Normally the cells in our bodies develop, age, die and are replaced by new cells. This normal cellular cycle was interrupted and corrupted in Janet's brain. Tumor cells grow even though the body doesn't need them (with the exception of Janet's body) and unlike normal old cells, hers didn't die, they aggressively multiplied. With Janet, the aggressive growth was not due to cells attaching to the original mass but the tumor grew in size from the accumulation of abuses, unwarranted beatings from both her mother and stepfather and bullying at school. A place she considered as her own personal Dachau; where she wore an invisible sign that read: 'Kick me.' Tumors are basically characterized as being benign, non-aggressive and non-cancerous or malignant which are cancerous, typically growing fast and aggressively invading surrounding tissues and organs, spreading death. Although brain cancer rarely spreads to other organs, it will attack other parts of the brain and central nervous system resulting in eventual death but Janet's tumor was sort of an enigma. Its mission did not involve discovery, spreading, surgery, chemotherapy, radiotherapy, a healthy diet and a hopeful recovery. The cells of her brain tumor were composed of dark, destructive, renegade hell machines careening along the dark, electric pathways of her brain. They weren't seeking healthy tissues to implant and destroy on a psychotic mission of death. Their mission was charged with self-preservation, defense and offense and no, this is not the way brain tumors are supposed to behave. There was a definite method to its madness and its reasons for coming into being. Janet's tumor was born and incubated for the sole purpose of compensating for Janet's inability to cope with the abuse and hate surrounding her in her young life. It had been silently incubating for years, not yet matured, when it found it necessary to poke it's one monstrous tentacle out for barely a second and touch the speech portion of Janet's brain and caused her to scream, "No!" to the probing fingers of Mr. Three Fingers of Death. Afterwards it went back to sleep for over ten years which was an extraordinary amount of time in which to grow many numerous, strong, malicious and dangerous tentacles that would make its debut years later in her high school hallway. She would be her own self defense mechanism although it was not always present and not to be counted on to rise to any occasion. It surfaced only in times of extreme emotional stress or fear. It would appear in the form of fear stimulating her fight or flight mechanisms. This tumor, enveloped within a cocoon of rage and anger would turn her into a vicious viper whose attack would be unannounced and deadly, struggling indignantly against its cocoon to get out; beating in a whirl wind of indignation that the web of its cocoon would dare stand in its way. It would be during extreme moments of fear that the tumor's actions would burst free and the conscience part of her mind would no longer exist. Janet would never know when she actually lost control of conscious thought but the tumor did and it would be in control. Its intervention wasn't always necessary in all situations that Janet would find herself involved in; but when it surfaced it was Janet's protector against all dangers even when the odds were insurmountable and she was totally out of her league. The tumor in Janet's brain was a lunatic cell; a splinter of wood destined to find a tender organ to pierce, infiltrate and destroy as it cruised along raising lots of inactive benign tumors. Janet could by no stretch of the imagination be termed a predator but through the actions of those around her she would learn to become one. As for now, in the beginning, she was just the shy, quiet, unobtrusive, mousey Janet Nelson trying to keep a low profile in the world.

Two

Janet's earliest memories of her childhood began at age six; before that there was nothing. Janet had no idea what she looked like physically because there were no pictures of her from birth to age six. The first picture she'd ever seen of herself was of the school photograph of her first grade class. There she was standing in the first row where all the shorter students stood and her shyness stood out like a beacon. Her long, dark hair was out and spread across her shoulders with long bangs that almost completely covered her eyes. She was a tiny, light-brown skinned girl with skinny arms and legs. Her cat like brown eyes could barely be seen as her head was slightly bowed as if she was afraid of being caught on camera. Wearing a plain white, knee length, dress with a red belt, ankle white socks and black and white shoes, she was the only child in a class of twenty-eight who wasn't smiling in the picture, she looked scared and vulnerable, as if her body would shatter into pieces at a yell. It was both strange to her that no matter how hard she searched her memory they always began at age six. She was the illegitimate child of a mother who represented nothing to her aside from hurt and alienation. Her mother never talked to her unless it concerned questions that required answers and her father was never mentioned. Janet was afraid of her mother's silence towards her and that silence was returned because Janet never really knew what to say to her or how to say it. She didn't understand what it meant when she caught her mother staring at her with disgust on her face and what seemed like hate in her eyes and it frightened her. It confused Janet that no matter how much she searched her memory she could find no instance of her mother hugging or kissing her and she kept these confused feelings locked inside of her. Her mother was a tall woman whose face showed signs of resignation at the world until she caught religion. Janet had never heard her laugh and smiles were few and far apart. She was a handsome woman with long dark hair, stern arched eyebrows and the same brown cat's eyes she'd passed onto Janet. Her mouth was always set in a stern tight line and she had a no nonsense approach to life and was extremely short on patience. This attitude deepened when she became a Jehovah's Witness. She stressed and maintained the rules of no engagement with the world unless it was with people of her religion. She labeled all holidays as pagan, so birthdays, Christmases and Thanksgiving were not celebrated in the home. Janet was made to study the bible Monday through Sunday and if she did anything her mother perceived as 'worldly' she was punished and had to write bible scriptures. They lived in a third floor apartment that opened up on a living room that led to the kitchen in one direction and her mother's bedroom and then Janet's bedroom off to the side. The furnishings of the rooms of her home were also a blank in Janet's mind. She could only recall the kitchen. Her memory was hauntingly clear and powerful of the kitchen and the day she came home and found herself alone in the house with her stepfather. This man came into her life from out of nowhere. All she knew was that one day while sitting outside reading a book on the front porch her mother called her upstairs. She ran up the three flights of stairs (it never paid to tarry when called) and into the house. She found her mother in the kitchen standing next to a tall, black man, a stranger, who was standing next to her mother with his arm around her waist. Her mother began speaking words that she understood; yet were alien to her comprehension. Janet understood English perfectly well but she couldn't quite grasp what her mother was saying to her, she wasn't making any sense. *Did she? Did she just say this is my new father?* Janet's mind questioned along with the fact that she'd never met her old father. Janet's eyes went slowly back and forth between her mother and the stranger with disquieting uncertainty and wariness. With her head slightly bowed, she cautiously peaked from beneath her long eye lashes at the man who seemed a giant; and not a gentle green one. She saw a huge, dark man staring down at her with a twisted, creepy, grin and a mouth of yellowed teeth. His presence in the not so large kitchen seemed to blot out all thoughts in her mind and light in the kitchen; darkness he was and darkness he would remain. Her mother repeated to her stunned child that this was here new father and at that mind numbing introduction no one said hello. The stranger removed his arm from her mother's waist, leaned over and lifted Janet up and hugged her to himself and she was speechless, frozen in his arms, her arms and legs rigid as he held her against his chest in a hug that made her skin shudder and she felt, lasted too long. When he finally sat her back down on her feet, his arm returned to the waist of her mother who seemed a little tense as she was propelled by that arm out of the kitchen. Janet, still bewildered, watched them walk out of the kitchen. Whenever the wedding of her mother and that troll of a man had taken place Janet didn't know; she hadn't been invited to the wedding.

Janet could vividly recall being six years old and running home after dismissal from her first grade class. She had run as fast as she could, her books clutched tightly to front of her white blouse and her checkered black and white skirt trailing in the wind. She was very anxious to finish reading a book called Tom Sawyer. She'd left the book on the kitchen cabinet and had last left Tom Sawyer rafting down the Mississippi River. She dashed up the three flights of stairs to her apartment, entered the living room and ran into the kitchen. At the kitchen door way she came to an abrupt halt and all thoughts of Tom Sawyer drained from her mind. She stood there in the door way; a tiny, brown skinned girl with two long, thick braids of black hair hanging down her back and long bangs covering her eyebrows, and brown cat-like eyes that were wide with indecision. Her tiny mouth was a complete circle of surprise swiftly followed by apprehension and fear realizing that she was alone in the house; in the kitchen, with him, the stepfather. She stood there clutching her school books tighter to her chest. It was the first time that she'd really taken a good look at him. He was a tall hulking man with a deep brown complexion whose huge head was completely bald, except for bristles of short stubbly hairs over his ears. He had a wide over hanging forehead with three deep grooves etched across it over almost non-existent eyebrows. His eyes were nothing short of frightening to Janet who'd developed the habit of never looking directly at them because she always froze under his gaze. There were no lashes that she could see surrounding his piercing black cobra eyes that had a sick, yellow, rummy look to them where they should have been white and puffy layers of eye bags hung beneath each eye. He had a thick neck with lots of tiny protruding moles and a powerful barreled chest from which large muscular gorilla arms hung and he was missing a thumb and index finger on his right hand. Looking at that hand always produced goosebumps in her and she'd mentally shut down whenever he touched. He made her skin crawl. It was that hand which led to her naming him 'Three Fingers of Death' and Janet had hated him from the beginning with a child's blended conception of fear and mistrust. She never spoke to him; always made herself scarce when he was home and no amount of beatings (of which there'd be many) could induce her to call him 'Daddy' When home he always wore the type of white tee shirt that was later given the auspicious name of 'Wife beater' tee shirts. The shirt was tucked into the band of his work pants which were held up with a thick, black, evil looking leather belt that Janet would come to know intimately through beatings yet to come. He had a deep booming voice that kind of grumbled deep in his throat when he spoke. Janet's fear of him was in all ways adult, primitive, with no pre-history; it just existed. She had come upon him sitting sideways at the dilapidated white kitchen table with its rusting legs held steady by pieces of folded newspaper beneath two of its legs. He was staring at her with those petrifying eyes and Janet, withdrawing into herself, remained frozen in the kitchen doorway. She cast her eyes down to the faded linoleum whose edges were curling at the ends as if they were trying to escape from the kitchen walls. "Come here." He rumbled at her when he saw her standing in the doorway and she whimpered inside at the summons which filled her with fear. She was alone and the thought to disobey never entered her mind as she took slow, apprehensive, robotic steps over to him. He was sitting sideways at the kitchen table, hunched over, his large hands dangled between his legs and his beefy forearms rested on his thighs. When she was within his reach, his arm suddenly shot out, grabbed her, turned her around and drew her backwards into the gap between his long legs. In one swift motion she felt his three fingered hand beneath her skirt, lifting the edge of her white cotton panties and pushing their way up inside of her and she froze in shock. The further he pushed up inside of her the more she rose up on her tippy toes. In her frightened, stunned mind a picture was forming of fat, hot, wiggling, worms pushing around the place where she peed; she didn't know the word vagina. Her revulsion and panic was dynamic but she didn't dare attempt to move away. It wasn't fear that held her still between his legs while his finders probed around seeking she did not know what inside of her, she just knew without a spoken word that she must remain still, and she did. She began trembling and her mind retreated to thoughts that told her that this was not happening and she should pretend it wasn't. She looked up at the kitchen ceiling and began counting the squares of the ceiling tiles from one corner to the other. She noticed for the first time that each of the ceiling squares had an 'X' inside of it and there were tiny ruffled flowers around the edges of each white connecting square. She felt his fingers moving inside of her and inhaling deeply she continued counting the ceiling squares. She was not in the kitchen of her home. She was not between this man's legs and certainly there wasn't anything going on inside of her panties. Her concentration suddenly shattered when she felt his scratchy beard on the side of her face, big slobbery lips against her ear and a coarse weathered whisper, "Do you like that?" A dizzying swoon filled with revulsion overcame her at the sound of his voice. She didn't like it! She didn't know if her response was due to his touch, his question or the sound of his voice in her ear; deep, dark and clotted as if broken branches, twigs and dried leaves were trapped in his throat but she screamed a child's horrified, frightened scream of one word, "No!" His whispering broke into the loud bellow of a wounded animal, "You're too sassy!" he screamed as he pulled his three-fingered hand from beneath her skirt and slapped her a blow that sent her spinning across the kitchen floor. She slammed into the sink cabinet where she crumpled into a heap of pain onto the floor as droplets of blood began dripping from her nose and the corner of her mouth onto her white blouse. At the exact moment of the slap Janet's mother had stepped into the kitchen. She saw her mother's face twice because the force behind the blow caused her to spin around twice as she hurtled towards the sink. Lying on the floor, she turned frightened, pleading eyes towards her mother and her mind sort of flipped-flopped because no emotion could be seen on her mother's face and her eyes were devoid of sympathy. There was nothing to be gleamed from her composed, unconcerned features. Janet continued staring incredulously at her mother, wondering why there was no outraged shock, no cry of anguish followed by rushing feet to come to the aid and protection of her child. Why wasn't she furiously attacking this man who'd dare do such a thing to her child? Why didn't she call the police? Her mother merely stood in the doorway calm and indifferent; as if she were watching a television program that she wasn't particularly interested in. Looking not at her husband; but at her only child bleeding on the floor she spoke saying incredible words that devastated Janet's mind for days. Her mother asked her in a blasé manner, "What did you do now?" Janet didn't know the word flabbergasted but that is what she was when she was asked that question. It was undeniable what her husband had been doing but she gave no indication of that knowledge. You couldn't misinterpret the scene, yet her mother dismissed it, her response was no response. Janet dropped her eyes from her mother's face too stunned to even cry. Devastating of all was the sight of her mother being led arm in arm from the kitchen by her stepfather, leaving her fractured and abused daughter bleeding on the floor. As they left the kitchen, Three Fingers of Death's eyes leered back at her over his shoulder and she shuddered at the look as he said, "Don't you have something to do besides sitting on the floor? Go clean the bathroom!" Still no tears came but they were there; as she stood up on unsteady legs that threatened to drop her back to the floor. It was then that the tears welled into her eyes and were about to fall when a voice spoke in her head, "Don't cry! Don't you dare cry!" Janet didn't know where that voice came from but it was both demanding and compassionate and she listened. It was in that moment that Janet began the practice of suffering in silence. She was on her own. And this was what she believed, while in the back of her mind she wondered if it would happen again. Somehow she knew it would and she was afraid. It was an adolescent beginning lesson that she carried throughout her young years, being afraid and to suffer in silence. And in silence she did suffer, letting anyone and everyone bully her, accepting every abuse against her in silence. If someone hit her she didn't hit back, if someone demanded money from her, she supplied it, if she was physically hurt or injured, she never went for help, and if someone purposely knocked her down on the ground, she would simply get up and go on her way. She never appealed for help from anyone in authority and worst of all she suffered all in silence.

Three

Years later, people were still talking about what happened at the high school. The story had acquired mythical status and its main characters were in the eyes of many, legends. Many students and teachers who were not there claimed they were and those who were claimed to have tried to break up the fight. Others claimed they were the ones that ran for the security guards; and still others claimed they were on the school's roof when the ambulance helicopter lifted off carrying a child's torn, bloody body. There had been one medic present on the school's roof top who would never forget (courtesy of reoccurring nightmares) the sight of the severely mangled child's body that caused him, a twenty year veteran, to violently expel his lunch. He'd never seen such desecration to a child done by another child and his brain suffered extreme difficulty accepting what he was seeing. He had been momentarily confused as to which part of the body to stabilize first; the thumb which dangled over the wrist, the arm which was twisted and lying at three impossible angles, the shoulder, which was shattered, the naked, exposed ribs of the chest cracked and protruding outward, the missing tip of the nose (missing?) the four bloody sockets where once living teeth lived or the eye that was dangling from a dark bloody hole.

The only thing they, faculty, students and security guards, all agreed on was the sound of running feet, slamming doors, cries of fight and the spine numbing sounds of agonized screaming. Many suffered nightmarish dreams of those screams from which they clawed their way out from, leaving them disorientated and just a little frightened. Many students required counselling, while some were transferred out of the school by shocked parents, faculty members quit, others were fired and there were lawsuits flying all over the place. There were different versions of what happened from the students and faculty but all who knew Janet Nelson and Alfreda Whitehurst agreed that it was bound to happen eventually. Alfreda was a bully and Janet was a victim.

Charlie Johnson sat behind the desk in the spacious Principal's office. Once this office, with it solemn atmosphere and paneled walls, had intimidated him with the responsibility it represented. Large portraits of former Principals sending silent messages that he'd better not screw up decorated the walls. His portrait would be next on the wall. The U.S. flag (which Charlie saluted every morning) drooped on its pole in one corner of the office next to glassed in articles and awards given over the years, a row of green file cabinets containing pertinent information on staff and students and a large revolving ceiling fan to keep everything cool. At first, Charlie took to comparing himself to King Sisyphus, who in Greek mythology was cursed to repeatedly roll a huge boulder up a mountain which summarily crashed back down every time he reached the top. Charlie Johnson had reached the pinnacle of his career, high school principal but suffered feelings of anxiety that it would all come crashing down around him. His fear of his job was as real as the night fears of children afraid of what they couldn't see in the dark corners of their bedrooms at night. He'd waited over ten years for this position and now he had it and he was terrified of the responsibility. He had been stunned to learn that he had been appointed to the position. He never knew of the many better qualified individuals with Masters Degrees (of which he was sorely missing) who had flatly refused the position. The Board of Education was at the bottom of the barrel with one lone marble rolling around inside it and that marble was Charlie Johnson. It was no small wonder why the others ran for cover when offered the position at Grant High school because it housed the bulk of the district's criminal youths, drug dealers, users, pregnant teenagers, bullies and victims. These were the children whose parents saw the school day as a chance to get the kids out of their hair for half a day. Parents who could care less what their kids did as long as they were out of the house. They weren't the type to take a day off if summoned by the school to discuss their child's activities; not if it interrupted their sleep, day time soap operas, game shows or their jobs. It was due to a combination of an overzealous witch hunt by the Board of Education, the fanatic zest of reporters reporting the catastrophe that left three students dead, dozens of broken limbs, concussions and the death of his own daughter (found buried beneath other fallen students) that he avoided termination. He was, after all the Principal and responsibility began and ended at his door. King Sisyphus's boulder had rolled back down the mountain literally crushing everything in its path. After eleven years on the job, the early intimidations had long since dissipated like the remnants of a nightmare whose strength waxed, waned and dissolved away as soon as you woke up and you could no longer remembered what had frightened you. His days behind the desk had coalesced into how many cross word puzzles he could solve before lunch or should he smoke his daily joint in his office or his car or how could he get his hands down into the blouse of his voluptuous secretary. All in all, he had handled the job with some measure of success until the end of one particular day. A still unexplainable day which began for him with a hysterical, wide-eyed teacher bursting into his office screaming his name just as he was in the process of putting a spit seal on his joint and ending with death of his daughter and his hospitalization.

Meanness and stupidity are a bad combination in any scenario to inflict on anyone, especially young children, but attach the features of a 'Gollum' (the creature from the Lord of the Rings) the adolescent fear of the boogey man in the closet, the bully in the school and archeologist theories on the existence of the missing link and you'd have Alfreda Whitehurst. To say Alfreda was ugly as sin was being generous and severely tolerant. She suffered an ugly to the bone type of continence that every day society at large pretended not to notice. Back in the sixties there was a comedy show called 'The Monsters' which featured the father, Herman Monster (Frankenstein) Lily Monster (Dracula's daughter) was the mother, their son Eddie Monster (The Werewolf) and the grandfather was Count Dracula. Their hunchbacked daughter (who missed the auditions) would have been Alfreda Whitehurst. On one episode, the family was assembled together practicing their poses in front of a large mirror for a family portrait. When they smiled into the mirror the entire glass depressed inwards away from their image, cracked into hundreds of jagged pieces and then exploded outwards. One look at that assembled caricatured group and you knew Alfreda Whitehurst would fit right in as the missing link. Adults were kind to Alfreda's shape, size and appearance. As to the children, they simply weren't stupid enough to make any comments, good or bad in front or behind Alfreda's back. It would be tantamount to saying the name 'Voldemort' in the Harry Potter books. In the book series (that spawned seven books, seven movies and its own culture cult) the spoken name was a beacon summoning the bad guy to you. None of the children wanted that recognition. The only safe place to talk about Alfreda was in their minds. It was just plain suicide to say anything out loud about her. If they did they knew with certainty that the result would be something far worse than their childish night fears. Even if her name was whispered in the confines of the school's bathroom to a fellow student, somehow Alfreda found out. None of the children were embarrassed or ashamed of their shared fears of Alfreda, because damn near the entire school, including faculty, were afraid of her. It wasn't a known fact, that she had faculty members on her payroll but it wouldn't have surprised anyone if she did and actually they were correct. Alfreda didn't come right out and say, "Give me some money for lunch!" to the teachers, instead she pleaded that she was hungry and had forgotten her lunch money. She had a smooth, malevolent way of fleecing money from the teachers. There was something in her face and voice that would brook no refusals. When faced with that misshapen head, chaotic features, darting, black, beady crossed eyes, massive hunch backed body, bad breath and body odor in their faces asking could she borrow two dollars for lunch, they were glad to give it to her if not for any other reason than to get her out of their faces. Besides, she always promised she'd give it back 'Tomorrow' which she never did and they never reminded her. Some teachers couldn't open their pocketbooks or fumble around in their pockets fast enough to get the troll out of their faces and class rooms. They knew, like the students, that they weren't going to get their money back. They were only concerned with hoping they had single dollar bills. It wouldn't do to have a five dollar bill. They wouldn't want to give it up but somehow they'd convince themselves that she would bring the change back when they knew she wouldn't. When they saw her later in the hall ways, Alfreda ignored them as they summarily ignored her. Alfreda had no problem laughing out loud as she looked into the eyes of her benefactors passing by in the corridors and they never reminded her of the change she hadn't brought back or the dollars she owed them.

Like all bullies, there was no method to Alfreda Whitehurst's meanness or her quest to dominate, crush, mangle and destroy. Begging or pleading for mercy to her was no more than an expected nuisance. No matter what the victims said there'd still be pain; whether they had money or not and woe to them if they didn't. She prided herself on creating an oppressive atmosphere around her victims. When she walked the school's corridors or entered the playground all activity momentarily ceased. All eyes watched the bully that was Alfreda and relief was energy draining as her popped eyes passed over them, fear followed by relief. Alfreda glorified in her supremeness. It didn't matter to her that she was hated. The only thing important was that she was feared. Alfreda preyed especially on the weak, quiet kids who were loners, never spoke unless spoken to and for all intent purposes were under the radar, invisible. They were her perfect lunch appetizers. They would never fight back or report her to their teachers, parents or older siblings. They could always be counted on and never failed to provide whatever she was seeking at that moment. When her eyes locked on one of them as she approached; they already had their money in their hands and she'd snatch it from them without missing a step. Alfreda generally arrived at school with no money but by lunch time she'd have amassed over twenty dollars from her ever ready to please subjects. Alfreda preyed on the invisible kids and Janet Nelson was one of her favorite temples. On this one particular day it would prove to be a religion she wished she had never subscribed to.

Grant High School was structured like any other school in a large metropolitan city. It was four brick stories high with the first floor demoted to administration, nurse office, guidance counselor offices, auditorium, teachers' lounge and assorted other rooms necessary for the running of a self-sufficient school environment. Its basement was delegated to the lunch room, gym, pool, changing rooms, gym lockers and the boiler room. Its top three floors housed the tenth, eleventh and twelfth grade classrooms. Each floor began and ended with a single set of steel double doors at each end of its corridor. The doors opened onto a steep set of fourteen steel steps, a small curved landing and another set of steps that ended at the steel double doors to the floor below. Each corridor on the top three floors was divided so that there were seven classrooms on both sides of it.

Student lockers lined the walls between the classrooms with a boys and girls bathroom on each floor. Janet Nelson was in her classroom on the second floor with her classmates, all of whom were twenty-five minutes into a forty minute math test and twenty minutes before the end of the school day. The classroom was quiet as is the case when students are testing. The teacher, Mr. Fires sat at his desk flipping through a magazine of cars he could never afford.

Janet was on the next to the last question which read 3/8 x 27/32, multiplying fractions. Janet loved fractions and the complicated steps involved in solving them. She murmured in her mind. First re-write the problem, transposing the second fraction. Now cancel out the available numbers. OK, find the common denominator which is 32. The re-written problem was 3/32 + 27/32. Add the top numbers which equal 30 and the problems answer was 30/32. Reduce the number to its smallest number and the answer is 15/17. As she was admiring her neatly written figures a whispered voice drifted over to her in the quiet, sunny, classroom. She recognized that voice immediately and intimately as well as its owner. Sitting at the desk across from her was Alfreda Whitehurst and a paralyzing chill streaked up her back. Whenever Janet had reason to give any thought to Alfreda, she was never just Alfreda, she was Alfreda Whitehurst. The whispered voice wafted over to her again only this time it was deeper more desperate, "Move your arm so I can copy." Janet knew any pretense to not have heard Alfreda would be taken as just that to Alfreda, a pretense and would be ignored. The voice came again, grittier, more insistent, "Move your fucking arm so I can get the answers!" Ordinarily Janet would have compiled. She had complied with this whispered request plenty of times for almost two years and today's response, she knew, would be no different, she would comply. Only something different happened on this particular sunny day. In the past, Alfreda's request to copy her work was justified by Janet as a 'Snafu' or 'Situation Normal all fucked up' Ordinarily, she would have moved her paper over to the edge of her desk and Alfreda would greedily (in the most illegible writing Janet had ever seen except that of struggling four year olds first attempts at writing) copy her answers and hopefully that would be the end of her torment for the day, if she was lucky. Frequently she wasn't even after giving Alfreda the answers.

The thing that happened was that Janet (although she intended to comply) for some reason didn't move her arm off her test paper giving Alfreda the view to her answers. She wanted to, she intended to, she knew she had to but her arm just wouldn't obey her mind. It was as if her arm belonged to someone else or was tremendously heavy. Either way her arm did not move. Alfreda's next words swept over her like a bucket of chilled water being thrown on her reducing her to a teeth chattering mess. "I'm gonna get cha after class!" Janet's entire being was stricken with fear, her stomach clenching, her bowels felt hot and watery and she peed herself a little. The fear those words unleashed in her was like that of a huge, rampaging bull elephant trumpeting loudly as it stomped and wrecked everything in its path, knocking down trees and squashing any unfortunate creatures beneath its huge feet on its way to crush her. She just sat there staring straight ahead, immobilized with fear and no coherent thoughts. Her eyes went to the clock above Mr. Fire's desk. It read 2:45, 15 minutes and ten seconds before the bell rang ending the day and her life she thought. She sat there, her mouth, dried of moisture, was hanging open and her breathing began coming in short, captured, frightened burst. Now the fear was tiny squeaking mice scampering around inside of her, scratching and drawing blood with their tiny sharp toes. Claws digging so deeply into her psyche that she couldn't think about anything but the little time she has left before... *What the hell!* A voice exploded angrily in her head. The entire racket of the effect of fear on Janet's mind woke up another part of her mind. Something alien, who yes friends and neighbors, could think very well and clearly. Janet thought she was going in sane having no clue where that angry sounding voice in her head came from. And what awakened inside of her mind decided not to go back to sleep. Not just yet.

So paralyzed with fear it was a few moments before Janet realized that the teacher was calling her name telling her to bring up her test paper if she was finished. Janet nodded in compliance, looking at the clock, ten minutes to three. She was a simpering, trembling mess holding back tears and her motions were stiff and wooden as she stood up and slid from behind her desk and stood in the aisle. Before she'd taken a step Alfreda's foot struck out in the aisle and Janet tripped over it and went sprawling down between the aisles banging her nose on the floor. Mr. Fires looked up just before she fell and he could swear, no he knew, that he'd seen Alfreda deliberately stick her foot out and trip Janet and then slide innocently back beneath her own desk. He looked Alfreda dead in the eyes and she glared, unperturbed and defiantly back at him as if daring him to say something. He didn't. Alfreda had the kind of face that even caused adults to hesitate and rethink their actions. Mr. Fires abhorred Alfreda Whitehurst. It wasn't just the fact that she; God forgive him, was coyote ugly, she was a bully. Whenever he looked at her, and he tried not to as often as possible, his testicles tended to itch and draw up inside of him and he inwardly shivered as he looked away from that face. His eyes could not avoid her massive head covered in clumps of coarse nappy hair that had only a passing acquaintance with a comb. That wandering left eye that was constantly circling in its socket as if it was searching for a way out. The cruel mouth he imagined was filled with pointy sharp vampire teeth and the awful raised mass on her back that formed a not so tiny hump on her back. To him she was a living abortion, a pompous anti-Christ with delusions of grandeur, strutting around creating havoc and destruction in her wake. He'd in the past, in a casual manner, spoken several times to the principal, guidance counselors and teachers, whoever was present in the teacher's lounge about her bullying, but their only interest was in Alfreda's latest exploits and the blessing that she wasn't in any of their classes. He was always ignored and this ignorance would prove fatal. He helped Janet to her feet and sent her to the nurse. Janet left the classroom five minutes before the bell rang. Once in the hallway, desperate eyes looked towards the end doors of the corridor trying to reason which way to go. She turned and limped (her knees had not recovered from the fall) towards the closest hall doors and into her destiny.

Inertia is the resistance of any physical object to any change in its state of motion including changes in speed, direction or state of rest. It is the tendency of objects to keep moving in a straight line at constant velocity. Once in the hall, Janet's desperate, frightened eyes tried to reason which way to go, right or left, to avoid Alfreda. She was not familiar with the word 'inertia' and actually it didn't matter because inertia and destiny were already in motion in the world of the tiny frightened girl who weighed less than 100 pounds soak and wet. She turned to the left and limped into her future towards the closest set of the corridor doors. Just as placed her hands on one side of the double doors, prepared to push it open a white hot sheet of pain exploded in her behind and she was lifted and propelled forward through the double doors by Alfreda's foot literally in her ass and somewhere behind her, seeming far far away she heard the metal clang of the doors shutting behind her.

Alfreda's kick was planned, timed and aimed with all the force she could muster. Her foot, which was encased in a steel-tipped boot connected squarely with the center of Janet's ass and lifted Janet's body up into the air propelling her entire body through the door. As the doors closed, what Alfreda saw was Janet's books flying and Janet suspended on her toes on the edge of the top stair. On the other side of that door, Janet was paralyzed with pain, perched precariously on her toes on the edge of the first set of fourteen steel steps leading down to the landing. Her face was a distorted mask of pain and surprise as wave after wave of dizzying, agonizing, white hot lightening, washed over her body from her assaulted behind. The agony settled into a metronome of throbbing pain; continuously pulsating from the point of impact. The torment was energy draining, leaving her nauseated and weak with sirens ringing in her head. On the other side of the door, Alfreda, her face, a rictus of pure evil, hell bent on destruction, gave no thought to the serious harm she could have done to Janet if she had plummeted down the steep flight of stairs from her cowardly attack. That didn't matter. Her only thought, as she placed both of her massive hands on either side of the doors and shoved them so hard they banged violently against the wall, was to beat the shit out of Janet Nelson. She burst through the open doors like a dark, fiery demon from the pits of hell to descend on Janet, whose back was facing away from her and this seemed to enrage Alfreda even more. She was going to mess her up, mess her up real bad. She gave no thought to the fact that she was going to do this thing simply because the girl hadn't given her the test answers. The only thing that mattered was that she had not given Alfreda what she wanted and that was something you just didn't do to Alfreda. It was not only unacceptable, it would not be tolerated. What kind of example would she be setting if she let Janet get away with denying her anything? So she, Alfreda, in the guise of some demented angel of justice was going to dish out some much needed correction and punishment.

Janet was still perched on her tippy toes barely balanced at the edge of the first step. Her mouth and eyes were perfect circles of a surprise and pain that showed no signs of dissipating. The anguish was excruciating and so instant that she hadn't cried out in pain. She silently stood there as lightning bolts of electric pain radiated in wave after wave throughout her body and she couldn't come down off her toes. Stunned, paralyzed and rigid with pain, she stood there, which in real time was really only a matter of about five seconds until she was brought savagely back into reality by a new pain clamping down on her shoulder and spinning her around. Janet dropped to her knees looking up at Alfreda. This new pain colliding on the heels of the still pulsating hurt in her behind was too much to endure as her shoulder and asshole struggled over which pain was the worst and her leg muscles yielded. Alfreda's right arm, led by a huge, balled, fist was already spiraling down (inertia) in a devastating punch that would surely knock her unconscious as opposed to killing her. As Janet was turned around to face Alfreda's perfectly thrown punch; Alfreda was already visualizing where the blow was going to land on Janet's face. She was patient and confident; savoring how her fist would feel smashing into Janet's face and it was all so satisfyingly perfect. The realization that the first and last thing Janet Nelson would see before her lights were knocked out would be Alfreda's face bought a perverse joy to her. Janet was yanked up from her knees but what Janet saw was not Alfreda's face. Her pain filled eyes had locked onto the dark, benevolent, force that was Alfreda's fist barreling down at her out of a dark, midnight tunnel, sparks shooting from its knuckles and angry tumultuous clouds streaming in its wake. Space and time evaporated, ceased to exist around Janet at the sight of that impending doom and suddenly in her mind she was no longer there in that stairwell with this deranged animal. Simultaneously what Alfreda saw and realized was that the frightened eyes of Janet, which she expected, were not the eyes looking up at her. She was momentarily confused and felt an all too human shiver go up her hump covered spine. The eyes looking up at her didn't belong to Janet but how was that possible? They were and weren't Janet's eyes and she was thinking. *Who is this and where did Janet go?* Janet had gray eyes but these eyes were darker, precluding something unfathomable to her (fear), something cruel and merciless. Suddenly all her plans to beat Janet senseless made no sense, and for the first time in her evil, miserable existence she was afraid. Her mind screamed at her fist, *Stop! Don't hit her!* Only the command was useless and much too late. Although she wanted to halt the forward motion of her fist, it was indeed too late. Inertia was already in motion and was not concerned with the self-preservation of neither Janet Nelson nor Alfreda Whitehurst. Inertia was acting as it should, a physical force, set in motion, resistant to force or velocity stopping it.

Alfreda's right arm and fist was unable to stop hurtling down towards Janet's upturned face which was slowly turning in the direction of the oncoming blow. The fist breezed past Janet's face and the only evidence that it had ever passed by was a low swishing sound and a small scratch on her cheek produced by the ring on Alfreda's finger. The momentum of Alfreda's punch carried her body behind it so that the fist, glancing Janet's face slammed into the wall above the railing with such force and velocity that the knuckles of her fist collapsed and shattered hitting the wall instead of Janet's face. Alfreda's mouth opened and she screamed in pain. Janet's hand, seemingly acting of its own volition turned into a fist and she reached up and punched Alfreda a devastating blow in her open mouth. Her fist uncurled deep in Alfreda's mouth and her finger nails clamped down and shredded deep gouges in Alfreda's tongue as it groped for purchase. The ripped, bleeding tongue attempted to retreat from the merciless, clutching fingers leaving torn flesh under Janet's finger nails which now latched onto the sensitive flesh holding Alfreda's bottom teeth. Janet's fingers locked onto Alfreda's bottom teeth and with uncompromising anger and strength yanked backwards and broke off four of her teeth at the gum line. Alfreda screamed in agony with blood dripping from her tongue and gums. She had arrived in a dark, sorry, state of affairs, out of the blue and into the black. Janet pulled her hand free still clutching Alfreda's four lower teeth which she flung against the wall where they clicked and clacked as they fell onto the stairs leaving small droplets of blood and gristle. Janet reached up behind Alfreda's massive head, entwined and buried her bloody fingers in the coarse, matted hair, pulled her head back and bashed Alfreda's face down into the wall above the railing. Alfreda collapsed to her knees, her face was a squashed, bloody mess with interesting new shapes and pending on your point of view, minus the blood and gore was an improvement. She would have happily drifted off to la la land if Janet had permitted it. She did not.

Janet's class mates knew something was up even before Janet left to go to the nurse. Several had heard Alfreda demanding Janet give her the answers as well as the threat when she was refused. They witnessed Alfreda tripping Janet and saw all the signs of a fight developing and they wanted to see it. Janet was going to get beaten up by Alfreda and although they truly felt sorry for her, they were extremely glad it wasn't them. At any rate, all compassion aside, they wanted to see the fight. As in all schools, when the word or rumor spreads that there was going to be a fight all normal operating procedures of hallway etiquette disappeared. When the dismissal bell rang, the class jumped up in unison and jostled each other to be the first out of the class room. There were approximately eight class rooms on each side of the corridor and approximately thirty students in each class meaning that well over two hundred students were entering the corridor with the single word, "Fight" telegraphing through them. The normally adjusted students morphed into an undisciplined, mindless, screaming mob infested with the expectation of seeing someone, it didn't matter who, get the shit stomped out of them. With that single word 'Fight' blood lust, thick and potent silently sneaked up and overwhelmed the students like a thick fog rolling in off the ocean.

Researchers theorize that humans crave violence just as they crave money, sex, food and drugs. This craving satisfies certain areas of the brain. This explains our fascination with brutal sports as well as our own penchant for the classic bar brawl. The brain processes and craves aggressive behavior as it does other rewards. Humans seek violence, picking fights for no apparent reason other than the rewarding feeling of a fight. The brain of the bully is only satisfied inflicting pain, fear and destruction. The brain of the crowd is satisfied watching the blood flow. Science has shown that humans are drawn to fights. Psychopharmacology reveals that the same clusters of brain cells, aided by Dopamine, are the same cells involved in other rewards as well as the craving for violence. An individual will intentionally seek out an aggressive encounter solely because they experience a rewarding sensation. Aggression occurs and is necessary to get and keep important resources such as mates, territory and food and the reward pathway seeks to satisfy or award the brain's lust for violence.

Thoughts of going home extinguished, the students experienced a kind of sick fascination and anticipation of a fight that involved Alfreda Whitehurst. *Oh this was going to be good.* The grins on their faces said and everyone wanted to be there. They already knew the victim was going to lose badly going up against Alfreda who would as usual retain her heavy weight title. There was no sympathy for the opponent, who everyone knew didn't stand a chance in hell. A lot of them had firsthand experience or extremely close calls going up against Alfreda and they felt better knowing they weren't the target. They all flowed out of their classrooms quickly becoming an undisciplined, mindless mob stampeding down the hallway screaming, "Fight, fight!" They saw the doors at the end of the corridor close behind Alfreda, they knew where the fight was and that was where they had to get to. No one wanted to miss anything. They had no idea of what was happening behind those closed doors but it was sure to be good. Students who weren't interested in the barbaric melee were unable to detach themselves from the crowd and were swept up, hustled, bustled and tossed about, driven along with the frenzied crowd towards the closed doors at the end of the corridor, towards their destiny.

On the other side of the closed doors Alfreda was barely conscious leaning against Janet and they were still perched on the edge of the first of fourteen steel steps leading down to the landing. Janet, who was much smaller than Alfreda, had begun to slide from beneath Alfreda's weight that was pinning her against the railing. Once she was free, Alfreda's head slid down lying on the top stairs. Janet reached behind the railing, grasped Alfreda's fat arm and began pulling it up backwards behind the railing. When she had pulled enough of her arm so that Alfredda's elbow joint was resting backwards behind the railing. Janet pulled the trapped arm away from the railing, and jumped up, bringing her full weight (which wasn't much compared to Alfreda's) down on the imprisoned arm. The bone snapped with a with a sickening sound and ripped through the skin, leaving a bloody, jagged mess of splintered bone and shredded flesh splayed open. Alfreda snapped out of near unconsciousness with a blood curling scream of pain. She was moaning on the edge of unconsciousness when Janet grasp the thumb of Alfreda's hand bend it backwards until the thumb joint snapped causing Janet to lose her grip once again as the mangled arm slipped out from behind the railing. Janet's rage boiled over feeling the loss of the broken thumb which to her, represented all the times that Alfreda with a Gollum's grin, had painfully bent her fingers backwards until the pain was excruciating, unbearable but bear it she did, because she had no choice until Alfreda was ready to let her fingers go. This ending would have been a much needed blessing and welcome reprieve for Alfreda if Janet had stopped there but unfortunately, it was not to be. Janet grabbed the destroyed arm and lost her grip again due to the massive of amount of blood (that fortunately for Alfreda was oozing instead of flowing) that was making the arm too slippery to grip. Janet seemed impervious to the blood, Alfreda's moaning, and the broken bones and for that matter the body of Alfreda which slipped yet again from her grasp. Janet screamed with silent rage in her head and Alfreda was in the land of darkness and possibly of no return. Janet positioned herself above the limp form of her tormentor, grabbed two handfuls of Alfreda's sweatshirt behind both of her shoulders and dragged her with a strength that was not only phenomenal but should have been physically impossible; Alfreda had to weigh at least 170 pounds and Janet barely weighed in at about 100 pounds. I suppose one could chalk this strength up to adrenaline, like the person who could in a moment of high stress lift a car off an injured child. Such feats are known to have occurred with no explanation other than mind over matter. Perhaps this is so, but in this case it was Janet over matter as she pulled Alfreda's bulk up the front of the stairwell wall. Using her knees and her hips, she worked like a dervish, the cords of her tiny muscles standing out as she positioned Alfreda's shoulder just below the railing, her mangled, useless, arm flopping along leaving a trail of blood and gristle. Pinning the shoulder against the wall, Janet reached down and grasp Alfreda's unbroken arm and pulled it up behind the railing until it could go no further and like before she dropped her weight on the arm. Alfreda was already unconscious when this happened and so felt nothing when the skin at her shoulder joint ripped open and the bone broke loose from the socket and the clavicle bone snapped. Janet watched, totally fascinated as the hump on Alfreda's back slowly drifted over to the side of the demolished shoulder and settled itself in such a way that it disappeared and her back now seemed physically normal, if you didn't count the broken clavicle bone. It was that disappearing hump that spared Alfreda any further injury for the moment. Janet was squatting, hypnotized over the crumpled, unconscious body of Alfreda, watching the hump on her back sliding across it. It was then she realized that the floor in the stairwell seemed to be vibrating with low thumping sounds that were getting stronger. She could feel the vibrations approaching, getting stronger and louder with each second. Crouching over Alfreda, she turned to face the closed doors where the sound was emitting from and in that instant the doors to the stairwell exploded open and about ten students with over a hundred behind them burst through the doors colliding with Janet and an unconscious Alfreda with nothing to stop their forward motion. Inertia!

The entire corridor was jammed with students trying to get to the fight when someone came up the idea to run down to the corridors opposite doors, down the stairs to the floor beneath, run the length of that corridor beneath the upper floor, and enter the stairwell from that direction. Students at the rear of the mob detached themselves, forming a second mob and took off for the opposite stairwell leaving over a hundred more stampeding students trying to get through the doors and into the stairwell. When the detached group entered the opposite stairwell they were met by students coming down from the upper floors and students coming up from the lower floor. The effect was immediately recognized. Fight! Now even more students joined the screaming mob although this second group had no clue as to who was fighting or where the fight was taking place. Putting the clues together they had all the facts they needed and the only conclusion possible was there was a fight somewhere and like their blood lusting peers they wanted to see it too; and they joined the already hundreds of stampeding students out to satisfy their blood lust. The first ten students on Janet's floor having no knowledge of what was beyond the closed doors, burst through colliding with Janet and an unconscious Alfreda who were both knocked into the air off the top stair.

When the bell rings ending a class period, part of the teacher's job description is to stand outside of their perspective classrooms to ensure a safe and orderly transfer of students from one class to the next; as it is also the responsibility of the security guards to be present in the hallways. Perhaps it was due to the years of employment that this duty relaxed and all but disappeared. Currently, when the bells rang teachers mostly remained at their desk shuffling papers, preparing for the next class or just closing their eyes succumbing to the knowledge that they had another thirty different children, six times a day, five times a week and how long before they could retire. There were no teachers present in the hallway when the bell rang on that particular day. There was no telling where the security guards were in the course of a school day. They could be counted on to be present when the school opened in the morning and when the school closed, in between those times it was anybody's guess where they hung out. Truth be told, if the teachers and security guards had been present it would have made no difference; you couldn't stop a speeding train by yelling at it to stop you'd just be crushed. This was the thinking of the teachers who didn't respond to the noise of screaming voices and pounding feet in the hallway. They peeked out of their classroom doors, saw what was going on and quickly ducked back inside the safety of their classrooms. There weren't any security guards on the floor and they weren't going out there, no way, not in their contracts. So they remained in their classrooms and the security guards remained where ever they were. The teachers knew there was a fight going on somewhere out there just from the yelling and sounds of pounding feet. There was an excited urgency in that pounding rush of feet that let them know that something extraordinary was going on or about to happen. The running feet represented spectators jostling each other for good viewing areas and someone could really get hurt just by being present or trying to get to a fight and that someone (the teachers felt) might just be them and they weren't getting involved. Some of the teachers fretted over their thoughts and imaginings. Feeling sorry for whoever was getting beat up; while other teachers thought that all the kids were animals anyway and felt it was a shame that youth was wasted on the young, may they all catch head lice and die in hell. As far as the one losing the battle (the teachers felt) it came down to the survival of the fittest. The Junior and High schools were political battlefields in session and open for business.

Everyone belonged to one click or another and if you have no connections then you were fair game for any bully or gang that came along. Teachers learned not to get involved because they could get hurt or even fired if they did too much or too little to stop altercations. Why take the chance. So they remained in their classrooms, absent from the scene. The security guards had their own priorities and that was obtaining popularity with particular students for drugs and sex. They were mesmerized by the young saucy girls, who not only flirted with them but were willing participants in quickie boiler room romances. Some of the guards used students for drug distribution. The guards set up the sales and got a piece of the action. The guards could always be seen (accept in the presence of school staff) flirting right back with the female students and developing buddy, buddy relationships with the popular and most notorious male students. There had been more than one firing when a female student marked a security guard as the father of her unborn child. It was generally known by those in the know, that a particular security guard was selling some of the best weed around. The guards formed their own click which provided hours of hilarity and back slapping among them as each knew who their peers were into (literally) regarding school romances and drugs. Whatever the case, the security guards too, were absent from the scene. In short, there was no one to project order on over four hundred rampaging students and the outcome was gruesome and horrific.

The first student to burst through the corridor door was little Peggy Johnson, a tenth grader and daughter of the school Principal Charlie Johnson. Peggy was the only one to get a clear perception of what was on the other side of the closed corridor doors just before she died. What she saw had little time to assimilate in her brain but was captured quite distinctly in her eyes before they closed forever. What she saw was two girls she didn't know, one (Janet) crouched over what looked like something resembling an unconscious or dead bleeding body (Alfreda). Thick, red, coppery smelling (she thought) blood was pooling around the two girls, spreading over the stairwell, down the stairs and on the walls. Peggy was catapulted into the air when she collided with them. Her body was suspended momentarily above the two girls giving her a view from above, then came crashing down onto the middle of the steep steel stairs, her neck landing directly over the edge of one of the steps. Kevin Spears, also a tenth grader, never saw the two girls on the staircase because he was following so closely behind Peggy Johnson whose collision with Janet and Alfreda caused all three of them to tumble down the stairs. He slipped in the blood and flew over Janet and Alfreda and landed knees first on a dazed Peggy's neck which was directly on the edge of a stair. His weight snapped her neck neatly and cleanly as he rolled off face first into the wall at the foot of the landing successfully breaking his nose and knocking him unconscious. Seven students behind Kevin also unable to stop even if they had tried slipped in the blood and tumbled down the stairs with nine more students following them. Although the students in the front were falling down the stairs, the students behind them were not aware of this and so group after group of students were actively pushing and shoving their way through the doors only to join the cascade of their falling peers, stumbling and tumbling down the long flight of steel stairs. Seeking to protect herself, Janet had the presence of mind to grab onto Alfreda's unconscious body and use it as a cushion against her fall. The students continued to push and shove themselves through the door unaware of what waited on the other side. Then they lost their footing on the puddled blood and being propelled from behind they too were thrust, slipping and sliding over the top stair down onto the growing mass of screaming, twisted, tangled, conscious, unconscious and slightly conscious bodies before them. The flow of bodies just didn't stop because those behind continued to force their way through the doors at a rushing rate. The pile of bodies became higher and higher until none of the fourteen steps were visible and yet the students continued tumbling in a cartwheeling flood that showed no sign of ending. Students on top, scrambling to get up were stomping on the body parts of those below them, poking eyes, ears, noses, throats and other various body parts below them. Students on the bottom struggled in vain to upright themselves in a hopeless cause as they were forced back down by those on top and still the bodies continued to fall. Janet found herself lying atop of Alfreda against the landing wall but she too could not get up but she was still on a mission. The weight of the falling bodies above her only served to make her angrier and she took the anger out on the still body of Alfreda beneath her and the things that happened out of sight of all eyes was unmentionable.

The flow of cascading bodies began to taper off as the pile of fallen students became too high to fall over. The stairwell was clogged with no room to proceed further. Everyone was dazed and horror struck and some were laughing hysterically because they had no way to assimilate what they were a part of in the stairwell. There was hysterical, chocked, laughter, intermingled with moans and crying. Then the screams of panic began. Some students attempted to help the students on top to get up but it was hopeless because outstretched helping hands were grabbed and clutched by the buried students and the helpers were pulled down onto the pile of twisting bodies. Somewhere beneath the pile one student was gasping for air that just wasn't there, cause of death, suffocation. All those able to maneuver began to do so by any means necessary. They clutched, clawed, stepped on and rolled over anybody beneath them in their efforts to get out from under. The high heel of a twelfth grader punctured the eye of one of the buried students, straight into child's brain which was further scrambled by the heel trying to free itself. If you have ever walked down a street and happened upon the body of a dead animal decaying in the sun; your eyes try to avoid the sight because you know what you're going to see; hundreds of swarming maggots churning like boiling water, slipping, sliding and oozing over and under each other in a frenzied mess. This was the scene in the stairwell, only it was struggling students, not maggots that were in that tangled frenzy. There was utter chaos when the schools fire alarm blared throughout the building galvanizing the teachers from behind their protective, closed, classroom doors and summoned the security guards from wherever they had been. Once the hallways were cleared, the teachers and security guards were met with the horrific scene in the stairwell and the task of extracting the mass of injured students who'd fallen and were desperate to get untangled from the conflagration. They were met with long agonizing wails of pain, shock, fear, panic, broken appendages, the conscious, unconscious and semi-conscious, bleeding bodies and three dead students. Their cries echoing throughout the stairwell increased the urgency of the trapped students trying to free themselves and the attempts to aid them by the teachers and security guards. There was blood all over the stairs and walls and of course the students, making it difficult to determine who was bleeding and from what injury. In shock the only thing they could do in their shock was attempt to extract the students as they appeared from the top to the bottom. Students were lifted screaming, crying and some made no sound al all, just stared blankly. Some were lifted who slid out of the grasp of the rescuers because of broken arms, others couldn't stand due to broken legs and some were simply unconscious. Finally, there were just four remaining students in the stairwell. When they reached the body of Peggy Johnson they were momentarily confused. They were looking into the face of a child whose eyes not only stared blankly out at nothing but the face seemed to be on her back. When they realized that the head was completely twisted around they screamed in horror at the sight. They didn't attempt to lift her but instead backed away from the awfulness of the dead staring eyes. One security guard fell back against the landing wall and began to jabber hysterically into his walkie-talkie, "She's dead! She's dead! On my God, her head! She's dead!" over and over he shouted into the shocked ears of the school's security dispatcher. When he managed to regain some control he ran down the stairs to the office and snatching the nearest phone dialed 911. A male voice asked indifferently, fire, police or ambulance? "No, no, you son of a bitch, we need ten, eleven, twenty fucking ambulances, hurry, hurry! Two bodies left and as they reached for Janet she screamed, "Ow, my arm, my arm, ow, let go, let go!" They gently released and lowered her back down unsure of how to move her but they had to because there was another student beneath her. Three teachers grabbed the back of her bloody sweater while trying to support the twisted arm and pulled her off of Alfreda and then discovered that her leg was broken. The normally and without a doubt, distinguishable face of Alfreda was unrecognizable and one of the teachers fainted when she saw Alfreda's nose was gone. There was just a gory, bloody, oozing hole. Two more teachers passed out and a third ran screaming hysterically down the stairs into the hallway headed for the Principal's office. Looking at the severely ravaged body of Alfreda the security guard's pale faces looked at each other and silently sent the same message to each other, *dead, definitely dead. Oh hell yea, she's deader than dead.* Then they wondered, *Oh my God, what the hell happened?* They didn't know. No one knew except one person, Peggy Johnson and she'd never tell.

Janet was about the twentieth student rushed to the hospital by ambulance followed by several other emergency vehicles that had been requested from area hospitals. All the injured, hysterical and dead students were taken away except for Alfreda Whitehurst, who despite having sustained brutal life-threatening injuries was still alive but had to be air lifted from the school's roof to a trauma center hospital in New York. When Janet next opened her eyes she was in the hospital emergency room in total confusion and in an extraordinary amount of pain. It felt like someone was screwing hot bolt nails into her head, arms, and legs and behind. Her only conscious thoughts were silent screams of, *Make it stop! Please make it stop*! Her sub-conscious mind, aided by heavy sedation, did as it was asked. The pain began to dull and she was floating away in iridescent clouds on the edge of complete unconsciousness. As she sank deeper and deeper into a soundless void she didn't rebel but another part of her mind did. This part of her mind was wide awake looking out through Janet's swollen eyes taking in the sights and sounds around her. The hospital emergency room was all hustle, bustle and urgency. Doctors and nurses running to and fro, stretchers carrying screaming children rolled in and she saw one roll out with a sheet covering a body. It was a mad house of movement and noise. The room before her eyes swayed, dissolved, came together, melted away and came together again as she observed it's hectic sights and sounds. Although Janet was for all intent and purpose unconscious, her conscious mind was fully awake and apparently that self could also feel pain and disorientation. She forced herself to relax and concentrated on soothing the pains that racked her body. It was only than that she realized she couldn't move her leg; it was broken and in a cast suspended from a bar attached to the bed. She curiously tried to reach out to touch it and found that her arm didn't respond to her command and there was a heavy, unyielding weight across her chest. It took a minute to realize that her arm too, was in a cast. She tried to quiet her panicking, questioning mind and began thinking back, trying to piece together what had happened. She remembered the refusal to give Alfreda her test answers *(what had she been thinking then?)* followed by the trip and fall, being sent to the nurse, that devastating kick in her behind and the blue black pain that followed (that thought was accompanied by the ghost of that pain) the pain in her shoulder as that hateful Alfreda grabbed her and the huge fist and then she was falling, falling and falling. Recalling Alfreda's abuse to her for some reason was followed by thoughts of her home life and hot, scalding tears began to first drip, the drip becoming a stream and the stream became a flood of painful tears and memories.

Dozens of hurtful memories rose in her tortured mind. Painful memories she wanted to turn away from but didn't. Like some deranged masochist she sought to relive them. It was inconceivable that she could have so many emotional scars. She began to relive them through a foggy mist that opened and closed on different scenes in her home life. The mist parted to reveal her mother forcing her to wear one boot and one shoe to church because she hadn't been ready on time and unable to find a match to either. She had been beyond embarrassment when the people saw her wearing one boot and one shoe and they had laughed and laughed at her. The mist closed over and reopened to reveal the time her mother took her shopping for a new coat that she'd been allowed to choose herself. The coat cost $99 dollars and her mother put down a deposit of $98.50 on the coat. The sales woman, a little perplexed told her mother that she only needed $.50 more to purchase the coat and her mother, looking directly into Janet's eyes said, "I know." She left the store with a stunned, teary eyed Janet in tow owing $.50 on the coat. The mist closed and reopened on the day Janet had an excruciating pain in her stomach. The pain so sharp she could barely stand up straight or walk. She had hobbled, bent over holding her stomach, into the kitchen to her mother who in an exasperated tone told her, "Well go to the hospital, I'm cooking." The mist closed and reopened on Janet playing kick ball with other kids in the park across the street from her house. As she was about to kick the ball her mother, standing on the steps to the house called her over to her. When Janet reached her mother, she was handed a toothbrush and told to go upstairs, the kitchen baseboards needed cleaning. The mist closed and opened (would it never stop?) on her stepfather yanking her butt naked from the bath tub and beating her with a razor strap for what she did not know. Her mother, hearing the screams came into the bathroom. She saw her daughter dangling in the air from her husband's hand around her wrist while her legs and one arm were thrashing wildly in the air as he hit her over and over with the strap. Her mother watched for a minute, turned and left closing the door behind her. The mist, closing then opening on her mother ignoring her pedophile stepfather, who on more than one occasion was caught by her leaning over a partially sleeping Janet's bed in the middle of the night fiddling in her under wear. Waking up from a dream where she was getting stung by bees only to discover that the stinging was coming from a belt wielded by her mother hitting her over and over. So many bad memories; coming and going in the mist. Her mother sending her to junior high school graduation in dirty, worn out sneakers, a sweat suit and her hair barely combed; the stopping of her piano lessons, forcing her to quit her little after school job behind the candy counter at the corner store and possibly the worst memory surfaced. For over five years she was a part of the neighborhood kids who teased and threw things at a dirty, urine smelling bum who everyday sat on the bench in the park. Hundreds of times; she and her mother had walked past that dirty disheveled, stinking man. Her mother never gave him a glance. One day her mother pulled her from school to attend a funereal. She took Janet up to a coffin and introduced Janet to the dead man in the coffin as her father, Joseph Coleman. The man in the coffin was the dirty, smelly man from the park! Before the mist could open again; Janet whispered, "Stop, no more." to her tortured mind, the merciless flashbacks and the empty room. . She wiped at her tears with her uncast arm that too was throbbing in pain, she didn't want to travel down the dark recesses of her past any longer. The memories, for her, were clear and powerful. Turning her head back and forth in negation, "No more." she whispered again though her tears in the bustling emergency room. There were a few more things she didn't want and one of them was to ever have to go home again. She was not an unintelligent child, spending all her available time buried in books. She read anything and everything and as a result; she'd gained quite an imagination. She was intelligent beyond her years and that coupled with a huge imagination she began to think about a plan that would make it possible for her not to return home. What she came up with was ridiculous. It wouldn't work in a million years but Janet clutched at it feeling as if it were her only hope. Acting on the developing idea she asked a passing nurse to call her mother. As the nurse walked away with the number, it occurred to her that the child looked strange. Having received heavy pain and sedation medication she would have thought the child would be groggy, slow and vulnerable. Instead her face was sharp, alert and set. The subconscious part of Janet's mind only knew that it existed and that it was the part of Janet tasked with protecting her.

That part of her mind just didn't know it was simply the minds instinct to danger, a mechanism that offered one of two choices, fight or flight. It did recognize that its time with or within Janet was limited and it needed to set the stage for the future protection of Janet. It was these realizations that were the basis for her plan. Essentially it was planning for the future, fight or flight, she chose flight.

Janet was alone, after being transferred to a semi-private hospital room; with a ceiling to floor curtain separating the two beds. She dozed lightly but uncomfortably with cast on her leg, arm and three fingers. The door to her room opened and the nurse escorted a woman into the room, a woman who wasn't Janet's mother, but her cousin, Elizabeth Nelson. Elizabeth Nelson was Janet's mother's niece. She was an attractive, tall and heavy set woman with a round, kind, attractive face. Her long hair was pulled back in a heavy bun lying against her thick neck. Although she was almost fifteen years older than Janet they were very close. Elizabeth was the only friend Janet ever had and Elizabeth loved her unconditionally. She always helped Janet when she was in trouble at home. Far too many times, Janet had run crying to her house from her own because her mother was beating her or her stepfather was either beating or was trying to touch her again. Elizabeth was aware of his antics, as she too, on occasion had been victim to his Roman fingers and Russian hands probing her as a teenager living with her aunt. Many a night Elizabeth had awakened to an insistent pounding on her door to find a hysterical, disheveled, weeping, Janet standing on the third floor landing outside of her apartment in pajamas and always she'd bring Janet inside never asking, "What's wrong?" because she knew. When she saw Janet lying in the bed with broken bones and bruises on practically every visible part of her body her concern and sympathy were snatched away like a leaf in a hurricane and was replaced by mounting white, hot anger. Automatically assuming that the stepfather was responsible and not caring what her aunt said or would do; she reached for the phone to finally call the police on that bastard. Janet weakly reached out grasped Elizabeth's wrist with her free hand and whispered, "No." Elizabeth tried to jerk her hand away but Janet held on. "No." she whispered again and beckoned for her to sit down. She gently sat down on the edge of the bed, her face a mask of concern and anger. Janet whispered a little louder and told Elizabeth what she needed her to do. Looking down at Janet, her heart breaking at the sight of the cast and bruises Elizabeth left the room agreeing wholeheartedly with Janet's request at first but not fully understanding the 'why' of the request.

Elizabeth went to the nurse's station and asked for a phone book. After a bit of searching the nurse came up with a thick phone directory. Turning the yellow pages to the section labeled lawyers and as instructed she looked for a large law firm that carried a full page ad and whose location was within the city, preferably close to the hospital. Locating the firm of Graves, Ritter and Reddick she dialed the number. She spoke briefly with someone, probably the receptionist, explaining the circumstances and reasons for her call and was told to hold on. When the receptionist returned she assured Elizabeth that an attorney would be at the hospital within an hour and a half. Elizabeth returned to Janet's room and Janet told her everything that had happened at the school and that she wanted to sue to school. Holding Janet's free hand she said compassionately, "You can't sue the school honey, you're a child, a minor." Elizabeth went on, "I suppose your mother could but not you." "I won't be suing the school. I know I can't do that." Janet whispered back. "Then why do you want a lawyer?" questioned Elizabeth. "I want to sue the school without my mother or stepfather knowing about the lawsuit." "What are you talking about Janet?" Elizabeth questioned amazingly. "I need to call your mother; she's the one that needs to talk to a-lawyer." "No!" Janet cut her off and painfully exhaling she continued saying, "Liz please listen, just listen. Let me explain something to you." and Elizabeth's eyes widened in astonishment at what Janet said to her. She told Elizabeth that she wanted her to pretend to be her mother when the lawyer arrived. Janet explained that if her parents knew she wouldn't get any of the money and the money was the most important thing because it would allow her to escape from home. No one had to know, it would be their secret. Elizabeth declined the suggestion and participation in such a thing vehemently while staring incredulously at Janet and protesting the obvious. "How could your injuries possibly be kept from your parents? Assholes that they are, they aren't blind. What you're thinking is crazy. You'll never get away with such a thing. No, no. I can't do that." Elizabeth tried to reason with Janet as she walked around the hospital bed her head twisting negatively. "It can't be done, sugar. I'm sorry. Surely you realize this and me pretending to be your mother? That's out of the question. It's insane! No honey, I could never do that. Where did you ever get such an idea? No, we'd both get in trouble. I do understand how you feel but this; this is just crazy." Janet waited for Elizabeth to get all her denials and reasoning's out then told her the plan in its entirety. She sealed the plan with the fact that no one would question her identity because they both had the same last name. She painfully reached over with her uninjured hand and lightly grasped Elizabeth's hand, "Help me, please. The only person to see you will be the attorney and if no one else knows, there is no one to find out. Help me Liz. Help me get away. Help me escape. You know what it's like at my house. You know this! That's the reason I want the money. I need to get away from them all. Help me please!" she pleaded tearfully and with that and apprehension around her heart Elizabeth consented. She was hesitant and wary, but in the end she was fully on board with the deception.

The attorney arrived (photographer in tow) and while he was introducing himself as Roger Wellington Lloyd he was looking in shock at Janet. Elizabeth played her part (her emotions fueled by sincere feelings for her cousin), as the hysterical, grieving mother so well the nurse offered her a mild sedative. Before any questions were asked, the attorney set the photographer, a disheveled looking young man with a shock of unruly red hair and quick movements to the task of taking pictures of Janet's injuries. Several pictures were taken of Janet lying prone, arm, leg and three fingers in cast, multiple, colored bruises about the face, torso, uncast leg and arm. After the photos the photographer began packing up his equipment when Janet, in a weak voice said, "Wait a minute." The photographer stopped packing his gear as Janet continued, "You need to take pictures of my rear end. I was kicked there and I can still feel it bleeding and burning." The photographer was hesitant to take pictures of Janet's unclothed buttocks but Elizabeth insisted. A nurse was called and Janet was gently rolled over onto her stomach and everyone gasped, the cheeks of her buttocks were red and inflamed and what they all viewed when her cheeks were parted was a badly bruised, torn, bloody, swollen anus. "Oh my God!" the nurse gasped when she saw the traumatic bleeding mess; she dashed out to get a doctor. The photographer's lunch flip-flopped in his stomach and started to rise into his throat as he bent close to snap the pictures. He didn't want to look any more and was thinking, *Boy, it's going to hurt like hell if she tries to move her bowels"* and for the second time his stomach lurched upwards. The angry, tightly wrinkled sphincter muscles were torn and ripped open, surrounded by congealed and fresh blood and mucus. If not for Janet's request that the area be photographed, the injury would have gone unnoticed and would have festered into an infection without the much needed cleaning, disinfecting and sutures needed to repair the damaged. Janet would be on a liquid diet for weeks because a regular bowel movement would rip open any sutures. Snap – snap – snap of the camera.

Roger Wellington Lloyd was young, fresh out of law school with a wife and two children. He was tall and slender with a thick mop of black hair brushed over his green eyes. He had a blemish free face with a straight nose and generous mouth. His voice was slightly deep but calming and he was dressed in a rumpled suit and tie that was definitely off the rack. This would be his first case and he meant to make good on it. He took out a tape recorder and asked Janet to tell him as best she could what happened and it was unbelievable what he was hearing. Janet began a story of how she was continuously bullied, hit, stolen from, forced to steal and reduced to humiliating tears by the same bully, Alfreda Whitehurst, for almost two years and all her teachers knew it but no one did anything to stop it. She was deathly afraid to tell herself because she had been threatened and warned what would happen to her if she did. She talked about these things in a sort of a trance like voice and her eyes grew wide as her story became more and more engrossing ending with Alfreda's request to copy her answers, the deliberate tripping in the classroom (witnessed by the teacher) the kick in the hallway and the hospital. The attorney had long since put away his legal pad and he, Elizabeth, the photographer and the nurse were transfixed listening to the incredible story. They were filled with sadness and an increasing anger at this tiny little girl's story of brutality, torture and who had been afraid to tell. Janet too appreciated being recorded because it added an extra dimension to her story being told in her own voice because all the emotion, hurt, pain, fear and humiliation in that tiny voice was both hypnotizing and tremendously compelling. Just listening to herself made her cry and she saw that Elizabeth was wiping her eyes along with the nurse and the photographer. Roger Wellington Lloyd reminded the nurse that what she'd heard in the room was private and confidential, not to be repeated to anyone. By the time Janet finished her story the doctor had arrived and Janet was taken down to surgery. Roger Wellington Lloyd was beyond pissed off, pacing the room. He had begun to wonder about his own children, especially his daughter, who never talked about school. *Was the same sort of thing happening to her? Could it be possible that she too was being bullied and keeping silent, afraid to tell?* He, himself, teared up as he put the recorder away, closing his briefcase his eyes and mind distant, thinking about his daughter. His oldest son talked too much, almost without a break between sentences but his daughter, his daughter; head down, concentrated on her plate and never really responded to the oft asked question by her parents, "How was school today?" He never gave any thought as to why she never talked about school just chalked it up to her personality, quiet and demure. He left the hospital driving like a bat out of hell on a mission that didn't involve putting a case together for Janet Nelson. He headed straight for his daughter's school before realizing that school was over for the day. In his heart he cried for little Janet who'd suffered such atrocities in silence and fear. *Don't you worry little one,* he silently promised himself and her. *They will pay for this! Oh they will most definitely pay!*

While the hospital was processing Janet's release, her mind was struggling with a problem and it wasn't a small one. It was serious, huge and with no solution in sight. In her rush to put her idea into action she had completely ignored what Elizabeth had called the obvious. *How were her injuries to be explained to her parents?* She had reached too far, too soon and had no back up. She had been successful thus far getting Elizabeth to masquerade as her mother and contacting a lawyer. She had no intention of letting her parents have any knowledge of the lawsuit. Neither the hospital nor the attorney questioned Elizabeth's identity but things would surely come to light when she came home with multiple cast and bruises all over her body. It was important that her parents weren't aware of the circumstances behind the injuries, because without a doubt, her stepfather would play the angry, aggrieved father who was suing the school for what happened to his most loved daughter. The incident at the school would most certainly make the papers and area news programs. She hadn't thought about these things at all. It would be front page news. She could visualize the headlines 'THREE STUDENTS DEAD, DOZENS INJURED IN TRAGIC HIGH SCHOOL RIOT' There was no way she could keep the papers from reporting it or the television news stations from airing the story. She wasn't too worried about the newspapers, her parents didn't read them. However, her mother did watch the six o'clock news every night, she never missed it. It she wasn't watching it, the sound was turned up loud enough for her to hear it in the next room. If they broadcast what happened at the high school and her mother connected it with Janet's injuries the deception and impersonation would be over and the lawsuit discovered. If her stepfather smelled a dime he'd spend nine cents to pocket it. And what about Liz, what trouble would she get into if her parents sued only to find that there was already a lawsuit on Janet's behalf by her mother, what would happen to Liz? She had never thought about these things when she began her deception. Now they were crowding in on her and she could see no way out. She was quiet on the taxi ride home to Liz's apartment which was four houses from her own. After being placed in Elizabeth's bed, she still never said a word except to have Elizabeth call her mother and tell them that Janet would be at her house for a few days. Elizabeth thought her silence was due to pain and depression. In the beginning her idea had seemed so simple. Have Elizabeth pose as her mother, get a lawyer and sue the school, simple. But now she saw the enormity of what she had put into motion and it was unstoppable and she was in a panic. What was she going to do? There was no way to stop the forward motion of her plan. Staying at Liz's house wouldn't be a problem. Janet's mother, for reasons unknown to Janet, hated her. She wouldn't be missed, she was invisible there, a non-person; but what about later when she'd have to go home, at least to check in? The cast wouldn't be off for months, how could her injuries be explained and keep her plans intact. She needed a plausible excuse for the injuries and there was none. She realized that she had taken a very big leap before she looked.

Neither Elizabeth nor Janet knew the reasons for the animosity her mother showed towards her daughter but it was blatant and out in the open. Janet never knew who or where her true father was and Elizabeth hated Janet's mother just as much as Janet's mother hated her. Elizabeth's hate truly began when Janet's mother took Janet, then fourteen, to a funeral, pointed at a man in a coffin and told her that the man was her father. Elizabeth herself had been shocked at the cruelty as she watched a stunned Janet looking into the coffin at a dead man introduced to her as her father. That had been the first and only time that Janet ever saw her father and her mother apparently felt that it was just fine to introduce her to her father lying dead in a coffin. She well remembered Janet's face. It seemed to be asking questions like: *Who are you? Where have you been? Why did you leave me?* Questions from which there would be no answers from the dead man in the box. His eyes remained closed and his lips would remain forever sealed. Elizabeth had been speechless as Janet's mother gripped Janet firmly across the shoulders, turned her away from the stranger in the coffin and paraded her around the mourners like she was first prize at a county fair. She was proud and her face glowed with pride that even though Joe was dead, she had his daughter to love. *What in the world?* Elizabeth thought as she watched this show of Janet being led from person to person in the funeral parlor. She was met with exclamations and questions swirling around her that didn't seem to penetrate her confused mind as she was held firmly in front of her mother. *I didn't know Joe had a daughter! She is so pretty! How old are you honey?* Her mother, smiling a glittering false smile, proudly showing off the prize winning pig and holding up the blue ribbon while she proclaimed that, "Yes, this is Joe's daughter" but Joe's daughter (Janet) seemed to be was asking herself, *Whose Joe?* Elizabeth watched as Janet kept attempting to turn back towards the coffin but her mother's firm grip and tour of fame didn't allow this. It was obvious to Elizabeth that Janet wanted to see the man's face again but she never did. He would remain a stranger to her. She hadn't been allowed to view the body long enough to remember his features and Elizabeth was sure that the brief glimpse was already fading in the child's mine. This proved to be the day that Elizabeth's hate for Janet's mother burst like a rotten egg whose shell had for years grown multitudes of cracks that were etched around a shell and that could no longer hold back its secrets. It was also the day Elizabeth became Janet's secret protector and stand in mother. If only she could have snatched the child up and bundled her safe in her arms out of the funeral parlor and out of her mother's life, but of course

Murder is against the L a w But . . .

she couldn't. All she could do was stand and watch the stunned child. She was glad that Janet wasn't crying but she was also afraid of the look on the child's face. It was like she was here but not here, disconnected. She was the person looking in the mirror at the person in the mirror and neither knew who the other was. This was one of the reasons why Elizabeth went along with the impersonation, she hated Janet's mother so very much.

Elizabeth knew she was deeply involved in Janet's deception, but she didn't care. The impersonation of Janet's mother, the lawyer, opening up a lawsuit in the guise of Janet's mother, signing Janet out of the hospital as the legal parent and the request to be taken to her house (not her own) were all entwined and she was the binding knot. It was Janet's and hers alone and she had no intention of letting Janet down. Once they arrived at Elizabeth's house she'd tipped the cab driver to get his aid in getting Janet up to the third floor and into Elizabeth's bed. She then hastily left for the pharmacy to pick up the prescriptions for Janet's pain and infection medications. She was extremely uncertain about the things she'd involved herself in and then she chose not to dwell on it. Circumstances would take care of themselves. The one thing she was adamant about was that she would do anything she could to keep Janet safe. That night, after taking the pain medication, Janet lay in bed not sleeping but wondering how to keep her plans a secret, at least long enough for the cast to come off but there was nothing that she could think of to explain her injuries to her parents. Although she was well under the radar, practically invisible at her home, the cast and bruises wouldn't be and there was no way of concealing them, none at all. There was only a minute degree of ignorance and time that could be forestalled by her staying at Elizabeth's house but there was no way she'd be allowed to stay long enough for the cast to be removed from her arm, leg and fingers. She lay in Elizabeth's bed, which was at the front of the house facing the street looking around at the familiar surroundings. The house couldn't be said to be nasty or dirty, it was more of a clutter of things accumulated over the years. On the bed there were five different spreads and numerous pillows with unmatched covers. The dressers were covered with perfume bottles, body powders and lotions, various lipsticks, Q-tips, cotton balls, bobby pins, tiny figurines, and old lottery tickets. The floor was carpeted with an old rug that was clean but cluttered as well with shoe boxes, bags of clothes and statues of animals, but there was order in the disorder. As Janet surveys all the signs of a lived in room her problem returned to her mind again and again hit a brick wall. It's purported that God watched over babies and drunks, perhaps, just perhaps, he watched over Janet too. It turned out that he did, but it came at a heavy price.

Sometime during the night of April 3, 1968, while Janet slept a drug induced sleep, the solution presented itself in the morning papers whose headlines Janet feared would scream '**THREE STUDENTS DEAD, DOZENS INJURED AT IN HIGH SCHOOL RIOT!**' but instead the city's largest newspaper proclaimed to a shocked nation in big bold black letters

'DR. MARIN LUTHER KING JR. SHOT AND KILLED IN MEMPHIS TENNESSEE HOTEL!'

Janet was dredged from the depths of a deeply medicated sleep by what sounded like multiple sets of fist pounding on her cousin's front door. The voices were excited, agitated, and angry repeatedly yelling, "Liz, Liz!" Janet tried to sit up, pushing off on her uncast arm and found her body was having none of that. The drug induced sleep still had her in its clutches and the room waxed and waned before her eyes. Feeling dizzy, nauseated and out of touch she collapsed back wearily onto the pillows. The voices had no clarity, so solidity, sounding as if they were fighting their way through thick mist or heavy waters to reach her ears. Her mind began to clear and she began to recognize near hysterical, angry shouts, repetitiously shouting the same thing: *They killed Martin Luther King! They killed Dr. Martin Luther King!"* She heard her cousin's heavy treads running to the door and the sound of the three locks being opened. A cacophony of voices and footsteps entered into the tiny living room still shouting, *they killed Martin Luther King!* She could hear her cousin's voice cutting in, "What? What are you talking about?" but her voice was cut off as she was dragged into the hallway and the entire angry crowd tried to tell her what was going on at the same time. Elizabeth was getting no coherent words from any of them but allowed herself to be dragged down the stairs and outside into a night that was alive, loud and angry with unrest. The sounds of whatever was going on began to fade in Janet's ears as their footsteps faded from the house and her consciousness and she again fell asleep with the voices fading away.

When she awoke the next morning she couldn't immediately grasp where she was or why she was still hearing the same angry, questioning voices of the night before only now they were much louder and powerful, more focused, angry and confused. She was disorientated and confused herself, in pain, ill at ease and her body throbbing like a rotten tooth but there was something else. There was an anxious, edginess seeping into the atmosphere. A feeling she couldn't quite describe, and while it was clearly present, it was coming from no perceptible area. Taking her time, she was able to, with difficulty, sit up. The pain caused her to gray over and she halted her movements until the sensation of free floating slowly dissolved and she called weakly for Elizabeth but there was no answer. She was alone in the house except for the rising, angry buzz that sounded like someone had disturbed the world's largest hornet's nest. That sound seemed to house something dark and sinister and was that chanting? As she tried to focus more on the sounds, it seemed more chaotic and did indeed appear to be chanting. *The natives were restless. What natives?* She wondered. She was totally confused; these were the same sounds she'd heard last night before falling asleep. It had been dark outside then with the same sounds just over the horizon of her mind but now it was daylight and the same sounds were crashing all around her. They were growing more urgent, more insistent in intensity like a symphony orchestra building up to its final roof shattering credenza. Suddenly the disembodied voices began to coalesce into an intelligent sentence, just one sentence and she understood that sentence. *They killed Dr. Martin Luther King Jr.*

Janet knew the name but couldn't, at that moment, place the significance of it. As her thoughts slowly began to come together she realized what had happened and it had happened to Dr. Martin Luther King Jr. He was dead, assassinated! The news of the riot and deaths at the high school was for the moment irrelevant and banished to the back pages of the newspapers and television news for days. Actually, it didn't see any print until almost two weeks later. The assassination proved to be a reprieve for her but for a nation it carried a heavy cataclysmic, dismaying price. It was an eye opening shock to the country, this great nation, resulting in riots across the country in over a hundred cities including Washington, D.C. Chicago, Illinois, Baltimore, Maryland, Kansas City, Detroit, Michigan, New York, Trenton and Newark, NJ and Delaware and was soon to be known as the "Holy Week Uprising' People, black and white, all over the country had taken to the streets burning whole city blocks, destroying everything in their path in their combined hurt, outrage, dismay and anger at the assassination.

The assassination of Dr. Martin Luther King Jr; who was born Michael King Jr. after his father a powerful southern Baptist minister who was inspired to change both their names after a religious retreat in the Holy Lands of Europe in 1934. It was an inspiration that would eventually inspire and change the world over with its message for equality. Dr. King Sr. visited a historical religious site where a Catholic priest named Martin Luther, in the 16th century defied the Catholic Church preaching for the need of reformation and equality. Michael King Sr. was greatly inspired by what he learned about the priest Martin Luther and upon their return home he changed both his and his son's name from Michael King to Martin Luther King to honor the German reformer. He and his son took up the fight for equality in the South and the world. It would be a name that inspired a call for Civil Rights and changed the world over. His son, now known as Dr. Martin Luther King Jr. after his father's death, took over the church and was soon to be known as the American Baptist Minister and activist for the Civil Rights Movement. He was an active member of the NAACP formulated to address civil rights and equality. He would be best known for using nonviolent, civil disobedience based on his Christian beliefs. Staging peaceful protest marches all over the South calling for equality for all. These marches were met with citizen and police brutality. The marchers were hosed with fire hoses, attacked by civilians, police and dogs and in many instances imprisoned. One famous protest, Janet remembered involved an African American, Rosa Parks who refused to give up her seat on a Montgomery bus to a white person. Dr. King Jr. helped organize a city wide boycott of the bus company. The case was repeatedly thrown out of court until a higher court ruled it was illegal to force segregation. The city of Montgomery was over ruled and a new law created making it illegal to force African Americans to go to the back of buses. In the state of Alabama it was not acceptable, according to then Governor George Wallace, for black children to attend school with white children. The National Guard was called out to escort the children safely through hundreds of angry, name calling white citizens lining both sides of the street, pushing against police barriers and guards in an attempt to prevent black children from entering into the school. Dr. King Jr.'s message for equality was brutally and cowardly ended by a man named James Earl Ray who shot and killed Dr. King Jr. on the balcony of the Lorraine Motel in Memphis, Tennessee. A shocked country (whites and blacks) exploded in riots, civil disobedience and controversy. There were 43 deaths, 2500 injuries and over 15, 000 arrests and property damage. The people, ignoring the posted warnings that looters would be shot, broke into stores, burning and looting until it was necessary to call out the National Guard in major cities to control a public who wasn't interested in being subdued. Someone near and dear to both whites and blacks had been needlessly killed and across the country angry people reveled in what was known as the greatest act of civil disobedience in the United States since the Civil War.

After remembering all she heard and seen of Dr. Martin Luther King Jr. and his famous "I Have A Dream' speech, Janet felt like she was suffocating in a cocoon of guilt, her breathing coming in short labored gasp. Raised as a Jehovah's Witness, she was taught that God knew what was in the hearts and minds of all men. He knew what you were planning to do before you actually did the act. If this was so, then he was in the hospital room with her and Elizabeth and the birth of her deception. God also knew she couldn't figure a way to hide the deception from her parents. Simultaneously, God knew that a man named James Earl Ray was finalizing his plan to assassinate the great personage of Dr. Martin Luther King Jr. So it stands to reason (in her mind) she rationalized that he, God, knew the problems surrounding her life and her planned deception; as well as the struggles for equality by Dr. Martin Luther King Jr. and James Earl Ray's plans to assassinate Dr. King Jr. If God chose to let Dr. King live it would present an implacable barrier to her plans. On the other hand, if he, God, chose to allow Dr. King to be assassinated it would

knock down the barriers allowing her deception to succeed. God chose her? Why?
She remembered a statement made by Dr. King that remained in her heart and
mind. His statement was, "The Ultimate Measure Of A Man Is Not Where
He Stands In Moments Of Comfort And Convenience But Where He Stands
At Times Of Challenge And Controversy" This statement unbeknownst to
her would later inspire inner strength and tenacity in her at a time when
she could see only a dark highway with no exit ramps before a lightless
tunnel. It would be a time yet to come, because the future was like the
past, immutable. It could not be changed nor denied and that statement
would come in handy when she locked horns with the Department Of
Dirty Tricks. Yet, her future had changed, altered in her favor by an
assassination of a great man, Dr. Martin Luther King Jr. It provided the
answer to how her injuries could be explained without divulging the law
suit. Janet's injuries were explained and accepted by her parents with the
reason being blamed on the out of control turmoil and violence on her
own street following the news of Dr. King Jr.'s assassination. The lie was
told by Elizabeth that like everyone else in the neighborhood, including
Janet's parents, she and Janet were outside watching the chaos in their
neighborhood that would eventually lead to Marshall Law being declared
two days later. They were outside Elizabeth lied to Janet's parents, when a
large crowd of people came charging down the street knocking Janet down
and she was trampled in the melee resulting in her injuries. The explanation
was accepted and not questioned by her parents who basically called her
stupid and blamed her for not getting out of the way. The problem was
solved, the lawsuit could proceed without her parent's knowledge but Janet
felt bad, confused and guilty inside. The discovery of her injuries and
probable lawsuit against the school by her parents would never materialize
because of the assassination of Dr. King Jr. His death was her reprieve. A
dirty reprieve, covered with lies, deception and for her, guilt.

Why did God sacrifice Dr. King for her? How could she feel good about an
assassination that provided a means to an end for her lies; ultimately freeing
her to pursue her deception but at the cost of the murder of one so dear to the
country? Was there really a God who loved her and if there was, didn't it stand
to reason that he also loved Dr. King too? Was she more important? There was
no greatness in her; past or future. She was barely aware of Dr. King and his

struggle for equality until her afternoon cartoons were repeatedly interrupted by adults changing the channel to Eye Witness News when the news was about someone named Martin Luther King Jr. She recalled pictures of black people, walking arm in arm singing, "We shall overcome." She saw people hosed with water, beaten by police and other people and bitten by dogs but at that time it really didn't mean anything to her. She thought the news was a made up program for adults. She felt somehow unclean, guilty and soiled and not understanding why she should have these feelings. What she couldn't put into coherent thought, what was actually troubling her, was that this man's death was actually giving her life and she was torn. Her thoughts were between herself, God and the guilt inside her. The path through the deception was now open but did she have the right to pass through? She was taught that Jesus died for man's sins. Had this man, Dr. King, died for hers? Was it a sin to have Elizabeth impersonate her mother and institute the law suit which would be hidden from her true mother? She was frightened not of her plans but of God. Life had been hard, even cruel and unfair to her but was it wrong to seek relief, happiness (albeit in the form of money) and if this relief was made possible by murder did that make it ok? She hadn't killed anyone, she argued to herself. She barely (and that was a stretch) knew anything of the man other than what she saw in the news. What did she owe him? Why should she be upset, why was this stranger's death upsetting her? Who was he to bring these troubling thoughts into her mind? Why should his death bring these unwanted thoughts tinged with guilt and remorse? Then the tears came, hot and stinging without concrete reason. She kicked impotently at the covers on the bed with her one good leg knocking the covers to the floor. It wasn't her fault if God chose her and not him. It was God's choice, God's decision, not hers. *I won't be blamed for God's choices. I won't take the blame! I won't feel this way! I didn't murder anyone!* Over and over she repeated these protestations, trying to convince herself to believe them. Just as her tear heavy eye lids were drifting shut with exhaustion another voice, an alien voice, speaking in her head snapped her eyes momentarily open again. *God has his reasons and all things, good or bad serve the Lord. Go to sleep;* and she did. She slept the night through free of anxiety, guilt and strange as it may seem pain. Her last thought was *who was that speaking to her?* And then she slept, her question unanswered.

FOUR

wo months later, Janet was still at Elizabeth's house. Her parents
weren't concerned with her and hadn't bothered to come over and
check on her. It was during this time that a letter arrived at her cousin's
house from the attorney. He needed them to come into the office and get
things started which included assigning her to several rehabilitative doctors
for her body as well as her mind. When they arrived at his office which
was more of a cubicle than an office, they were informed that a case had
been opened, the Board of Education notified and all necessary papers
and forms filed with the courts. It was his wish, he told them he wanted
to get things started as quickly as possible because there would be other
lawsuits filed from parents of deceased children. He'd surprisingly (and
pleasantly) had been contacted by the State Board of Education's attorneys.
They wanted a meeting, feeling it would be prudent to address the matter
as quickly as possible. In other words, they didn't want the media to get
wind that a lawsuit had been filed, which would cause others to follow
suit. They were of course expecting lawsuits from the parents of the three
dead students, the parents of the physically injured students, claims from
parents whose child, although not physically injured but were mentally
traumatized and the teachers, some claiming injury and others mental
trauma. They wanted to move quickly to calm the community and reassure
them (somehow) that the school was a safe environment and to provide
answers to all the questions that would arise from the parents, the media
and the State. By agreeing quickly to the first lawsuit, they would put forth
the dubious picture of great remorse and concern and that they were doing
all they could to put everyone at ease and to get things back to normal
as quickly as possible even though following the incident the school had
been closed for a week. Janet's attorney, Roger Wellington Lloyd knew
her injuries would heal but he'd insist the trauma would affect her life
both physically and mentally for years. He'd be asking for a substantial
award. In his ambitious mind he toyed with the idea of asking for a

million dollar settlement, which of course he wouldn't get but it would outline the seriousness of the lawsuit and set a standard for the lawsuits that would follow. The fact that they had contacted him for a meeting was both interesting and encouragingly in his favor. Such profound, life threatening injuries that arose from ongoing bullying that was ignored by the teachers and staff would undoubtedly result in changes in the schools policies against bullying, which currently didn't exist. The case would also generate new State laws concerning bullying, there would be terminations, training for teachers and counselors to recognize or suspect bullying and their responsibility to report and act on it. He knew it and the Board knew it. The State would want to shy away from the media fallout while he wanted to add as much flammable fuel to the media as possible. Each was aware of the others game. What they weren't aware of was the ambitious, tenacious, manipulative and imaginative mind out to set the world on fire with his first case, Roger Wellington Lloyd.

Janet set silently in a padded chair next to her mother impersonating cousin Elizabeth Nelson, who was inwardly worried that her identification would somewhere along the way be challenged. After producing her legal identification, Elizabeth signed document after document with her own name. Janet understood why they were there but confessed she didn't remember everything about how she got hurt. She well remembered Alfreda's threat, being tripped in the classroom and she could without a shadow of a doubt recall with total mental and physical clarity the white hot pain of being kicked in the behind in the hall way by Alfreda and the punch that was headed for her face but after that there was nothing else she could remember. She was listening intently to everything that was said and when he asked if they had any questions Elizabeth didn't, but Janet wanted to make another recording of everything that had been happening to her at the hands of Alfreda Whitehurst and the second recording proved to be worse than the first one taken in the hospital. Elizabeth and Roger Wellington Lloyd could hear the tears and fear in her voice but there was no emotion in her eyes as she related the entire story of being tormented by the same individual for almost two years. She had been teased, shoved in the hallways, punched, pinched, made to bring money to school (which at times she stole from her mother) to give to the bully every day or get beaten up, she was spit on, slapped, had food thrown in her face, if it wasn't taken, forced to steal from other students who incidentally would beat her up if she got caught, glue and paint in her hair and this was only half of her torment. There was the awful name calling that followed her as she walked home, seeing rocks fly past her head and wondering how much it would hurt when one, probably a big one, would hit its mark. She spoke of the many flying missiles that did strike her head, back and neck so hard they brought stinging tears of pain, fear and humiliation yet she was afraid to run because they would certainly chase her down then beat her senseless for making them run. She spoke of the teachers, by name, who failed to do anything when they witnessed her being tormented. Once a teacher told her to change her seat and when she stood up and began gathering her things, Alfreda the bully had whispered, "You better not move!" Janet feared the bully more than the teacher and did not change her seat and was summarily yelled at by the teacher while behind her Alfreda laughed and laughed.

Elizabeth and Roger Wellington Lloyd stared at her as she talked into the tape recorder, emotions flitting across their incredulous faces, bewilderment, shock and anger. It was incomprehensible that these things could be true but there was no lie in Janet's eyes. More to the point there was nothing in her eyes. She stared straight ahead at a point over her attorney's head speaking in an eerily, unhappy, depressed and frightened voice that raised goosebumps on their arms. It wasn't a conversational tone, it was more trance like. She appeared to be going back in time to bad times and places. They were not far from the truth for Janet had regressed in time in her mind. She was in that scary, wet, dark place where invisible things lurked and slithered across moist stagnant leaves and water dripped from slimy invisible walls, a place of evil silence. Her face was immobile; her eyes blank. Her words were a monotone soliloquy, droning on as she regressed into her tortured past. He recorded it all while imagining how best to manipulate the tape to Janet's advantage.

Roger Wellington Lloyd's hand reached across his desk and switched off the recorder. He pulled a handkerchief from his pocket and wiped his eyes and blew his nose as he handed Elizabeth a tissue from the box on his desk. He and Elizabeth had listened closely to her story and both of them were quite angry and hurting for Janet. He couldn't wait for the meeting next week with the State attorneys. He would open the meeting with the playing of the disembodied voice of a tortured child, his client, Janet Nelson. He wanted (in his aspiring fantasies of legal greatest) to be notorious for only taking cases that would generate large settlements and would turn down cases, that while they were legitimate, wouldn't be worth his exorbitant fee of $900 an hour. In a moment of epiphany, he recognized that he would have taken this case even if he had been an established, sought after attorney-at-law, whether there was a big pay off at the end or not. When it came to Janet, a settlement offered was no longer what mattered; what did matter was a settlement that fit the crime. He repeated to himself the promise that he'd made the first time he's seen the tiny, broken, body of Janet in the hospital bed with her arm, leg and fingers in cast, the blazing black and blue bruises about her face and visible body parts and the damage to her anus area. He was so pissed off after listening to her story of torture, fear, hopelessness and humiliation that he didn't realize that his fist were clenching and unclenching with rage. When he did register this, his only thought was Janet couldn't clinch or unclench her muscles down there without inviting the possibility of tearing the stiches that were holding her anus together. With that thought he became even more incensed, if that was possible. He was a lighted match seeking a short fuse. He was visibly trembling with rage. There were dark thunder clouds in his handsome face; his mouth was pressed together in a flat thin line as he repeated the vow he'd made but this time he said it aloud to Janet, "Don't you worry honey. They will pay! Oh yes, they will most definitely pay!"

The meeting with the State Board of Education attorneys was schedule for Friday morning but Janet's attorney against the wishes of his firm, called a press conference for Tuesday, three days before, on the steps of City Hall. There were throngs of reporters, television cameras from all the major networks, city officials and a curious public on hand and around the steps of the City Hall building. All just as he planned. He exited the doors of City Hall alone with his dead bowed, looking unhappy and dejected. In fact he looked like he was barely holding back tears. The press ate his planned performance like starving beggars given a side of beef with mashed potatoes and gravy. As he slowly approached the podium, the jostling reporters with their instruments of reporting; cameras, pencils, pads and microphones poised, he was immediately assaulted with questions, "Who was he representing?" "Was it one of the students killed in the riot?" "How did the State Board respond to the charges?" "Was it true that a large group of teachers and security guards had been terminated? "Was the daughter of the Principal really killed in the Riot?" "What was her name?" "Who was the person air lifted from the schools roof in the helicopter?" "Was the Principal spared termination because of his daughter's death?" Roger Wellington Lloyd held up his hands to quiet the rush of questions and when he had complete silence he spoke, "I have called this press conference today not to address your questions for I have no answers to any of them at this time. I have no knowledge of the State Boards actions or responses nor do I have any information regarding any terminations at the high school. At present, these things are unimportant to me. What is important and most egregious to me is my client whose name I withhold because of her age. What I do have ladies and gentlemen is a recorded statement from a fifteen year old girl who was tormented, tortured and bullied for almost two years at a school that ignored her plight. The final assault against this child who was almost beaten to death by this bully now lies with cast on her arm, leg, fingers and numerous other injuries to horrid to mention and this beating is what capitulated the riot. A final brutal attack, whose beginning was witnessed, ignored and dismissed by her teacher. You may feel this helpless child is less important because she wasn't one of the deceased students but this is not true. She is the most important person in this tragedy because it brings to a light a situation that has gone under the radar in our schools far too long. Bullying! Now ladies and gentlemen, I ask for your complete silence and to just listen. Let it be known that this child's statement is also a reflection of my own, Roger Wellington Lloyd attorney for the defense on this matter" He pushed the play button on Janet's recording and the result was fantastically more profound than he could have imagined. Unabashed shock washed throughout the silent crowd as Janet's tear filled unhappy and frighten voice drifted out over a set of one of the best speaker systems in the world, Bose. Camera men had stopped filming, reporters had stopped jostling for better positions, people's mouths hung open and more than one person was wiping their eyes, some were openly crying and reporters who had begun speed writing the words stopped, pencils poised above tablets. All were captured and enthralled as they listened to the sad emotional voice of a tormented, tortured, frightened voice of a young child drifting over the crowd on that warm Tuesday afternoon on the steps of City Hall. Normally, Roger Wellington Lloyd would have been turning gleeful handstands at the reception the tape received but he was again taken away to the dark, torturous, endless, shadowy world of a tormented child. Janet's over stressed, tearful voice floated out and over the powerful Bose speakers and invaded the hearts and minds of those listening. She spoke of all the horrible treatment she endured for almost two years, leaving out nothing. Roger Welling Lloyd was going to give his assistant a bonus for suggesting the Bose speakers being placed on the steps around the entrance to City Hall. Those speakers even captured and carried the sound of Janet's inhaling between her astonishing statements of torment, fear and humiliation. There was a devastation in that voice that brought numbness and deep sympathy to the hearts and minds of the media, television reporters, City Hall officials and the gathered public. God it was beautiful Roger Wellington Lloyd thought as he wiped at his own eyes. He was a genius, absolutely brilliant and Janet would be the most beloved child in the country tomorrow. If he asked for a million dollar settlement the world would demand three.

That evening, television news stations and radio news played and replayed Janet's tape. Day after day for over a week her voice filled the homes of citizens all over the country. People in their homes watching the news called their family members to come and listen when the tape was being played. Children from all walks of life were questioned and re-questioned on whether things like this was happening in their schools and not surprisingly, there were hundreds of tearful confessions from children to their parents about 'stuff' that they were experiencing. Editorials flooded the major papers, letters were written to the Board of Education from hundreds of communities, television phone lines were jammed with calls wanting to know more about the girl on the tape, politicians huddled to put together statements to address the tragedy and show their support for Janet Nelson and all bullied children and a call went out for changes in the schools systems to recognize and address the problem of bullying. There were tearful radio confessions from parents of children who committed suicide because of bullying. It was a media frenzy that did not go unnoticed by the partners of the law firm who hadn't been thrilled with him holding a press conference for an injury case in the first place. People began to send sympathy cards, letters, flowers and even money to the law firm. Bags and bags were delivered to the firm for Janet Nelson. Roger Wellington Lloyd humbly thanked all the writers with hand written letters and as another stroke of genius; he returned all the money that was enclosed in the envelopes explaining that Janet didn't need their money but desperately needed their support. The writers were urged to write to City Hall, their legislators and school officials letting them know that bullying was unacceptable and should not be tolerated in our schools. News of the letters and the returned monies was anonymously leaked to the media (courtesy of Roger Wellington Lloyd) and the public lapped it up with praises for the lawyer, the firm and prayers for Janet. Imagine a lawyer returning money! Unheard of, everyone knew lawyers were about the 'Bling, bling" siphoning as much money from their clients but not this one! It was indeed another brilliant ploy and endeared the people and the media even more to Janet, Roger Wellington Lloyd, and of course the law firm, who was brave enough to take up the fight against the government for Janet's rights. The publicity, which he, as well as the firm received, propelled them both into celebrity status with book deals, television and radio appearances and even talk of a movie where he'd play himself. It all served to make him one of the countries most publicized and sought after attorneys in the country. Any other time, Roger Wellington Lloyd would have been popping the champagne cork, dancing a naked jig on the ceiling and wallowing in his new found fame but celebration was the furthest thing from his mind. There was only Janet.

Janet's parents, without any fuss or muss, allowed Janet to remain at Elizabeth's house to avoid the constant attention she required. Roger Wellington Lloyd became a regular visitor at the house he believed to be Janet's home. On his visits he would sit on the edge of the bed or in a chair if she was on the living room sofa and taking her un-cast hand in his own, he'd ask, "Hey Monkey Face, are you awake?" He was falling in love with her as a father to his adoring daughter and not so strangely, she loved him as what she termed her 'fantasy father' His heart always melted when she opened sleepy eyes and smiled a bright, contagious smile that he couldn't help but return with his own. They enjoyed each other's company and she would miss him sorely on days he didn't stop by. Her bruises had faded away revealing a very pretty face. Along with her strikingly long, black hair, Janet had beautiful, soft, brown cat-like eyes under pencil thin arched eyebrows. Her clear brown complexion was perhaps a shade darker than her eyes and a tiny upturned nose over a wide sensitive mouth. She had a babyish, angelic face that would mature into a heart breaking beauty; but it was a beauty Janet didn't see. Perhaps this was why the bully Alfreda Whitehurst hated her so, because of her quiet beauty. Janet believed herself to be hideously ugly when she looked in the mirror. She felt this about herself because that was what her mother and stepfather constantly called her, ugly, and she believed them. Roger Wellington Lloyd had gotten into the habit of talking to her about himself, his hopes and dreams and his desire to become a great sought after attorney and the types of cases he'd handle. He told her she was his first case and he was a little scared hoping that he'd do well by her. She had assured him that he was of course the best ever. He'd smile at that and soon they were both laughing and it didn't stop until she reached over with her uncast arm and hugged him tightly. Tears welled up in his eyes as he returned the hug while stroking her long hair. He'd gotten permission for a private tutor for her, who would come to her home to keep up her lessons. She would be out of school for months and he didn't want her to have to repeat the eleventh grade. He proudly announced to her that he'd be sitting in the front row at her graduation where she was sure to be valedictorian. Janet was ecstatic loving her fantasy father.

Janet loved Roger Wellington Lloyd and often imagined being his little girl. A father who'd greet her with a smiling face and wide open arms at the sound of her running feet approaching him after school. He'd snatch her up, swing her around into a giant bear hug saying, "There's daddies little girl!" She imagined locking her arms around his neck, smelling the daddy smell of shaving cologne, screaming with laughter and happiness as he held her close and she held him even closer. On many occasions her heart ached for want of a real father's love. She completely dismissed the need for a mother's love, only daddy that was important. It was daddy who'd love, protect and smother her with hugs and kisses and this was what was building in her heart for Roger Wellington Lloyd; a father's love, Roger Wellington Lloyd's love. He came practically every day and they'd talk for hours about anything and everything. He began teaching her to play chess and once understanding the pieces and their movements, she quickly began giving him a run for his money. He discovered she was quite intelligent and had a pretty extensive vocabulary for a sixteen year old. He introduced her to the study of law saying anyone as intuitive as she was must study law or medicine. Both areas appealed to her and she began to question him about the laws, courts and people's rights. He was impressed with her retention skills and began to wonder if she had a photographic memory. He showed her how he was putting her case together and the importance of information, contacts, confidentiality and manipulation of situations, facts and witnesses. He told her how he manipulated the media with her tape recording. You've got to get society on your side; the rest would fall into place he'd told her. He showed her blank legal forms, filing petitions and answered a question that she'd had for years like just what is Habeas Corpus? He laughed explaining that it was basically holding a person against their rights. He'd made up mock cases, leaving blank forms and a legal pad for her to put together her case for homework. When he returned, he'd find that the only thing hindering her work from being accepted in a court of law was that the forms were filled out in pencil. She was very good and intuitive and he told her she was unofficially, technically a sixteen year old para legal. She absorbed it all never knowing that the teachings would save her years later. She was of course, well aware that he wasn't her father. Her father was a stranger, a dead man in a box, buried she knew not where and whoever he had been, he'd been replaced by an evil, nasty ogre of a stepfather that she'd never did or would call daddy.

Over the course of the next six months Janet's cast were removed from her leg, arm and fingers. She started regular sessions with a psychiatrist and progressed smoothly with her tutor who wondered why she wasn't in advance classes. The only issue was the painful physical therapy. When her attorney called to check on her progress he was informed of her failure to adapt and comply with the exercises because of the severe pain. She didn't understand that the pain was a necessary part of the healing process. No pain, no gain. After receiving these reports Roger Wellington Lloyd began showing up at her sessions offering encouragement and with him there the pains had become just a little more endurable. The new school term was already in session and having done well with her tutor Janet was passed into the twelfth grade from home. After one particular grueling session of physical therapy, they sat down and talked about her returning to school and she became quiet and despondent and this puzzled him. She told him that she wished she didn't have to return to that school, ever. She understood that in order for her to attend a different school her family would have to move to another district and that was totally out of the question. Janet was silent, digesting his words. Roger Wellington Lloyd said he'd look into having her transferred to another school but not to get her hopes up. Schools did have bussing programs where children from one school district attended school in another district; perhaps under her circumstances she'd be allowed into the program. She brightened up with hope, crossed her fingers and smiled. "You can do it. I know you can. You can do anything!" With a chuckle he believed her believing that he could do anything.

It was December, eight months since the fight and Janet was returning to school on a cold, blustery morning. Resigned, she stood on the corner waiting for the approaching bus when a car, horn blaring demanding attention pulled up in front of her. Out jumped Roger Wellington Lloyd with a big Kool-Aid grin on his face, "Hey Monkey Face, where are you going?" Janet, as always happy to see him for the moment forgot her woes of returning to school, laughed out loud and said, "To school, I guess. Are you here to give me a ride to the house of horrors?" "Nope." he replied opening the passenger side door for her. "I'm here to escort you to the Montclair School for the Gifted, located in scenic Montclair, NJ hop in!" Janet stood there speechless while he laughed hustling her into the toasty warm car. Roger Wellington Lloyd had indeed given his full attention to getting Janet transferred without the need of the family moving. He found that it hadn't been all that difficult. With the publicity surrounding her, the case and her exemplary grades, he'd gotten her accepted to the Montclair

School for the Gifted to complete her final year of high school. The school snatched her up free of charge for the humanitarian publicity it would generate for the school. She was overcome with surprise and joy. He'd gotten her accepted into the school over a month ago and was bursting with excitement to tell her but he held on to his secret, only Elizabeth knew as she had to sign the admission papers and she promised not to tell. He wanted her to find out in just the manner she had. He knew what day she would be returning to school and where she'd pick up the bus. He was parked half a block from the bus stop so he could see her and the arriving bus. He could barely sit still has he spied her walking to the bus stop. "No." he told himself, "Not yet, wait until the bus is coming." He was so excited for her and the anticipated effect of his secret that he couldn't stop smiling. When he saw the bus approaching he screeched out of his parking space and left skid marks when he braked in front of her. He was full to bursting with pride and love for Janet and his secret gift to her. He loved his children dearly but again found himself wishing she was his daughter.

They pulled away from the bus stop headed for the Parkway entrance and Janet was chattering away like the proud goose that laid the first golden egg. He listened in silence with a smile. When they arrived at the school, he escorted her inside to the administration department and after hugging him good bye, she was given a list of classes, taken to the school's book and supply store, her identification picture was taken and her uniforms would be supplied later and she didn't have to pay for those either. She was escorted to her first class in a school for the gifted and best of all there was a bus that would provide round trip service from her home. Was all this really happening to her? Her new class mates didn't know anything about her; she was simply the new girl in class. The teachers however, knew exactly who she was and practically fell over themselves to make her feel comfortable and at home in her new surroundings. Her classmates she found were easy going and helped each other with their lessons and she was sucked into their mist with no fuss on the first day. She discovered they were indeed gifted, very smart, but they weren't snobbish about their talents. The classes were all geared for college bound ambitions. She was amazed at the lessons, which were difficult but not out of her league and she fell right in with the work load which was nothing like her high school studies. She was the world's happiest girl thanks to Roger Wellington Lloyd.

After dropping Janet off he was navigating the morning traffic to hopefully get to work on time. At same time the directors of his law firm were already pass their coffee and donuts and were well on their way to the brandy while discussing Roger Wellington Lloyd. The law firm of Graves, Ritter and Reddick was an old prestige's firm over eighty years old representing old and new money. It dealt with all forms of law foreign and domestic and made millions of dollars for its clients. One didn't just call them for legal services. A prospective client had to be referred by a current client and before accepting a new client a dossier was compiled on the individual or company, which included background checks, assets, societal standing and even their politics and they never accepted personal injury lawsuits. The firm would never consider representing anyone or company no matter how much money they'd pay, if they had questionable backgrounds or affiliates. Nothing was allowed to tarnish the firm or its history. They were a shrewd bunch of 'Good ole boys' but they were honest with themselves, their clients and their billable hours. Their investments spanned the globe and it was always ready and eager for more because money represented political power. If one ever questioned the existence of an organization called the 'Blazer Club' they could, with proper introduction, heritage, wealth and age be allowed into the catacombs of the firm. They'd find such an organization existed and how it represented itself as an extensive, wealthy and powerful law firm. Few were ever invited in and no one ever resigned from the club accept in death and in that event it was already prearranged by that member who would succeed in his chair (No Women Allowed). Of the twelve directors on its board only one was a member of The Blazer Club. Junior partners weren't considered for membership and associate attorney's names weren't even known by the partners but they knew Roger Wellington Lloyd's name. He had been the subject of discussion for months and now the issue being discussed was how to keep him from being lured away to another firm, they desperately wanted to keep him. He had been hired as a law researcher for their legal library and no one could quite figure out how a researcher got the Janet Nelson case. They couldn't even figure out how the firm accepted a personal injury case; when as a rule they didn't handle such cases. Actually, it had been a fluke how Roger Wellington Lloyd got the case and a gamble by him accepting it. When the call came in from Elizabeth at the hospital looking for an attorney, the regular receptionist was on lunch and an office secretary took the call. The receptionist kept a file on available attorneys at the firm. The secretary didn't know the firm didn't accept personal injury cases and when she looked through the receptionist file she saw no one available accept a Mr. Roger Wellington Lloyd. She contacted him in the library and gave him the message from Elizabeth whom she had on hold. Even though he had passed the bar (with the lowest score in his group) he knew it was a mistake for the call to come to him but he answered it anyway arranging the hospital meeting and things just rolled along from that point. When he showed up to work the next day to brief the partners they were all set to toss his ass out the door, terminated. One of the partners noting that they were committed to the case, pushed to allow Mr. Roger Wellington Lloyd to carry on with the case saying to him, "Young man if you know anything about this firm you'd know we don't accept personal injury cases," he paused looking sternly at him and continued, "but I admire your balls for actually contacting the client and your fanatic need to prove yourself out of the library. So I'll tell you what, go ahead, let's see how you handle yourself. We don't play with the law or our clients or words in this firm, so I'm letting you know now that if you fuck this up, you're out of here and out of a job you should have never had in the first place. "Imagine," he said sarcastically, "Scoring the lowest on the Bar Exam. You're dismissed." He said with contempt to Roger Wellington Lloyd. Roger left for the hospital on weak legs and the seat of his cheap trousers on fire calling himself stupid for what he tried to get away with at the firm. The rest as we say is history.

Roger Wellington Lloyd had not only impressed the firm but succeeded in impressing the country. The twelve directors, none of which were less than fifty years of age and wore nothing less than $1000 dollar suits; were astonished at his approach to the case and where blown away at his performance at the press conference at City Hall which they'd watched in their boardroom. The request for him to meet with the State attorneys a day later with talks of a settlement in so short a time was unheard of, unexpected and impressive. It was sheer brilliance playing that tape publicly, it was dynamite. They were, at first, obstinate about him returning the money people sent in for his client but he insisted on running the case his way, after all they did say to him, "Let's see what you can do." Then they saw the imaginative logic of returning the money in hand written letters. It sent the message to the public and the media that the firm wasn't interested in money, their interest was in their client's rights. They had no doubt that it was him who tipped the media about the returned monies. The firm was besieged with praise by people, organizations, reporters and institutions of higher learning who thought that was a fine gesture, a great thing to do. Then innocently putting pressure on the politicians by telling the letter writers to write to their politicians and legislators was another stroke of genius. The firm's phone lines were jammed with calls from Congressman, Senators and he even Washington D.C. where they were being set up to meet the President of the United States to thank them for bringing the problem of bullying in schools to light. Everyone was eager to join the firm's fight against bullying in the schools (which incidentally brought out the situation of bullying in the work place) and the push by the firm for new legislative laws to address bullying was fantastic. Marvelous! Roger Wellington Lloyd (they loved his name) had single handedly accomplished what no one in the history of the firm had ever done. He bought the firm into high media profile, had them leading the charge for new legislative laws surrounding bullying (which would undoubtedly be instigated into law) had the public, societal organizations and the media praising the firm and the public at large practically worshipping them. Remarkable! Now he and the firm were in high demand for representation, speeches at colleges and law universities, television interviews, even talks about one on one sit down with interview in the Washington Review; and all along the mail room of the firm continued to receive cards, letters, money and flowers for Janet and praise for the firm and Roger Wellington Lloyd. The firm was also aware of the dozens of calls seeking to lure Roger Wellington Lloyd to their firms and the partners had no intention of letting that happen.

Roger Wellington Lloyd wasn't aware that he was the subject of the day being discussed up there on the 22nd floor of the building. He was currently at that moment getting bawled out by the office Manager for being late and receiving his final warning not to be late again. But nothing could upset his mood after the morning he'd had with Janet. He walked into his tiny cubicle and was about to sit down when the office manager returned looking very pleased. "They want to see you upstairs." he said to Roger. As he walked out of the cubicle the manager added with a nasty sneer, "Take your things with you, I don't imagine you'll be back." and he was right. When Roger Wellington Lloyd left the Director's office on the 22nd floor it wasn't with instructions regarding his termination, it was with the keys to his new Junior Partner corner office on the 21st floor complete with receptionist, private secretary, two paralegals and a fantastic view of the city included. Roger Wellington Lloyd looked around the huge office taking in the large, shiny mahogany desk, the plush leather chairs, polished tables, sofa, private bathroom, kitchenette, a wall of glassed in empty book shelves and he was quietly elated. All this was due to Janet. After staring out of the large, sun glare resistance windows at the city sprawled below him for about half an hour, he sat in the soft leather chair behind his desk, sinking into the luxurious feel and smell of the rich leather. He picked up his phone with its numerous buttons, which he thought wouldn't be connected but when he heard the dial tone he pushed the intercom for his private secretary. There was an immediate soft knock at his door and a slightly overweight woman, professionally dress with well styled greying hair and spectacles perched on her nose entered his new office and he liked her immediately, there was a reassuring quality in her composure and grandmotherly stature. He introduced himself and then asked, "So how does a new Junior Partner start his first day?" The woman, Ms. Harris, smiled a motherly smile and pointed at a metal basket on his desk. "Those are all new cases. You need to go through all of them, pick the ones you feel are representable, discarding the rest, with a written reason of course, of why you feel you can't represent the client. The discarded cases are forwarded by me to the Director's office. They will either agree or disagree with you. If they disagree, the files will be returned to you and you have to prepare a case for the client. Now to start this all off, I first ask what your preference is when you arrive in the morning; coffee or tea. Since you're already here," she smiled, "I'll take your order, return with it, give you as much time as you need to review the cases in the basket and then you call me back in and give me instructions on anything you need in relation to the cases." she concluded. Roger Wellington Lloyd looked at the imposing, intimidating stack of files and anxiety was written all over his face. "Don't worry," Ms. Harris smiled, "The work is difficult, time consuming but not to worry, you've got me!" she said indicating herself, "And I'm the best damn paralegal in this building. Lots of people put in to work with you but I got the job because this firm knows I'm good and that you're a genius. What choice did they have but to team us together? I was quite impressed with your work on the Nelson case. You'll do just fine. Did you know a settlement offer came in on the case? I don't know the amount offered but I hear it's a whopper! You earned this office Mr. Roger Wellington Lloyd. It's a nice office isn't it? And I'm here to see that you keep it. So, let's get started." Roger Wellington Lloyd nodded and then added, "Thanks for that welcome." "You're welcome, now coffee or tea Mr. Roger Wellington Lloyd. I love your name; it's very aristocratic." He laughed, chose hot tea and reached for the top file and started reading as she quietly left the office for his tea. He opened the file and was half way through it when Ms. Harris returned with his hot tea. He read the file slowly and meditatively with minute intervals of tea sips. His excitement of the appointment was already behind him. He loved the challenges of defending the law and dove in head first.

FIVE

F ive months had passed so quickly that Janet didn't realize they were in the first week of May and she'd been progressing well at The Montclair School for the Gifted with a G.P.A. of 4.00. She was expected to be in the running for valedictorian at the June graduation, although her counselor told her not to really expect it because other graduating students had put in three years at the school and she had only been there for a few months. It wouldn't be fair not to recognize those students. Janet didn't mind, she was grateful for the opportunity to be at the school period. During her months there, she had gained a new level of confidence. She was a member of several clubs and had lots of friends. She wasn't able to attend after school activities due to her sickly mother, she had lied, but the school was set up so informally that the clubs met during the course of the school day. She saw Roger Wellington Lloyd very infrequently now, due to his important new job but they often talked over the phone. The last time she'd seen him was last month when he came to the house with a blank job application and a duffle bag full of letters addressed to her in care of the firm. The job she was applying for was his off duty secretary and her duty was to answer all the letters in the bag by hand. Some of the letters contained money. She would be paid $10 for each answered letter and when she came across money in the envelopes she was to write the amount down and return the money to the sender. He in return would give her the returned monies from his own pocket. It was a great arrangement; she was making her own money and now had a savings account. She really appreciated the correspondences and a lot of the letters, surprisingly came from out of state and she enjoyed answering them and thanking the people for their support.

Near the end of class one day, a message came over the PA system instructing all graduating students to report to the auditorium after school for graduation practice. At 2:00 p.m. Janet reported to the auditorium where they practiced entering the auditorium, seating and then walking across the stage to receive their diploma and exiting the stage. The practice ended at 4 p.m. and she was on the bus headed home. Janet walked up the stairs of her real home, a four story brick apartment building and knocked on the door. It was yanked open by an angry, growling stepfather demanding to know where she'd been; as if he really cared. Before Janet could open her mouth and explain about the graduation rehearsal, his hand lashed out and smacked her a tremendous, crushing blow to the side of her head causing it to slam violently into the cement hallway wall. Bright lights and stars exploded in her head and a haze drifted over her eyes as her vision doubled, then tripled wavering in and out and she started drifting downwards towards the hallway floor. She was on the precipice of passing out from the horrendous, vicious blow she never saw coming. Her vision began to clear and the three men in front of her became two, then one, then her stepfather. Through tear filled eyes and an unforgiving throbbing in her head, she saw her mother standing a few feet behind her stepfather looking at her and as usual saying or doing nothing at the vicious attack on her daughter. Janet's head was pulsating with unending pain and flashing multicolored lights. A small trickle of blood had begun flowing from the ear that smashed against the cement wall and a much wider stream was flowing from her nose and mouth. The pain was incredible and all-encompassing and without realizing that she was doing it Janet leaped onto her stepfather, raining blow after blow about his head and shoulders. Her forward lunge pushed him back along the long hallway of the apartment that ended at the refrigerator in the kitchen. Her stepfather, who expected nothing but the usual silent tears from Janet, was stunned at the totally unexpected attack that propelled him back into Janet's mother and the three of them staggered unbalanced down the hallway from the force of Janet's attack. Like Alfreda Whitehurst, the bully, he was in the dark zone. He never stood a chance to defend himself as he was struck over and over by Janet's fist that had amazing force behind them. He tried to grab her arms but it was useless. Her assault was as vicious as his blow to her head. She heard nothing except silent screams in her head. She saw nothing accept him and she'd had enough and was determined to strike down his poison right there, right now. She let loose a loud primitive yell and for the first time tears streamed down her face as her attack intensified, and the backward motion of the three of them ended when they crashed against the refrigerator at the end of the hall momentarily rocking it on its foundations. Her mother, attempting to scramble from behind her husband, was now free and trying to restrain Janet. She grabbed her from behind and the cowardly stepfather took the opportunity to grab Janet by the front of her torn bloody blouse and the top of her skirt and was attempting to lift her up over his head and slam her to the floor. Sensing what he was coming, Janet locked her legs around his chest and both arms around his neck. Then leaning sideways with all the weight and strength she could muster from her 95 pounds she twisted sideways pulling both of them down onto the floor and her tiny fist resumed pounding into his face and his now his exposed chest. She saw fear in his rummy eyes as she continued battering him with her tiny fist. Suddenly she was again yanked from behind and thrown across the kitchen floor where she slammed against the cabinet that held plates, bowls, and glasses that clicked and clattered violently. The cabinet had lower drawers that held eating utensils forks, spoons and knives. "Knives" the word flashed in Janet's mind like a bright beacon. Turning she snatched open the knife drawer and her eyes settled on the large butcher's knife with the serrated edges and she reached for it. Elizabeth had been visiting friends in the apartment across the hall was just leaving when the commotion started. She didn't see the blow to Janet's head but she saw and heard her head hit the wall with a sickening thud and she came running to Janet's aid. Enough was enough and she'd be damned if she was going to let that man beat Janet again. Her pudgy hands were balled into fist the size of small hams, her face a mask of furious indignation as she waddled down the hallway to the scene of Janet atop of her stepfather beating the holy shit out of him. A malevolent grin spread across her face at the sight and inside she smiled to herself, *about time baby, kick his ass!* And Janet was doing just that; kicking his black ass and he couldn't get up to make an attempt at fighting back. Waddling as fast as her thick legs would allow her down the hall way to where Janet, her stepfather and her mother were entangled, she saw that the fight was out of control. Just before she reached them, she saw Janet's mother grab and fling Janet across the kitchen and Janet was now digging deep in the cabinet drawer. Elizabeth, Janet's mother and stepfather all saw her pull the large evil looking knife from the drawer. The three of them seemed to simultaneously receive the same telegraphed warning/message and their eyes bulged in horror and fear at the dark determination in Janet's eyes as she lifted the knife over her head in a death plunge. She was open for business and that business was the murder of her stepfather. Janet's mother leaped up and shoved Janet violently backwards and she again fell against the same cabinet narrowly missing impaling herself on the sharp upended knife in her hand. Elizabeth saw Janet raise the knife again and she screamed, "Oh my God, Janet no. Don't do it!" Elizabeth wobbled swiftly across the kitchen floor and tried to grab the knife from Janet's hand. "Let it go Janet! Let it go!" Elizabeth yelled but she was ignored by Janet as she fought to get to her stepfather; the huge serrated knife high above her head again in a position for killing. While her stepfather was trying to back paddle away from the blade, Elizabeth grabbed and twisted Janet's arm that held the knife. A bolt of pain streaked up Janet's arm and it was immediately paralyzed and the knife fell from her grasp. The knife was kicked away by Elizabeth but trying to hold Janet was like trying to hold a wounded gorilla. She was all thrashing arms, legs and snapping teeth. Janet's mother began yelling at Janet, "Get out! Get the hell out of here!" Elizabeth with tremendous effort pulled a still struggling Janet down the hallway, out the apartment, down the stairs and over to her house. The last thing Janet saw (a thing she would never forget) was her mother kneeling over and consoling her husband, supporting his head while she administered several blast of medicine from his asthma bottle. She had apparently beaten him into an asthma attack. The sight hurt Janet profoundly seeing her mother helping and comforting him when she had witnessed him punching her in the head. He had started this thing, not her. Yet she went to his aid. When they arrived at Elizabeth's house Janet was quiet, shaking and despondent. She lay across Elizabeth's bed and it was more frightening to Elizabeth that there were no tears, she just laid there, eyes open looking disconnected from things and Elizabeth cried for her. The child was hurting pretty bad inside and not from the fighting. Her spirit was broken, she was a crushed tragedy and Elizabeth was very concerned when Janet suddenly curled into a fetal position. This alarmed Elizabeth even more than her silence but she didn't know what she could do for her. She picked up a book, sat down next to the curled body of Janet on her bed, pulled Janet's head onto her lap and began reading to her in a soft, soothing voice. Janet appeared not to hear but she remained still until her eyes began fluttering and she fell asleep. Elizabeth sat in a chair next to the bed all night intermittently crying as she watched over her. Inside, she too, was hurt and despondent over Janet. Elizabeth wanted to return to Janet's house and give her mother a piece of her mind but she didn't want to leave Janet alone. When Elizabeth awoke the next morning, her back aching from sleeping in an upright position, Janet was up and dressed preparing to leave for school. Janet looked at her and said that she was fine and that she would see her after school and left. Still feeling uneasy, Elizabeth called out sick from her job and hour or so later she called the school to find out if Janet was there; she was. She wanted to be home for Janet when school let out. Janet stayed at Elizabeth's house for three weeks. When she returned home nothing was mentioned about the fight. Janet avoided her parents and they likewise avoided her. Needless to say, he never laid a hand on her again but there were other ways to get her. Yes, there were other ways.

After doing her homework, Janet went back to responding to the letters from well-wishers received at the law firm as Roger Wellington Lloyd had requested and paid her to do. One letter contained a newspaper clipping about a fifteen year old boy from Connecticut who had been driven to suicide due to constant bullying. Cal Paltry committed suicide after his first day of high school. His friends reported that he'd been unrelentingly bullied for years by his class mates in Junior high school and it carried on into the first day of high school. After returning home that first day he shot himself to death. He had written several warnings about what he was going to do to end the bullying but no one listened. He was found dead in his bedroom from a self-inflicted gunshot wound to the head authorities said. His friends reported that in the eighth grade he was sent to the hospital for stitches after his head was bashed into a school locker. Faculty members called the incident an accident and refused to show the hall camera video of the attack. In his biology class, his phone was taken from him and smashed to the floor. Walking home from school he was frequently shoved into prickly bushes. One former classmate was quoted saying, "When you think of all the hard stuff he went through day after day, you realized he was suffering through some really hard stuff." His parents were blindsided, never knowing or suspecting what was happening to their son until police showed them the things he'd written about killing himself because of the bullying. They blamed the school. There was no return address on the letter and Janet tearfully wished there was because she wanted to write back. Instead she saved the clipping for her attorney. The letter sparked her interest in just how many kids, like her, were bullied day after day. They actually killed themselves because of school bullying and she broached the subject with Roger Wellington Lloyd on his next visit. He too became curious and researched the subject.

Roger Wellington Lloyd was astonished at the amount of adolescent and teen suicides all over the country all due to bullying. The list was incredible and when he was called into the Directors office of his firm and was told of a settlement offer of $187,467 for Janet Nelson, the Directors were stunned when he flatly turned down what was an amazing offer. He handed each of them four sheets of paper with a list of the names of children under age 18 who had committed suicide from bullying. The list was long, shocking and dismaying. He planned to present it to the State attorneys with the message that Janet Nelson had missed being on that list. Her cause of death would have been recorded as being beaten to death by a known bully; who tormented his client for years with the staff's direct knowledge of the bullying. He also had the names of those teachers and eye witness accounts from students. He planned to publish the list. The partners continued looking at the list, which amazingly began in the year 1877!

1877 – Arthur Gibbs, age 12, cause of death suicide due to bullying.

1884 – Jane Oldman, age 13, Allentown, Derby. Cause of death listed as bullying.

1986 – Mary-Western age 14, Canada. Cause of death suicide due to bullying.

1984 – Nicky Ralph, age 15 suicide due to bullying.

1990 – Patrick Helmsman, age 13, Vermont suicide due to bullying

1993 – Margie Gant, age 13, Missouri, suicide due to bullying

1992 – Sladjana Vymur age 16 suicides from bullying.

1995 – Patrick Prood, age 15, Massachusetts, suicide due to bullying.

1992 – Tom Flements, age 17, Piscataway, NJ suicide due to bullying. The list went on and on.

The Directors agreed with Roger Wellington Lloyd's request to refuse the offer and true to his word, he presented the list to the State Attorneys on their next meeting with the threat of publication. In that meeting Roger Wellington Lloyd had them twisted in a bind shut completely down. Fearing the backlash of publicizing that list; that infamous tape recording, names of the teachers and student witnesses, the hot button issue of bullying, the media and the support of politicians and the public, the State attorneys crumbled and made another settlement offer to Roger Wellington Lloyd himself; along with an offer to join their firm.

And so it was, three weeks later, with the wind behind his back and beneath his wings, Roger Wellington Lloyd arrived flushed and out of breath, after charging up the three flights of stairs to Elizabeth's apartment. He was supporting himself on the hallway door, trying in vain to catch his breath and talk at the same time. His breathing was labored, sucking in too much air and releasing too little in short, frightening gasp. He was overcome with emotional excitement and couldn't get any coherent words pass his mouth. Elizabeth and Janet put an arm under each of his arms and guided him into the apartment to an ugly stuffed, baggy chair with tuffs of cotton sticking out of its arms and supported with a telephone book beneath one leg. He sat or was rather forced down and he immediately leaped back up into Elizabeth's arms. He encircled her wide waist with arms that didn't quite reach around her bulk and began kissing her about the face. When he released her, he turned and lifted Janet up into the air, laughing and spinning her around. "We won! We won!" he shouted breathlessly overcome with emotion. "The case is over, we won!" he told them again in a breathless stutter of words. "Won what?" Elizabeth and Janet asked simultaneously. His excitement became contagious, enveloping the both of them and they too became excited and celebratory even though they had no idea what the celebration was all about. Roger Wellington Lloyd sat them both down and pulling a lop-sided kitchen chair up to face them both he sat down and told them that he'd just left the State Attorney's office of the Board of Education and a settlement had been offered on Janet's case and if it was alright with them he'd like to accept a settlement offer of $787.485! He was still trembling with excitement as he looked at their incredulous faces but all was quiet in the tiny apartment. He looked back and forth between the astonished Janet and Elizabeth who sat stunned and immobile, saying nothing. With a giant Kool-Aid smile on his face, he took one of both of their hands in his and with a huge Kool-Aide smile asked, "Well, shall we accept the offer?"

It was, the Directors of his firm agreed, an extraordinary offer. It would have been a dicey move on the Board of Education's part to risk the matter in open court and the hands of a jury. It might have settled for a hell of a lot less if not for Janet's tape recording. They doubted if there would have been a dry eye in the court room after listening to that tape recording which they too had been overcome by. That coupled with that list of child suicides due to bullying, names of teachers, witnesses and all the publicity surrounding the case it would have been a done deal. They wouldn't be able to select twelve jurors who hadn't heard that tape recording of the tortured child. Add to that the hundreds of sympathy letters (sure to be introduced by Roger Wellington Lloyd in court) and finally the noose around their neck was that list of adolescent suicides all proven to have been the result of bullying. It was a no win case. Almost a year later, the firm was continuing to receive letters and support for Janet and praise for the firm. Everyone, including school age children knew about the 'Girl on the tape' Then there was the involvement of publicity seeking politicians who booked a seat on the gravy train as supporters of Janet Nelson (in reality they wanted to look good for upcoming elections) and the new legislative laws regarding 'Bullying' that had already been drafted and publicized before the ink was barely dry. The only issue left the Board of Education and the State recognized was how much it would cost them. The State and the Board knew that in court the settlement amount would be up to the jurors. That might go into the millions with the way Roger Welling Lloyd was setting up the case and if the Board appealed the juror's settlement the public and media uproar would start all over again. The Board and the State would be the bad guys, unfeeling, uncaring, unsympathetic to a child almost beaten to death by a known bully and what was currently going on in schools around the country that were supposed to be safe. And let's not forget the media who just wouldn't stop bringing up the issue of bullying and periodically playing that tape when any child was involved in an altercation at a school. The continuing letters to government officials and school boards all over the country continued to be a thorn in their side. They definitely couldn't allow Janet Nelson to testifying or risk that infamous tape being played before the jurors (which they knew Roger Wellington Lloyd would definitely do) while the jurors eyes were on the tiny child who narrowly escaped being killed by a bully. Any potential jury, along with the entire country was already sympathetic towards the child even before a trial date was set. There would be standing room only at the trial with most of the seats taken by the media. The probability of selecting twelve jurors who were unbiased or unaware of that tape was millions to one. It was an explosive public issue and they knew Roger Wellington Lloyd was going to milk it for all it was worth. He'd proven this by rejecting the first and second settlement offers. If this thing went to a public court he would come out with two six guns blazing and let all sissies get down below. He'd already indicated that he planned to include testimony from noted psychiatrist to testify to the lasting effects of bullying on a child nearly beaten to death, eye witness accounts from class mates and the embarrassing testimony from teachers whom Janet had named as witnesses to her bullying incidents in class, gym, the cafeteria and hallways. The Board and the State's case crumbled and the only cap put on the settlement offer was that the amount would not be made public.

When Roger Wellington Lloyd heard their offer at the meeting and he was jumping for joy inside. He was well aware that a court trial would be in his pocket from the moment faceless people around the city began receiving notices to report for jury duty. He didn't know it but there were hundreds hoping they'd be selected. He wasn't greedy for himself or Janet but he wanted the settlement to fit the crime and a settlement stretching over $700,000 certainly did that. He accepted the offer on Janet's behalf but of course would have to get her mother's approval. He couldn't get out of the Director's office of his firm fast enough to suit him after informing them of the offer. He tried to restrain himself from running to his office to gather documents and head for Elizabeth's house. The elevator, he felt, was taking much too long to reach the 21st floor, so he took the stairs two and three at a time all the way down to the building lobby. Outside the building on the crowded sidewalk, he couldn't remember where he'd parked his car. He settled for hailing a passing taxi, gave Elizabeth's address and tried to settle down and relax for the over thirty minute drive. His thoughts were solely on Janet and what that amount of money would do for her and her mother. With $787,435 dollars they could afford to move out of that third floor fire trap apartment into a new and better neighborhood. He thought back to his first meeting with Janet Nelson, all broken, bruised and barely conscious in the hospital bed and his silent promise to her, that he'd make them pay for what happened to her. Roger Wellington Lloyd eyes closed with a smile on his face and whispered to himself into the back seat of the taxi, "Promised kept Janet"

During the ride to Elizabeth's house, Roger Wellington Lloyd was thinking how in less than a year his life had changed. After graduating from law school and applying to take the Bar Exams (for which he almost didn't show up for) as just another white boy with a wife, two kids and dreams of grandeur. He had wandered aimlessly up one street and down another ending up in the park trying to figure out where his life was headed. He didn't expect to pass the exams because he was a lazy student as proven by his class work. He'd gone to law school because he genuinely wanted to practice law. The work had been nothing short of grueling and time after time he asked himself what he was doing in law school. He struggled through and when he reached his final year his G.P.A. had still never topped 2.07. It was hopeless, but he could think of nothing else he wanted to do in life and over all he had a family to support. He showed up for and took the Bar Exams and wasn't a bit surprised when he discovered in the mail that he'd passed ranking in the bottom 1% of his group. No law firm would hire him. He found this to be true when he wasn't contacted for an interview by any of the dozens of firms he'd contacted. When he came across an ad seeking a law researcher for the firm of Graves, Ritter and Reddick he applied for and got the job. His family had to eat and he at least had one foot in the door. And now, less than a year later, he was a Junior Partner! Life certainly was strange and filled with unexpected twist and turns but it seemed that sometimes your dreams did come true. His dreams and Janet's destiny were entwined, although at that time they weren't aware each other existed; but once they met great things happened for the both of them. He settled back into the lingering smell of old tobacco in the cab and napped until they reached his destination. He just couldn't get over the impossibility of a law student banished to catacombs of a firm's research library, had somehow become not only a junior partner but a much sought after celebrity.

While Roger Wellington Lloyd was napping in euphoria in the cab headed for the Nelson home, the Directors of his firm were no longer discussing him. They were brain storming how best to capitalize on the huge publicity surrounding the firm, curtesy of Roger Wellington Lloyd and of course Janet Nelson. They had solved the issue of keeping him with the firm by not offering, but giving him a junior partnership. After his brilliant, imaginative maneuvering and astonishing victory on his first case he was now a money magnet to the firm. He was praised and popular with everyone who knew about his case and what he'd done for his client. Imagine a $787.435 settlement on his very first case! The people, the politicians, the city, hell, the country loved him. The firm would be credited with leading the fight for new legislation against bullying and when the laws were enacted the firm would receive the credit. They needed to capitalize on the publicity yesterday. The sky was the limit as far as a publicity campaign was concerned and Roger Wellington Lloyd was the force behind it. Perhaps they could even feature Janet Nelson in a series of television, newspaper and magazine ads. They'd have to speak to Ms. Nelson about something like that because she was in no way obligated to do any such thing, but they figured she'd do it if her attorney asked her.

SIX

Roger Wellington Lloyd left Elizabeth and Janet dumbfounded in an apartment where the only sound to be heard was from the ticking clock on the kitchen wall. They had separated into different rooms. Elizabeth went into the kitchen where the sounds of washing dishes could be heard and Janet remained in the living room where she sat on the sofa with a pencil and paper on which she'd written and twice circled $787.435 and was tapping the figure with her pencil. Elizabeth, hands submerged in suds and dishes couldn't believe that Janet's plan had worked, and so much money! They had gotten away with the deception which had plagued her many nights but how were they to explain the money! This too, had been on Janet's mind after her attorney left and she came up with a simple solution and definite plans on how to use the money. Going into the kitchen, she had had to call Elizabeth's name twice before she got her attention. She told Elizabeth that the check would undoubtedly be made out in her name because she was the parent and that she had no intentions or dreams of shopping sprees and stuff. She was thinking how best to make the money last and work for the both of them. She had it all figured out and that the most important thing was that nobody, absolutely no one could know about the lawsuit or settlement money. She told Elizabeth that it wouldn't be wise for everyone on the block to notice sudden pricey spending because questions would follow especially from Janet's parents, who must never know about the deception or the money. The solution she came up with was the State Lottery. Everyone in the neighborhood knew that Elizabeth religiously played the lottery almost to the extent of addiction; always dreaming of hitting the big one. She'd played the games for over ten years and had never succeeded in winning more than $50. It wasn't unusual for her to spend $20 to $25 dollars a day on tickets and scratch off cards that never failed to win. The only thing more abundant than roaches in her apartment were losing lottery tickets and scratch off cards and everyone who visited her home knew this. Losing tickets and scratch off cards were scattered all around the apartment; on the kitchen and living room tables, dressers, the bed and bathroom, on top of the refrigerator and on the floor in some cases; where they remained until checked and re-checked for the losers that they were and finally tossed out in the garbage. Well, one day, to her shock and surprise she, Elizabeth, had won the State Lottery grand prize on a scratch off card! Elizabeth laughed and laughed until tears were streaming down her face. "We just have to get the word around that you won." Janet said thoughtfully. Elizabeth, who was still laughing said, "That's easy. I know just who to tell, Gertie Jenkins, that woman can speed rumors and gossip over backyard fences faster than a purse snatcher chased by the police." She asked Janet, "How much did I win?" "Why you won $250,000 dollars on a scratch off card." Janet replied still writing on her piece of paper. "Huh?" Elizabeth's laughter dwindled off. "Yes, that's what I'm giving to you and you deserve it. Oh not for the part you played in all this but you've always been there for me." Elizabeth was looking incredulously at Janet when she noticed a single tear drop onto the paper she was writing on. It was followed by another and another when Janet suddenly dropped the pencil and paper on the floor and ran into the comfort of Elizabeth's abundant flesh and began to cry in earnest. "You've always been there for me, always." she cried. Elizabeth held her tightly as she too began to cry.

A month later, Roger Wellington Lloyd was giving Elizabeth and Janet a tour of his office of which he was very proud of and they were much impressed. He introduced them to Ms. Harris who he declared was he right arm and that he couldn't find his ass with two hands and a flashlight without her. They all laughed as he led them up to the Director's office, where for the first time the partners met Janet Nelson. They were captivated by her beauty. She was tall and lithe with long dark hair and a slightly pixyish face. Up tilted light brown eyes offset the darker brown of her skin that was fresh and young. She had a bright wide contagious smile that they all succumbed to. They remembered the photos taken of her in the hospital and found it incredible that this beauty was buried beneath all the cast and hideous bruises. She was absolutely enchanting in their eyes and (completely out of character for the stodgy good ole boys) they fell over themselves welcoming her, offering them seats on the plush chairs and something cool to drink. While they talked with her about her health and schooling, Elizabeth was showing identification and signing documents for the release of a check totaling $614,638 dollars, the amount left after their fees and deductions. The partners didn't fail to notice that after receiving the check, Elizabeth asked for an envelope in which she inserted the check and although she couldn't cash it, she handed it over to Janet. They were impressed that her mother felt the money belonged to Janet as she was the victim. Janet turned to Roger Wellington Lloyd and asked, "What am I supposed to do now?" He replied with his patented Kool-Aide smile, "Well, if you want, I can take you guys to a good bank and deposit the check." So everyone said their good byes and left. An account was opened with TD Bank and the check was broken down in the following manner as pre-determined by Janet. Two accounts (checking and savings) were opened in Elizabeth's name and $125,000 dollars was deposited in each. A savings account for Janet was opened with a deposit for $20,000 dollars and the balance of $344,638 dollars was locked away in a trust fund for Janet which would mature in fifteen years. With that being done, Roger Wellington Lloyd asked, "What next?" Janet grinning happily replied, "Lunch on me!" The three of them went to lunch at Spain's Italian restaurant and enjoyed a fantastic leisurely meal. Afterwards, he dropped them off at their apartment with promises to call him if they needed him. Janet hugged him making him promise that he wouldn't forget her and they parted amid hugs and kisses.

The following morning Janet's next deception began. Elizabeth dressed in her finest suit of clothes which consisted of a white waist length jacket and skirt, faux pearls, ear rings and white heels was looking out of her living room window waiting for their pigeon, Gertie Jenkins, to take up her accustomed seat in her rocker on her front porch, which was directly across the street from Elizabeth's house. Gertie could, weather permitting, always be found sitting on her porch rocking and knitting, from 8 a.m. to 5 p.m. with intermittent meal and bathroom breaks. She sat there knitting and spying on her neighbors, with her telephone perched on a tiny table next to her enabling her to speed up to the minute breaking gossip to and on her neighbors. She kept constant surveillance on everyone and everything on the block, from corner to corner. She was the block's self-appointed crime watch and gossip patrol. She knew what time everyone came or left their homes during those hours and if any hanky-panky was going on the inhabitants of the block knew to use their back doors. Gertie didn't fail to notice Elizabeth emerging all dressed up from her house and called her over asking where she was going looking all classy on this fine Tuesday morning. Elizabeth crossed the street, climbed the four steps to Gertie and sat down on a chair next to the little table. She told Gertie her destination was a secret and that was enough to stop the knitting needles from clacking together. Gertie was about sixty years old but no one really knew her true age. Her hair was completely white and cut short to her head and whatever her age it didn't show on her. Her shiny brown face was wrinkle free and smooth behind her thick bifocal glasses held up by a bulbous nose and her wide mouth was full of white even teeth. She was tall and sparse and few would have guessed the strength in those legs encased in brown support hose because Gertie could run really fast for her age. The eyes behind her glasses where sharp and bright, never missing anything within sight of her porch and when she sighted Elizabeth she wanted to know what was going on. Elizabeth smiled and let Gertie press and press her on the nature of her secret until finally appearing to give in she told her that she was going to meet a friend who would be taking her Trenton. What was in Trenton, Gertie pressed not bothering to hide her nosiness. Elizabeth looked secretively around to see if anyone was near, seeing no one, she began to open her pocketbook. Gertie's ball of yarn fell to the porch and she almost tumbled out of her rocker trying to look into Elizabeth's pocketbook, which she drew back from Gertie's eyes. Elizabeth slowly took out a white envelope which she opened and revealed to Gertie the top of a lottery scratch off card that was actually over a month old. Gertie's eyes widen as Elizabeth revealed the entire card and told Gertie that she'd won a lot of money on the card, $250,000 dollars and her friend was taking her to Trenton to cash it in. Gertie's knitting fell off her lap following the ball of yarn and the chair ceased its rocking. She tried to get a closer look at the scratch off card but Elizabeth quickly returned it to its enveloped and sealed it closed. Looking at her watch, she did something she'd never done before, she leaned over, kissed a stunned Gertie happily on the cheek, stood up and sped as quickly as her bulk would allow her, off the porch calling back that her bus was coming and she didn't want to miss it. Waving her hand over her head, she quickly walked away. The phone was in Gertie's hand before Elizabeth had gone ten steps and she was dialing as fast as her arthritic fingers would allow, her list of memorized numbers already lining up in her head. Janet, who was sitting in the upstairs window recently vacated by Elizabeth, was watching all this and was rolling with laughter. It was just a little after 9 a.m. and Gertie would have the news all over the place by 10 a.m. that Elizabeth Nelson had hit the lottery for $250,000. She wouldn't go into long conversation with her listeners because she had to hurry onto the next person on her gossip list.

Janet left the window and the house by the back door. Climbing over the backyard fence to the neighboring street behind the house, she ran to meet Elizabeth at the bus stop. With all the money they each had in the bank neither one of them had bus fare. They found this hilariously funny and started walking the five blocks to the nearest TD Bank laughing uncontrollably at the game they'd just played on old Gertie and agreeing that by the time they returned home the news of Elizabeth winning $250,000 dollars in the lottery would be everywhere except posted on the side of passing buses. After withdrawing a few dollars and getting an ATM card, they discussed what they were going to do with the money. Janet said she needed some new sneakers, jeans and a wrist watch. Elizabeth sat back and dreamily said she'd like to go to Path mark and buy all the food she not only needed but the items she just wanted. Janet laughed as they agreed to go food shopping.

True to Janet's speculation and Gertie's hotline, the neighborhood knew that Elizabeth had hit the lottery for $250,000 dollars before they returned home hours later. It was just what was needed to avoid questions about the money and spending to all her nosey neighbors. If there was any question of proof that Elizabeth had indeed hit the lottery it was silenced by the two taxi cabs that pulled up in front of her house late that afternoon. Bags and bags of groceries were removed from both cabs and carried upstairs to Elizabeth's apartment. It looked like everyone on the block had camped out on Gertie's porch waiting for Elizabeth to return, including Janet's mother and stepfather. Out the corner of her eye Janet saw her stepfather give her mother a nudge in their direction. Her mother crossed the street smiling and clapping her hands and then (surprise, surprise) hugged Elizabeth. "I heard what happened. Did you really win $250,000 dollars? Oh my God, I'm so happy for you. Come on let me help you carry those bags upstairs. My goodness," she exclaimed "You must have brought the whole store out!" "Damn near." Elizabeth replied pulling away from the hug and taking two more bags upstairs. The kitchen, living room floor, stove, tables and counter tops were fast becoming covered with grocery bags of food. Janet had begun unpacking them but could hear her mother and Elizabeth talking in the living room. Janet smile to herself feeling good inside until her stepfather's thick frame stepped into the open hallway door blocking out the hall light and a hood of darkness seemed to slowly settle around her head. She froze and time momentarily ceased to exist as if she was waiting for an unexpected beating. He continued to have that effect on her whenever he was near her. Her movements putting the groceries away suddenly became stilted and robotic but he paid her no attention, going straight into the living room. Janet had been able to clearly hear her mother and Elizabeth talking, but now the voices became muffled as if her ears weren't meant to hear. Her mother entered the kitchen and began helping put the groceries away. The entire affair was a first; they never came to Elizabeth's house, ever; even though they lived only four houses apart. Sometimes she'd stay over two weeks at a time at Elizabeth's house but she was never missed or called home. She was a non-person there. Now, here they were. It was the money of course that drove them to Elizabeth's house. Her parents left about an hour later and Elizabeth came into the kitchen carrying some of the bags from the living room floor in stony silence, her face an unreadable mask. As she began arranging meats in the freezer she suddenly started talking. "Would you believe that bastard was hinting that perhaps he was owed some of that money for allowing you to practically live here? He said how much you were needed at home and how you were missed but it was worth the sacrifice to help me out because I was sickly. Sickly!" She growled shoving a ham into the freezer. Janet responded that perhaps it was his logic that was sickly from too many blows to the head and they laughed remembering the fight in the hallway that started with the blow to Janet's head from her stepfather and ended with her trying to stab him. Elizabeth laughed so hard she dropped a pot roast on her foot and Janet laughed saying, "That belongs in a pot you can't cook it on your foot." They finished the task of putting all the food away and then Elizabeth cooked a dinner of baked ham, mashed potatoes and gravy, string beans, corn on the cob and apple pie for desert.

The following day, without Elizabeth's knowledge Janet withdrew $8,000 dollars from her savings account. When she returned to the house, she gave the money to Elizabeth with instructions to take it to her mother. Elizabeth asked for no explanation and Janet gave none. When Elizabeth returned she told Janet that she gave the money to her mother and her stepfather immediately snatched it from her and that her mother snatched it right back. When she left they were glaring angrily at each other and she couldn't figure out who'd hit who first. He was a bully but Elizabeth knew Janet's mother wasn't the type to take a hit and not hit back. He'd have his work cut out for him trying to get that money back in his hands, she laughed and Janet laughed half-heartedly with her. She was glad Elizabeth hadn't asked why she'd given them the money because she had no real explanation. There was however, the conscious thought that she was in some symbolic way buying her freedom from them. She had no idea what she'd do after graduation but she knew for certain her parents were not in the equation and she'd never return to that house. When Janet returned from school the following day she went to her own home essentially for the last time. She found her mother and stepfather seated at the kitchen table drinking coffee. She handed her mother the graduation packet from the school. It contained information when and where the graduation would be held, Montclair School for the Gifted, Montclair, NJ and four guest tickets. Also enclosed was the cost of graduation pictures and the class ring. Somehow she knew there'd be no graduation preparation for her and she was right. Her mother returned the information to its envelope without comment and her stepfather growled, "What do you need pictures and a ring for, where are we supposed to get the money from?" Her mother placed the envelope on the kitchen shelf above the stove and went back to her coffee. It was still there a week later. There were no plans (and allegedly no money) made at her home for Janet's graduation but it was all pomp and ceremony at Elizabeth's house. Janet, insisting on using her own money, went to the bank and got money orders for the cost of the graduation pictures and the ring. An appointment was made at the beauty salon to have her hair and nails done and then they went to the mall to shop for a gown, shoes and accessories. When they returned home exhausted with their purchases, Janet had had one more task to perform. From the graduation packet she had withheld two tickets, one for Elizabeth (meaning they had to return to the mall for her dress and accessories) and remembering his promise to be seated in the front row for her graduation, one for Roger Wellington Lloyd, which she placed inside a letter addressed to him at his firm's office.

'Monkey Face' Roger Wellington Lloyd smiled remembering his nickname for Janet. He hadn't thought about her in months. He hadn't forgotten about her, but he was so busy. He was hip deep in litigations, depositions, arbitrations and court dates. He barely had time for a piss and a spit as he put it. The firm's prediction that he'd bring in clients had come true, he was a money magnet to the firm. His handling of the Nelson case had made him a celebrity, the adoption of new legislative laws (initiated by him aka the firm) regarding bullying also added tremendous prestige to the firm. New clients besieged the firm for their law issues, all requesting him and had to be told that his calendar was full and there was a waiting list for his services. His personal assistant, Ms. Harris, true to her word was the best the firm could offer. Arriving for work before him, she had everything he needed and things he didn't know he needed on his desk when he arrived along with a fresh pot of hot tea and cream cheese bagels. She never failed in having key information on some case, client or adversary and always had a dash of legal gossip to add to the mix. He recognized he would have been lost in the papers, research, filings and court motions without her. His work load was so heavy he had been afforded three extra paralegals for his office.

The last time he'd seen Janet had been months ago when he'd presented her with the settlement check for over $600,000 dollars. He was still smiling to himself as he fingered the gold embossed invitation to her graduation when Ms. Harris entered carrying stacks of briefs. She looked at his smiling face and said, "Ah, good news, huh?" He handed her the invitation and in less than five seconds she said, "This is scheduled for the same day as the litigation on the Buxton case" She took the invitation and left his office and returned fifteen minutes later to report that she'd contacted the school regarding his desire to attend the ceremony and asked the approximate running time of the ceremony and discovered there was no way he could attend both. She proceeded to contact Mr. Buxton, she apologized, informing them that something unavoidable had come up and they needed to postpone the litigation on his case until the following week. Rather than lose the best representation in town, the postponement was accepted and he was now free to attend Janet's graduation. She returned the invitation to him along with an updated schedule for the following week and left. Roger Wellington Lloyd made three phone calls: first to Elizabeth telling her to tell Janet, when she returned from school, that he would not only be attending the graduation but would be her escort. The second call went to a florist where he placed three orders for three dozen roses, one for Janet, one for Elizabeth and one for Ms. Harris. The third call was to a jeweler who would of course have no problem coming to his office to discuss a purchase.

Gertie Jenkins was sitting surveillance in her usual place rocking and knitting on her front porch. She was thinking there had certainly been a lot of goings on across the street at Elizabeth's house. She attributed that to the recent lottery winning by Elizabeth for $250,000. She had of course told everybody by phone she could about the money and to passersby whose number she didn't have. She never mentioned the $1000 dollars Elizabeth had given her; after all people didn't need to know everything about a body, did they? Still when a florist truck pulled up and a man got out with two huge bunches of roses and went up Elizabeth's stairs she felt the neighborhood needed to know about that. She couldn't begin to speculate who would be sending Elizabeth such a bunch of expensive, beautiful roses. Did she have a man friend? Must be, a woman wouldn't send a woman flowers. How come Elizabeth hadn't told her about any special man friend? Who was he and where did he come from? Gertie burned with curiosity. She pulled herself from her rocker, crossed the street, climbed the three flights to Elizabeth's apartment and went to find out for herself.

A week later Gertie was in her spot knitting when the longest car she'd ever seen (accept on television) pulled up in front of Elizabeth's house. A uniformed driver emerged and proceeded to open the door and a well-dressed, handsome, young, white man (?) stepped out and went up the stairs and rang Elizabeth's door bell. Before the bell was answered Gertie was jabbering into her phone on the table next to her. She watched, slacked jawed as Janet came out of the door and fell into the man's arms. Gertie was completely stunned at how beautiful Janet looked dressed in a dusky, rose colored, off shouldered gown, whose coloring next to Janet's caramel skin, seemed to shimmer in the morning sun light. She wore matching high heeled sandals and her hair was stylishly done up in a high princess chignon and topped with a tiny tiara. Elizabeth came out next and she too was hugged by the handsome young man. Elizabeth, for her all her size and bulk, was wearing a beautiful, flowery, ankle length dress of silk with white high heeled shoes. Her hair was classically styled in falling finger waves about her face. Gertie throwing all caution to the wind; dropped her phone on the step leaving someone on the other end yammering about what was going on. She crossed the street approaching the handsome party on the porch. She exclaimed how gorgeous Janet looked and how fine Elizabeth was in her dress and how her hair was so pretty. All the time she was chattering at the two of them, she kept cutting her eyes over to the handsome white man, waiting for an introduction but none was offered. They left her open mouthed on the porch as the driver of the limousine opened its doors and all three were handed inside and the limo pulled off. Gertie hurried back across the street heedless of the horn blowing cars attempting to avoid running over her. She reached her porch, picked up the phone she had dropped on the steps and there was still someone yammering on the phone wanting to know what was happening. Gertie's heart was hammering so hard (it had been doing a lot of that lately in connection with Elizabeth) in her chest that she couldn't make it up the stairs to her rocker just yet and sat down heavily on the step and began gossiping. She could barely talk as her words tripped and stumbled over each other in their rush to catch up with a brain that was about to burst a blood vessel with everything she'd witnessed. She left out not one detail. She talked on and on to numerous people who in turn called their fellow gossipers and all the chickens clucked for hours. It was unanimously decided, over the grape vine, that the white man was someone rich and important and that the flowers that came last week were sent by him for

Janet (they got that part half right) A rich white man was Janet's boyfriend and she was obviously in love with him. You could tell that by the way she leaped in his arms and he hugged her and coming to pick her up in a limo, oh my! And Elizabeth not only knew about the relationship, she obviously approved of her cousin dating a white man! It was all too much for Gertie's circle of gossipers and their words were still flinging back and forth over the telephone line hours after the limousine had left.

Inside the limo, Elizabeth was hard put to calm Janet down, warning her repeatedly that she was going to destroy her hair do and wrinkle her gown. Roger Wellington Lloyd was enjoying it all when he looked at Janet his heart skipped a beat she was so beautiful, like a little fairy princess. He reached into his jacket pocket and produced four little boxes and handed two to Janet and two to Elizabeth. Janet's boxes contained a pearl necklace with a charm pendant of a capital 'J' surrounded with tiny diamonds, matching earrings and bracelet. Elizabeth's contained the same set with the exception of the initial being a capital 'E'. He put his gifts around Janet's neck, into her ears and around her wrist and produced a small mirror allowing her to see herself. Janet didn't wear any make up, her natural coloring didn't need it but if she had, her made up face would have been ruined with tears. She was so happy and only Roger Wellington Lloyd and Elizabeth noticed how she was a truly beautiful young lady. Yes she was and he was the proud of her. The graduation wasn't an overly large ceremony and was held outside under a pavilion on the school's lawn. There were approximately forty students graduating and prior to the ceremony Janet took them on a tour of her school introducing them to her peers and teachers. They found that Janet was very popular at the school and the teachers would be sad that she would be leaving but happy that she was graduating. The ceremony was short and dignified without all the unnecessary pomp and hoopla of larger schools. There was an opening welcoming speech, the valedictorian's speech, the presentation of awards, scholarships (of which Janet received one) then the walk across the stage to receive their diplomas. When Janet's name was called it was greeted with cheers and applauds and leading the cheering section was Elizabeth and Roger Wellington Lloyd who was snapping pictures of Janet. Neither of her parents attended her graduation. After picking up her class pictures

(Roger took the largest) and class ring they returned to the limo and he took them for a nice leisurely lunch at a very posh Manhattan restaurant in New York. Before leaving, Janet excused herself and went to the ladies room. While she was gone, Elizabeth was in deep conversation with Roger Wellington Lloyd. Driving back to Jersey, Janet noticed that they had driven right pass Elizabeth's house. They drove on, the conversation light and gay, until they stopped in a neighborhood of colorful, one family houses with manicured lawns circling a large pond in the center of a park. Janet wanted to get out and look at the large white birds gliding slowly in the water and so they did. Elizabeth and Roger Wellington Lloyd lounged on a bench while Janet walked around the pond looking at the swan like birds and then she followed the short path onto the tennis courts in the park. In her beautiful, rose colored, off shouldered gown she created an idyllic vision of an affluent southern girl out for a leisurely stroll in the park. The only thing missing was a large floppy hat adorned with flowers, a parasol and white gloves. Elizabeth couldn't help snapping picture after picture of her which Roger Wellington Lloyd made her promise to send him copies. When Janet returned to them, Elizabeth pointed at a house directly across from the center of the pond. It was a small, colorful two story cottage. Its second floor had a house length balcony that faced and over looked the pond. There was a manicured lawn and flower beds on either side of the walk-way leading to the steps.

Janet thought the small house looked like a fairy tale cottage nestled deep in a forest. "I wonder who lives there." she said and Elizabeth, looking over at her responded, "I do," and continued, "You do too, if you want. The first floor is mine and the second yours; if you want. What do you say? Would you want to come and live there with me?" Elizabeth asked taking Janet's hand and leading her to the side door of the first floor. She opened it with a key and the three of them went up the stairs to the second floor. The door opened on a moderately sized dining room with hardwood floors, two carpeted bedrooms, a bath and kitchen. Opposite the dining room was the living room which connected with a slightly smaller room that featured a wall length fireplace. There was a door in the living room that led out onto the balcony that sat directly in front of the pond and tennis courts. Janet walked out onto the balcony thinking that she'd never seen anything lovelier and her heart was full to bursting with the view. Could it be possible that she could live here in this beautiful place? Elizabeth and Roger Wellington Lloyd joined her on the balcony and she turned to them asking incredulously, "For real? This is yours and I can live here with you? Oh, yes! Yes! Yes!" she cried running back inside the apartment with her heels clacking on the hardwood floors into the room with the fireplace, then the bedrooms, bathroom and kitchen. And so it was settled. Janet needed no permission from her parents, she'd be eighteen in less than four weeks and if they put up a fuss (which she doubted) about those weeks she'd simply wait the time out. "When can we move? Can you afford this? I wish I hadn't locked that money away, it would have helped but I can get a job and help pay the rent and stuff. When can we get started?" Elizabeth laughed and told her that the house had practically been a steal. The elderly couple who owned the house had plans to move to a retirement community and wanted out of the house as soon as possible. They were asking $90,000 for the house. Roger Wellington Lloyd spoke with a realtor (who was incidentally a satisfied client of his at the firm) and haggled the price down to $80,000 and Elizabeth put $50,000 down, papers were drawn and signed, and they could move in whenever they were ready. She had a $30,000 dollar mortgage whose monthly payments were $25 dollars more than her current rent and thanks to $250,000 dollars she received from Janet, she could afford it quite easily. Janet was so excited. It was all too much, the good things that had happened to her in the last year and she owed it all to Elizabeth and her fantasy father, Roger Wellington Lloyd. She didn't say this aloud but went to him and gave him a humongous hug and then Elizabeth too was embraced with an even tighter bear hug. They returned to the limo and as they pulled off Janet looked back at the little house receding in the rear window thinking, *I live there, me!* Roger Wellington Lloyd dropped them off at Elizabeth's house with a kiss and a promise to keep in touch. They walked him downstairs, where they found their neighbors standing outside the limo looking into it. They commented on her dress and Janet told them that it was her graduation day and laughed off the undercover questions designed to get to the meat and potatoes of who the white man was, and why he came in a limo. Roger Wellington Lloyd, with a final kiss on Janet's and Elizabeth's cheeks drove off. Elizabeth and Janet's neighbors followed them (uninvited) upstairs and it was there that Elizabeth announced that that she would be moving at the end of the week. She would be having an open house in two days and anyone would be welcomed to anything that she wouldn't be taking with her free of charge. As expected she, Janet and the white man were no longer the subject of interest. Her neighbors were busily claiming items and furniture of interest to them and securing promises from Elizabeth that she wouldn't give away the things they'd picked out. Elizabeth promised for they had no way of knowing that she intended on leaving everything in the apartment except her personal items. She was done with the apartment, the neighbors, the neighborhood and her relatives. The following day the shopping spree, on Elizabeth, she had insisted, began. They purchased not what they could afford but what they liked. The utilities (water, electric and gas) were turned on and phone and cable service appointments acquired. Elizabeth insisted on paying for all their purchases after all she had over $200,000 dollars to work with, curtesy of Janet. They purchased full living, dining, kitchen and bedroom sets, televisions, stereos, stoves, refrigerators and air conditioners for their apartments to be delivered in three days. The next day they purchased utensils for the kitchens, curtains, linens, rugs, bathroom supplies, pictures, knick-knacks and book cases for Janet after their stop in Barnes and Nobles where Janet purchased over fifty books. These purchases they immediately took to the new house and begin to turn their perspective apartments into homes. Two days later all the furniture was delivered and set up and they went on the biggest food shopping spree ever. The freezers and cabinets were jam packed with food and it wasn't long before Janet could smell baking cakes from down stairs. Afterwards they admired each other's apartments agreeing that there really is a happy ever after. Janet adored her apartment and still could hardly believe it was hers. A few months later, Janet decided she wanted to look for a job having decided that she didn't want to go to college just yet. Elizabeth suggested that she apply for work at her job at the mental health institution. If she didn't mind the grudging work of working with the mentally disabled and could stomach having to clean, feed and bath mentally retard adults who soiled themselves. Outside of these duties, it was a well-paying State job with benefits, paid vacation, sick time, 401 K plan; the perfect job. Janet agreed to put in an application the following day and Elizabeth would take her there. Janet filled out an application for the position of direct care worker at the Sawyer developmental Center on Tuesday, was called for an interview on Wednesday, was hired, and began work the next day on the 3:00 shift and life for her would never be the same or her perceptions of human behaviors and its cruelties.

SAWYER
DEVEVEOPMENTAL
CENTER

SEVEN

The Sawyer Developmental Center founded in 1965, was a 65 acre Intermediate Care Facility designed to accommodate 576 residents of various levels of mental retardation who resided in one of 19 buildings on its grounds. Each building was home for 32 patients of various ages ranging from twenty-five on up and over seen by a Head Supervisor and two floor supervisors for each of its three shifts. The Division of Mental Health and Addiction Services (DMHAS) served adults with serious and persistent mental and behavioral problems. Central to the Division's mission was the fact that these individuals are entitled to safe, dignified and well cared for lives at the institution. What a joke! The Sawyers Developmental Center, Janet discovered in her first week, was the State of New Jersey's answer to Dachau. Janet arrived for her interview dressed in a 2-piece green skirt suit and matching shoes. She was nineteen years old, tall, slim young woman with long, black hair that enhanced her caramel complexion that was a shade darker than her brown cat like eyes and delicate facial features whose sensitivity announced its presence to the world. The interview didn't include a drug test, background check, employment history, credit check or physical. In short the State was taking anyone who cared to apply. During her interview she was given a brief tour of her work site, building thirteen which consisted of three huge area rooms, two of which were called dayrooms and the third was the patient's sleeping area. One half of one day room served as a dining area with tables and chairs and on the other side was a sitting area consisting of no furnishings other than two orange, hard plastic sofas. Seating availability was secondary to the staff and the patients sat on the floor. There was a small television bolted high up on its brick wall and a wall of curtain-less windows around the entire perimeter of the building. The next large room was the same minus the dining area and television set. It's only contents were one picnic table and benches. Behind these sitting areas was the 'Wet Area' featuring a huge bathing area unlike anything she'd ever seen. There were sixteen lidless toilets bolted to the floor with no doors or walls for privacy or tissue for cleansing. Across from the toilets, were two large tubs, one shower and a long counter containing three sinks. Behind the wet area was the sleeping area which consisted of a huge gym sized room with thirty-two military style cots placed side by side each having two sheets, a thin army blanket and one green, cracked, plastic pillow. The only difference between the treatment of the patients in her building and the unfortunate, legendary inhabitants of 'Dachau' was that the residents weren't shot or gassed and they didn't have numbers tattooed on their skin for identification, but huge, nasty looking bruises served just as well for identification.

Janet was shocked at the many instances of beatings, torture, forced labor and unreported injuries, slip shod medical treatment and theft perpetrated by the staff and nurses. There were numerous cases where a head was busted open and bleeding, fingers or toes broken and injuries that required sutures that were never received. These injuries were conveniently (with the approval of the supervisors) blamed on other patients who staff claimed attacked the injured patient, when they were the actual culprits. The patients were trained to do the staff's duties or else be punished. The patients did the laundry, cleaned soiled patients, cleaned the day rooms, dining areas, kitchens and bathrooms, made beds, mopped floors and took out the garbage; while the staff watched television, knitted, ate their lunches, smoked and drank alcoholic beverages, ran personal errands or slept. They received paychecks for doing nothing. If a client refused to do the work their toes were stepped on, fingers bent back, hit with broom sticks, slapped, pinched, punched or refused their meals. Their treatment was deplorable, accepted and covered up by the staff and supervisors as needed. Janet was to discover that cruelty was an everyday thing within her building and no staff person ever told on another or intervened on the patient's behalf even when they were direct witnesses to the patient assaults. At bathing time, it was demonstrated to her how to put a cake of soap in a sock, soak it in cold water (so as to not leave a mark) and beat the clients. She was also shown how to wet a towel with cold water, twist it into a rope that was then wrapped around the client's neck and twisted until their faces went blue. Dinner was delivered by the food service trucks and once it was set up for distribution in the client's kitchen, the staff was the first to par take of the client's food; preparing plates for themselves, and the patients were fed what was left. If there wasn't enough food left the clients were given a small box of cereal or a bowl of Jell-O or bread and butter. It was not uncommon to see staff take entire crates of milk, cereal, boxes of ice cream, loaves of bread and desserts home. On Christmas Eve the staff stole the patient's gifts putting them into large garbage bags that were placed in the trunks of their cars. Most of the patients had no family visitors and no one outside the building questioned the injuries and thefts and all was ignored by the supervisors who participated in the abuse and thievery. Janet's duty was to monitor, feed and bathe a group of 8 clients which she never abused or stole from them; she also never told or intervened on things she saw. She was a passive employee who kept herself apart from the apart from the rest of the staff. She did her work and no more. It wouldn't be long at the institution before it would be discovered she wasn't a team player when it came to abuse against the patients, therefore she was a liability. With that recognition, things aimed at getting her fired began to happen to her. Things she couldn't understand or avoid. She was on a six month probationary period and there were two attempts to terminate her in her first month.

Janet's peers were women and all at least fifteen or more years older than her. Having nothing in common with them conversation was practically non-existent. At first they asked her questions like:" Are you married? Do you have any kids? Where do you live and if one could believe it, are you a virgin?" She always gave one word responses and gave no indication of expanding on the questions. Her peers adapted the impression that she thought she was too good to associate with them and this aggravated them for reasons unknown. Within her eight hour shift, there were only three instances where the employees actually got up and worked: meal time to distribute meal trays, bath time and putting the clients to bed. In between there were really nothing to do. Janet, who had always been an avid reader, began bringing books to read and this appeared to be another irritation to her peers and she didn't understand what the problem was. They didn't talk to her and she likewise didn't converse with them. She was an oddity among them and the only thing they could surmise from her personality was that she was very intelligent and this too proved to be an irritation.

Janet had become in every sense of the word, a true commuter. Getting to work involved a bus, train and taxi and reversed this order to return home. Her punctuality was always at the mercy of those three modes of transportation and if one was late then so was she (in most cases no more than fifteen minutes) and she had to fill out a late slip. Three late slips resulted in a disciplinary action. Three disciplinary actions equaled suspension days and anything more was subject to termination. In her first month she was late more than three times and was recommended for termination. On numerous occasions, she observed that her peers arrived an hour or more late for duty, but never received late slips. She was sent to the CEO's office who would decide whether to terminate or not. The CEO was a tall scraggly looking man with long, blonde hair and an emaciated look about his facial features. His clothes had a disheveled look and the sleeves of his jacket were too short for his long gangly arms. He appeared bored and disinterested as Janet explained to him that this was her first job and what it took for her to get to work. She asked that he take in consideration that she had no control over the transportation schedules but had to depend on them to get to work and the fact that she did show up albeit a few minutes late. Perhaps it was her open honesty and determination to get to work that persuaded the CEO to drop the termination recommendation and send her back to work. This did not sit well with her peers or supervisor who asked her why she was back in the building and when told, they called personnel to check. Janet couldn't understand why her coworkers wanted her to lose her jo or what she'd done to make them feel that way?

During her second month, Janet received a notice informing her that she was eligible for promotion to a higher title and pay (performing the same duties) if she passed an on grounds exam. With an operating budget of over $974,785,000 that year the state of New Jersey had plenty of money to throw around and politicians had not yet gotten into stuffing their own pockets with perks and tax payers money. She had a starting salary of $14,500 a year and if she passed this exam her salary would increase to $16,400. Janet had been dumb founded when she discovered that her peers were circulating a petition (that they all signed) that she shouldn't be allowed to take the test because she hadn't been there a year.

What kind of people was she working with that would not only be upset about a raise in her pay but would actually canvas for it not to happen? Her coworkers put such malice in their mission that they even sought signatures from employees outside of her building. People she didn't know existed were signing the petition. The petition was submitted to the CEO, who for reasons unknown to Janet, ignored it and she was scheduled to test. She ranked number one at the institution and the natives were pissed. Three weeks later, she received a raise in pay but was called into the Head Supervisor's office and informed that she was being recommended for termination for not properly getting a patient off the toilet. The patient had fell and now had a bruise on his arm. Janet had no idea where the lie came from but she blurted out that the patient weighed over 200 pounds and that she herself weighed 105 pounds. No one would help her and she fell hitting her head on the floor trying to prevent the patient from falling. The Head Supervisor knew she couldn't fire an employee who was injured in the course of performing their duties. Janet was given an employee incident report to fill out. She returned the completed form to the head supervisor who read and tore it up. She gave Janet another blank form informing her that she couldn't write down the patient's weight or hers, nor could she put down that no one would help her lift the client. Not questioning these omissions, Janet did as she was told, rewrote the employee incident report and was sent to the hospital. It was somehow determined that she had a mild concussion and was given three days off to recuperate. During those days off Janet went to personnel seeking an opening in another building in her new title as Cottage Training Technician. She found and applied to several openings but was not accepted and in many cases not even interviewed. Her peers were industrially at work slandering her to perspective interviewers. It was over two years before she was accepted in the building next door to her own. The new building, she found was staffed with people around her own age and for the first time since her employment at Sawyers, she was happy with anticipation at being out of the hell hole of her current building.

On her first day in the new building, Janet discovered that abuse was alive and well there too only much worst because the abused were the staff! Building twelve was not just a job it was an adventure! Here the patients attacked the staff, each other and themselves. There wasn't a day when a staff person or patient wasn't assaulted by one of the patients and when neither was available the patients attacked themselves; banging their heads against the concrete walls, biting themselves until the skin broke, punching themselves about the head and one patient constantly pulled out his hemorrhoids and wrapped the bloody, feces covered coils around his body. In between avoiding physical attacks, staff had to be on the lookout for flying feces, shoes, crash helmets, soiled under garments, tables and chairs. The patients threw anything at anyone and the staff, knowing the warning signs, knew when to duck, usually. The staff surprisingly took all this in stride, finding the antics of the patients amusing and never sought retaliation against them. They understood that their patients had mental issues and a total lack of control over their actions. The staff accepted that they were casualties of war. They worked with them as best they could; understanding that there was no understanding to the assaults. When they were assaulted they simply filled out employee incident reports, had a day or two off and returned to work laughing about the incident. Janet had to admit that although the clients were somewhat dangerous they were also funny in their assaults. One day, staff couldn't stop a patient from repeatedly throwing shoes at whatever target unknowingly presented itself and sometimes if it didn't. One staff member commented that the client had better not throw a shoe at her and just as she finished the sentence a boot came sailing through the room and smacked her upside the head. The patient, the staff and the assaulted staff person, rubbing her head, burst into uproarious laughter. Assaults were a form of twisted entertainment for patients and staff alike. Like the Romans who gathered in the Coliseum screaming and yelling for blood, blood and more blood. Janet loved her new building, over the years she'd been hit in the face, head, been bitten, kicked and slapped but it was what it was, she hadn't been paying attention. She never read books in the work area, there was a cost for not paying attention to where and what your patients were doing. The staff treated the patients with patience; donated clothing to them, brought them fast food sandwiches, fries, sodas and candy. On Christmas it wasn't unusual for them to bring in small gifts for the patients.

Janet was right at home with her new peers. She'd made arrangements with one of them for transportation to and from work. They partied together, celebrated birthdays and holidays and went on trips together and hung out at each other's homes. Her relationship with her job and peers was so cool she hated when she had to miss a day of work. Four years later she was notified that she was eligible to test for the position of Cottage Training Supervisor. Janet wasn't interested in being a supervisor but changed her mind about testing when she learned that she'd get the day off to take the test. She signed up along with just about the entire staff. The exam, open to all residents of the State of New Jersey was held three weeks later. Janet sat for the three hour test and afterwards accompanied her peers to the beach and amusement park. The test scores came out with Janet ranking number one in the State and that was just fine but she wasn't interested in being a supervisor. Ranking number one didn't affect her with feelings of superiority over her peers. She'd always looked at any test as an enemy that wasn't going to defeat her. Even in her school subjects it wasn't acceptable to score anything less than an 'A' on a test and anything lower would be a major disappointment to her. Three years later when she did apply for the position of supervisor she discovered that Sawyers wasn't interested in her. Positions were supposed to be based on your test rank Janet was denied interview after interview regardless of her ranking on the test. What she didn't know was that positions were politically based on who you knew and what people thought about you. She had left disgruntled enemies behind in her previous building and they had no problem spreading lies and negative comments about her to prospective interviewers. She didn't care; she was satisfied where she was in life. She was now making $26,400 a year, liked her job, and had her own apartment. She had great friends and co-workers and was saving to buy a new car which she wanted to pay for with cash. About eight years later, Janet was approached by the Head supervisor and offered an upcoming supervisors' position in her own building and on her current shift. Janet was surprised at the offer but didn't jump at the job and was given until the end of the month to decide. Janet didn't have to tell her peers about the job offer, they already knew and encouraged her to take the supervisory position but she still hesitated having doubts about supervising her own peers. She continued to decline the offer saying to her peers, "Yea right! Supervise you guys? It'll never work." "Of course it will," they chorused, "We'll help you. You already know us and we all know our jobs. Girl you better take that job!" Their continued encouragement was the deciding factor and she accepted the position never realizing that there was a method to their madness for her to take the offered position.

On her very first day as supervisor Janet found that the entire staff, her friends, were suddenly inflicted with amnesia regarding their assignments and no one went to their assigned work areas. The patients were unattended; running around creating chaos but the staff remained lounging against a. table staring at her and she had no idea what to do. *Why were they just standing there?* She wondered, everyone knew their assignments, had for almost ten years but they were acting as if they didn't have a clue as to what they should be doing. Janet nervously turned away from their staring eyes and went into her new office, a small room with barely enough room for the desk and file cabinet, wondering what that was all about. She was soon to find out. During her first year the staff (her friends) had on many occasions reduced her to tears of frustration and confusion. Her position as supervisor was completely disrespected and ignored by her staff/friends. They took two hour lunches, attended to the patients' needs in their own good time and just made the position a living hell and things showed no sign of improving and she was unable to get them to comply. She knew she had the power to enforce the rules through disciplinary actions but didn't want to make her friends angry, so she didn't use that power and the staff capitalized on her weakness. They showed absolutely no respect for her or her position. For instance, the food service worker was two hours late and wrote on her late slip that she was late because she was having sex. The staff, along with the worker, found this outrageously funny but Janet was shocked at what the worker had written. It was Janet's responsibility to co-sign it and forward the disrespectful late slip to personnel. *Did the employee really not care or was she comfortable in the knowledge that she knew Janet wouldn't sign it?* Janet was seething with the knowledge that she was being taken for granted again. She began wrestling with the decision to sign the late slip against concern over what would happen to the employee if she did. On that day Janet gathered the reins of her job and took control deciding that if the employee didn't care why the fuck should she. Janet called the employee (a friend for years) in, after her cheering section had dispersed, she signed her name to the late slip, and handed it to the employee for her signature and asked, "Do you really want me to send this down"? Shamefaced the employee said, 'No, don't send that. I'll get in trouble." "Yes, I think you will." Janet said in her new stern voice while staring at the employee. She gave her the opportunity to re-write the late slip. That day Janet learned just what the staff thought of her as a supervisor. In their eyes she was not only a joke as a supervisor but was under their control and she would cover for them no matter what they did or didn't do. They were confident that she wouldn't allow them to get in any trouble because of their friendship. With the realization of these things, Janet began to take took control of her job and her staff. For months afterwards, her staff/friends didn't speak to her unless necessary but they did their jobs. Janet learned that being a supervisor was a lonely position and that friendships had no place in the equation. She accepted this along with their silence. After almost two years of rough riding, the staff grudgingly accepted her position of authority over them as well as recognizing her responsibilities and their friendships mended. They had to respect her position, responsibilities and most of all; they now understood that she would discipline the hell out of them as necessary and wasn't about to sacrifice her job behind their bullshit.

Five years later the institution suffered major reconstruction of all its buildings after asbestos was discovered in the attics of the buildings and OSHA declared it a health hazard A Class Action law suit was filed against the State because the staff in all the buildings had been for years, inhaling asbestos which could result in respiratory cancer. In the end the Class Action law suit just disappeared and no one in the State seemed to have any knowledge of it. Under the reconstruction all the asbestos material was removed from every building on the institutions grounds. The buildings were then divided into four separate units each with its own director and assistant director. Janet discovered this when she arrived for duty one day and was called into the nurses station where the supervisors of her unit were assembled. She was handed a petition by a supervisor she didn't personally know and told to sign her name. When she asked what it was for, she was told that a woman named Julia Mead, was given the position of Assistant Director and the petition was to stop the appointment. "Do I know her? I don't recognize the name." Janet had said and was told, "Never mind that, just sign it!" Janet looked at the list of names and handed it back saying, "Why should I sign a petition against someone I don't know; who hasn't done anything against me?" The response was, "I knew she wouldn't sign it!" The instigator snatched the list from Janet's hand and she summarily turned and left the office remembering the petition against her being signed by people she didn't know to stop her from getting a raise and promotion. She asked herself the same question that she had asked herself back then, *What kind of people were these at this institution, when they would band together to stop a person from a promotion that didn't affect them"* They were like live crabs dumped into a steaming hot pot of boiling water. Mindless crabs grabbing, clawing and dragging each other down. Back then she had felt that it was terrible thing to do and her feelings hadn't changed. Walking out into the corridor an unknown woman was approaching her. She was a short, well dressed, dark skinned woman with her long hair stylishly done. As they passed each other, Janet turned and asked, "Are you the new Assistant Unit Director?" "Yes." the woman replied turning to look at Janet. Janet smiled at her and continued walking away then casually called back over her shoulder, "You better watch your back." The woman stared at Janet's retreating back and calling to her, she asked her who she was. Without turning around Janet replied over her shoulder, "I'm your 3 p.m. shift supervisor, Janet Nelson and I was just told to sign a petition against you. I didn't sign it, why should I? I don't know you?" and she walked on leaving Julia Mead staring at her retreating back. Although they both worked in the same building it would be over two years before their paths crossed again because Janet Nelson would be what Julia Mead needed to keep her boss, the Unit Director happy.

EIGHT

Two years later, two exams were offered by the State Civil Service Department, Head Cottage Training Supervisor and Institutional Superintendent. With ten years supervisory experience under her belt Janet was eligible and signed up for both exams strictly on the basis of the days off that came with taking the exam. When the results came out for Head Cottage Training Supervisor Janet ranked number one and on the Institutional Superintendent exam she ranked number three in the State of New Jersey. There were only nineteen positions available on grounds for the Head Supervisor position and they were permanently filled by employees who held them so long they could only be waiting for retirement or death. Besides with the animosity surrounding her from her beginning years there wasn't a chance in hell of her getting one, dead or alive. In the twenty years she'd worked there, there had only been one superintendent and that wasn't likely to change. You had to be appointed by the State which basically meant it's not what you know but who you know. Although her scores would be good indefinitely; she had no ambitions of power and was not impressed with titles. She was satisfied where she was holding the record of being the youngest supervisor in the history of the institution.

After the appointment of the new Director and Assistant Director Ms. Mead, rumors were running rampart throughout the building that the Ms. Mead (who was married) got the position because she was sleeping with the Director, who too was married. Janet, after hearing the rumors dismissed them wondering why people even cared about who was sleeping with whom. It had been over two years since she'd met the Assistant Director Mead in the corridor and she'd never met the Director or knew his name. It wouldn't bother her until years later when she discovered that she was being groomed to be his next mistress but before her there was Gloria Pitts, the current Head Cottage Training Supervisor. Janet had neither applied for the spot nor was it offered to her. Gloria Pitts was a short, big boned, light skinned woman who wore a white doctor's smock that apparently had never seen the inside of washing machine and chained smoked got the position.. That smock was covered with coffee and greasy food stains that were almost indistinguishable from burn holes from the cigarettes that always dangled from her smoke blackened lips. She had dreams of high titles and power and felt she was too intelligent to be working as a Head Training Supervisor. She could always be found bragging about having an Associates' degree from an unnamed college but ignored questions pertaining to her job such as: "If you're so smart; why was she cleaning shit for a living?" Janet worked the night shift and Gloria Pitts the day shift, so they seldom seen each other except at the monthly supervisor's meetings. When their paths did cross again it was under somewhat disturbing circumstances.

Gertrude Fleming was a day shift supervisor in Janet's building who had a round, dark, greasy looking face that could wreck a thousand ships. She had short, spikey, greasy hair that was always littered with lint and never laid down. Large frog-like eyes protruded over a bulbous nose and enormous shapeless lips she habitually covered with striking red lipstick. Her body was a bulky, shapeless mass that jiggled when she walked. Her pudgy fingers competed for attention with the stubby toes she insisted on cramming into toeless sandals and the bottom of her feet, were white with crust. She favored spandex clothing that squeezed her bulk into waves of over-lapping flesh. If Gertrude were in the spy game she would be known as a 'Deep Mole' and a double agent, working for both sides and personal gain. She was a snake in the grass who gathered information and passed on anything that could potentially create problems for others and make her seem essential to her superiors. She sought rumors, gossip (fact or fiction) from all kinds of sources at the institution and carried it where it would bring about the most damage and/or amusement. Her hidden agenda was meant to bring her closer into the confidences of the power people. She had nothing to recommend her as a part of the elite other than her gossip and she wanted very much to be within the pantheon of power. Gertrude craved their attention, wanted power and was glamorized by high titles which continued to elude her. She was allowed into the circles of the power people, lunching, conversing, passing information that never failed to interest her listeners but they had no illusions about her and used her for just what she was; a liaison to what went on out of their sight. They purposely divulged only enough information to wet her file banks and then released her onto unsuspecting employees to see what she'd come back with. She thought they were her allies; as well as the quickest route to promotions. She wasn't aware that the general consensus among the elite was that she was physically repulsive, intellectually retarded, a sloppy, ghetto dressing, grinning monkey whose credo was, 'Hear evil, speak evil and tell evil' and she stank. After dropping some venomous information about someone to her superiors and leaving, her bosses would laughingly spray air freshener to rid the office of her body odor. Gertrude Fleming had set herself up as everybody's friend and confidant and strangely enough lots of people flocked to her for aid or assistance with job issues or unfair treatment and she always presented a willing ear and sympathetic smile. If nothing else she was a wealth of information regarding the rules, regulations and policies of the institution. The troubled never knew that their problems were being telegraphed as quickly as possible to the Director and CEO and the information always resulted in severe retaliatory action against the troubled employee ending in disciplinary actions or terminations courtesy of Gertrude Fleming.

Janet had been assigned to the day shift for the day with Gertrude and was eating her lunch in the office when Gertrude entered the office looking mischievous. Janet looked up at her briefly wondering what this clown was up to now. The office was a small affair that was meant only to be functional, containing barely enough room for the desk, file cabinet and coat rack and its walls were empty of any decorations. There was very little walking space between the desk and the cabinets as Janet watched Gertrude squeezed her bulk between them to reach her. She leaned down over Janet and her smell caused Janet's lunch to lurch in her stomach and leaning away from her she held her breath as long as she could. Leaning away from Gertrude impeded the smell of her breath but not her body odor which was wafting over Janet's face in sickening waves causing her nose to wrinkle in disgust. Gertrude asked Janet if she wanted to see something. She was grinning like a sardonic clown while pulling lightly on Janet's arm. Janet followed Gertrude out of the office, into and around the corridor and out the rear door of the building. As she followed Gertrude she asked her what was going on. Gertrude didn't respond just pulled Janet along behind her. It was warm and sunny outside as she followed Gertrude around the outside of the building towards the front entrance. Just before they reached the corner of the building, which was surrounded by low hedges, Gertrude put a fat stubby finger up to her red colored lips and whispered for Janet to be quiet. They were standing behind the bushes that grew outside of the Director's office windows and Gertrude directed her to look through the window. When she did she blinked and then blinked again. There was the Head Training Supervisor Gloria Pitts, stretched out atop the Directors desk, naked below the waist and the maintenance supervisor was atop of her thrusting himself between her thighs. Janet was shocked but didn't pull back from the scene and got an eye full of the office and what was going on. Gertrude whispered into Janet's ear that Gloria had agreed to have sex with the man if he'd buy her a shrimp platter from Red Lobster and a fifth of Tequila. Janet surmised that James Brookes, who also worked in the building, accepted the offer, made the purchases and Gloria was upholding her end of the deal along with her legs. Janet realized that Gertrude was giving everyone a quick look when she saw her leading other staff persons up to the window and the scene inside, no admission cost required. She had no idea why she did it but she looked in again, mesmerized at what she was seeing. As she took in the details of the scene they became more and more minute. James Brookes was totally focused on what he was doing with both of his hands supporting Gloria's buttocks, lifting them to meet his thrusting hips. Her legs, on either side of his shoulders, flopped in unison with his thrust and Gloria lay casually beneath him smoking a cigarette. Janet watched Gloria take a long drag off her cigarette and exhale watching the smoke drift upwards. At that moment she casually turned her head looking towards the office windows and looked directly into a shocked Janet's face. Janet was caught in the act of spying on her but it seemed to her that Gloria dismissed Janet's face with a glance that asked *May I help you?* Janet was embarrassed at being caught watching but still couldn't move away. She wasn't familiar with the word erotic but that's what the scene represented to her and it fascinated her in her present stage of virginity. Part of her reluctantly accepted that she didn't want the image to fade; she curiously wanted to remember and study what she was seeing in all its detail. At the same time, she shied away from the image because it brought back unpleasant memories she associated with what her stepfather had been doing to her for years. Although he never penetrated her sexually, he like the maintenance man; was concentrating on that spot between the legs. She knew the names of these body parts but they'd never set up residence in her mind. At thirty three years of age she was still unbroken, a virgin and what she'd seen stirred up a multitude of mysteries within her that was both physical and mental. It was early afternoon and the sun's rays were shining directly into that window. Its light beams seemed to be concentrated on the maintenance man's penis and bare buttocks. Every time he withdraw flashes of light seem to sparkle on his glistening member giving it a high shine and when it disappeared between Gloria's thighs the sun's rays flashed, sparkled and traveled across his sweating buttocks. Janet tore her eyes away and began looking around the office and did indeed spot a large shrimp platter and huge bottle of Tequila but her eyes strayed back to the writhing bodies. Janet was embarrassed at what she was seeing, ashamed for having seen it and yet curious with something else that eluded her inexperienced mind and body. She finally backed away from the window and turned towards Gertrude who was just then sliding up to the window with another group of people. Not looking at her, Janet walked past them to the rear of the building and back to her office. After that day Janet didn't see Gloria for over a week but she couldn't avoid her as Gloria was her immediate supervisor. Whenever she chanced to run into her; she had at first avoided eye contact until she realized that Gloria wasn't the least concerned or bothered by what she'd done in the office or what Janet saw through the office window. It was as if it never happened and as far as Janet was concerned, aside from the lingering images, it was no concern of hers. She had no idea that almost two years from that day, she'd be at that same window, looking at the same act and taking pictures.

. Janet was summoned to the Director's office by the Assistant Director Julia Mead. She had never been in the front office other than peering through the window at that peep show months ago. It was a large, spacious office with a wall of curtained windows, waist high sliding door cabinets against two walls, a row of three file cabinets and two large, desk placed caddy-cornered to each other. Ms. Mead sat at one and an unknown man at the other. When she entered the office the man stood up from his desk and rushed over to her so quickly it seemed his feet never touched the floor. He reached over, grasped her hand in both of his and shook it while introducing himself as the Unit Director, Barton Cleese and said to her that Mead was right in saying that she was a pretty little thing. He was an older white man in his fifties perhaps with just enough hair left on the top of his head to cover his mottled scalp. He had deep red splotches of high up on both his cheeks that were separated by a large, red, bumpy nose, and a greying, handle bar mustache that down hung down from the corners of his red lips. His arms and hands were covered with age spots but the nails were well manicured. He seemed a jolly sort of person with dancing grey eyes and a generous welcoming politician's smile that seemed deceptive to Janet and his words felt slime covered. Goose bumps rose up on her arms at the touch of him and she disliked him on sight. There was something creepy about him and she resisted the urge to wipe the hand that he'd shaken on her dress after he released it from his grasp. He continued smiling as he said that Julia had told him all about her and he wanted to meet her. Janet smiled but said nothing. She couldn't imagine what Ms. Mead could have said about her because she had met the woman once over two years ago and that had just been in passing each other in the building's corridor. "What I'd like to know," Cleese continued, "Is would it be a problem for you to work day shift for the next two weeks? We have State inspections coming up soon and I need more experienced supervisors on dayshift." Day shift for Janet meant getting up 5 a.m. and the thought didn't excite her, but the off shoot was that she'd be off at 3:30 which was cool. She asked if she could think about it or was it mandatory and Barton Cleese had replied with a smile, "Of course the shift change isn't mandatory but it could be; if necessary," His hidden meaning wasn't lost on Janet. "But let's not think in those terms shall we. I would rather you simply volunteered." he smiled again and Janet imagined there were worms slithering behind that smile. She had just been given a hidden ultimatum; she knew that, and slowly replied that she could start the day shift the following week if that was ok. It was agreed and she left. She returned to her office thinking it strange that although Ms. Mead had summoned her, she never said a word; in fact she hadn't even looked at Janet. All of her attention was focused on the green blotter on her desk as if she was mesmerized by its color. The entire meeting was strange. She'd never met the man and yet he knew all about her. When she entered her office a smiling Gertrude beamed up at her asking, "So when will you be coming on my shift?" And Janet, who didn't particularly care for Gertrude, felt she was always too willing to please, looked at her, shrugged her shoulders and walk back out of the office wondering how Gertrude knew about the transfer and then dismissed the thought. After lunch Janet entered the supervisor's office just in time to hear Gloria Pitts and Gertrude talking about her coming on day shift. "I don't give a fuck whether they chose her or not but I'll tell you one damned thing, I won't be training that skinny bitch to do shit!" Gloria was declaring just as Janet entered the small office. With her head up and hands clinched into fist in her pockets, Janet casually looked first at Gertrude sitting behind the desk grinning from ear to ear, the red lipstick looking like a bloody slash across her face and then her eyes settled on Gloria. Taking a step towards Gloria, not close enough to be perceived as a threat but close enough to make her believe she could be one. She locked eyes with Gloria, her face representing just what she thought of her and in a quiet menacing voice she said to her face, "The day I become your bitch will be the day you kick my ass and we both know that's not going to happen. And to the best of my knowledge no one has stooped so low as to ask you to train me to do a damned thing!" Janet said contemptuously, "And if they did," she continued looking Gloria up and down, "I'd have to inform them that the only thing you could possibly teach me would be how screw a man 25 years older than me on a desk for a plate of shrimps and bottle of Tequila!" "Lastly," Janet said emphasizing each word with a poke of her finger in Gloria's face, "Fuck you bitch!" Standing her ground, breathing calmly while staring in Gloria's abashed face; waiting for her to say something, anything. Gloria couldn't have said anything even if she had been arrogantly stupid enough to do so. She was speechless, her tongue glued to the roof of her mouth, which wisely stayed shut. She would have never imagined such language from the quiet, passive Janet, whose voice never rose above a conversational tone. Having been caught with her foot stuck squarely in her mouth there was nothing she could say plus Janet had intimidated the hell out of her with her quiet ferocity. With her tail tucked firmly between her legs, Janet watched Gloria stand up and she stepped a little allowing her to walk pass her out of the office leaving a still grinning Gertrude sitting behind the desk.

"Anything you'd like to say?!" Janet snapped un-expectantly at Gertrude. Her question cracked through the office like a lion tamer's whip with acid on its tip. Gertrude could have sustained a whiplash injury with the speed in which her head snapped into the direction of Janet's dark face which was now focused on her. Her facial muscles were frozen into a rigor mortis grin; as she too had been caught off guard and stunned by Janet's not so delicate speech. Janet could physically see the signs of Gertrude cunningly changing sides in her face, about to throw Gloria to the lions. Janet hadn't heard Gertrude say anything against her, but she knew the conversation hadn't been one sided and that Gertrude had been had been adding her bits and pieces. Janet listened as Gertrude retreated into anonymity stating, "Nope" and grinning replied, "I think you just about said it all and very well I might add." she laughed and true to her back stabbing ways threw Gloria to the lions. A week later, Gloria was gone. Rumor had it that she had been promoted but whatever the reason for her absence, she and Janet would meet again and it wouldn't be good.

It had been two weeks since the confrontation between Janet and Gloria and also the end of Janet's (allegedly not mandatory) stint on day shift. Gertrude was itching to tell somebody about it but it couldn't be told to just anybody. She kept her explosive, dirty, little, nasty secret in a noxious smelly chamber of her heart where it scratched and clawed to be let out. Passing such information needed to in some way benefit her, but how? Janet wasn't a threat to her ambitions but Gloria was; but now Gloria was gone. Each day after signing in, ensuring the patients were dressed and fed breakfast, Gertrude would leave the work floor and go up to the Directors office. She'd gotten into the habit of preparing coffee for Mead and Cleese and they'd gotten used to being served. Every morning while she waited for the percolator to perk she'd let slide some rumor or in some cases fact she knew would be of interest to her bosses. Something that would lead them to question her about her information she was relaying. She'd casually make them all a cup of coffee, take an unoffered seat and began spilling her guts, in detail, about what she'd heard or knew. She knew that it was expected that she'd have something of interest to tell and she never disappointed them. The hot item concerning Gloria and Janet was gagging her in its attempt to be let out especially about Janet cursing and threatening Gloria but she had to be careful with that information. Janet wouldn't have been able to make the statement about Gloria having sex on Cleese's desk if she, Gertrude, hadn't brought it to Janet's attention. Damn, she sighed, deciding that Cleese wasn't the one to be told but Mead, his assistant was and if she chose to tell Cleese well then that would be on her. Gertrude's goal was to break up any forming relationship between Janet and the Assistant Director, Julia Mead.

Gertrude was extremely interested in the fact that Janet had not been returned to her regular shift and was correct in her assumption that Janet hadn't approached Cleese concerning her return to her regular shift. Gertrude too noticed that Gloria's office door was closed and locked; had been for three days now. Everyone assumed she was out sick because no one on the work floor knew that she had been promoted or about the now vacant position. No one accept Gertrude that is, who was so ecstatic with anticipation and longing that she could barely contain herself knowing that she was the logical person to fill the vacancy of Head Training Supervisor. Why else would they have brought Janet down to day shift accept to take her place as the day shift supervisor. She was going to be promoted into the vacancy left by Gloria. Gertrude decided that the telling of the confrontation between Gloria and Janet had best be set aside, but just for the moment. She couldn't very well attack her replacement. She had a better idea, she'd train Janet. She'd have no problem doing this because Janet would be working under her and she'd make sure she was well trained. Gertrude was feeling extremely generous. She couldn't wait to finally get her own office and a real title representing power. It was finally going to happen! After fifteen years of waiting she was getting promoted or so she thought in her mind morning, noon and night. She was close to joyous tears in her eagerness and excitement; as if she was preparing to give her acceptance speech for winning the Nobel Peace Prize. Throughout the day, she repeatedly walked down the corridor that led to the door of the Head Training Supervisor's office, pausing for brief seconds to lovingly caress the oak door which she imagined responded to her touch in a silent welcome. She, like the Jefferson's, would be 'Moving on Up' not to a deluxe apartment in the sky but to Head Training Supervisor. She found herself, sometimes out loud, humming the theme song from that show. The smile on her face was for once actually genuine and as real as it would ever get. Instead of having a spring in her step, she was a bouncing ball. Everyone noticed this strange happiness and fell over backwards when Gertrude came to work with enough coffee and donuts for the entire staff. "Did you hit the lottery or something?" they asked remarking on her generosity. Gertrude replied with a secretive smile "Nope, something much better." she would reply. "And what was that?" the staff inquired. "Power" she breathed to herself as she stepped spritely towards the front office her arms carrying coffee and donuts for her benefactors while wondering if today would be the day she was given the position. Up front they partook of her generosity and she spent almost two hours with them just socializing but when she returned to her office she was still a supervisor. This was fine with Gertrude, she could wait because when all was said and done; she would finally be where she wanted to be; with the "Big Boys'.

Gertrude was confident in the knowledge of her upcoming promotion. She began inundating Cleese and Mead with praises of Janet. She naively brought up the subject of Janet and how well she was working out on day shift. It was a difficult shift to handle because all essential patient appointments, meetings and training occurred on that shift. She remarked how quick Janet was to grasp and implement information, how willing she was to learn and how the direct care staff accepted her so easily. She, Gertrude, said would be an asset to the shift and the unit. Luckily, Cleese and Mead hadn't been flies on the wall a few weeks earlier when she and Gloria were trashing Janet. Cleese boosted Gertrude's expectations even higher when he raised his coffee cup to her in a toasting manner and complemented her on taking the initiative to train Janet. Returning the statement with a toast of her own she informed Cleese that she'd make sure Janet was properly trained. Gertrude's smile was so wide that the corners of her red lips almost touched her ears. And then he had complemented her again, saying he knew he could count on her and that he had made the best and only choice possible to complement her staff. Gertrude clung to those words 'Her staff" and just barely contained herself from quivering like an excited, frolicking puppy being stroked by its master. His words could only mean that the decision was made and the position was hers. She was floating in euphoria as she finished her coffee and left the front office and that was when she began telling people that she was about to be formally promoted to Head Training Supervisor.

After Gertrude left the office Mead, sitting at her desk was looking at Cleese who was saying with a laugh, "Isn't she a happy camper?" Julia didn't immediately respond, then seeing Cleese's pale eyes on her she responded drily, "Any particular reason she shouldn't be happy, Chief?" her nickname for him. She listened with mixed feelings as he repeated that he had made the right choice and she couldn't help but think that the choice had been hers, not his. She, as well as Cleese, knew Gertrude was thinking that she had been chosen for the position but this was not the case and in his perverse form of humor this amused him.

NINE

Julia Mead could think of plenty of reasons why Gertrude was running on cloud nine, but she wouldn't voice them any more than she would ever speak (under any circumstances) against her boss/lover/Cleese. He'd owned her affections and loyalties for years; lock, stock and barrel as the saying goes and there was no way out for her nor had she ever sought escape from him. She didn't want out and today, years later, she felt the same. He wasn't much in the looks department but he was a very dynamic, charismatic man that exuberated charm, power and energy and she had been irrevocably drawn to him. That had been years ago and although he continued to hold the same attractions for her, she didn't protest his desire to replace her and that was just what he was doing. She would continue to be his Assistant Director but was being dismissed as his mistress. She wasn't hurt or angry about his plans for defection from her; any more than his wife, who had for years known about their affair. In fact, she was sort of proud that he had chosen her to pick his new mistress. She was not only privy to the inner workings of her boss's scheming, power mad mind; she was a willing participant when lies were necessary to back some devious ploy of his. She became a completely different person, morally, after having been for years, tarnished by his vindictive shenanigans that were never done with good intent. All things served God and in his absence they served Cleese! If anyone ever wanted to question the validity of the saying 'The idle mind is the playground of the devil' they had only to meet Barton Cleese.

She'd met and fallen in love with him over twenty years ago when the institution first opened and they were both assigned to the same building. He was a supervisor and she a direct care worker and their mutual attraction had been immediate with her only drawback being that she'd never been with a white man. Back then, she had been a beautiful charcoal colored young lady, short in stature with thick beautifully styled hair and dark bedroom eyes under long lashes. She had a tight body with sculptured curves in all the right places. She had been vivacious and flirty with a quick mind, willing attitude and in the mind of the married Barton Cleese she was sexy as hell. Today, her aging years had added a sedate handsomeness and charm to her maturity and at fifty-two years of age she was still sexily gorgeous and her body hung in there right along with her looks. Julia had married young, produced no off spring and was stuck with a husband who had abandoned her for his own mistress, alcohol. He was a 24 hour drunk who liked to fuss and fight, although he never struck her. Yet she was happy, full of life and open to adventures with men that came her way. She was careful to keep her affairs under cover and had done so for years after losing her place in her home to drink, which began in the second year of their marriage. The affairs never lasted more than a month or so and contrary to popular consensus, she was the one who always broke them off. When she met Cleese, the affair began two weeks later and lasted for over twenty years and counting. Well not exactly counting, because he was arrogant and straight forward enough to let her know that his interest in her was done and he wanted new amusements. He was not only replacing her; he left it to her to fill her own spot. He charged her with finding and grooming her own replacement. "After all" he'd actually said to her while chucking her affectionately under her chin, "Who better to do the job than the person who knows what I like!" Yes, it was her assignment and her first step had been to select Janet Nelson. It was for this reason that she, Janet, had been transferred to the dayshift; to give Cleese easy access to her. He would be able to get a good look at his prospective bed fellow and also ascertain that her level of intelligence, which was almost as huge a necessity as the sexual attraction, met his own egotistic levels. He liked to surround himself with intelligent, fast thinking people because it enhanced his status as he liked to brag to his constituents how good his staff was, holding them up for display, wanting others to want what he had. Julia's job, essentially as his pimp, was to ensure the mistress looked good, was intelligent and could be ensnared with the first step being to bring Janet Nelson closer to the precipice and to Cleese. It was the only way for her to ensure Cleese would have daily access to Janet and she presented this option to Cleese who loved it so much he wanted her to put it in action yesterday. The same day Mead came up with a plan that would begin with transferring Janet Nelson to day shift, she had cautioned Cleese that they had to take things slowly. She had no idea what type of woman Janet was morally; she only knew that she was intelligent and attractive. Time would tell if she could be seduced but Cleese had no patience for waiting and he let Mead know that he liked what he saw and wanted it. Later that same day, she discovered that he had not only changed his mind but her plans for ensnaring Janet. He'd told her that he'd decided to be the one to start the seduction through Julia's plan but he wanted to speed things up and without Mead's knowledge, he made his move.

The designs of the buildings at the institution were such that the work areas were well separated from the front office by a locked door and a short corridor and only supervisors had this key. The direct care staff of all nineteen buildings on grounds was 99.99% black and whenever a white person (male or female) entered into the work area everyone snapped to attention ensuring that everything was in order. Any white person who entered the work area was automatically thought to be someone of importance and so it was a week later when Cleese came strolling into the work area at 7 a.m. in the morning with a hand full of large vanilla envelopes. He didn't bother to notice or acknowledge the direct care staff as he (thankfully) passed them by and went directly into the supervisor's office. The shift was just changing and two mid-night shift supervisors and two dayshift supervisors (Gertrude and Janet) were present in the office. His appearance had the same effect on them as it had on the direct care staff, everyone came to attention. Cleese didn't bother with such trivial things as 'Good Morning' as he stood there smiling down at Gertrude. She had been explaining a procedure to Janet, who was leaning over her shoulder. All four supervisors looked up at him and without saying anything, Cleese lackadaisically, placed the envelopes down on the desk in front of Gertrude. On top of the pile was a huge ring of keys that seemed to glide in slow motion off the stack of envelopes and jingled down to rest in front of Gertrude. Everyone, accept Janet, stared at the keys knowing what they represented, the keys belonging to the Head Training Supervisor's office. Gertrude's heart caught in her throat as she greedily snatched up the keys that had landed directly in front of her. Suddenly the most shocking thing happened. Cleese, with a devious smile on his red cheeked face, leaned over and neatly plucked the keys from Gertrude's sweaty palms and handed them to Janet. There was an audible gasp among the two night shift supervisors as they quickly deduced what was happening. Cleese turned and left the office laughing and thinking to himself; "I'm such a stinker!" He left three shocked supervisors and a puzzled Janet, holding a set of keys she had no idea went to what, and a stunned Gertrude with the same smile frozen on her face.

When Cleese dropped the keys down in front of Gertrude her heart skipped a beat and when she picked them up; she felt like she was holding the winning ticket for the mega millions lottery. In Gertrude's head the sun was bright, the birds were chirping and somewhere glorious carnival music played on and on; until suddenly a huge, almighty, dark cloud descended upon her when Cleese suddenly plucked the keys from her pudgy hands and gave them to Janet. Gertrude's face looked as if it had been held together with invisible screws that were slowly unscrewing. Her features began a slow drooping motion like the paintings of that artist's melting clocks, until her mouth dropped opened in a perfect 'O'. She could feel the eyes of her peers staring first at Janet then sliding cautiously over to her. Their eyes barely concealing their humor at what had to be the greatest slap in the face ever. One of them laughed nervously and then guiltily slapped a hand across her betraying mouth. It took all of her being for Gertrude not to release a primitive yell of betrayal; to halt the hot tears of embarrassment from flooding down her shocked and broken features. After the weight of the keys had been cruelly and she bet purposely removed from her hands and given to Janet (right in her face mind you!), her mind was speedily trying to comprehend and yet refusing to accept what had just happened. It felt like a ton of bricks were tumbling down onto her heart and the pressure, hurt and embarrassment was getting heavier, showing no signs of letting up. She had to get out of there but she couldn't move, she was paralyzed with embarrassment and there was no way to make a graceful exit. She had bragged to everyone about being the new Head Supervisor. Now she had to face these same people, who liked her just as much as she liked them, knowing what had happened. She knew there would be amusing stories of her humiliation told all over grounds by lunch time about how the keys were given then literally taken from her hands and given to Janet Nelson.

She bit down on her lip so hard she drew blood at the excruciating position Cleese had left her in and her eyes narrowed with hate for that bastard. She hated and despised him with a passion that was now orgasmic. She spared some of that hate for Janet; whom she now believed knew that she was getting the position all along. Well, maybe, just maybe, it was time to release what she knew about Janet and Gloria. While she was plotting sabotage against Janet the phone rang, it was Cleese and the sound of his voice in her ear was like hot churning gravel. He cheerfully apologized for interrupting, but would she please send Janet up front with yesterday's attendance sheets thank you and he hung up before she could choke out a peanut butter thick reply. She weighed the pros and cons of whether or not to deliver the message then decided against it. She reasoned with herself that if she didn't deliver the message he might possibly come back there himself and she certainly didn't want that to happen. She informed Janet of the request without looking at her. She couldn't look at her without having to restrain the urge to rip that pretty face to shreds and she knew her feelings would show on her face. Janet took the attendance sheets and left. The remaining two supervisors studiously avoided Gertrude's eyes and collided with each other as they jostled each other in their rush to get out of the office; each wanting to be the first to start spreading the news of what they'd witnessed. And much sooner than that and for the first time, Janet would be entering the zone of darkness in Cleese's office as an unknowing virginal sacrifice. It was then that a thought entered her bruised ego as to why Janet was given the position. She wasn't exactly on point but had no idea how close she was to the reason why.

When Janet entered the office Mead was the only one there. She said hello to Janet and proceeded to show her how to transfer the information on the attendance sheets to the building attendance book. Afterwards, Janet accompanied Mead down to the business office where she introduced her to the head of payroll, who handed Janet the payroll checks for all four buildings of her unit, showed her how to count and record all the staff's pay checks and after signing for the receipt of the checks, they returned to the building. Arriving back at the office, the checks were separated and counted out to each head supervisor for their prospective buildings. Janet was seated in a chair at the front of Mead's desk when she asked Janet if she would accept the position of Head Training Supervisor because Cleese really wanted her in the position. Janet wasn't stupid enough to jump at the offer. She pulled the keys Cleese had given her out of her pocket. Holding them up by the ring on one finger she looked at Mead and asked, "Is that what these keys are for, the keys to Gloria's office? Cleese was in the back this morning. He gave them to Gertrude, then took them from her and put them in my hands." And she was thinking, *Wow!*"

Mead said nothing; just looked placidly at Janet, her hands folded under her chin noting that Janet wasn't at all excited about the position, so titles didn't impress her. She was also thinking about how she acquired the keys. She thinks before she leaps, interesting but conceivably problematic. Cleese could be such an arrogant bastard. *Why'd he do that?* She was thinking but she knew the answer. He knew, full well, that Gertrude expected the position. He had, according to his usual sadistic form of humor, set out to deliberately humiliate Gertrude and in front of an audience for his own amusement. Janet, according to her plan, was to be transferred to day shift for two weeks. At the end of that period she would be informed that Gloria was leaving and offered the position. That was how it was supposed to go down. She also believed that Janet was thinking about the pros and cons of accepting the position, in fact she appeared to be downright hesitant. This was also an unexpected turn of events. She was supposed to be excited, all smiles of anticipation, yet she just sat there quietly looking at the keys. "I don't know anything about the job." Janet said cautiously. "Cleese and I will train you." Mead countered. "Suppose I mess up, will I be able to return to my original shift and keep my supervisors position?" "Sure, that'll be no problem." Mead lied. She knew in her heart that if Cleese didn't get what he wanted from Janet he'd see her either demoted, terminated or both. She knew Cleese was not a good person. He was cunning, knowledgeable, manipulative and highly vindictive. He possessed all the quaint qualities that make up the typical tyrannical, irrational boss and all things served him. His motto was 'My way or the highway!' and he meant just that. "What if something happens and you know I'm right and he is wrong, what will you do?" Janet asked. "Side with him." and there she told the truth without hesitation. They were now studying each other. *Wow!* Janet thought again. "Can I take a day or two to think about it?" she asked. "Sure but in the mean time you will perform the duties of Head Training Supervisor and your first assignment while you're thinking about it will be to clean that rat nest of an office of Gloria's as its your office now. That's all." And Janet was dismissed.

Janet didn't miss Mead's statement informing her that the office was now hers. There was no mistaking the point that she was in the position whether she wanted to be or not. After being dismissed she took the long way around to her new office. She wasn't ready to run into Gertrude just yet and she avoided her for the remainder of the day. She didn't particular like Gertrude and no way would she ever trust her; but what Cleese had done with the key business was nothing short of cruel, totally fucked up and deliberate. Even Janet knew that the job should have gone to Gertrude. She did, after all, have seniority over her and in the same building. Cleese's early morning visit to the office and the business with the keys had all been pre-planned and had been amusing to him, that's why he was laughing when he left. It had been sadistically funny to him to see Gertrude's reaction. He had to know that doing such a thing to her was bound to hurt and embarrassed her deeply and that had been hilarious to him. Did she, Janet, want a part of these types of doings? No. Did she have a choice? No, she wasn't being given a choice. If she turned down the position she had no doubt that there would be some sort of repercussion. Now she really didn't believe Mead when she said everything would go back to normal if she turned down the position. Nothing, she would come to learn, could be considered normal when dealing with Barton Cleese. She would also come to understand why Gertrude had nicknamed the institution Cleese's Plantation."

After trying several keys, she found the right one and opened the door to the office and the smell coming out of the opened door literally shoved her backwards. She found Mead was right, the office was filthy. It was littered with leftover food, half-filled soda bottles with drowned roaches inside of them. Empty crates, cigarette boxes, papers and more papers were all over the place. The surface of the desk was littered with Styrofoam cups with coffee dregs and cigarette butts, leftover plastic plates and forks with fungus growing on long left over food and roaches were scurrying from the light. Janet went to the maintenance closet for a several large garbage bags and a pair gloves and started cleaning and disinfecting the office. Two hours later, she was mopping the floor when two unknown women knocked on the open door and entered saying they were there to interview for the dayshift and evening shift supervisor positions. Janet needed no further proof that her supervisor's positon was gone and she didn't know anything about the job placed on her or conducting interviews. This was not surprisingly handled for her when the phone on her desk rang. It was Cleese informing her that he'd already hired the two women that were currently standing in her office waiting to be interviewed by her. Janet felt a stab of panic in her heart and it had been on the tip of her tongue to ask why they'd been sent to her if he'd already hired them, but she thought better of it. He asked her what she thought of them and she replied she didn't know, she hadn't had enough time to actually speak with them. He laughed and said, "Don't worry about that, they'll be starting next Friday." and hung up and Janet again felt that stab of panic as an icy chill streaked up her back. What had she gotten herself into and was there a way out?

Janet had no options regarding the acceptance of the position she had been railroaded into and settled into doing the best job she could do, on a job she knew nothing about. After the interviewees left she sat behind the desk wondering what to do. There were lots of things she always said she would do if she was running this building and now that she was, she set about doing them. She went to the client's personal closet, a huge room containing all the personal items of the 32 patients including, clothes, shoes, coats and things. She emptied the room of its contents and set about arranging and assigning the clients names alphabetically on the shelves and then went through all the clothing and placed them on their now alphabetized shelves, making a list of who had what and who needed what. Next she called down to the supply building and asked if they had curtains to put up to all the empty windows of the building. They did and she placed several huge orders for curtains, personal hygiene supplies for the clients, soap, shampoo, razors, wash cloths, towels, cologne, deodorant, toothbrushes, tooth paste and mouth wash. Her orders where approved but forwarded to Cleese's office for confirmation and she was called up to his office. She went with notebook and pencil in hand. He asked her the reason for the enormous order and she told him backing up her explanation with the things she'd written down. He laughed, but was impressed with what she'd accomplished in her first day as Head Training Supervisor and confirmed the orders. He was, in fact, so impressed that he had the other head supervisors of his unit inventory their client's supplies, and make necessary orders including curtains for their buildings. In the over thirty years of their existence none of the buildings on grounds had curtains up to the windows of their buildings (accept the administration building) and they all followed suit. Over the following months, many of Janet's suggestions and request were approved including cable television, piped in music and a public address system. She was doing exemplary work and Cleese brought the assistant superintendent, Paul Dunning up to his office to show off the building and to introduce (show off) Janet. Janet barely stifled a giggle when she met him. Mr. Dunning was Santa Claus's twin come to the Sawyer Developmental Center. He was over six feet tall, a huge rotund man wearing pants held up with red suspenders. He had a full head of thick wavy white hair, a white mustache and full white beard that that covered his cheeks and neck. At the introduction from Cleese, he merely nodded his head in Janet's direction and she said hello and sat down. Dunning continued staring at Janet as if she were an insect under a microscope and it made her just a little uncomfortable. Cleese was going on about what a good worker she was, setting trends all over grounds. He began making statements about how attractive she was and Janet sat there embarrassed up to the roots of her head and when Cleese dismissed her she got the hell out of there in a hurry.

TEN

Gertrude Fleming succumbed to her defeat and carried off the impression that she knew before everybody that Janet was getting the position. She never indicated by word or deed that she hated Janet and surprisingly true to her word, helped her with necessary procedures Janet wasn't aware existed. For all intents and purposes, she was happy for Janet but this was by no stretch of the imagination true. Gertrude was sitting back waiting for a chance to derail the train. She couldn't do anything that would appear as a blatant attempt of sabotage to Janet. She, like everyone else, knew Cleese stood firmly behind his new protégé and to get caught plotting against Janet would incur his unforgiving wrath. No, she'd have to wait for the right moment and the best situation to turn Cleese against Janet. So as if nothing unusual or unexpected had occurred, she resumed her habit of preparing coffee in the front office for Cleese and Mead every morning. She kept a firm smile pasted on her face as every morning the topic was Janet; Janet, Janet! Inside she was throwing the world's most insane tantrum; kicking, screaming, throwing and breaking whatever she got her fat, stubby hands on. Cleese found Gertrude's fake acceptance hilarious and when Gertrude left the office he cracked nasty jokes about Gertrude's endeavors to assume business as usual. Mead just sat there smiling at his nasty jokes.

Building fifteen was undeniably the worst, nastiest building on grounds with the most destructive and dangerous clients. Whenever a building was short of staff and staff from other buildings were sent there to cover the shift, the selected employee refused to go, argued that it wasn't there turn to go or simply signed out and went home. All the employees opted for disciplinary action against them as opposed to working in building fifteen. After Janet took over as Head Supervisor and changed the face of the building and its clients, people all over grounds wanted to work in her building. Whenever there was a direct care vacancy, her mail box was packed with request for interviews. Under her supervision, all acts of favoritism, unfair treatment and deceitful disciplinary actions ceased. Everyone was treated with respect, fairness and no disciplinary actions went past her desk without her thoroughly investigating the charges with the staff person and the supervisor. Absenteeism and lateness that led to suspension days or termination were dealt with an understanding of the employee's circumstances. If the situation was plausible she would reduce a termination to a suspension and a suspension to a warning. Building fifteen was the best building on grounds and competition to get in there was fierce and the interview, with Janet, was no joke. She checked the interviewee's record of attendance, disciplinary actions and strangely enough their communication skills. Recognizing that as well as having a constitution strong enough to handle her raucous clients, her staff also needed communication skills to speak with families, health care professionals and outside disciplines and they needed to be able to express themselves orally and on written assessments, evaluations and recommendations. It wasn't her job or her supervisor's duty to teach reading and writing but it was one of her requirements. She was tough but fair. Over a year had passed since taking the position and everything was on point in her building with State inspections coming up in a month. She had just received permission to redecorate the dayrooms. Each day room held sixteen clients, four hard plastic sofas and a long wooden table with bench chairs. She requested a divider to split the room in half having eight clients on each side and threw out the plastic institutional furniture and replaced them with real living room furniture. She wanted two real sofas, two reclining chairs, coffee and end tables and a large throw rug for the floor. If the room was called a day living room it should look like one she said presenting her idea to Cleese. He not only loved it but approved the furniture purchases and room dividers; he threw in requested monies for large scenic pictures and plants to be placed around the bare walls of the building and corners of the corridors for all four buildings of his unit. Her next request was to split the two large dorm rooms into four separate rooms and each room divided in two. This resulted in four patient beds to a room. The request to purchase nice, colorful comforters, dusters and pillow cases to match the curtains for each bedroom was also approved. The changes in Janet's building were modern and eye catching and the other eighteen buildings on grounds hastened to copy off Janet's building which had took on the look of realistic living areas which added to Cleese's bragging rights on his star head supervisor.

Perhaps it was his dreams of the previous night that threw Cleese completely off the deep end. His sleep had for weeks been plagued with luscious, hot visions and fantasies of chasing and catching a scantily dressed Janet, who willingly performed heart stopping erotic antics on his willing body that drove him beyond the boundaries of ecstasy. In his dreams, he could not only see and touch her; he could hear her sultry laugh, and smell the scent of her sex all around him. He closed his eyes, inhaled deeply and would suddenly come fully awake, disappointed, unsatisfied, drenched in sweat with a rock hard erection convincing him that he would wait no longer for Janet's body. Almost two years had gone by with him secretly lusting after her and like Popeye the Sailor 'he had stood all he could stand, till he couldn't stands no more! He wanted her. He wanted her NOW! He shaved, showered, ate breakfast and still his erection did not fully deflate. It throbbed and ached in his loins until he felt he'd have to grab and throttle it into submission. This perhaps might explain why, with dream laced memories of Janet, he masturbated himself while driving to work. He knew fully well that he couldn't just get a hold of her and bang her into a fine powder to satisfy his lust. His big head told him he had to take it one step at a time, his little head was indignantly yelling at him to cut out the middle man. "We have to do this now!" his little head screamed and punctuated the ultimatum with an electric, spine numbing orgasm that caused him to momentarily lose control of the steering wheel and he drifted out of his lane with tires screeching against the curb. He pulled over, flushed, weak and gasping for breath from the strength of his orgasm. Fifteen minutes later, after cleaning himself with tissues from the glove compartment, his breathing back to normal, he pulled back into traffic and continued on to work and Janet.

Julia Mead and Gertrude Fleming were both aware of Cleese's sexual interest in Janet. Mead knew it as a work in progress. Gertrude knew it because she could read the signs from Cleese whenever Janet was present in the office. Janet had simply sensed his attraction for her. Cleese didn't care who was present when he said or did inappropriate things to Janet which she stoically ignored. The one thing Mead, Cleese and Fleming could all agree on regarding his pursuit of Janet was that she in some way knew and had begun to make her presence scarce in his office and had changed her style of dress completely. Instead of the attractive dresses and skirt sets; she began wearing jeans, sweat suits and pants with baggy sweaters. When summoned to his office she always stood well away from his desk. She never engaged in conversation unless it was work related and never lingered in his office. Although she was offered, many times, to stay, sit down and have a cup of coffee, always she declined.

When Cleese arrived for duty, he threw all caution to the wind and had barely sat behind his desk when he ordered Mead to call Janet; he needed to speak to her. Janet had long before developed the habit of prepping herself before going to his office. She'd calm her anxiety (which always occurred) at his request for her presence in his office, adjust her face (on which she never wore makeup) into placid, slightly bored lines, had taken to wearing her long dark hair in a single pony tail and she never, ever entered his office with a smile upon her face. This summons somehow felt different and she was sorry that she hadn't had time to change out of her dress into her sweat suit. Her anxiety increased as she entered the office standing as always in the center of the office with Cleese's desk in front of her and Mead's desk off to the side. Not looking at her Cleese said, "Janet hand me the schedule book." The book was a top a file cabinet that was situated between the gaps in their desks. Just after she walked through the gap she heard the sound of a book hitting the floor and then Cleese's voice, "Janet would you hand me that please." It was ridiculously obvious that he'd purposely shoved the book off his desk. Janet turned, looked down at the book, then at Mead who was carefully studying her. Janet tilted her head slightly to the side as a thought flashed in her head and she thought incredulously, *Oh my God! He wants me to bend over and pick up the book so he can look under my dress! Son of a-bitch!* She experienced an intense desire to turn around and punch those red splotches off both sides of his grinning face but of course she couldn't. She did know that a response was needed. A strong response that would carry an even stronger no nonsense message that said; *I know what you're doing and I don't like it"* She had to send a convincing message that was respectful and indignant, clear-cut, nice and nasty. Yet, she could think of nothing to say; so she went with her gut feelings which were how she felt about his tasteless action and request. She turned completely around with her back now facing Mead. She bent over, picked up the book and placed it gently on his desk. Locking eyes with him she quietly and firmly said, "If you do that again I won't pick it up." Her jaw almost dropped open at his response which totally ignored her words. He laughed uproariously slapping himself across his knees and said, "Damn, I wanted you to turn the other way!" Janet was shocked at this supercilious response and not without effort; she dragged her eyes from his and with hips swinging indignantly she stalked out of the office. In her office there were no words she could think of to express how belittled and pissed off she felt although she had plenty of adjectives. *How dare he do that to me! Who does he think he is? What kind of egotistical, narcissistic, self-centered, arrogant, self-important, pretentious, pompous ass little anti-Christ, son of a bitch was he?* She was upset that he'd actually done such a thing; but was even more incensed that he felt she would comply. She couldn't calm down or concentrate on her work so she took a Release of Duty form from her file cabinet, filled it out and took it up to his office but he wasn't there. She handed Mead the form which she co-signed without comment. Janet accepted her copy, signed out and left for the remainder of the work day. She didn't know Cleese had also relieved himself of duty.

Mead knew that Cleese had gone too far and much too soon. She too, wondered what was wrong with him doing such a thing. She was both shocked and embarrassed that he done it and in the course of his act made her a witness, but that was neither here nor there, because if necessary she (as well as Cleese) knew she'd lie saying she wasn't in the office or had been in the office but hadn't seen anything. He hadn't even considered what Janet's response might be, whether or not she'd file a complaint of sexual harassment. In his conceit and arrogance, he just did it and had the unmitigated gall to be upset that he hadn't gotten a chance to look under Janet's dress.

Completely ignored and/or forgotten by Cleese and Mead was the presence of a fourth person in the office. Gertrude Fleming was standing in her accustomed spot (which would have been behind Janet) making coffee and watched the entire scene and her mind was busily making backup copies of what she'd seen and heard. She'd witnessed Cleese sexually harassing Janet, witnessed Mead witnessing the entire incident and she hated them both!

Janet called out sick for the following two days which led into the weekend. She needed the four days off because she was afraid to return to work and afraid not to return. She loved her job but knew it was impossible to endure such treatment from Cleese on a daily basis. Only two options were available under the circumstances and both were unacceptable. She couldn't just quit her job and she felt confident that any attempt to transfer would be blocked by Cleese. She'd been extremely agitated over the weekend about how things would be on Monday morning. It wasn't as if she could avoid Cleese, her day began and ended in his office. She brooded over how she should act, whether to speak or not, pretend nothing happened or bring the situation up for discussion. She just didn't know what to do or where to turn. What does a woman do when her boss does something like that?

The next morning Gertrude stood outside the closed door of Cleese's office. She was just about to knock and go in to prepare their coffee when she heard the muffled sounds of an argument on the other side of the door. She pressed her ear to the door trying to hear better but the thick door provided no clear conduit to what was being said in there. She had an idea that the argument was about Janet and what Cleese had done to her the previous day. *Damn!* She thought failing to clearly hear what was being said. Then an idea came to the snake in the grass. She quietly left the front lobby, went through the building and left it through the rear door. She crept around the outside of the building until she came to the front of the building. The windows of Cleese's office were open just as she hoped and she could hear them as clearly as if she was in the office. "Don't blame me!" Mead was saying, "It was a stupid thing to do. What were you thinking?" "Obviously, I wasn't, now was I?" Cleese shouted. "Do you have any idea what could happen now? When she released herself from duty I knew repercussion was coming. Janet's not stupid, you know this. Yet you did this thing to her? What the hell were you thinking? You act as if the world revolves around you and that you can go around crashing peoples' lives to pieces at any whim that rips around in your head. Flash point, it doesn't! I've watched you manipulate people for years and sure they dance to your tune but that's because they're afraid of losing their jobs but Janet is different. I told you this! I warned you that if you planned to get in her pants you'd have to go extremely slow, gain her trust and confidence; but oh no, not the cock of the woods. I can't help but wonder if she's going to tell what you did and if she does, who will she tell it too? You were stupid, stupid, stupid!" "Don't you call me stupid, don't you ever call me stupid!" Cleese's voice was rising. "You got a better word?" Mead came back. "Have you given no thought to the position you put me in or don't you care? You made me a fucking witness! I agreed to set her up in the position for you, not to be on the opposite end of a sexual harassment complaint as a witness against you! I didn't sign up for that shit, no way!" "Who says there's going to be a complaint, have you heard something?" Cleese sounded nervous. "No, but you should have considered these things in that almighty brain of yours." Mead said. "If she does make a complaint, you'll back me up, won't you. With both of us denying anything happened or better yet, just say you weren't in the office at that time. Yes, that's better. You don't know anything because you weren't there!" "You got me on this, right?" his voice sounding slightly menacing. "You know I will, but there is one other problem that you forgot to consider." she said. "What's that?" he asked. "Gertrude Fleming!" she spat out angrily. "Gertrude Fleming?" he repeated. "What does she have to do with anything?" he asked nonplussed. "She was in the office, you fool. Making coffee and I bet taking notes!" Mead replied somewhat satisfactorily. When Gertrude heard her name a crippling chill went through her. Heart thumping she stumbled away from the window and wobbled back to the rear door on trembling legs. Her mind swimming with what she'd over heard and the possibilities that presented themselves and blackmail wasn't far behind. If Janet did file a complaint, she, Gertrude, would be the star witness to prove the harassment happened and prove Mead and Cleese guilty of perjury in any testimony they gave. She'd have to be extremely careful because they now knew that she was a witness who had a gift of gab. Gertrude decided that she would lie down, play dead, and let them come to her. The person here that she'd have to manipulate with her knowledge was Janet Nelson. She needed to be persuaded to file a complaint against Cleese, with her and Mead as witnesses. Cleese would need to find a way (or position) to placate and silence her, Gertrude, the star witness! Or, Janet could be persuaded not to file a complaint, thanks and courtesy due to Gertrude which most would certainly earn her a grateful reward. Either way it went, she'd be on top. Just where she wanted to be holding the power!

When Janet arrived for duty the following Monday, Mead immediately noticed a difference in her that caused her to raise her eyebrows contemplatively. Firstly, Janet had entered the office with a smile on her face; she'd never done that before and the smile, she noticed, didn't reflect in her eyes. There was a new look there, a no nonsense glint in her eyes. Secondly, her long, dark hair was out, cascading down towards her waist and she wore an attractive lime green skirt set. She never wore her hair out anymore nor did she wear skirts or dresses. Mead studied her and had to admit that there'd been a definite change in her and the change was on the outside. She would have paid money to know what had changed in Janet on the inside. Mead watched Janet closely as she began updating the attendance sheets and she had been completely surprised when Janet made herself a cup of coffee and sat down making small talk while she sipped the coffee. If Janet held any feelings against Cleese she was keeping it to herself. It was as if the book incident had never happened. Mead was extremely wary of this noticeable change in her behavior and was more than a little uneasy. Prior to Janet's arrival, Mead had suggested to Cleese that he bring up the incident and apologize for being a jerk. She insisted that he pretend that he had just been joking around and was sorry he had done it and that nothing like that would ever happen again. Mead felt this was the best road to take to avoid a complaint of sexual harassment and would leave nothing for Gertrude to be a probable witness to. She had watched Janet closely when Cleese walked over to her with a contrite smile, hugged her and apologized for what he'd done adding that she was like a daughter to them. Janet had laughed, again the humor not reaching her eyes, saying that was just what she'd thought and that she later felt silly taking the incident too seriously, going home and calling out sick for two days. She continued saying that she knew neither of them would ever deliberately do anything to make her feel uncomfortable but she was making Mead uncomfortable. Mead had the unsettling thought that Janet was lying her ass off. She didn't believe a word of what she'd said. She observed Janet's body language when Cleese hugged her and that too, she felt was a lie. Janet's body had gone rigid and wariness swiftly crossed her features and then disappeared just as quickly but Mead saw the change in her face. Mead breathed a silent sigh of relief, although she hadn't been convinced with Janet's performance she was sure any complaint of sexual harassment had been avoided. Just as she was sure that Cleese, being the egotistical asshole that he was, was thinking he still had a chance and she was right, but she had no idea of the extent of Cleese's desire for Janet.

Only Cleese was aware of the effect of holding Janet in his arms, up close and personal. He was exactly in a state where a man is most likely to do something stupid to a woman and knowing all that time that it was stupid. With her in his arms, albeit in a fatherly manner, time had stood still for him and he restrained himself from letting the arms holding her to him slide firmly down her back, grab both sides of her behind, lift and pull her up and into his sex. It was a momentary thought fueled by his lust and had to be forcefully deleted from his brain. Fortunately, common sense raced up into his lust saturated brain and prevented his hands from the movement. That Janet accepted the hug was a big thrill for him. He was holding her close, could smell the scent of her perfume and he was just a little dazed. He didn't notice that his hug was not returned or how quickly she pulled away from the embrace that he knew was unnecessarily, overly firm. When she disengaged herself from his embrace he felt the lost profoundly as if a part of him had been unfairly snatched away from him and all he could do was watch her leave the office pleading that she had reports to write.

Walking out of the office she felt soiled by his embrace and wished for a shower. As she was locking the door to the front office corridor Gertrude slid up behind her, "Are they up there?" she asked grinning, looking for an opening. Janet played stupid, "They who?" "Cleese and Mead, are they up there?" Gertrude repeated. "You should be the first to know that as you make their coffee every day." Janet replied drily. Gertrude didn't appear to notice the barb and went on, "I wouldn't have thought he would be after what happened." Gertrude prodded. Janet had no recollection of Gertrude being in the office when the book incident occurred but somehow she knew that was what she was referencing. Janet didn't take the bait and feed into a conversation that seemed to be more of a trap designed to seek information. "Well, he has to make a living like the rest of us." Janet replied as she unlocked and opened the door for Gertrude. Janet knew Gertrude was feeling her way, trying to get her to talk about what happened and when she didn't, she noticed that Gertrude wasn't particularly perturbed by her lack of response. She simply smiled and waddled through the door heading for the front office. Janet locked it behind her and walked to her office wondering what that scheming clown was up to now. She dismissed Gertrude from her mind and thought about her performance in Cleese's office. One thing she was sure about was that Cleese gave no thought to her level of intelligence or of the extensive training he'd had personally given her. She would make a formidable adversary that could lead to his downfall if he tried something like that again. She was aware that getting into a fight with her would essentially mean fighting himself for he had trained her well. It was him who taught her how to manipulate a bad situation into her favor, how to put an adversary at their ease and then go in for the kill. When that future time unfolded, it would be comparable to Muhammed Ali and George Frasier, two heavy weight giants, 'A Rumble in the Jungle' and it all began quietly with the inappropriate placement of a fifteen year old boy at the mental institution and in Janet's building. This placement would lead to broken bones, black eyes, elopements, suspensions, terminations and three demotions for Janet Nelson.

ELEVEN

Janet was seated in Cleese's office along with Mead and three unknown suited men from the State Department of Human Services. There reason for being there, they explained, was to do an emergency placement for a fifteen year old child with behavioral problems. The child was to be placed temporarily at the institution until an opening in one of the State Group Homes became available. They spoke about how very intelligent the child was. He could care for himself independently, read, write and use a computer. Janet listened quietly to all the praises and adulation for the child with warning bells chiming softly in her head and she proceeded to upset the apple cart. If the child wasn't State classified as developmentally disabled with severe behavioral issues, why was he being placed in a mental institution? Her building was definitely no place for a fifteen year old child. Her clients were third level behavior clients who could potentially harm this child and most importantly, what were his negative behaviors? All eyes turned to her and the symphony of warning bells were growing into their credenza when she noticed that her questions especially the last one, was met by down cast eyes and silence by the three men. A silence that was much too long for her. Something about the child was being withheld and she wanted to know what they were not being told. Janet had repeated her questions regarding negative behaviors a second time before the men elaborated further. They essentially talked loud and said nothing; ending with a weak statement that everything concerning the child's behaviors was in his records that were on Cleese's desk. Janet looked at the records suspecting that there was something bad between those pages but none of them had any idea of just how bad. The men from the State left and the next day, Daryl Campton was brought to Janet's building and the direct care staff immediately fell in love with him. He was a light brown skinned boy of fifteen about five feet tall, with thick, black, curly hair and long girlish eyelashes over large soulful brown eyes that were almost too large for his tiny face. He had a wide mouth with a bright smile and was full of compliments for everyone. He was thinly built; quick and light on his feet. All four group leaders were responsible for eight clients and their groups were full but they were all willing to accept Daryl Campton into their groups. He was sweet, cute, smart as hell and eager to show off his abilities. The staff excitedly gave him books and papers and called their peers over to see how well he could read. The staff doted all over him on his first day but Janet continued to be suspicious of him and whenever time allowed she would just sit and watch him. Some things were too good to be true.

Marjorie Jenkins was the oldest employee in Janet's building with over thirty-five years of service. Everyone called her 'Granny' because she treated the staff and patients as if they were her children. She was a kind, helpful and considerate worker whose age showed on her kind face and in her grey hair and the only disciplinary actions on her record were for lateness. Due to her seniority and age she worked the midnight shift and all of her clients were already asleep in bed when she arrived for duty at 11:15 p.m. She was assigned to the easiest group of clients in the building and had never had any instances of client abuse. The morning following Daryl Campton's first day, two clients, who slept in the same room with him were discovered with both of their eyes, black and swollen shut and Marjorie Jenkins had no explanation as to how the two clients were assaulted or any idea of who could have hit them so hard in both of their eyes. She explained that when she checked the clients at the start of her midnight shift everyone was fine. It was in the morning, when she was getting them out of bed that she made the discovery. Hence, she became the first person to be suspended with a charge of corporal punishment, termination pending an investigation. Everyone knew Marjorie would never perpetrate such a thing but it didn't matter. Although black eyes were common in the building, none had ever been so severe. The staff knew which clients had a history of such acts and there was always an explanation. Assaultive clients were kept separate from their peers because their assaults were so quick and unannounced that the staff seldom had the time to intervene. None of those assaultive clients were in Marjorie Jenkins' group but she was suspended on the spot at 7:30 a.m. Cleese, Mead and Janet didn't arrive for duty until 8 a.m. and when they received the report of the injuries and who the group leader was, they knew it wasn't possible that Marjorie Jenkins was guilty, this had to be a mistake but there was nothing they could do and the suspension stood.

The clients' in Janet's building had high threshold levels for pain. Injuries that would cause a normal person to scream or pass out didn't affect her clients. When injured they never cried out in pain or attempted to get away from the source of the pain. This would explain the reason why Marjorie Jenkins didn't know her clients were being assaulted. Still the institution had to follow its regulations; removing the client away from the suspected source of harm or in other words, removing the employee. It was Janet's responsibility to do an investigation and report to Cleese. She found this to be extremely difficult but it had to be done. She started her investigation with James Litten, the other direct care worker on the floor with Marjorie Jenkins the night of the incident. He too, had heard nothing during the night. All clients were asleep except Daryl Campton. He'd said he wasn't sleepy and wanted something to read. Nothing else unusual happened. A forewarning flashed through Janet's mind when she heard that Daryl was not only in the same room as the assaulted clients but that he was up and about. Was it possible that that little boy had assaulted the clients? Janet didn't know but she broke off her interrogation with Mr. Litten and went to the nurse's station. She needed to know everything about Daryl Campton. She took his medical charts and six separate files to her office and began thoroughly reading them. The material enclosed was shocking, explosive and had been intentionally omitted during his intake. The institution had been deceived by the men who brought Daryl Campton to them by withholding his dangerous, anti-social behavior. She couldn't wait to bring what she discovered about the 'sweet child' to Cleese's attention. The following morning Janet was observing breakfast before taking Daryl's files to Cleese's office when she noticed that one of the clients was refusing to take his tray. This was unusual for him because he was known as a 'shoveler' a staff connotation meaning that once he was given his tray he began shoving the food into his mouth. Once his tray was empty he would, if not watched snatch another peer's food and shove that too into his mouth. Yet he was not taking the tray handed to him. When the staff called his name he quickly turned around and Janet noticed with a sickening sensation that his entire arm had flapped almost entirely around his back when he swerved around. She called the nurse and they took the client into the nurse's station where it was discovered that his arm was broken at the shoulder. Such an injury would have a normal person down on their knees in excruciating agony but for this client, who had an extremely high thresh hold for pain; the pain simply didn't register in his mind or body. Suspension numbers two and three, termination pending for an unexplained broken arm, which it was noted by the hospital, had been twisted with a great amount of force in order to cause the bone to be broken at the shoulder. It was a horrible injury and in such cases the institution was responsible for notifying the family of the client. The institution didn't notify the family because for years they'd never visited the client and it was basically decided that what the family didn't know wouldn't hurt them. The institution was also responsible to investigate (from the bottom up) to come up with an explanation and a guilty person who of course would be immediately suspended, terminated pending a hearing and possibly face criminal charges. The staff was in an uproar and angry at the second suspension in two days. The time of the incident couldn't be pinpointed between two employees, so one from the mid-night shift and one from day shift were suspended, terminated pending an investigation. The supervisors and the staff knew their peers were not capable of the injury they were charged with but all this was all to no avail, someone had to take the responsibility and Janet had no choice but to uphold the suspensions. She felt confident about who was responsible for the injuries but she had no proof. All staff on duty wrote statements yielding no knowledge of the incident and vouched for the innocence of the suspended employees, yet again, to no avail, the second and third suspensions of Steven Lotts and Phyllis James were upheld.

In the front office, Janet found Cleese, Mead and the assistant CEO Mr. Dunning in conference discussing the three injuries. Mr. Dunning didn't care for Janet and she didn't like him. Before the book incident in Cleese's office she'd been in her office with her back to the open door when she felt like she wasn't alone. When she turned around Dunning was standing there staring at her. He stated that Cleese had called him to come up and see how nice she looked that day. Janet's mouth dropped open and she turned her back on him thinking, *And you came? You left your office and came all the way up here to see 'how nice I looked?!* She was beyond embarrassed and without turning around she quietly said, "I wish he wouldn't do stuff like that." When she turned back around he was gone. Since then he had few words for her whenever he was in the building and if it were possible she had even less for him. Cleese, like Janet, believed the incidents were at the hands of the child, Daryl Compton. "Nothing like this has ever occurred in this unit or even on grounds for that matter until he was placed here. You know this Paul. I have three staff members up for termination and everyone else is suspect. It has to be noticed that these incidents began the day after he was admitted to my unit and I want him out of here!" Cleese demanded. "He won't be removed!" Dunning calmly said, "I can tell you that now. There is simply no where to place him until the State removes him. Until then, he is our responsibility!" Dunning stated adamantly. "What about our responsibility to the clients and the staff of this building?" Janet interjected placing Daryl's medical charts and history on Cleese's desk. "I stayed last night and read his entire file. Were you aware that he's been kicked out of six State Group Homes? Each place reported broken arms, legs, fingers, black eyes and in one place a stabbing. He has never spent more than two weeks at any of the group homes and now he's in our building and the same types of incidents are occurring here! When those men came here praising this boy, if you recall, I asked about his negative behaviors and they mentioned nothing when they knew full well what he was capable of and they conveniently omitted this information and the reasons why he was removed from those six group homes. The common denominator is this child who you say we can't get rid of." What happens if someone dies from an assault from him? What we are essentially doing is waiting for the ultimate assault!" Janet concluded. Cleese and Dunning examined the files which didn't lie. A dangerous, hostile, sociopath in the guise of a fifteen year old child had been placed in their mist with no fore warning but the information didn't alter the facts and the facts were that he couldn't and wouldn't be removed until the State found somewhere to place him.

If one could believe it and one had no choice but to believe their own eyes but the following day another client was discovered with three severely bruised toes which were later determined to be broken. It couldn't be determined on what shift the injury occurred and Dunning wanted all the group leaders on all three shifts suspended pending an investigation. The staff backlash at this suggestion was nothing short of verbal violence and subsequently there were no suspensions for the incident. The next day another client was found with two broken fingers. Four severe injuries, in four consecutive days, and still Daryl Campton remained in the building. Janet requested and received permission to place put him on one-to-one supervision. This created a situation of around the clock overtime which didn't thrill the Assistant CEO Dunning or the staff. Although it was easy time and a half money, no one wanted to work with Daryl Campton. A mandatory overtime list had to be created and staff took turns supervising him. The incidents stopped but then a new plague of elopements began. Daryl was quick when he bolted away from his group leaders, running out of the doors or jumping out of the windows. Although he was on one-to-one supervision he was somehow managing to get away from the staff. He not only left the building; he left the institution's grounds. He'd been returned by the state police four times and suspension days began to be passed out again.

On Daryl's sixth day in the building, in protest the staff had a sit in. They got their clients up, dressed and fed and then the entire staff sat down in their day areas and refused to do any work until something was done about Daryl Campton and their union representative, Sharon Nesbit had been contacted. Sharon Nesbit could best be described as a smoldering volcano subject to explode at any time. She was short, slightly overweight, dark skinned woman with long dreadlocks surrounding a round, expressive face whose emotions (whatever they might be at the time) always showed on her face. She was extremely knowledgeable of the rules, regulations and policies and was known to throw them out at any level of administrative employee who was caught breaking the rules against a union member. She was never intimidated or backed down when her back was up and was known to hurl loud, colorful expressions as freely as the wind blows. The administration hated to see her coming but they had to accept and respect her knowledge. She came to the building and was presently in a meeting with Janet who suggested that the meeting be moved to Cleese's office. When they entered the office they were faced with the unbelievable scene of the security guard holding the child, Daryl Campton, in a head lock with his arms pinned behind him. Cleese was yelling in his face that if he didn't stop hurting the clients he was going to go to jail, where he'd be beaten and raped. Janet stumbled backwards trying to back out of the office at the sight and collided with Sharon who saw and heard the same things as Janet. Cleese looked up, saw Janet and shouted at her to come in and Janet replied, "I don't think I want to watch this." Cleese yelled "I'm giving you a direct order—sit down!" Janet reluctantly sat down keeping her eyes on the floor. The union representative, Sharon Nesbit had disappeared. Janet was summarizing in her mind what would happen next. If the staff were suspended with terminations pending for assaulting a client, what would Sharon do or say about what the two of them had witnessed the Director and security guard doing? This was bad, bad, bad. Janet wanted no parts of it but she was already ass deep in it as a witnesses. Worst still; it was her responsibility to immediately report what she'd seen. She couldn't begin to guess what Sharon's response to what she'd seen and heard would be. Seconds after Sharon left, the security guard released his hold on Daryl and he ran out of the office back towards the day area. Cleese and the security guard looked frightened and Cleese yelled at Janet, "Don't just sit there. Go after him!" Janet ran in the direction that Daryl had fled but couldn't find him. No one could find him, until Janet went to her office and found her door locked from the inside and she could hear Daryl on her phone yelling and screaming. Janet ran back up to Cleese's office, the security guard was still present and they were deep in a hushed conversation; no doubt scheming up some explanation when she burst in and told them that Daryl had locked himself in her office. Joined by the Sharon they all rushed to Janet's office and could hear him yelling into the phone. After repeatedly banging on the door, requesting that it be opened it finally was and out stepped a smiling Daryl asking if lunch was ready. There was nothing any of them could do except watch helplessly as he walked pass them into the dining area. They all looked helplessly at each other as Sharon walked away to the room where the protesting workers sat refusing to work. No one knew what she said to them but they broke off their protest and returned to their normal duties. Janet was staggered with all that was happening: The injuries, suspensions, staff' sit in, the abuse at the hands of the Director and security guard, the witnessing of said abuse by the union representative (whom everyone knew abhorred Cleese) and no idea who Daryl had called on her office phone. It was all too much and she felt herself going into a sort of mental fugue where she couldn't put two coherent thoughts together. She was dazed at the enormity of the events and she wouldn't allow her mind to venture into thoughts of the possible repercussions. It was all too much and she walked away from Cleese. He in turn yelled, "Where are you going? Get back here!" Janet ignored him and kept walking towards the back door of the building. This time he screamed, "Did you hear what I said. Get your ass back here, now! I need to talk to you!" Whirling on him Janet shouted, "No!" and walked on, "Leave me alone, right now. I need to be alone right now" "I didn't ask what you needed. You don't tell me, I tell you! Now get your ass back here right now or," "Or what?!" Janet challenged him a second time and shoved open the backdoor so hard it shuddered on its hinges as it struck the brick outer wall of the building, She stalked out on weak legs seriously contemplating to just keep right on walking straight to her car and driving away from Cleese, the union representative, Daryl Compton and her job. Her cup was full but unfortunately it hadn't run over yet.

TWELVE

Daryl Compton was literally born to be bad. As a three year old he would rip the heads and legs off his toys and smash the ones with un-removable parts against the walls. At the age of five, in kindergarten class, his teachers marveled at his intelligence. While the other children built unrecognizable structures with building blocks, Daryl constructed buildings, bridges and castles which he summarily dashed against the wall once completed. When unobserved by the teachers he would strike the other children unmercifully until they cried and when the teachers came they found him crying along with the other children and he'd run to them for comfort. No one ever noticed that his crying was never accompanied by tears. When he was ten years old, his mother left him in the house while she hung clothes outside on the line. When she returned to the house she was assaulted by a strange unpleasant smell coming from the kitchen. On the stove she found her huge cooking pot, lidded and boiling madly away under a high flame with hissing steam and hot bubbles condescending down the sides of the pot into the flames. Holding her nose she ran to turn the stove off and burnt her fingers lifting the hot lid off the pot. She began screaming and screaming in a high pitched wail that brought her husband running into the kitchen. He could see nothing that could have so alarmed her, just the boiling pot on the stove but his nose wrinkled at the stench. His wife pointed to the pot with shaking hands and when he fanned some of the rising steam away and looked into the pot his stomach lurched and he vomited violently onto himself, the stove and the floor. Cooking away in the pot was the family cat with most of its fur boiled off and parts of its skull visible. That was the moment they agreed that something was desperately wrong with their child and something needed to be done, but what? They looked at an unconcerned Daryl who was oblivious to his mother's screams, his father's vomiting and the smell in the kitchen, contentedly watching the television. Over the years there had been many 'incidences' in the home that could only be attributed to Daryl. There was the bath tub which somehow was covered in baby oil and his father took a nasty fall when he stepped into the tub. There was the strange smell coming from lemonade in the refrigerator which turned out to have had bleach poured into it. There was the middle of the carpeted steps leading upstairs that had been saturated with lard. There was the fork in the toaster just waiting to be plugged in and so many other instances that could have led to serious injury or even death.

Daryl was taken to the family doctor who finding nothing physically wrong recommended he be seen by a psychiatrist. He was given all kinds of intelligence test that revealed that he had an extremely high IQ, was very perceptive and imaginative but there was nothing to support the things his parents reported because he was a very illusive, cunning charmer. Anyone meeting him was immediately taken in by his large, innocent, soulful eyes, enduring smile and eagerness to hug everyone. He was very good at compliments and manipulation, making all who met him wanting to just hug and kiss him wishing that he was there darling boy. There was nothing to indicate the sociopathic monster inside of him. His sadistic behavior came to light in junior high school when he was found holding a student's head down in the toilet and repeated flushing the toilet while laughing. He was of course suspended and assault charges were filed against him and his parents. The judge ordered a stream of psychiatric test which he couldn't manipulate and it was found that he suffered from extreme destructive behaviors and had very little remorse for his actions. It was determined that he was too dangerous to remain at home but not mentally impaired enough to be institutionalized. He was admitted into a State Residential Group home and that's when the fun really began. Not only did he assault the other clients in ruthless, extreme attacks he tore up the house, breaking dishes, kicking in the television screen, breaking two large picture windows, slashing the tires of both house vehicles and started a fire in the oven. Perhaps the most dangerous thing about Daryl was that he knew staff knew that he was the perpetrator and he didn't care that they knew. He knew exactly what he was doing, when he did it, and he never denied his actions and had the audacity to blatantly dare the staff to do something about what he'd done. He had been transferred six times to six different State Group Homes until finally, after the stabbing incident in the arm of a staff member; he was soundly dumped at the Sawyer Developmental Center, symbolically bringing with him the ten plagues of Egypt. Daryl was too young for incarceration with the criminally insane (which had been suggested) but he was extremely happy with his new home at the institution, just look at all the new toys (clients) he had to play with!

An hour later, Janet returned walking through clouds of unreality, feeling as if she'd been beaten about the head and face with pillows saturated in chloroform. She found to her surprise that everyone had returned to their assigned duties and Daryl sat securely in a chair in the supervisor's office. What had the union representative said to them to make them return to work? The only thing she could surmise was that Sharon had told them what she and Janet had witnessed; leaving them with the impression that what was good for the goose was going to be good for the gander. Janet returned to her office but could get nothing done, her mind was bolt locked on the consequences of not reporting her boss for client abuse and the repercussions (which would come whether she told or not) if she did. Failing to report the incident made her just as guilty. Conspiring to withhold incidents of abuse was exactly what she was doing at that very moment and she didn't like anything about it. She didn't know what to do; she had to report the abuse, yet didn't dare. And what about the union representative, would she report it? And why had Cleese left leaving all this on her? Was he perhaps feeling confident that nothing would be reported against him, especially not by Janet who he'd done so much for? All the damning questions, revelations and possible outcomes were too much for her overwhelmed and bewildered mind. Without realizing that she was doing it, she dropped her head onto her folded arms on her desk and her mind simply shut down and she drifted into a mind exhausted, anxiety filled sleep. Her last coherent thought before sleep overcame her was strangely enough a statement made by Dr. Martin Luther King: *The ultimate measure of a man is not where he stands in moments of comfort and convenience, but where he stands at times of challenge and controversy.* If there'd been room for anything else in her tormented mind, that thing would have been thanks for having locked her office door before she fell asleep on duty. She slept for over an hour and when she awoke she remained locked behind her office door until the end of her shift.

Arriving home feeling abused, dazed and exhausted, Janet took a shower which left her feeling a little like herself physically but the events of the day clung tenaciously in her mind. There was no chance that they'd go away and in truth she couldn't let them. She'd have to face them eventually but for now she relaxed. She fixed herself a dinner of fried fish, baked sweet potatoes and green beans. Curling up on her soft, green, leather sofa, she turned on the television and began eating ravenously. She had just about finished eating when her doorbell rang. Getting up she crossed the room to the living room door and walked out onto her balcony to ask, "Who is it?" when she spied the union representative, Sharon Nesbit and a man, Kevin Banks, from her three o'clock shift. Their upturned faces looked up at her and then Kevin spoke in a shocked voice, "They fired me!" and the once comforting feel of the hot meal in her stomach turned cold, hard and sour. *Now what?* She was thinking, followed closely by, *I don't want to know,* as she walked down stairs to let them in. They sat across from each other in her living room, Kevin and Sharon on her vacated sofa and Janet sat down on a round, matching green ottoman. She waited for them to speak. Instead of talking; Sharon Nesbit pulled a tape player from her bag, placed it on Janet's glass coffee table next to her almost empty plate and pushed play. Janet listened in stunned disbelief and shock to the recording with growing horror as the angry voice of Kevin Banks filled her living room drowning out the sound of the television. "Mother fucker, where the fuck have you been?! Bitch, I should kick your fucking ass! You do that shit again and I'll break your mother fucking legs! Bitch I should kick your fucking ass right now, bitch! Get your fucking ass over here! Mother fucker trying to make me lose my job! Bitch you fucking run away again and see if I don't fuck you up!" This tirade went on for almost three minutes and was followed by the sounds of several sets of running feet and then dead air. Sharon turned the tape off. "This occurred half an hour after you left." Sharon supplied. Janet sat speechless looking at Mr. Banks, a young, handsome, dark-skinned man with natural, black wavy hair, dark eyes and a mustached mouth. He was an excellent employee, always carrying a joke and a smile. He was kind and helpful with staff and his clients. The young man sitting in her living room was totally opposite the young man portrayed on the tape. *.What on earth had happened?* She thought. Kevin began relaying the following story. After shift change,

Daryl was placed in his group because everyone refused the one-on-one supervision of him. When his group was called into the dining area, he lined them up with Daryl in the front of the line next to him. As soon as they entered the dining area Daryl bolted away from the group, ran across the dining room towards the windows. Knocking out one of the screens he jumped out the window and ran off. Mr. Banks was yelling for him to stop. He told the food service worker to get the supervisor and then he jumped out the window after Daryl who was nowhere to be seen. In the case of an elopement the building has twenty minutes to locate the eloper and if the eloper is not found security must be notified of a runaway. Security has thirty minutes to locate the runaway. If they are unsuccessful the state police must be notified. An hour later, staff, security and the police still hadn't located Daryl. Unbeknownst to them, after jumping through the window, Daryl had climbed up into the branches of a large tree near the building and he was smiling down on them as he watched them searching for him. An hour later, the searched had extended off grounds and local police were called in to help. In the meantime; Daryl had climbed down from the tree, crept around to his dorm window, removed the screen and slipped into his room. Mr. Banks was frantic searching and researching the same areas. He returned to Daryl's dorm room and found him smiling and leisurely lounging against the window sill and Mr. Banks had exploded. The client was reported found, incident report filed and employee statements taken. An hour later Daryl was gone again but this time he was found in the canteen building using the pay phone. Minutes later, police and security arrived and everyone wondered why, no one had called them after they'd left the first time. Daryl ran up to the officers crying (dry eyed) profusely as he handed them a tape recorder. While everyone was out searching for Daryl; he'd returned to his dorm room, climbed in and planted a tape recorder under his bed. He then simply waited to be found. The officers played the tape and listened to the terroristic threats made by Mr. Banks. Mr. Banks was terminated on the spot and the last thing he saw as he was escorted out the building by security was a dry eyed, smiling Daryl gaily waving bye-bye. Sharon Nesbit had been on grounds assisting with the search for Daryl. After Mr. Banks was taken off grounds she picked him up in her car and here they were at Janet's house. Janet asked Kevin one question, "Did you hit him?

149

It's obvious that you wanted to but did you?" "No!" he shook his head vehemently near tears, "I never touched him!" He was still stunned and shocked as they all were that Daryl had planned this entire thing that left him fired. Mr. Banks, holding his head down, turning it negatively from side to side just couldn't believe what was happening to him. He knew it was wrong to say the things he'd said to Daryl but he made him do it. "I panicked, sure. When he jumped out that window I went right after him. After searching and searching and finding nothing, I became more upset and afraid and that little mother--he climbs back into his room's window. I was so relieved to see him; scared for my job and mad as hell that he'd run away and then popping back up with a smile on his face. The words just came out. I wouldn't hit him. I didn't hit him. I never hit any client, ever!" Janet could see he was close to tears and turned away not wanting see him break down. He just didn't believe that after over twenty years of service he no longer had a job. Janet was thinking there was perhaps hope for him but not at the institution, they would do what they had to do. His chances laid in the Administrative Law courts and they were pretty lenient and understanding in matters such as this but for the time being he was definitely, profoundly, fired and there was nothing to be done about it.

Janet stood up, walked through the living room door out onto her balcony which looked out over the city park. Her cousin Elizabeth had purchased this house years ago with money ($250,000) Janet had given her from a childhood lawsuit against the Board of Education. She had fallen in love with the house on sight when she first saw it back on her graduation day over twenty years ago. The house faced a large pond surrounded by a cement walkway surrounded by park benches, trees and opposite the pond were the city tennis courts. There had been three large white birds gliding peacefully on the pond's surface back then and she wondered abstractly if the three birds she now watched floating serenely on its surface were the same ones. *Did birds live that long?* She wondered abstractly when Sharon came up behind her. "Impressive view." she said. "Yes, yes it is. Why did you bring Kevin to my house?" she asked Sharon contemplatively, not looking at her, "Did he ask you to or was it your idea?" Sharon appeared to think the questions over and then responded, "I didn't know where you lived but seeing as you and your staff have been friends for years I figured he knew. I asked him and here we are." "But why, what do you hope will be accomplished by your bringing him here? What is it you think I can do? I can't revoke the termination" Janet said quietly. "No, no you can't but I'm sure that you are aware that you and I are faced with a unique situation here that can't be ignored." Mincing words was not Sharon's style, she never did and she continued, "Cleese, the Director, your boss and the security guard are both guilty of the same actions, terroristic threats plus assault against the same client as you know we both witnessed. Kevin alone is charged with terroristic threats and terminated. Four other employees have been suspended, termination pending. I find this to be extremely interesting and definitely discriminatory. The fact is that they terminated the subordinate African American employees and will definitely look the other way for the Caucasian superior and security guard. It stands to reason that Cleese and the security guard's actions were not reported by you. True?" Janet saw a noose over her head. "True." she said. "It was your duty to report what you observed, true?" "True." she felt the noose lowered over her head to rest around her neck and across her shoulders. "It's also a fact that you didn't report what you witnessed, true?" "True." the noose tightened. "You know, this is all such wonderful news to me!" Sharon said to Janet smiling. Janet turned to her and said without anger, "You are I take it, a woman without scruples." "That's true, entirely without scruples!" Sharon agreed. "Cleese is a foul, evil, little cockroach. He has gotten away with egregious, illegal, unfair treatment and acts against employees for years. His evilness has resulted in transfers, suspensions, demotions and terminations and he has never been challenged or caught but now I have him. I call him 'The Fox' because he is not only good at what he does; he's cunning, sneaky and smart. He sees himself as being above the traditional morals of 'Good and Evil' in his eyes those traits are reserved for the average man, the inferior man. Right and wrong have no place in his world because these things don't apply to his superiority. You seem to be trembling dear. It's a warm evening or could it be," she said leaning towards Janet, "that my words against Cleese are disturbing to you?" Sharon peered deep into Janet's eyes and said, "I hope they are because I have a lot more to say. They will be words that I hope will dispel any sense of loyalty you may feel towards Cleese, as I'm betting that's what derailed you from your duty to report what you saw." "You also were a witness." Janet cut in smoothly without anger. "True but I have the ability to step back and say that I was behind you and therefore didn't get a full view of anything except the presence of Cleese and the guard." Sharon stated. Janet looked incredulously at Sharon who put up both her hands as if she was being held up by a mugger on the street and said, "Please, don't remind me that I have no scruples. That's already established." Janet stood up and headed for the living room door. Looking back over her shoulder she asked Sharon if she'd like something cold to drink, she had some iced tea in the refrigerator. Sharon nodded yes. While Janet prepared the drinks for the three of them, Kevin was still sitting quietly in the living room, hands clasped between his legs looking dejectedly at the floor. Janet was thinking of what Sharon had said to her and the bottom truth was that Sharon was going to sacrifice Janet to get Cleese! Janet's mind wasn't in defense mode because she couldn't deny anything that Sharon said. There was something else coming and she needed not to be defensive against Sharon's allegations but to hear her out, get all the information she could, then think about offense. She returned with three glasses of iced tea, stopped and gave Kevin a glass. He lifted his head as if it weighed a ton and accepted the glass. Janet lightly touched his shoulder and said, "It'll be alright. Things will have to run its course but I'm positive you'll be ok." He didn't respond.

Sharon twirled her glass of ice tea around in her hands, the ice cubes clucking against each other as Janet sat down. No one said anything for a few minutes as they watched a pair of teenagers playing tennis, hitting the ball back and forth over the net. Janet was thinking that she was that ball. "This is really good, homemade?" Sharon asked. "Huh." Janet said. She hadn't been listening. "I was just saying that the tea was good." They sat side by side for a few more minutes when Sharon asked Janet, "How do you think you got your position Janet?" she asked taking another sip of the delicious tea. "I passed the test with a high score." Janet replied. "That test is bullshit!" Sharon intimated then said, "Let me clarify that. The test is legitimate but when it comes to getting a position that test doesn't mean diddly squat. Your score simply means that you passed but the selection is all political. It's a matter not of what you scored, positions here are based on who likes or dislikes you at the institution. In all fairness the highest score on the test is just that, a high score. Your position rightly belonged to Gertrude Fleming. She passed the test, has ten years seniority and experience over you, neither of which you possess, but Cleese isn't interested in her. Now just why do you think you got the position? Everyone knows about Cleese giving the keys to Gertrude and then taking them from her and giving them to you. Why do you think he did that?" She asked twirling her glass of tea again. Janet clearly remembered the day that had happened and confessed she had no idea why. She hadn't even known what the keys were for. Sharon twirled her remaining tea in her glass and just before draining it and she said in a lackadaisical manner. "You got the keys and the position because Cleese wants to fuck you dear." Janet jumped up, knocking her chair backwards onto the floor. "What? What did you say?!" she almost shouted. "Oh do sit down, dear. I didn't stutter. Read my lips. The reason you got the position over Gertrude is that you are picked to be his new concubine, for lack of a better word and Mead is the one who selected you. Listen to me. Mead and Cleese have been having an affair for over twenty-five years; everybody knows it and it's never been denied. Word is that he is technically using Mead (willingly) as his pimp. Before you were given the position where you notified to come in for an interview? No. Did you see the opening posted in your building or personnel as is the normal procedure for openings? No. Were you ever even interviewed? My guess is no. You were just out of the blue transferred to dayshift. And let's not omit the book on the floor incident. Hadn't he laughed and literally told you he wanted you to bend over with your ass to his face?" Sharon asked not unkindly. "How did you know." Janet began and Sharon cut her off, "How did I know about that nasty little stunt? Word gets around. She leaned over, took Janet's cold hands in hers and looked her not unkindly in the eyes. "Think about it Janet, not now but later because I have to go but there is one or two more things I need to say. You're a damn good head supervisor. You've done a lot to improve your building. In fact, the changes you've made have been adopted in other buildings throughout the grounds. What I noticed is that everything you've requested was approved by Cleese even against the CEO's opinion. Didn't know that, did you? Dunning has no liking for you. Unheard of things that no one has ever requested of any director have been granted to you because you are Cleese's golden girl but everything has a price. Last year when you requested that some of the clients be allowed to go on a cruise to the Bahamas, what happened, Janet?

It was approved; as long as the group leaders and the nurse agreed not to request any overtime. No one has ever requested such a thing because they knew it would be ludicrous to even ask but not for you. Open your eyes little naïve girl. He's giving you everything you want because he wants you. But one thing you can trust and believe is that when something happens that affects him all bets and loyalties will be off, he will chew you up and spit you out to protect himself." Janet thought about when she had asked Mead if something happened and she knew Cleese was wrong what would she do and Mead had replied she would side with Cleese. If nothing else she saw that Sharon wasn't lying to her. The realization of all she was saying to her was not only chilling but was mind boggling in its reality and looking back she believed every word. The last thing she said was just as intimidating. Sharon said, "I'll be going now but understand this I will be leaving no stone unturned to get Kevin and the other four suspended employees reinstated and you are essential to making that happen. You need to be on my side on this, there is no middle ground and actually no place safe for you because you'll be damned if you do and damned if you don't, sorry. But you are in a position where you can talk to that bastard before I have to get a hold of him. Throw it in his face that he did the same thing and it's not fair for staff to be punished and he get away with his actions. That psychopath of a client, Daryl Campton, has a history behind him and word is that Cleese is going to let the terminations stand in order to force the removal of the client from his (your) building. I'm not going to sit by and watch that happen; especially with what you and I have in common." Janet's heart double-clutched for a second and she gently removed her hands from Sharon's and looking her in the eyes quietly said, "And you'll be throwing in just a touch of blackmail against me to make it happen, right?" "Right on." Sharon said without hesitation or the slightest hint of a stutter as she stood up. There'll be a hearing scheduled for Kevin in a few weeks and just so it doesn't come as a surprise to you, I will be calling on you to be there to represent my case. Before leaving, she turned and looking Janet straight in the eyes and said, (or threatened?) "Convince Cleese to get the staff reinstated or otherwise there's going to be big trouble in little China!" (Definite threat) She and Kevin left. Janet sat down in the chair on the balcony never noticing that the sun had gone down. The moon was out, large and bright and the large, white swan birds were gone from the pond and the tennis courts were empty when she finally went inside.

Following her usual procedure when she arrived for duty the next morning; Janet read the supervisor's log of the previous day, collected the time sheet and any incident reports and employee statements. The log recorded Daryl Compton's elopement, subsequent return but there was no report on Kevin Banks termination or any incident reports or employee statements. *Where were they?* She wondered. Technically, she wasn't supposed to be aware of what occurred until she returned to duty the following day but in this case, she did due to Sharon Nesbit and Kevin Banks visit to her home. She asked Gertrude for the incident reports and statements and was informed that Cleese had taken them. He came in at 7:00 a.m., an hour early and collected all the statements and incident reports. Janet played it off like it was nothing unusual but it was. It was huge and had never happened before. Janet needed them to start her investigation of the incidents. *Why would he take them?* She wondered. She gathered the time sheets and went up front where she found Mead and Cleese sitting at their desk. She glanced down at both desk and saw no reports or statements on them. And again she thought, *Where are they and why are they being kept from me?* As she transferred the employee information into the building payroll book, she kept expecting one of them to bring up the incident but neither did and this scared Janet more than a little. She wondered what was going on. Any and all incidents were discussed the morning after and plan developed to ensure that the incident wouldn't occur again. This morning there was nothing presented to her, no reports, no statements and no discussion. Sharon's words were coming back to her again, *'If something affects him that involves you, he'll chew you up and spit you out!'* Janet inwardly shuddered and Cleese asked her if she was cold. No she'd replied beginning to feel paranoid and left the office. Keeping the reports and statements away from her and not mentioning them was beyond wrong, suspicious and unnerving. By the end of the shift there was still no mention of the incident from Cleese or Mead. *Two, three, four days later and still nothing mentioned, why?* On Friday morning Janet was instructed to pack together all Daryl Campton's belongings, the state was moving him out of her building and the institution. She heard that

Daryl had called his parents who were filing suit against the institution for what happened to their sweet baby. None of the other injured client's families had instituted any law suits because they had not been notified of any injuries on their family members. It would be months later when notifications were sent to the families, instigated from an unknown source. By 11 a.m. that morning Daryl Campton was gone, off to terrorize some other State facility. Janet would have breathed a sigh of relief accept there was still the issue of the terminated employees, what she'd witnessed, Sharon's threat and the memo she was currently reading which gave the date and time of Kevin Banks hearing, in two weeks. It was to be held at the Office of Administrative Law and she had been subpoenaed not only by Sharon Nesbit but the State.

Janet had decided (somewhat angrily) that if they were withholding from her, she would do the same. She would keep Sharon and Kevin's visit to her home to herself. That unnerving visit and it's portents of doom continued to unnerve her. When the thought of informing Cleese and Mead of the visit entered her mind her inner senses screamed "No!' The information Sharon laid on her was intimidating, damaging and dangerous to her position. If she informed Cleese what would he say, what would he think and finally what would he do to her? "Plenty." she said to herself. No, it was better not to mention the visit. Although it represented blackmail; it seemed extremely valuable for self-preservation. She decided to lie down and play dead, she wouldn't tell. The time Janet spent deciding whether or not to tell Cleese about the visit was actually a work of futility; he already knew about the visit and wasn't thrilled to know that Janet had kept it from him. In essence, she'd chosen Kevin and that damned Sharon Nesbit over him. How fucking dare her!

After leaving her home, Kevin was in a state of panic, hopelessness and anxiety over the loss of his job. He began making phone calls reaching out to his peers for information concerning him and his job. He wanted to know what, if anything, they had heard. After all, no one told him not to talk to anyone at the job and who better to talk to than his peers. He knew nothing regarding the rules of engagement and confidentiality and with his first call he opened a door that caused Janet to lose her position and gave a new name to the term "Hostile Environment' His first call to the job was answered by the worst possible person, Gertrude Fleming, who was working overtime on his now defunct shift. She had no problem delaying her lunch and was more than willing to listen to him especially when the first thing he said was that he and his union representative, Sharon Nesbit, had just left Janet's house. He informed her hot, wide open ears and thumping heart about the over an hour long talk between Janet and Sharon. No, he didn't know what they discussed but he was confident that Janet was on his side and would be doing everything possible to get his job back. Hearing this, Gertrude was now frantically trying to get him off the phone without appearing to actually be doing so. She impatiently transferred the phone back and forth, from one ear to the other, thinking all along that she could just hang up and blame it on a bad connection, but thought better of it. There might be more information forth coming at a later date. She did like Kevin and was sorry this had happened to him but his dilemma didn't hold a candle to what he'd told her about Janet! She was on her feet beckoning an employee to come to her. When the employee (Kevin's peer) came into the office Gertrude thrust the phone into her hand and dashed out of the office. She went running around the corridor towards the front office door so fast that her huge feet became entangled and gravity pulled her bulk down onto the floor with a loud splat! The pain from her humongous body crashing onto the floor didn't matter to her. She heaved herself up so quickly one couldn't be sure if she had actually fallen. On bruised knees that buckled when she attempted to walk too quickly, she stepped, hopped and limped as quickly as she could up to the front office. She stopped outside Cleese's door for a moment to get herself together and then snake in the grass that she was, slithered into Cleese's office with a smile on her face to plant the seeds of doom and destruction on Janet.

Gertrude delivered to Cleese and Mead, everything she'd that she'd gotten from Kevin, which was actually very little but was jam-packed with jeopardy, trouble and threat for Cleese. As he listened with a small smile on his face, he appeared not to be overly concerned which was one of his tools of manipulation, a good poker face, but on the inside he was a wreck of chaotic fear, and emotional anger. Of the three of them in the office no one but him knew about what Janet and Sharon had seen him and the security guard doing to Daryl Campton. The news of Sharon's visit to Janet's house was not bad; it was extremely bad as he knew how Sharon felt about him. Maintaining his composure as best he could, he thanked Gertrude for her information and told her he wouldn't forget her help as he escorted her to the door and out of the office. As he turned back around he slammed the door shut with such force the windows rattled in their frames. His entire face had gone pale and his eyes carried the look of a frightened, trapped animal. "What is it?" Mead had asked him in alarm but he didn't respond. "Chief, what's wrong?" she asked again getting up from her desk and going over to him but again there was no response but what she saw on his face was fear. "Chief?" she ventured. "Be quiet!" he yelled sitting down for barely a second then springing back up; he walked unsteadily out of the office and the building.

Gertrude had lingered in the corridor outside of Cleese's office not to ease drop (for once) but because she was really in pain from the fall. Her knees were throbbing like a rotten tooth and the palms of her hands were flaming red and stinging. The slamming door had made her jump. Minutes later she heard Cleese yell at Mead to be quiet. Gertrude hobbled quickly to the corridor door, unlocked it and locked it behind her. She had no doubt that she (and her pilfered information) was behind the slamming door and the yelling at Mead and uneasiness began to settle over her. For the first time she was experiencing remorse for passing information designed to hurt someone. Apparently there was something more involved in the meeting between Janet and Sharon, something she of course, didn't know about. Whatever that something was, it had not only pissed Cleese off but she had unwittingly involved herself with her knowledge of the meeting. Passing off her information would definitely affect Janet's relationship with Cleese but what would it do to her? She had been planning on adding the confrontation between Janet and Gloria but Cleese had ushered her out of the office so quickly she didn't get a chance. Now she was thinking that was a good thing. She felt that it was pre-destined that she had been the one to receive Kevin's call. Janet's position should have rightly gone to her and now the Gods (who at been asleep when Janet was given the position) were arranging her fate to put things as they should have been in the first place. Believing this, the slight remorse she had felt earlier melted away and she was again in ecstasy and anticipation at being made the next new Head Supervisor.

In the world of the angry employer and the offending employee there is a term used that refers to the confrontation between the parties involved. It was called 'Tearing a new asshole' and this is what was occurring as a result of Gertrude's revelation to Cleese. Sharon Nesbit the union representative was tearing a new asshole into Kevin for telling Gertrude about going to Janet's house. Mead (after Cleese confessed to her what Janet and Sharon had witnessed) was tearing a new asshole into Cleese. Cleese was not only tearing a new asshole in the security guard but accompanied it with threats to deny all. Assistant CEO Dunning was tearing a new asshole into Cleese, who had no choice but to confess what Janet and Sharon had witnessed and the CEO Ms. Klein was royally reaming Cleese and Dunning. She ended her tirade with an ultimatum that they'd better fix this somehow and her name was not to come up in any way. As of that moment she was denying any knowledge of the entire affair. There was a whole lot of shaking going on but to the uninformed nothing unusual was happening. Tempers were soaring and high positions were in jeopardy and for those involved there was nowhere to run to baby, nowhere to hide and no one had a 'get out of jail free card' High anxiety and trepidation danced and twirled in the minds of all the superior officers of the institution including Janet's. Thanks to the grapevine (where nothing was sacred or secret) it was all over grounds how Cleese and the security guard had abused and terrorized a client. When the story reached Gertrude the pieces all fell into place for her and she decided that the shit was too hot to handle and she wasn't fucking with it. There was no mention of how Cleese found out about Janet's meeting with Sharon but that knowledge was now precarious and dangerous to Gertrude. If it should be discovered that she was the one who told Cleese, it would not only entangle her in the conspiracy but she would be guilty of withholding information. Her information didn't include knowledge of what Cleese had done because she hadn't known anything about it but it would be so assumed. Why else would she pass information on about what the union was doing regarding the terminations? It was a mess and everyone was playing for keeps except

Janet who had no knowledge anything at all was happening or that she was about to be made a pawn that needed to be somehow controlled or perhaps neutralized. A week before the court hearing, Janet was called down to Assistant CEO Dunning's office to go over the testimony she was to give at the hearing. His office was huge and spacious with one desk that was swallowed by the size of the room, file cabinets and numerous chairs. In the office was Dunning, Cleese, and a new player, the institutions Employee Relations officer, Dick Kahn and two unknown women and a man, all dressed in three piece suits, who turned out to be the State's attorneys and it was them who briefed Janet on the questions she would be asked at the trial. When it was over Janet could find no words to describe what went on in that meeting. Essentially, she was told what questions would be put to her by the State attorneys' and unbelievably what her responses were to be; and they were all lies. She was being set up and instructed to perjure herself in a court of law. There were no direct threats to her or her job, just instructions to lie under oath. In her hands, as she walked backed to her building, was the list of questions and the pre-programmed responses (lies) that she was told to memorize. Her mind was in a state of paralysis, having no thoughts or feelings other than fear, which soon changed to anger. There was no choice other than to comply or was there? Upon returning to her office, the first thing she did was to make copies of the questions they had been stupid enough to not only put into writing but to give her a copy. So confident were they of their duplicity and her compliance.

THIRTEEN

O n the day of the hearing at the Administrative Court of Law, Janet was surprised to learn that the hearing for Kevin Banks had been expanded to include the four previously suspended employees. Sharon had subpoenaed damn near the entire staff, the security guard, representatives from other State facilities, family members of clients who were injured at those facilities by Daryl Campton and a psychiatrist to speak on Daryl Campton's behavioral profile and of course Janet Nelson. The State was represented by the three attorneys plus Barton Cleese, Julia Mead, Employee Relations Officer Dick Kahn and for some unknown reason they had included Gertrude Fleming. Janet was also on their list to testify but on the State's behalf. The State attorneys noticed that Janet was accompanied by a man who they immediately recognized as the famous trial attorney Roger Wellington Lloyd and their jaws dropped knowing exactly who he was and a hood of confusion fell over them.

After receiving subpoenas from both sides Janet had called Roger Wellington Lloyd's office but was told he was unavailable and was tied up in cases for the next seven months. Janet left a message for him. The following day when Ms. Harris was going over the calls, memos and appointments she came across Janet's urgent message and immediately contacted Roger Wellington Lloyd who was in Barbados representing a high profile client. He was a very busy man these days with cases in and outside of the United States. He was preparing a case for court in Barbados when he received the call from Ms. Harris relating Janet's urgent call. He immediately called Elizabeth, who had no knowledge of what was going on but gave him the number to Janet's office. Her machine picked up the call and he left the message that he would call that evening around ten, thankfully they were in the same time zone. It had been almost fifteen years since he'd seen Janet but they talked often over the phone and always sent holiday and birthday greeting cards to each other over years. Their mutual affection for each other had not lessoned, he was still her 'fantasy daddy' and she contacted him for help and as always daddy was there. When his call came that evening they talked for quite a while about what was going on in their lives and then Janet told him what was happening on her job. She told him about Daryl Campton being inappropriately placed at the institution, the behaviors that were omitted, the assaults and terminations, the meeting with the union representative and her threats and hint of blackmail, the information her boss kept from her and the meeting where she was instructed to lie in court. She left out nothing accept the book incident in Cleese's office. She didn't know why she left that out, she only knew she didn't want tell him about it. Roger Wellington Lloyd had laughed asking her if she was joking and when she replied no, he became very serious and professional. He informed her first and foremost that she was under no circumstances to lie in court, even if it sadly jeopardized her job. He asked her when the court date was scheduled and assured her he would meet her there.

Roger Wellington Lloyd arrived at the Administrative Court House and saw Janet waving and running towards him as he got out of his car. He stopped in his tracks, slacked jawed at the sight of her. The last time he'd seen her was just after winning a half million dollar lawsuit for her and attending her high school graduation and that had been years and years ago. She had grown into a beautiful, caramel colored Barbie doll with waist length shiny black hair blowing in the mild breeze as she ran across the parking lot. Her hair was held back with a lime green headband and a darker green, matching leather choker was around her neck. She was tall, almost regal in stature, with an unbelievable figure that all eyes turned to watch as she ran towards him wearing a dark green, two piece silk cotton skirt set with matching shoes. Her beauty was raw and unapologetic with its light brown cat-like eyes, amazing cheek bones and full lips. "Monkey face?" he asked stunned. "Yea, it's me. Oh how are you? It's been so long since I've seen you." She said hugging him tightly. "I can't believe it! Is this the same seventeen year old kid from way back when? Look at you. Wow!" He said admiringly astonished as he twirled her around amazed at her beauty. "I guess I should stop calling you 'Monkey face' huh?" he smiled. "Don't you dare, oh I've missed you so much." she laughed hugging him a second time. In her heart and mind he was still her fantasy father and protector. "Come on." she said latching onto his arm, "Let's get out of this heat."

Inside of the court house, the atrium was crowded with people assembled for the case of the suspended Sawyer employees versus the State. There was a large, round, closed in security station in the center of the atrium manned by several police officers answering phones and pushing buttons and they all turned to look admirably at Janet as she checked in presenting her identification. There were several long benches in the corridor outside of several numbered court rooms. Taking up three of these benches was Sharon Nesbit, the four suspended employees, the terminated Kevin Banks and her entourage of special interest persons. The only person Sharon was waiting for was Janet. The benches directly across from theirs was taken up by the three State attorneys, Cleese, Mead, Dick Kahn (Employee Relations Officer) and the institution's security guard, the State police and Gertrude Fleming. They too, were waiting for Janet Nelson unaware that she'd also been subpoenaed by Sharon. When Janet and Roger Wellington Lloyd entered the corridor, Cleese noticed marked agitation among the State's attorneys. Their faces had paled and their mouths dropped open. What he wasn't aware of but the attorneys were; was the identity of the man walking with Janet Nelson. Roger Wellington Lloyd was one of the most respected and sought after attorneys in and outside of the country. He had in his first case, single handedly, instituted new legislative laws not only in his State but the country. *What was he doing here and why was he with Janet Nelson?* They whispered to each other but of course; no one had any idea or explanation. Janet was waylaid by both opposing parties when she entered the corridor. She was unsure which side to go over to until Roger took her arm and led her over the State's group. Sharon Nesbit, uninvited, headed for the group too; Janet was her witness and she wanted to know who the man with Janet was. He was certainly distinguishing looking. Tall, tanned with a thick mop of black hair greying at the temples. His eye brows were almost as pencil thin as the moustache that hugged a mouth that looked as if it was holding back hilarious laughter. His piercing green eyes were both kind and unsettling and he was the handsomest, most charismatic white man Sharon had ever seen in the flesh. He was impeccably dressed in an expensive, white designer suit that screamed money, success and business. He was also the only suited man she'd ever personally met who had a folded handkerchief in his breast pocket, cuff-linked shirt sleeves and a tie clasp.

The man with Janet smiled and introduced himself all around the group as Roger Wellington Lloyd attorney for Janet Nelson. The State attorneys were dumbfounded, acknowledging how it was indeed an honor to meet him while secretly wondering about the reason behind his appearance with Janet Nelson. There were no charges against her, why did she need an attorney? Hell, how could she even afford him? He was billed out at over $2,000 an hour. His presence made them extremely nervous and uneasy. .Sharon Nesbit too, was curious wondering what Janet was up to bringing an attorney. She had only hinted at blackmail to Janet. She never made it a fact. After introductions, Roger Wellington Lloyd informed them that he'd had a rather disturbing discussion with his client Janet Nelson about these proceeding and charges. The State attorneys respectfully informed him that there must be some misunderstanding, Janet wasn't on trial, she was here as a testimonial witness. Roger Wellington Lloyd's brows lowered, his voice deepened and all traces of his earlier humor disappeared. He agreed that there had definitely been a mistake when his daughter was being coerced and/or forced to perjure herself under oath in connection with her testimony. Everyone's head turned in his direction when they heard the word 'perjure' and the much more astonishing words declaring that he was Janet Nelson's father. The attorneys blanched and their stomach muscles clenched. Roger Wellington Lloyd, the humor returned to his face and voice, suggested that before the hearing that they all sit down and have a little chat. A court employee directed all of them into a conference room and left closing the door. Everyone, Janet, Sharon, the employees and Cleese, Mead, Kahn and the State attorneys took seats around the table and Roger Wellington Lloyd wasted no time on preliminaries or a mincing of words and shot straight from the hip.. He stated that he was prepared to charge the state attorneys, the institutions Director Barton Cleese, Assistant CEO Paul Dunning and Employee Relations officer Dick Kahn with conspiracy to force Janet Nelson to perjure herself, under oath on the stand. That's called witness tampering and he backed his words up by placing a Motion on the table. His eyes grew menacingly darker as he continued, "No one does this to my daughter!" He then passed a copy of the questions and answers given to Janet to each person representing the State and Sharon Nesbit. The State attorneys, trembling in their skin, appeared violently ill looking at copies of the damning questions and answers they'd given to Janet. They knew their careers were not only over but that they faced disbarment, severe charges and possible jail and fines for what they'd attempted. Everyone was stunned and Sharon went ballistic leaping to her feet, opening her mouth to speak when Roger Wellington Lloyd held up his hand in her direction to silence her and she sputtered into silence. He continued saying that if the suspended employees and their union representative (he nodded and winked at them) didn't object; he was predisposed to represent them all in this strange, compromised and corrupt matter. Everyone's mouth, including Janet's, dropped open when he announced his fee of $2,200 an hour would be waived. He continued placing another document before the paralyzed State attorneys stating that he had already prepared a second Motion requesting postponement of this matter to give him time to put his case together; unless of course, the entire matter could be dismissed right here and now. He then placed a third Motion on the table whose hidden language was recognizable only to attorneys and it dripped with the triple threat of disbarment, jail, conspiracy and witness tampering by the State. Finally he handed the attorneys a fourth Motion in which he recommended a dropping of all charges against all five employees, reinstatement of their jobs with back pay and a specified amount to be set aside for mental pain and suffering in lieu of a promise not to sue the State for wrongful termination, in a case he would handle. The room was silent and silent as beneath the table, out of sight from the others, the five astonished employees and the union representative clutched hands. The State attorneys asked for private moment to confer and discuss the offer, as if they had a wing and a prayer. It would be suicidal to even consider turning down the offer. They were in fact, extremely relieved and one of the women was wiping tears from her eyes at how close they had come to the destruction of their careers and their lives. They understood why Roger Wellington Lloyd was the best money could buy and that he was tough but fair. He was giving them a chance to redeem themselves with an offer, which would be costly to the State but couldn't be refused without damning themselves. The discussion lasted two minutes but for face, they didn't come out for about thirty minutes. Everyone, except Janet and Roger, waited in anticipation and anxiety. Finally, they all went before the Judge (who before the start of the trial was telling Roger Wellington Lloyd how much he admired him) all charges against the five employees were subsequently dropped and all settlement terms accepted. The employees were reinstated with back pay and would receive an undisclosed amount for compensation. It was over for all of them except Janet. At the plaintiff's table, papers were silently being shuffled and stuffed into briefcases; while at the defendant's table cheering, hugs and celebration had erupted. Everyone celebrated accept Sharon Nesbit. She observed Janet and this Roger Wellington Lloyd talking quietly together. *Who is he really?* She wondered and being Sharon she walked over and put the question directly to him, shaking his hand she introduced herself and said, "You know something Mr. Roger Wellington Lloyd, game recognizes game and you've got plenty." Roger Wellington Lloyd laughed loudly and pleasantly. "Who are you really?" she asked peering into his face. Roger Wellington Lloyd and Janet both laughed. "I'm Roger Wellington Lloyd, junior partner with the firm of Graves, Ritter and Reddick." Putting a protective arm around Janet he continued, "And this beautiful young lady is my daughter Monkey Face. Oh excuse me, Janet." he corrected himself and then said to Janet, "Right monkey face?" Janet didn't answer; she just smiled, burying her face in his chest as he hugged her to him and they walked out of the building. All who heard those words gasped with the knowledge that Janet's father was not only a famous attorney; he was a white man! Perhaps Gertrude was right in her somewhat disillusioned belief that the Gods intervened into the fates of mortals to make things right. This intervention spared the lively hoods of five unfairly terminated employees, cleared away charges of conspiracy, witness tampering and perjury against the State and eliminated charges of abuse by the Director and security guard. Perhaps Gods do intervene when it seemed that all is lost, but in this case his intervention was through the hands of Roger Welling Lloyd.

Roger Wellington Lloyd and Janet were mobbed with adulation and thanks following them to his car. Janet whistled when she saw the car, a midnight blue convertible Jaguar. Roger pointed to the license plate which they all saw read 'JANET' "Oh wow. That's so cool, my name on your car. I feel honored." Janet laughed. "No, you're loved Monkey Face. None of what I have would have happened without you." He said seriously. Waving good-bye to the others, they drove off with the top down on the Jaguar. Roger Wellington Lloyd talked to Janet in a way he'd never spoken to her before and he was all business. He told her that there would most certainly be repercussions against her on her job and he was introducing her to 'The Rules of Engagement'. "Power people and organizations don't like to lose. Although people's lives were made whole again and rightly so, that won't matter to the higher powers. What will matter is that they lost big time and it won't sit well with them. Although very serious charges against the State were averted they will not be thankful to you or me for the reprieve. Your employer will most certainly come after you through your job. From this day on you will have to watch yourself on the job. You must be very careful to ensure that everything under your charge is done according to all their rules, regulations and procedures, no short cuts or omissions, because this is where there're attack against you will begin. And have no doubts, they will come for you. Start keeping a log of your activities at work including all assignments given and completed. Make copies of everything and it wouldn't hurt to notarize anything they give you and everything you submit. You can apply to become a Notary Republic yourself for less than $50 bucks. Buy yourself a pocket recorder and camera. Record all meetings and instructions given to you verbally. Discreetly take pictures you feel may be necessary and make backup copies of all the tapes and pictures. Arrive on time and never leave early, and Janet you must never let anyone know that you are doing these things. No one at this point can be trusted because when faced with choosing between you and their jobs, friends or not, they will not choose you." It was an hour and a half long ride home and Roger Wellington Lloyd spoke on preparing Janet for what would definitely come and he was never more right. He asked her if she remembered when he showed her how to prepare mock law cases and told her this is the way she must think, as if you are preparing a case for court. He told her the most essential thing needed to win cases was information. In order to survive she would need to be the best of the best. She needed to recognize that when dealing with persons of power; those people generally had strong affiliations behind them. He talked to her about alliances and to make it her goal to try to break apart their alliances as best as possible; divide and conquer. Manipulation is a powerful tool on both sides as long as the things manipulated by you are true and provable. If some false claim or discipline arises against you, research the charge and try to turn it against them. Remember the same rules, regulations, policies and disciplinary actions that are used against you can be used against them. If they do something shady to you on Monday morning make it your business to prove them wrong and submit your evidence or proof by the end of that same day; but not to them, but to their boss and allies. Remember that time will not wait on you and they will soon turn against each other. There are two main things that will help aid you and they are charges by you against your employer for 'Abuse of authority' and a little know State law called the 'Whistle blowers Law' and get a copy of their disciplinary actions book. If they discipline you for something that you know is not right; challenge it, you are always able to fall back on the charge of Abuse of Authority against them. Most importantly when the fire gets too hot under you, redirect their attack. Put them in a position where they have to defend themselves to a higher authority against something else. They won't have time to waste on you because they'll be too busy explaining something else they did, to say for instance, the Commissioner of Human Services. And don't forget the power of the 'Bluff" it will get you out of all sorts of problems if they think you possess something that you don't. Don't hesitate to go to your State representatives but don't use that route often, only at times of extreme entrapment. Lastly, use that amazing imagination of yours. Roger Wellington Lloyd pumped Janet with so many defensive moves regarding hostile work environments and employment laws that she felt empowered and confident to face her employers on Monday. Pulling up to her house, he left with a kiss and stern admonition to follow his instructions and a quote: 'Never fear them and take no prisoners!' He kissed her cheek again and pulled off heading for the airport and back to Barbados. As she watched him go he suddenly stopped, honked his horn and backed up to her. "I just remembered something." he said with a smile. Almost fifteen years ago you opened a trust fund worth almost $400,000 from that lawsuit. If I'm correct, and I always am," he said with a mischievous grin, "This is the fifteenth year and that money should be available. Use it wisely "Monkey Face'." He leaned over and kissed her cheek once more and pulled off. Roger Wellington Lloyd had never been so right she was soon to discover. She remembered what Sharon had said to Roger at the court house. 'Game recognizes game' and Cleese and the institution's games would be looking very familiar as Roger had foretold her: "They're going to come after you through your job." he'd said and here they were, bright and early Monday morning after their defeat in court notifying her that she was being recommended for demotion and the incredible thing about the recommendation was that there'd been no disciplinary actions against her to back up the recommendation for over ten years!

Over the weekend the grapevine at the institution was alive and producing. Everyone was talking about the court hearing. People couldn't decide what was more amazing; the fact the hearing was won without a trial and everyone reinstated with back pay and compensation monies or the juiciest tidbit being that Janet Nelson's father was a white man and a famous attorney. Sharon had looked him up and discovered his background and realized that she too had been spared serious charges of coercion and blackmail. If Janet had testified about their meeting at her house, she would have most certainly been fired from the union as well as her job with charges of attempted blackmail. When she tapped into the grapevine's gossip and told people about the hearing she judiciously omitted that part. The State attorneys, Cleese, Dunning and Kahn had gotten their asses royally kicked and were the laughing stocks at the institution. The almighty Cleese, beaten and retreating with his tail stuck firmly between his legs was an early Christmas present.

It had never happened before and people were cheering at Cleese's defeat and he didn't like it, refused to tolerate it and everyone within his sphere of things stayed out of his way. He couldn't get Janet's treachery out of his mind. He didn't care who her father was, all he knew and thought about was getting even with Janet. If he had taken the time, like Sharon, to look into Roger Wellington Lloyd's background perhaps he would have be persuaded to back off, leave it all alone. Unfortunately, he hadn't, that wasn't his way. He could think of no immediate way to get back at her other than taking what he'd given her, her job but it wouldn't end there, he salivated in his mind. Oh no! He'd see her demoted all the way to the bottom and then terminated. He didn't bother to confer with anyone about his plans for revenge. He just jumped right in on Monday morning. When Janet came into the office to do the time sheets he stood up behind his desk, looked at her and said, "Tell her Julia!" Janet inhaled, straightened her back, looked at Mead with her head up without fear the way Roger Wellington Lloyd had told her. So when Cleese said, "Tell her Julia!" Janet interrupted before Mead could speak. Looking Cleese in the eyes she quietly said, "If you have something to say, why not tell me yourself? Don't be shy." This seemed to derail him momentarily. People didn't talk to him like that! Ignoring her and not taking the bait he yelled at Mead, "I said tell her!" and sat down with a smile that would have made Hitler smile in hell. Mead said something that Janet couldn't hear and she said as much. "You're being recommended for demotion." Mead repeated never looking up from her desk. Janet again scrambled Cleese's plan by respectfully asking, "Under what charges?" This too was an unexpected response for which Cleese had no answer. He began to mumble and bluster under his breath wondering why she hadn't gone into surprised shock quickly followed by pleading for her job. Instead she stood there looking nonplussed asking for an explanation and this made him even angrier especially since there were no charges to speak of. When none were given she went to on with her duty of recording the time sheets. Before leaving the office she informed them both that she'd like to have a copy of the recommendation for demotion and a date of the alleged charges and/or disciplinary actions involved before the end of the day As she was leaving she added, "Is this about the trial?" There was no response given to her question and she was in no way as confident as she acted. She was profoundly shocked, not expecting such a thing. She expected her duties to become suddenly difficult or overwhelming but not a demotion! She loved her job. Returning to her office, she removed the tape recorder from her blouse pocket and rewound the tape and replayed it. She was following Roger Wellington Lloyd's instructions to the letter. She set about to do her job extremely well and on the lookout for any errors or mistakes. She remembered his suggestion that she apply to be a registered Notary Republic for her State. She made a call to Washington DC from her office and discovered that it was an easy and simple procedure to be a Notary Agent. All she had to do was fill out an application, submit copies of personal documents, identification and send a check or money order for $30 for the notary equipment and stamper.

Janet was a minor hero at the institution, a full celebrity in her building and a thorn in the administration's side. The staff was just a little shy of worshipping her. The reinstated employees were punished by being separated, and placed in three separate units courtesy of Cleese who refused to allow them back in his unit. The only reminder of his defeat he wanted and needed was Janet Nelson. This didn't sit well with anyone but there was nothing to be done, reinstatement was the goal. The news of her recommended demotion (purposely leaked to Gertrude by Cleese) buzzed angrily through all three shifts of the building. Everyone knew Cleese was out to get Janet and the staff rallied around her with invisible support. They knew that back stabbing, sneaky bitch Gertrude was the enemy. That fat, diseased looking hypocrite couldn't be trusted so they kept a close eye on her because she was in a position to purposely screw up any number of things and Janet would get the blame because she was the supervisor. They watched Gertrude like a hawk zeroing in on its prey. At the end of each week staff documentations were recorded and checked for content and completion by Gertrude. Yet she seemed to have forgotten to check the 32 client medical books the first week after the trial and demotion recommendation. Before the end of the day, the staff bought it to Gertrude's attention. Gertrude was caught trying to sabotage Janet. Each staff person sat in the office with her as she sheepishly checked and signed for each of the books completed documentations but Gertrude was not stupid, untrustworthy yes, stupid no. She figured out what the staff was doing and reported to Cleese that the staff was trying to protect Janet. This was fine with Cleese who laughed and said they'd best be protecting themselves from you (Gertrude) and they had better not try that sit down strike business again. It was his will and his will alone that was running the unit and he'd suspend and replace them all in a New York minute. The atmosphere on the work floor was tense, edgy, and anxious. They adored Janet but Roger Wellington Lloyd was right; when it came to choices; they knew in their hearts that they would step away from Janet in order to keep their jobs and this is what began to happen. If they were engaged in casual conversation with Janet and Cleese came by all conversation ceased and they drifted away from Janet like cats melting into the night shadows and they kept away from her as if she had the plague. This hurt and confused Janet deeply realizing the depth of their fear of him. Yet this was his plan she knew, to make her feel deserted and alone. She knew he could bring grief to her staff just by association but another part of her felt that they were cowards. These feelings came to a heart stopping peak when one day she was standing outside next to her car when a voice she didn't recognize came from behind her and a body pushed up against her back and said, "Hey Janet. Don't turn around. I don't want anyone to see me talking to you, You can't see or hear it," the voice continued, "but a lot of people are clapping and cheering for you standing up to that magnificent bastard Cleese. I've got to go, see you." Janet's heart was mortally crushed and tears came to her eyes at the thought that the owner of the voice wanted to remain anonymous, was afraid to be seen talking to her. The thought that people she'd known for over twenty years were afraid to be seen associating with her was inconceivable but true. Cleese's plan was working beautifully, she felt extremely isolated, alone, deserted and she did as the voice requested and didn't turn around to see who the retreating footsteps belonged to.

Cleese was infested with an insane hunger for revenge against Janet. His desire was like a battalion of dark, renegade cancer cells, industriously eating away at his mind and more critically his ego and no amount of chemotherapy could halt or delay its course. In his craving for retaliation, he didn't trouble himself with any thoughts of possible negative consequences. The only thing important, absolutely crucial, was the satisfaction of having his revenge against Janet. Closing his eyes to the truth, he just dived in head first merrily and haphazardly devising schemes with no other thought in mind than the satisfaction of her destruction. He began laying the ground work for a series of incidents designed to trap Janet in acts that would lead to disciplinary actions against her. He only needed three valid disciplinary actions to facilitate and backup a request for demotion and subsequent recommendations for termination. This was the goal in the best laid plans of mice, men and Cleese. He'd completely forgotten that one of the main reasons for giving Janet the position of Head Training Supervisor (aside from his desire for sex from her) was her level of intelligence and especially her knack for thinking before acting. When one trap failed, he'd simply set up another and another without realizing that every incident that failed was a record of his abuse of authority and employee sabotage. A record that Janet kept religiously, recording dates, times and descriptions of each incident. After the demotion recommendation that day, he waited for her signature on the sign in and out sheet. Janet's shift ended at 4:30 and for almost three years at approximately 4:15 p.m., Janet went up front to check her mailbox. If there no mail for her she'd sign out on the sheet recording 4:30, fifteen minutes early but always returned to her office until 4:45 before leaving for the day and Cleese knew this. Janet did as she usually did at 4:15 p.m., went to check her mailbox. Mead was alone in the office. She didn't look up as Janet passed her desk. Her relationship with Mead had quickly deteriorated after the trial and they now had zero conversations. Their relationship ended with Cleese's insistence that Mead treat Janet as the enemy. Janet's mail box was empty, she said, "Goodnight" to Mead; who didn't respond and went to sign out. She had just written in the out column the number four, when something stayed her hand and Roger Wellington Lloyd's voice blasted into her head. "Do absolutely everything by the book, everything!" Janet realized with a cold chill streaking up her back that signing out fifteen minutes early was technically against the rules although she'd been doing it for years without a problem. It had been at Cleese's suggestion so that she wouldn't have to come back fifteen minutes later to sign out. Realizing what she'd almost done Janet dropped the pen as if it were a red hot poker burning into the flesh of her palm and walked unsteadily back to her office beating herself up thinking what a stupid thing to do, signing out early in the current climate of her job. When she returned at 4:35 she happened to glance into Cleese's office and her mail box that was previously empty fifteen minutes earlier was packed with papers. Janet was dumbfounded as she went into the office and pulled the papers from her mailbox. She looked incredulously at Mead, "I was just here fifteen minutes ago and my mailbox was empty. What's all this?" she asked shaking the papers at Mead who never looked up or responded. Janet looked through the papers and each one was a separate request for some documentation or report and each ended with the incredible statement:

'If the above matters are not submitted by the close of the day disciplinary action will be requested for failure to complete assignments. There were seven assignments all due by the end of her shift in five minutes. Janet knew it would only take three of them to equal three separate disciplinary actions and a request for termination and she was shocked that Mead and Cleese would do such an evil thing. Knowing that she signed out early every day and assuming that today would be no different; they placed the assignments in her mailbox after she had left the first time. Janet was reading through the requested assignments as she stomped angrily off to her office. She had only ten minutes s and the threats of disciplinary action would be warranted for failure to complete assignments. For the average employee there was no possible way the deadline could be met but Janet wasn't the ordinary employee. Whenever she had spare time she'd work on assignments that would be due in the future. Every report they'd requested had already been completed and stored in her files weeks ago. Janet removed the completed assignments, made copies and then did one more thing before returning them to Mead who was preparing to leave for the day just as Janet walked into the office. She handed her all the requested assignments and firmly but sarcastically stated, "These are the assignments that were requested from my once empty mailbox. Please note that on the back of each, I have stamped my Notary Republic seal which is dated and signed by me the Notary Republic Agent. I've made copies for myself and employee relations." She turned and walked out of the office leaving Mead shocked and silent holding the completed assignments that weren't actually due until the following month.

Cleese couldn't fathom the workings of his own mind. Even with his current mission in life being to destroy Janet's career by hook or crook, he continued to desire her sexually with an intensity that was all consuming and driving his little head quite insane. He couldn't go a day without pausing for a few minutes of sordid sexual fantasy encounters with a frolicking, skimpily clad Janet dancing just out of his reach. It seemed to him that he was somehow tethered to her body by some invisible tentacle that dragged him along on an invisible track towards her. He was not aware that he was entangled in what is termed as "The scent of a woman" The natural scent of a woman's body is not naturally related to sexual organs but it is described as being an amazing, indescribable aroma. Oft times a man will complement a woman on some amazing perfume only to discover the woman is not wearing any perfumed product. This secret scent is more intense just before a woman's menstrual cycle by the release of certain hormones believed to attract males. Cleese knew and he knew Janet knew, that he was after her job; yet he continued to desire her. Now to a man of sound mind and body, this dual desire represented a complete and dangerous conflict of interest; a total parting of intelligent normal thinking. It wasn't possible to have both (her job and her body) but Cleese's thoughts weren't normal when it came to Janet. He actually found nothing wrong with his plans to simultaneously destroy her career and to get into her pants before that happened. She just wouldn't leave his conscious mind and frequently invaded the depths of his dreams, always just out of his reach. He would wake up from these erotic excursions of wet dreams angry, sweating, heart thumping, unfulfilled and even more ravenous for her sex. Perhaps these hormonal imbalances were the cause of the completely insane, cataclysmic act that sent him over the edge about a month after he'd demoted Janet. It was the stupidest act of insanity that he could have done and afterwards he couldn't even justify his actions to himself but he had been helpless to stop himself. It was as if he was on the outside, above the scene, looking down on the egregious act and he was the puppet master. It wasn't him who did that thing that woke a long buried beast inside of Janet that would eventually cost him dearly. The cost was high and resulted in a complete reversal of roles. Cleese would now be the victim and Janet the predator.

What was most egregious about Janet's demotion was that the entire affair took affect without any charges, disciplinary actions or a hearing, and the fact that her record had been blemish free for over twenty years didn't matter. Janet had been officially demoted from Head Training Supervisor to Cottage Training Supervisor. What Cleese wanted, Cleese got. Against the wishes of assistant CEO Dunning, Cleese returned her to her original position and shift in his building; which was the dumbest thing ever but it was the only way for him to maintain access to her career and her body. "What the hell were you thinking leaving her in your building? What are you trying to do?" Dunning yelled at Cleese in his office. When he'd discovered that Janet was being kept in Cleese's building he went ballistic. "Why are you keeping her in your building? Never mind, I know why. You're still trying to get in her pants, aren't you?" Cleese laughed, "Now Paul, use your head. "No, you need to stop thinking with your little head!" Dunning screamed at him. "With her here I can keep an eye on her." "Yea but which part of her are you planning to watch; huh? It's stupid to keep her in your building. You need to stop fucking thinking with your little head, Cleese. I'm telling you!" Dunning reiterated. "Me? Me? What about you? You wanted her just as much!" Cleese countered. "Yea, well that was before but unlike you, I let it go. You've got to let it go dammit. No good is going to come of you keeping her in your building. Let it go!" Dunning pleaded with him. "No!" Cleese said quietly. "It's my decision, my building and it stands. She will remain here!" "Where you can get your hands on her?" Dunning concluded and Cleese laughed. "Now I never had such a thought in my mind." he lied and standing up he turned Dunning towards the door and escorted him out, "Listen Paul, I got this horse, you just hold his head." He laughed again as Dunning stalked off shaking his head at Cleese's arrogance and stupidity. What Dunning was pleading made perfect sense but not to Barton Cleese's mind. He wanted Janet simply because she was what he wanted, and he was going to have what he wanted and that was reason enough for him.

Two weeks later, an hour before the end of Janet's shift, Cleese called the supervisor's office sounding extremely angry and irate, "You come up here right now and I mean now!" and hung up. Events of the last few days rushed through Janet's mind as she tried to pin point anything that she'd done wrong. There was nothing she concluded as she walked up to his office. When she entered, Cleese was sitting behind his desk. He jumped up from his chair and was across the office floor so startling quick, it seemed his feet never touched the floor. He was suddenly directly in front of Janet with hands on both sides of her shoulders he pulled her into him saying, "I didn't get my birthday kiss!" and suddenly without warning his tongue was past her lips and into her mouth. It seemed to Janet at that moment, that time stood still and things were happening in slow motion. Cleese gripping her about her shoulders, his tongue was coming out of his mouth (she could see its deep redness and tiny little bumps covering its surface) and then the tongue was between her lips and in her mouth. She began shuddering as she slowly turned her head to the side and thought she would surely drop dead as his tongue slithered across her cheek from the corner of her mouth to her ear. She shoved him ferociously in the chest and he fell back against his desk. Janet ran from the office, down the corridor to the locked door and was fumbling to put the key into the hole and get out of there. Over her shoulder she could hear him laughing and began to wonder if he was going to follow her. She imagined his hot hands clamping down on her shoulders and her knees weakened as she struggled to unlock the door. The slimy, wet, spittle filled trail his tongue left on her cheek horrified her and seemed to burn and itch as she finally got the key in the slot and rushed through the door and into the patient's bathroom. There she began soaping and scrubbing her entire face so violently it was a wonder that she hadn't scraped off the surface of her skin leaving a shocked looking white skull. After she dried her face, she stared in the mirror at her stunned reflection. It seemed she could see the wet path left by his tongue on the side of her face and she felt a scream of disgust rising in her chest and began frantically scrubbing her face again and again and again.

After drying her face for the final time, she was again staring at her reflection and reliving what had happened. She watched her own eyes narrow into slits and her mouth curved into an evil sneer. Her features took on strange and interesting new shapes. Her reflection seemed to melt and reform into the shape of a demon face, a doppelganger, the ghostly counterpart of a living person, an alter ego it's said. Janet was emotionally upset and stunned but her alter ego was incensed, infuriated and enraged. Janet was prepared to let the incident fade into obscurity like the book incident; but her alter ego was nowhere near as tolerant or accepting. The beast was out and staring back at Janet from her own reflection. Knowing who its prey was, the beast inside of Janet stepped onto the path of revenge. If it was at all possible she would kill him. Some people need to die. These thoughts were buried deep inside of Janet's subconscious and erupted like a capped volcano. She wasn't aware of her brains fight or flight mechanisms. While Janet chose to dismiss the incident her alter ego had other plans for that son of a bitch. It would fight back. That night Janet slept fitfully. Her dreams were disquieting, disconnected and filled with evil people, dark places and catastrophic events. But her alter ego was wide awake contemplating the many facets of murder like how it could be done and how she could avoid being a suspect. In the early morning hours, just as the sun was coming up, her last dream surfaced as a plan in progress and that plan was to destroy Cleese, body and soul. After all, her alter ego laughed viciously, you got to give the people what they want and many, many people wanted Cleese gone; if not dead, at least banished to the fiery pits of hell. The conscious and subconscious had combined.

Janet had accepted the demotion quietly and without anger. Her mind was on other things, namely revenge. She already had thoughts of a way to do it but it would take time, lots of time and money. She didn't know how much time she'd have but she did have over half a million dollars in the bank. She hadn't complained about the demotion because it worked in her favor and the stupidity of letting her remain in the building was a fantastic error. She wondered only briefly, if it was wrong to pray for God's aid and guidance to do what she planned, then dismissed the prayer remembering from long ago that all things served the lord. She received her guidance from the doppelganger, her own alter ego, the new Janet. Things came to her in her dreams and she saw that they were good things, wonderful, hilarious things and Cleese would die one way or another, preferably the other.

Janet began to actually contemplate killing Cleese, if not physically, mentally. Her first idea proved absolutely insane, impossible and maybe just a little funny but the more she thought about it; the more it intrigued her. She really wanted to get that arrogant son of a bitch and if what she was thinking could actually be done it would kill him without spilling his blood. She didn't, after all, want that on her hands or conscious. Medical examiners call deaths that didn't involve foul play natural causes and his death would appear to be from natural causes if she could actually succeed with the idea that wouldn't leave her mind now that it had settled in for a long, long nap. If Cleese and his 'good ole boys' wanted to shake hands with the devil, she'd ensure that they'd do it in hell from first class seats.

She thought about a line from a movie where the bad guy asked his victims the infamous question just before he shot them: "Did you ever dance with the devil in the pale moon light?" Then bang! Janet was smiling sinisterly to herself. She was the devil and Cleese and his posse would be dancing with her.

FOURTEEN

When the 3 p.m. shift arrived for duty and found Janet in the supervisor's office handing out assignments they assumed she was filling in for an absent supervisor. When they arrived for duty the second and third day and again found Janet delegating assignments they were more than a bit curious. On the fourth day their curiosity was satisfied through a grinning Gertrude Fleming, who informed them that Janet had been demoted to supervisor. The staff was only a little stunned but not overly surprised. They were realist to the perils of crossing Cleese. They of course knew all about the court trial with Cleese and the State lawyers backing out, the employees reinstated with back pay plus compensation. They even knew that Janet's father was a white man and a famous attorney; as well as they knew there'd be repercussions against Janet but no one expected she'd be demoted. The State would be no more forgiving than Cleese at Janet's defection. It didn't matter to the State that their lawyer's attempted to have Janet perjure herself. The only thing that mattered was that because of Janet, the State would be paying out a lot of money to settle things without a reasonable explanation to explain the cost of these things to the State Commissioner of Human Services. It was common knowledge that Janet had gained a much more powerful enemy, the State. They wondered how long it would take before she was terminated and under what form of bullshit. They knew Cleese wouldn't accept losing lying down; it was too much of a tremendous blow to his ego and they accepted Janet's demotion as a given and treated her no differently and asked no questions. They were realist. Gertrude on the other hand was again eyeing the vacant position of Head Supervisor but this time she held her anticipation and desire in check. No way was she going to suffer another humiliation at Cleese's hands. With the demotion, Janet was no longer her enemy or a threat to her ambitions. When she tried to breach the subject of the demotion with Janet, she was ignored and her questions left unanswered, "The hell with you too!" Gertrude thought to herself. She was quite content to sit back and watch the continuing fallout against Janet. No way would Cleese send her back to her original position and shift unless he had some deviousness planned for her and for that he needed to have her within his reach. But like Dunning, Gertrude too, felt it was stupid to let Janet remain in the building. No good was going to come of it she was certain. He obviously hadn't learned anything from the disastrous trial or the skill of Janet's lawyer father. She had strong suspicions that when Cleese did come after Janet he was going to get a huge surprise and all hell was going to break lose and that was just fine with her.

Meanwhile, hell was continuing when Janet opened an inter-office memo from Employee Relations officer Dick Kahn informing her she was being charged with theft of overtime and a hearing was scheduled in four days with a recommendation for termination. Dick Kahn was a 'Yes Man' and whatever he was instructed to do he did without question. He was a tall, skinny, pinched face man behind gold framed wire glasses and his beady eyes always seemed to be running for cover. Heeding Roger Wellington Lloyd's instructions she immediately responded with a letter of her own addressed to Dick Kahn Employee Relations Officer, Paul Dunning Assistant CEO and just for comic relief and to speed the word around at supersonic speed, Gertrude Fleming, she purposely omitted Cleese. In the letter she attacked Cleese's charge of theft and addressed a charge of sexual harassment against Mr. Cleese and assistant CEO Paul Dunning. Kahn was just as guilty allowing the disciplinary action to proceed without investigation but she wanted to save him for later. Per Roger Wellington Lloyd: Divide and Conquer!

TO: Mr. Dick Kahn Office of Employee Relations.

Dear Mr. Kahn: I am in receipt of your memo informing me of a hearing to address the theft of overtime by me and I am shocked! On the indicated date of this alleged theft I received an angry call from Mr. Cleese summoning me immediately to his office. This call has been recorded. When I arrived Mr. Cleese said to me and I quote: "I didn't get my birthday kiss." He grabbed me and proceeded to stick his tongue in my mouth before I knew what was happening. This is his second instance at sexually harassing me. Ask Julia Mead about the first, she sat there in the office watching. I should like to know who I can speak to regarding the filing of Sexual Harassment charges against Mr. Cleese and Mr. Dunning for the above incidents.

I will attend the hearing with my attorney (a bluff) Mr. Roger Wellington Lloyd, I believe you are acquainted with him. While we wait for the hearing, I should like to file charges of theft, embezzlement and corruption of State legal documents against Barton Cleese. Every morning Mr. Cleese enters the client's kitchen and steals no less than four boxes of the client's Rice Krispies cereal and five cartons of milk for his breakfast. Further, there is a receipt in the Purchasing Office and mine, for a pair of rubber galoshes; raincoat and pants (purchased with client funds) and currently under Cleese's desk. I have a picture of them (bluff). He told me that he needed them for fishing. The high backed, brown leather chair delivered to Cleese's office spent only half a day in the building. It was removed by him, placed in his car and taken to his home. Lastly, some stone brained idiot sent me a copy of the sign in/out sheet allegedly recording this theft of overtime. If this stupid person had looked closely at the time sheet they would see my signed name and in the approval column they would see Cleese's signature. Would you believe some butt head attempted to white out Cleese's approval signature, but the ink and his name rose to the top. Tsk, tsk! I look forward to the hearing Mr. Kahn of Employee Relations. The theft of client supplies, client's funds (embezzlement), institutional furniture, corruption of legal documents and sexual harassment will of course certainly not be tolerated on these holy grounds. I forgot to include an explanation for the sexual harassment charge against Paul Dunning. Mr. Dunning informed me that Cleese summoned him from his office to come and see how nice I was dressed. Would you believe actually came and stood behind me without my knowledge looking at me. You can only imagine how shocked and embarrassed I was. I'm making a recommendation that Barton Cleese and Paul Dunning both be terminated pending a hearing. I know you're probably thinking how dare she! Well I do and I did. If I can be terminated for breaking rules, regulations and policies, then so can the both of them; unless the rules, regulations and disciplinary actions only apply to African American employees and not Caucasian superiors who terrorize, brutalize and threaten clients (Daryl Campton). All aboard the good ship lollipop! And she boldly signed her name.

Janet notarized and printed four copies of the letter. She personally handed Gertrude Fleming a copy and submitted a copy to the Employee Relations receptionist. Lastly, she taped a blown up copy to the wall of the mailroom in the administration building. And so it was; that every person working in the administration building read the letter posted to the mailroom wall. No one dared to remove it but some anonymous person made a copy of it and it was circulated all over grounds. Three days later, the posted letter on the mailroom wall was brought to Dunning's attention and he rushed to the mailroom. Reading the huge letter addressed to him as 'Dear Paul' taped to the wall his mouth dropped open and he was beyond rage, infuriated and embarrassed as he ripped it down in three pieces. It was soon all over grounds that Cleese was stealing client food, client funds and institutional property, abusing clients, sexually harassing Janet Nelson and Paul Dunning assistant CEO was a Peeping Tom. The posted letter of course made Cleese (someone sent him a copy) and Dunning both the laughing stock of the grounds again. The kitchen workers began serving the client's Rice Krispy cereal first thing before Cleese came into the kitchen. On his first and last trip to the kitchen after the letter, he found the client's for the first time in years eating their cereal and he suffered the laughter of the staff behind his back as he left the client's dining area empty handed, fuming, furious and embarrassed.

One could imagine the rip roaring laughter that followed that single circulated letter all over grounds (without Janet's knowledge) one could only guess at the effect that it had on Cleese, Dunning and Kahn. An employer, with over 500 employees, laughing at them proved extremely intolerable to Cleese and Dunning and they both disappeared from the grounds (emergency vacations) for a few days. Janet's hearing for theft of overtime was postponed and never heard from again and one could frequently find Janet alone in her office or walking the building laughing her head off. As Roger Wellington Lloyd drilled into her, "When they come after you, you go after them, give them something else to think about and keep the pressure on' This is just what Janet did, she wrote to the State Commissioner of Human Services and told him everything starting with the coercion to perjury herself in superior court and she filed complaints with EEOC and Civil Rights and both were accepted. She sent copies of the confirmation letters from both agencies to Dick Kahn in Employee Relations to let him know the heat was on and who was bringing it. The union representative Sharon Nesbit stopped by Janet's office laughing and asked her if she planned this stuff or just made it up as she went along? She also had to concede that the matter was too big for her to handle and arranged a meeting with the President of the union chapter. Unfortunately for Cleese, this particular President also hated Cleese with a passion and now she had this Janet Nelson and she believed her story and got on board. Rubbing her hands together like a gold hoarding miser, she assigned Janet an attorney. The rains were coming and no one had an umbrella. To make matters worse Dunning began receiving anonymous letters where the sender described what clothing they were wearing, someone was leaving boxes of Rice Krispies cereal outside Cleese's office door and Kahn's office was flooded with anonymous queries about Janet's charges and what was he going to do about it. Years ago Roger Wellington Lloyd, while working on her case, had drummed up immense sympathy for Janet's case through manipulation and publicity and Janet well remembered his tactics and incorporated them into her fight. There was nothing Cleese, Kahn or Dunning could do and the CEO Ms. Klein made the intelligent decision to stay out of it. Janet put the crowning touch on her retaliation by calling the Governor of the State and with real tears and a whispered, trembling voice, she told everything that was happening to her. She suddenly she broke off the call saying fearfully that someone was coming and hung up. The disconnected call did not go unheeded; whoever it was she spoke with at the Governor's office immediately phoned the institution and soon the true rumor that Janet had called the Governor's office was being talked about in awe. Janet had successfully covered her back with definite higher authorities and she sat back and waited for the fallout between bouts of laughter. While she laughed; State officials contemplated how best to keep these things out of the papers, and how to silence Janet Nelson who it was obvious wasn't going to go down without a fight.

After being burnt on a hot stove, a child learns to stay away from the fire. Even a bruised and bloodied boxer knows when to throw in the towel. Unfortunately, some creatures of higher intelligence just don't get the message. With the over powering heat unleashed on the institution by Janet one would think the power boys would back off but stupidity, egotism and pride won out over intelligent reasoning. Instead of backing off, the administrators came at her again and suffered a terrible, humiliating lost at her hands. The problem was that this loss came with strings attached to innocent bystanders and would rip the roof off the entire institution. Weeks after her infamous letter, accepted EEOC and Civil Rights complaints, the call to the Governor's office and the Commissioner of Human Services, Cleese still refused let go. Dunning and Kahn thought him insane to keep up the attack against Janet but Cleese wouldn't budge even though Janet was fast becoming a swollen, smelly, burning hemorrhoid and the pharmacist was out of Preparation-H. Cleese developed a new plan against Janet which began with Gertrude's suggestion to move Janet to the midnight shift and a devastating newspaper article, supplied by Gertrude, who was making another bid for the Head Supervisor position Janet had been demoted from. What she'd discovered in the newspaper would surely secure Cleese's gratitude and as a reward he'd appoint her to the position with his sincere and grateful thanks. After all, no part of what he was planning for Janet would have a chance in hell of working without the newspaper article in black and white on Janet Nelson. Gertrude had discovered the article in the paper weeks ago but withheld it until she could find a way for the damning information to benefit her. She gave the newspaper article to Cleese and he was ecstatic. This was just what he needed to get that bitch. He showed the article to Dunning as he wanted to act on it immediately. Dunning was just as thrilled with the unforeseen information but Kahn had reservations. Cleese ignored Kahn saying that his plan was full proof. It would give Janet no way out no matter how many complaints she filed or letters she wrote. After hearing Cleese's entire plan Dunning was thoroughly on board but Kahn had reservations. He was against the plan and said as much indicating the possibility of it backfiring in their faces. "You will do as you are told! This won't work without you!" Dunning threatened Kahn. Kahn continued to insist that he wanted no part of it and attempted to leave Cleese's office. He was given a direct order from Dunning to sit down and he did, but immediately stood back up and voiced his opinion of their plan. "This plan, this vision of yours is juvenile,

Cleese. It's over dramatized, cruel and lacks any sense of moral character, structure or aristocratic training and your bullying tendencies are in full bloom. I implore you, don't do this thing!" In the end Kahn wasn't given a choice. "It will be done and you'll do your part. Am I making myself clear Kahn?" Dunning reiterated glaring at Kahn. "Yea, you're coming in loud and clear all the way to hell." Kahn complied, sitting back down and listening as Cleese and Dunning spun a web of lies, deceit and humiliation against Janet which was beyond horrifying, it was cruel.

Following Gertrude's suggestion Cleese's transferred Janet to the midnight shift with the idea being that it would relax her guard and give him the time needed to put everything in place for his coup de grace. It was two months before Cleese, Dunning and Kahn began the implacable assault against Janet and it began with the receipt of a letter at Janet's home.

Janet fingered the white business envelope with slightly trembling hands. Anxiety and foreboding descending over her as her eyes drifted over to the sender's return address. It was from the Employee Relations office. Apprehension and uneasiness made her feel claustrophobic and caused a dark hood of panic to descend over her and she found breathing difficult. She weighed whether or not to open the letter; it would most certainly not contain anything good. She had to know its contents to stay in touch with their deviousness, needed to know what they were up to but she was afraid to open it. Finally with trepidation, she slowly tore the envelope open. It was a notification dated two days prior informing her of a meeting scheduled in the Employee Relations office at 9 a.m. the following day and failure to appear would result in automatic termination. Her fear disappeared only to be replaced with anger. Her thinking was that they knew the letter would take 1-2 days to reach her and the plan must have been for her to get the letter the same day of the meeting or worst, the day after. Then Instead of fighting to keep her job; she would be fighting to get her job back. "Bastards!" she mumbled aloud. They were never in their offices before 10 a.m. yet they scheduled this meeting for 9 a.m. As luck would have it, the letter arrived the day before. Janet called her union representative Sharon Nesbit, but the machine picked up her call. She would have to arrive extra early tomorrow and hope she could find Sharon before the meeting although she was rarely, if ever, in her office.

Janet arrived on grounds forty minutes before the meeting time and went directly to the union office.

The door was locked. She exhaled desultorily and left, going upstairs to the Employee Relations office and was told the meeting was downstairs in the conference room. She didn't have time to check the Union office again so she went alone to the conference room. The door was also closed and locked. Returning to the Employee Relations office she was then informed that the meeting was in conference Room two on the other side of the building. She went there and found another closed, locked door. She returned to the office and was told the meeting had been moved to the conference room in the hospital building which she also found closed and locked. It was now 9 a.m. and she was in turmoil and growing desperation. The words of the letter echoing in her mind took on the rhythm of her footsteps: Failure to appear will result in termination. Suddenly she realized this was a part of some plan, having her running from place to place was eating up time and they could say she hadn't shown up at the appointed time, the meeting would be adjourned and she'd be terminated for failure to appear. *What do I do?* She thought desperately. "Well first," she responded to herself, "You calm down, get yourself together and think about this." and the answer came to her. Go over the Employee Relations Officers head to the CEO and tell what was happening. She was no longer nervous or afraid, she was thoroughly pissed off. When she walked through the revolving door of the administration building she came to an abrupt stop. "Son of A Bitch!" she whispered aloud, because standing there instead of at one of the four places she had been sent, was the Employee Relations officer, Assistant CEO and others. 'Son of a bitch!' she thought again. She stiffened her back and just as she moved towards them she heard her name called. It was her union rep, Sharon Nesbit and she was winded and fit to be tied. Janet was ignored, as Sharon brushed past her leaving thunder and lightning in her wake straight up to the Employee Relation Officer and . his group, who were standing there with surprise and guilt written all over their faces. She began yelling before she even reached them and when she did, she got right up into their faces. "I've been running around for almost thirty minutes looking for this bogus meeting you set up, going from place to place and found no one and no meeting. And now I find you all here! What the hell is going on here? You scheduled a meeting with no advance notice, don't bother to deny it. You sent not only her but me on a bull shit, wild goose chase to four different places knowing full well you wouldn't be there. You think this shit is funny?" She stepped even closer into their faces and said, "Now I find you all huddled together in a completely different place doing what, planning her termination because she didn't show?" She now stepped directly into Dick Kahn's face. "You fucking knew that was wrong four ways to Sunday and I'm going to nail your ass to the wall for it!" she said in a voice meant only for him to hear. Turning to the rest of the group, she stated loudly in a voice that carried all around the lobby, "Know this, you're formally notified, by me," her voice amplified even more. "I'm, yea me, will represent Ms. Nelson on these grounds and you can trust and believe that I will be filing a complaint with the State on what was done here this morning. Now just where the hell is this damn meeting, if there is one, taking place? And let's not bother about that bull shit 9 a.m. appointment time, we all know it was bull shit and purposely arranged for her to be a no show. Well, she's not and she's not alone. Now, let's get this party started right! Where is the meeting to be held, Australia?" she asked sarcastically. She was told to wait a minute. "Why? Wait for what? To give you time to regroup? Fine, but let me tell you all right here and now," she stated, nostrils flaring, blowing invisible smoke and steam. "I know you and you know me and if you even think about spitting in her direction; it had better be accompanied with a permission slip. I'm watching her and I'm damn sure going to be watching you. Have I made myself perfectly clear!?" She tossed her long dread locks over her shoulder, then plopped her short, plump frame down in a chair. She folded her arms across her chest like Chief Sitting Bull and whispered to Janet, who had sat down beside her. "Why didn't you tell me you were going through all this shit?" Janet wanted to reply but she suddenly became chocked with tears. Sharon knew the answer to her own question. Over the years, she'd made no secret of the fact that she didn't like Janet. It was true, she didn't like her, never had and her reasons were her own. But what she thought about Janet was one thing, how she felt about what was happening with her was another.

Sharon Nesbit showing up had indeed thrown a monkey wrench in their plans and was completely unexpected. They knew all bets were off when she came storming through the revolving door of the administration building. Thunder was coming and lighting was on its ass and they wished for a place to get out of the way of the storm. They hated 'That Bitch' as they referred to her. All fire and brimstone but they had no choice but to respect her spirit and knowledge, although they could do without her endless bag of whimsical, eye opening catch phrases. She knew her shit; just as well as she knew there power games as sneaky, devious, downright nasty and vindictive. She was fond of stating 'Game recognizes Game' motherfucker! and just like that she'd seen through their conspiracy and 'Woe unto thee. Get thee down below and fasten your seat belts, it was going to be a bumpy ride. They knew she figured out what they had planned. She'd said as much. The only thing she didn't know was that prior to her arrival, they'd just finished admiring and celebrating the typing up of Janet's letter of termination for failure to appear for the pre-scheduled meeting. They were passing it among themselves admiring the form and imagining her face when it was handed to her. It had all been so flawlessly and hilariously planned with the best part being there was no one to prove she had been sent on a wild goose chase. Only the receptionist knew and she'd like to keep her job. No, there was no one to vouch for Janet having arrived on time nor the fact that she had sent her from place to place. She was also right in guessing that they had to wait to start the meeting because they had to regroup and present a meeting that was never meant to be. They went to plan B, C and D and it was the worst embarrassing mistake ever. They were so busy covering their offense they completely forgot their defense, which was totally shut down, devastated, decimated and demolished not by that fire breathing dragon bitch of a union rep. but by little quiet Janet Nelson. It was half an hour before the meeting began and an hour later when Janet closed the meeting and dismissed everyone with their tails tucked firmly between their legs.

Janet needed to use the bathroom. Her stomach was cramping and her bowels felt hot, loose and runny. Afterwards, while washing her hands, she looked at her reflection in the mirror. Surprisingly, her face held a peaceful countenance. There was no stress or agitation showing in her eyes, her entire body felt relaxed. She actually felt kind of good. She chuckled to herself as she suddenly thought about the actor Bruce Willis. He was from her hometown in Penns Grove, NJ and had become a successful actor in Hollywood. In his early years he did commercials for Ban deodorant. She recalled the commercial where he faced the camera with that cute, mischievous, infectious smile that always made her smile and said, "Never let them see you sweat!" "Never let them see you sweat." she said aloud. She looked at her reflection in the mirror and said it again, this time with strength and conviction, "Never let them see you sweat!" Then she asked herself aloud in the empty bathroom, "Why the hell am I hiding, yes hiding, in the bathroom from those assholes? Never let them see ME sweat!" she said aloud as she exited the bathroom with firm decisive steps.

When Janet entered into the board room she noticed that the atmosphere was thick with anticipation and curiosity as all heads turned to look at her and she was captivating. Her hair was out cascading down over her shoulders and she wore a blue three piece man's pantsuit and carried a brief case and a duffle bag. The boardroom itself suggested nothing in the way of ambience, its name followed Its function; a place for meetings. It was a cold room devoid of any decorations or frills or even curtains at its large windows, there wasn't even a telephone in the room. There were no pictures on the any of its four walls or even a coffee machine. Its only contents were a large, long, heavy walnut table which was rounded at the corners and surrounded by seven non-descript swivel chairs on either side of it and one large, black swivel chair at its head. Every chair was occupied except for the two which Janet and Sharon took. The Assistant CEO was standing against the wall by the windows. Of the twelve seated people, Janet knew only one of them, the Employee Relations Officer, Dick Kahn, the others were all strangers. The atmosphere in the room was charged with electric expectancy; *but expectancy of what?* Janet wondered. Who were all these people and why are they here? She pulled out her chair, sat down next to Sharon, closed her eyes and inhaled deeply. These actions were viewed as a weakness but when she opened her eyes she was calm and collected. No one could have envisioned the explosive outcome of the meeting nor that they'd all be wishing that they were somewhere else, anywhere but where they were. They had no idea that they were about to have their heads ripped and torn from their shoulders, dripping blood and tossed wide eyed into their laps. They still believed she was nothing of consequence and they were the omnipotent Gods of Mount Olympus. They were not concerned, but should have been, when Janet removed a large tape recorder from her duffel bag and placed it on the table and before they knew what was happening she opened the meeting, just before she pushed the record button. She had their attention and the theme for the meeting was 'Divide and Conquer" courtesy of Roger Wellington Lloyd. In a voice that demanded attention she began, "Ladies and gentlemen you have me at an unfair disadvantage, I don't know any of you or why you're here." She looked into the face of the man directly across from her and asked, "Who are you?" in a voice that demanded a response. This turn in events was obviously unexpected and unheard of; her taking control of the meeting like this. The man looked at the Employee Relations Officer as if to ask what he should do. Janet grinned, "Sir?" she snapped in his direction, "Again, who are you and why are you here?" The unknown man lowered his eyes and said, "I'm Joe Leslie from the business department." "Speak up, I can't hear you. There's nothing to be afraid of here." she paused and then added, "Accept Me!" He blurted out his name and said I was told to come here." Janet eyebrows raised questionably at him and went on to the next person. "James Mason, file clerk." "Larry Melton, mail clerk." *She went around the room only to discover none of them was a part of the meeting or had a legitimate reason for being there; they were spectators, an audience called in for amusement at her expense.* She raised her hands above her head like a barker in a side show "Come One, Come All and see the show!" she said softly but audibly. Janet took them for what they were, spectators, and she was the main attraction. She bristled inside. She asked them who told them to be here and how much did their ticket cost? She looked all around the room at them but no one responded. She laughed a little and shrugging her shoulders said "Cowards" slightly above a whisper. She then turned to the Employee Relations Officer and dropping any show of respect for his position (they'd given her none) she called him by his first name, 'Dick' in such a way that he was accurately and justly named. "Dick, why are these people here? Is this some show you're staging? Is this a part of your program of planned behavior? Are you planning to harass and humiliate me, perhaps make me cry, boo hoo for the audience? Are you Dic ka! Making two syllables of his one syllable name as sarcastically as she could. She waved her hand in the air. "Oh never mind. It's not important, yet." letting the word suggest that worst things were yet to come. Dick Kahn the employee relations officer was completely thrown off balance and embarrassed by her manipulation of his name. He was seething inside, his thoughts reeling. He had no idea of how they had come to be in this sad and sorry state of affairs where the accused was now the accuser. *What happened or was happening? How did the meeting come to be chaired and opened by her? How did that happen, when did it happen? Why was she asking all the questions?* He looked to Dunning who at the moment chose to look out the window. "Ok." Janet said leaning back in her chair, "You have my permission to take it from here Dic ka." Again he felt like a prick and he wouldn't have been surprised to discover that the others in the room saw him the same way as they lowered their heads. He began shuffling papers and then with a forced smile on his face that took such strain to maintain it might have caused him a stroke he slid a check for $2000 dollars across the table to Janet saying, "I've been authorized to give you this check in exchange for your dropping the Civil Rights and EEOC complaints." He was smiling so hard it caused a tick in the corner of his mouth to jump. To Janet, it felt like each word was dripping with dark, oozing slime. She reached over, picked up the check and as she looked around at the spectators (again that feel of rushed electric expectancy) *It's some kind of a trick.* She thought. She studied the check which appeared to be a legitimate check made out to her from the State Department of Human Services but it wasn't in the usual form of a payroll check. *In that moment she surmised several things: (1) She had a strong Civil Rights and EEOC case (2) They were attempting buy (bribe) her off the lawsuits. (3) They were expecting her face to erupt in a gigantic Kool-Aide smile and (4) The lawsuit was worth much more but they expected her to get excited by $2,000.* She said nothing; just studied the check and slowly eyed each of the spectators. *They just knew they had her. They could scarcely hide their maniacal glee as they waited for response to the check. And Janet was wondering what would be next on their agenda. Something bad was coming. Something that was undoubtedly expected to smack the Kool-Aide smile off her face at receiving the check. Her glance fell on Mr. Dunning, who had a rather creepy Cheshire cat smile on his fat bearded* *face. What's up with that smile? Surely this throwback from a department store Santa Claus display wasn't happy for her.* She made a decision that was more of a bluff and acted. She picked the check up and tore it up into tiny pieces and tossed them into the air and as they fell like little bits of snowflakes back to the table she watched their faces. The pieces of the check slowly fluttered down across the table like drifting snow in front of their flabbergasted faces. Janet waited until the last piece landed and after a pregnant pause quietly and innocently stated, "I'm not for sale Dic-ka!" The effect was galvanizing on Dick Kahn as he jumped up from his chair in shock. Incoherent words tumbled and jumbled in his mouth but never made it past his lips. "Ah" Janet thought, "Better dial 911; here comes the stroke." She giggled to herself. The others in the room were summarily astonished and shocked as well, as with bulging eyes and slacked jaws; they looked back and forth between the ripped pieces of the check, Janet and Kahn. All was silent and silent until her union representative Sharon, who was sitting beside her burst out with a gut busting laugh. After a few seconds, Janet innocently asked, "Does anyone need a break or shall we go on?"

Mr. Kahn again tried to clear his throat which resulted in an embarrassing spray of spittle on the Table and Sharon reached into her purse and offered him a tissue and his anger quadrupled. Ignoring her, he began straightening out the papers he had crumpled between his hands. When he finally got himself under some control he went on and Janet did indeed have the wind knocked out of her sails. "I'm notifying you that you are being recommended for termination for sleeping on duty. You were discovered by two supervisors asleep on the floor underneath a client's beds." he concluded with more paper shuffling. Again all eyes focused on her and she was now certain why they were assembled. *They had been assembled as spectators to watch her reaction to receiving the $2000 check and then a smack in the face with a termination recommendation. They expected a great big Kool-Aide smile when she was given the check and then shock at the termination recommendation.* Janet maintained herself, fighting hard to maintain her composure and her facial muscles. She continued to sit serenely looking at the pieces of the destroyed bribe. "Where is the written disciplinary action form to record this event?" she asked. "What?"

Mr. Kahn asked looking greatly perturbed. "The written notification of this sleeping while on duty. If it happened, I was supposed to be called to the office by the supervisors, who allegedly discovered me under a bed, the matter discussed and then I would sign for a copy of the disciplinary action. Where is the original write up and my signed copy Dic-Ka? Janet sneered at him. She was livid inside and her eyes narrowed, shooting hot daggers at him and was hard put to remain seated and Sharon knew this. She grabbed Janet's hand beneath the table and said, "Don't you dare give them what they want! Go on. I don't know what you're planning but you're doing just fucking fine." Janet swallowed her frustration and looking at Mr. Kahn she said, "You don't have one do you? If you did, you would have thrown it in face like that nasty, bribery check. I'll tell you why you don't have one, it never happened. It's because every night, every night (she repeated for emphasis) I wake up those two supervisors. One sleeps in the nurse's office, the other in the supervisor's office. If you have a problem believing this," She paused and pulled something from her purse. "This is a video/voice recorder and camera and I've got both of them on video and still pictures asleep in their usual places. The pictures and the video are dated and can't be tampered with. I can have them developed if you want to take a recess (This was a bluff) Or we can wait for termination hearing. That's why they didn't report it because they knew I was always waking them up, every night!. Someone else reported this lie to you, someone who couldn't do the disciplinary write up. Furthermore, the first infraction for sleeping on duty is six weeks suspension. Why are you recommending a termination for me Dic-Ka?" Plus the woman working with me comes to work to sleep. She was found sleeping seven times and was only given six weeks suspension on the last instance. When she returned, from that suspension she was promoted to a supervisor! I'll accept the charge until a hearing is scheduled and you will give me six weeks suspension like the regulations specify and when I return from the suspension you will promote me to Head supervisor!" Sharon burst out laughing again. It was all too hilarious. Tears were streaming down her face as she slapped her hands on the table. "What the hell, you didn't need me at all. You go girl! Go on with your bad self!" She laughed and laughed. Janet was genuinely concerned when she looked at Mr. Kahn and asked, "Are you OK? Do you need a doctor or something?" Kahn's neck and faced went from red to purple with smoldering rage. He actually wanted to hit her and Janet saw it in his eyes and she sent him a silent message of her own "Bitch You just go ahead and try it!" Khan did want to hit her, smash her face right in, rip her eyes out of her head and skull fuck her to death. He felt like at any moment now he would burst into hot scalding tears. He was so humiliated and most of all beaten. He was hard put to control himself and he proceeded to screw up again shouting, "You'll never be promoted here!" Sharon leaped up adding her two cents to the melee, "Do you realize you're being recorded? Oh my God! You forgot didn't you?" and he had forgotten the recorder on the table. He was livid with rage. "You don't and shouldn't," Sharon continued looking at the Assistant CEO, have anything to do with who is or isn't promoted. You forget yourself Dick and that's abuse of authority and another complaint I'll be filing against you! And let's not get it twisted because it's all on tape!!" she said tapping the tape recorder. She sat back down and saying, "Perhaps, If no one objects, I'd like to suggest we take Ms. Nelson's suggestion. "Does anyone need a break or shall we go on?" And as in the case when Janet asked the same question the response was the same, silence and more silence.

The eyes of Mr. Kahn's audience, feeling sorry for him, dropped perceptively when they realized they weren't getting the first class show they'd been promised. They were here to see Janet Nelson get excited over the $2000 check and then shocked and dismayed, on the verge of tears over the termination recommendation. In the beginning they wanted to see her humiliation and tears, crying and pleading. Instead all they perceived about themselves was an increasing respect for her. Unease began to creep into their minds. Janet asked in a matter of fact tone, almost seeming disinterested and bored, "Is that all?" She knew it wasn't when she observed with her peripheral vision Kahn pulling out yet another set of documents. Kahn was angry, he was the one being humiliated and embarrassed by Janet. He lips were pressed tightly into a thin line trying to hide his anger. He was very unsuccessful and his feelings glowed across his face. He expected shock and outrage. Instead he got nothing but was forced to go on. While inside he was thinking. *We fucked up! We messed up bad. I don't quite know how, but we did.* Dick Kahn, more commonly known in his position as a 'Yes Man', he was given orders from his superiors and he followed through on those orders, whether they were illegal, unfair or just plain cruel. He would do his job. He'd had nothing personal against Janet (at first) In fact, he actually liked her. She was smart, unobtrusive, of good humor, easy going and always to be seen with a smile on her face. On occasion when their paths crossed they always chatted for a while and she always managed to send him on his way chuckling at some amusing remark she'd made. He had liked her immensely but he also liked his job. He knew he had to make a good showing of being a team player and was failing miserably. He hated and abhorred his instructions. He was charged with humiliating, demoting and terminating Janet, he had no choice. Once he'd had a good working relationship with her and now couldn't even look her in the eyes. Initially, he had hoped she knew and understood that these things were beyond his control; he had his orders and a job to do. There was no question or doubt that that he wouldn't do as he was told. She had made him; in fact all of them, look like fools. It was that fact that burned and twisted in his crawl and it no longer mattered how he felt about Janet prior to these proceedings, not any more. Now it was personal. She had indeed made him look like a fool and to add insult to injury, she made him look nothing less than stupid, discriminatory and vindictive and it was all true.

From the moment Janet showed up followed by that mountain troll from the Union everything was washed up and out the door! He should have known this and backed down but now his pride was firmly involved. *Everything was lost except this one last attack, he thought with malice in his heart and mind.* He was paralyzed with indignation mostly revolving around the insulting manner in which she pronounced his name, 'Dic-Ka!' With a flourish he began reading, "You were arrested for possession of crack cocaine and are hereby suspended without pay until your hearing in superior court. I know you don't have a court date yet but until that court decision you are immediately suspended." A profound silence followed his words as he continued, "If you are found guilty you will be immediately terminated." Hoping he was putting on a good show for his audience, he said the last with triumph dripping from his lips and cold, hard eyes staring in her face. "You'll be notified by us for you to come in and take a mandatory drug test which may or may not be before the court trial. Now,

I've known you for years and I know you don't use drugs but we have to respond to the arrest and a drug charge is a felony and unacceptable for employment with the State." All was silent as Janet stood up and excused herself to use the bathroom and she walk out wondering how they had found out about that arrest. Kahn was confident that he had her. It was the crowning point of Cleese's and Dunning's plan to deliberately save this action for last. Although she had tapped danced around the previous charges there was no way out of this one. They had her and they knew it and the spectators should have been ecstatic but the feelings among them had subtlety began to change in favor of Janet. They now secretly wanted her vindicated after seeing that this was an unfair and cruel game against her. They felt she was a courageous, knowledgeable and fearless fighter. With all the odds against her, she was holding her own and hadn't faltered once until now they thought sadly. They thought her brilliant the way she manipulated the meeting, the charges, smoothly and impressively and with the foresight to record it all; no one had expected that. Where did she get her knowledge and imagination? Where did she acquire the nerve to turn Mr. Dick Kahn's name into a backroom joke? (Imagine changing Dick into Dic-Ka) that was hilarious; although no one would have dared laughed. She had tenacity realizing that when out-numbered, strategy would win out over force. They had to give her that, holding her own like a champion. They'd been assembled to watch her humiliated and broken but things change and they were now drifting towards silent encouragement for her. They wanted her to best Kahn, Dunning and Cleese but that wouldn't happen now. None of the fourteen of them were stupid enough to voice this but there was a definite change in the atmosphere of the boardroom and they feared what was going to happen when she returned. Unfortunately, there was no way she could manipulate the drug charge. If only it didn't exist. The spectators no longer looked at her as a spectacle but as a champion, David taking on Goliath. Mr. Kahn had watched her push back from the table, get up and walk out and he was confusedly tormented, happy, insulted, torn inside. He hated having turned against her. He hated his participation in this travesty, hated his job, hated what she'd done to him in the meeting, hated all the spectators but most of all he hated Cleese and Dunning under whose instructions he acted. As he was commiserating these thoughts Janet returned, sat down and looking down at her folded hands on the table she began to speak.

"I won't be offering any information on the arrest matter but I will await your letter notifying me to come in for a drug test. I am, however, curious about why you, Dic-Ka, are seeking termination on me, a black employee for probable drug use. Do you recall telling me about that white employee, Hunter Lewis? He was arrested buying drugs from an undercover cop. You said you sent him to a six week drug rehab program, with pay, mind you, and he returned to work. Do you recall that conversation? I do; and it seriously concerns me why the white employee is sent for treatment and returned to work but this black employee is to be terminated. Seems a little prejudicial and discriminatory to me Dic-Ka and I can see from your expression, that you remember that conversation." Pausing for dramatic effect she got up from her seat and began slowly walking around the perimeter of the long table and their backs as she continued, "In as much as I will submit to taking your drug test to prove that I'm no drug user there are a few other employees on these grounds that I must insist you also give mandatory drug test." Every heart in the boardroom seized up and frankly, no one wanted to hear any more but it was too late, much too late. "Let's start with Mary Leeds Unit three Director, she smokes so much weed the thumb and index fingers of her right hand are permanently stained with Cannabis secretions. Walking around her building wearing dark shades, laughing and giggling, asking me if I have anything sweet because she has the munchies so bad. Test her! Her boyfriend or lover, how so ever you may want to put it, is James Talbot. You may have seen him strolling around the grounds with a black briefcase. That brief case contains ten and twenty dollar bags of cocaine. I know because he once asked me if I wanted to buy some. Test him! On to Unit five's Director Melba Watley, also a known marijuana smoker and cocaine sniffer and one of James' clients. Test her! Your Director of Food Service Calvin Coleman is rumored to have the best marijuana on grounds and holy smokes he delivers. Customers make orders using the phones in their buildings and their packages are delivered by the pot smoking food service delivery guys Calvin Hartman, Jose Maldanado and Reese Budding. Your RN, Betty Wright has taken to selling the clients medications, psychotropic drugs I believe; twenty dollars a pill." As Janet slowly walked around the length of the boardroom table, all their slack jawed, eye bulging faces, turned up and followed her progress as she ticked off names. These were people some or most of them knew. People they associated with on and off grounds. People whose homes they'd visited, even partied with. People who just might know about their own indiscretions. "I believe alcoholic beverages are not allowed on grounds. Feel free to check the filing cabinet of Head Supervisor Dee Louis, building five. She keeps a fifth of Jack Daniels in the lower, third drawer of that cabinet. Bill Tory, your payroll clerk, drinks and smokes weed. Amazing isn't it? Working right here in this building and no one knows, or do they? Most of these individuals are your top managers. How many, do you imagine, Direct Care workers within and including 19 buildings, a hospital, maintenance, food service and laundry departments are using drugs on these grounds? I won't hazard an estimate but you will drug test them, mandatory!!" she said placing emphasis on the mandatory. "And oh yea, before I conclude, after we adjourn this meeting you really must stop at the front receptionist desk, its right outside this room. Your receptionist Gail Myers, has an eighty dollar a day crack cocaine habit. She is also one of James' customers and he likes to brag about how much money he's making." Janet paused and looked at each person individually around the boardroom table. "If you fail to drug test these individuals, that's on you but you can trust and believe," she said looking directly at the Dunning, "That when I leave this room I'm going straight to that pay phone in the lobby and calling the Commissioner of Human Services and tell him everything that has occurred from the time I received your letter inviting me to this meeting up to the list of names I've just shared with you all and will also inform him that I will be forwarding a copy of the tape recording to his offices. I will also be contacting the police who might see fit to call in the DEA." She had circled the table three times before reaching her seat again and sedately sat down. All was silent but none could escape the bomb blast she'd detonated. In the silence, Janet brushed away some of the littered pieces of the check she had shredded and sat a small square box on the table. All eyes locked on the box as she slowly lifted its top off. Inside were seven blank cassette tapes. She reached over and pushed the stop button on the recorder and then the rewind button. The room was so quiet everyone could hear the whine of the tape recorder rewinding the tape. Some even flinched when it clicked at its end. She pushed play to not only test the recording but to ensure that everyone in the room knew the recording existed. She proceeded to dub seven copies of the taped meeting while they all watched in silence. As each blank tape was dubbed, she removed it from the recorder and labelled it speaking aloud.. "Sharon Nesbit Union President, Dick Kahn Employee Relations, Human Service Commissioner, Assistant CEO Paul Dunning, the Daily Journal newspaper, Governor Hailey and finally Eye Witness News. She distributed copies to all the named individuals seated at the table, except for Assistant CEO Dunning. She placed her thumb on the center of the tape with his name on it and putting a little English on it, send it sliding across the boardroom table's to the far end where Dunning was seated. As she intended the tape skidded into the empty space beside him and clacked to the floor and continued sliding until it struck the wall. Janet looked him square in the eye and said, "I won't say excuse me nor will I pick that up. It's just your copy if you want it and I'm sure you do, you can pick it up yourself. If not-" she shrugged her shoulders with an added huge Kool-Aide smile. No one spoke. "Is this meeting over or does someone wish to discipline me for littering with a bribery check?" Janet asked, or perhaps you have something else for me in your magical bag of tricks? Silly rabbit tricks are for kids." No one responded. Janet looked around at their astonished faces and repeated, "Can I leave?" Again, there was no response. "Hey Mr. Dic-Ka, is the meeting over, can I leave?" Janet asked impatiently yet again. Dick Kahn mumbled something. "Excuse me sir, I didn't hear you. Is this meeting over or what?" Janet snapped. "Yes!" Kahn shouted in a shell shot sort of voice and mind and Janet mockingly said to him, "Temper, temper." as she and Sharon stood up and headed for the door leaving all the spectators, none of whom wanted to be the first to leave, sitting quietly around the table after the door closed behind them. Sharon silently followed Janet out into the lobby. The receptionist waved to Sharon and she'd dazedly waved back while thinking, *She's got an eighty dollar a day crack cocaine habit!?* Her mind was reeling with the over twenty names Janet had dropped on the unsuspecting group and the probable repercussions that would follow. If it was all true and knowing some of the names, she knew in their particular cases that Janet hadn't lied there was going to be a huge backlash. She and Janet walked to the parking lot together saying nothing to each other. Sharon kept cutting her eyes up at Janet who appeared to not notice that she was there. When they reached Janet's car and she opened the door and was about to get in when Sharon asked, "Are you going to be able to pass a drug test?" Janet looked at her, bent over, pulled her pants leg up, put her hand down into her sock and pulled out a skinny rolled joint. She lit it, inhaled and looking at Sharon exhaled and said, "Nope." She got into her car, started it up, rolled down the window and then she pulled off leaving a stunned union president standing in the hot sun of the parking lot looking after her unknowledgeable about a simple thing called 'A bluff'.

FIFTHTEEN

The drug charge and pending court appearance was for the record true. She had been to New York on numerous occasions with some friends, who she knew went there to buy drugs. She never brought anything accept marijuana on their trips to the Big Apple which were always great. On these trips they always visited places of interest. They toured Washington Square Park, the United Nations, The Statue of Liberty, The Metropolitan Museum, the Bronx zoo and Coney Island. The enjoyed the view from the top of the Empire State Building and walked the streets of Park Avenue, Wall Street, the Village and shopped on Canal Street. She did smoke weed but didn't use Cocaine. On the day in question, Janet had driven her car with three friends to New York. They each brought (or so Janet thought) a $3 dollar bag of weed and then after lunch headed for Washington Square Park. Back then, park inhabitants were allowed to smoke weed in the park as long as it didn't bother anyone and they respectfully extinguished their joints when a police officer was in the vicinity. The same for alcoholic beverages as long as it was concealed in a bag it was ok to drink in the park. There was a small outside amphitheater in the park and people would sit around it listening to jokes told by the comedian of the moment. After their show the comedian would pass around a hat and people would put money in if they felt he or she was funny. Janet and her friends were pleasantly high on this particular beautiful day in New York and as darkness descended they wandered the streets of the Village where all types of people and stores were on display. They had spent a large amount of time at a store that only specialized in selling Barbie and Ken dolls. There were Barbie dolls on sale that never made the main stream markets. There were several Barbie dolls at various stages of pregnancy, Barbie the prostitute in an outfit made entirely of chains, a black Ken doll depicted as a pimp in zoot suit and wide brim hat, cross dressing and gay Barbie and Ken dolls with highly protruding male organs and they were all done in good taste and very expensive, some sold for as much as $800.

It was well pass eleven o'clock that night as they made their way back to her car headed for the Lincoln Tunnel and New Jersey. They crossed over into Jersey and instead of going home Janet detoured to her job to get some files she needed to have completed and on Mr. Cleese's desk come Monday morning. She arrived at the institution, went to her building for the files and left. Just after they pulled off of the institution's grounds and onto the street the flashing lights of a police car pulled them over. Janet wasn't concerned, her papers were in order and she never allowed the smoking of weed or cigarettes in her car. The officer asked them to step out of the car and requested identification from her three friends. After the two guys got out of the back seat the officer shined his flashlight in the back seat and asked, "What's this? He reached into the back seat and pulled out a small bottle containing a white powder. He guessed it was drugs and called for backup. All four of them were hand cuffed and Janet went ballistic when she heard both of the guys deny any knowledge of the bottle. With that said, the possession charge went on Janet because it was her vehicle. They were read their rights and all transported to the police station which was about four blocks away. When they arrived at the station Janet was charged with possession of a CDS (controlled dangerous substance) She informed the officer that she did not use any drugs other than smoking weed now and then. Looking directly at the both of the guys, she told them that they could give her a drug test and wouldn't find anything in her system besides weed. The drugs belonged to the guys who obviously tried to hide it in the back seat of her car when they were pulled over. Of course, the guys denied this and she was the only one charged with possession of cocaine, given a summons to appear in court the following day and they were released. The officer was nice enough to drive them back to her car. In front of the officers, Janet adamantly refused to allow the guys back into her car berating them on letting her be charged with something they knew she didn't indulge in. She got in her car and left them standing there with the police. She didn't care how they got home any more than they had cared about stuffing their drugs into the seat of her car and letting her take the blame.

Janet showed up for court the following morning. The judge was a real joker in a humorist mood as he read her the charge of possession for personal consumption. An examination of the contents of the bottle had revealed its content as cocaine. Janet explained the course of her and her friend's actions on that day, that the drugs were not hers and that she was willing to do anything she could to prove that including taking a drug and polygraph test. The Judge laughed saying that for some reason he believed her but couldn't dismiss the charge because it would be in superior court, his court was municipal. She would receive a court summons and a letter from a court appointed attorney to represent her. Janet asked the judge where she could go that day to have a drug test taken that very day. She wanted to present the test results on court day. The judge said he could request a drug test and Janet said please do. She took the test and had the results in her hand. It read no traces of cocaine in her system and a small amount of marijuana. Janet left with the instructions that she would be contacted by a Public Defender and then be given a date to appear in Superior court. After leaving the court she noticed that she had plenty of time to report to work but she chose not to, she had called out sick for the day and would stay out sick. If she had chosen to report for work she would have discovered what people at her job already knew. The city paper always printed an item in its own column called the Police Blotter. On the same day she went to court, people on her job were already reading and showing copies of the Police Blotter that carried her name, address and charge. With a price on her head and an unnamed reward offered for anyone or thing that could bring help to the persecution of Janet Nelson up for grabs a copy of the newspaper was given to Cleese, courtesy of Gertrude Fleming, and he forwarded it to Dick Kahn, Employee Relations Officer and Assistant CEO Paul Dunning.

A month later, Janet still had not been contacted by the court appointed lawyer but it never left her mind. She felt like she was hanging by the tips of her fingers on the edge of a sliding precipice. She could lose her job with a felony drug charge. She had absolutely no idea that the administration was well on their way to doing just that. They'd contacted the police department and asked about the arrest. Finding it to be true they wanted to know the court date but were told that although the court date was public knowledge it had not yet been scheduled by the Superior Court. They set about contacting the courts every day to get up dates on Janet's court date.

They just couldn't wait. They were salivating with the prospect of getting her terminated on a felony drug charge. So great was their impatience that they just had to act against her immediately. Instead of waiting for a court decision they suspended her from duty without pay pending the outcome of the drug charge at that boardroom meeting. This was the fail-safe plan Cleese had put together, approved by Dunning and Kahn chosen to deliver the coup de grace. Janet pictured them in her mind plotting her downfall. She imagined three huge, hairy troll like men and one woman. They'd all be huddled in a close circle under the moonlight with unkempt hair, disfigured faces and filthy, smelly bodies surrounding a photograph of Janet. There'd be spittle dripping from their huge, grinning, blubbery lips surrounding a mouth of gap-toothed, blackened teeth with several missing. Huge bulbous, eyes glittering as they rubbed pudgy, hairy, wart covered hands together like a gold hoarder coveting it's his gold.

Janet received the letter from the Public Defender's office scheduling an appointment to meet the court appointed attorney almost two months after the arrest and that date was over a month away. She'd be out of work for almost three months prior to the hearing. She had no choice but to face reality and she began searching the classifieds for work. She felt assured she wouldn't go to jail for such a small amount of cocaine (that wasn't even hers) she'd probably get probation or something. But what kind of job could she get if she had a felony conviction for drug possession? She began to lose sleep, couldn't eat. Food felt like saw dust in her mouth and attempts at swallowing left her gagging. She was an emotional wreck. Three days before the appointment with the public defender she received another letter rescheduling that meeting for a month and a half later. She wouldn't reach court until the middle of November five months after the arrest. The waiting was anxiety filled and exasperating and never entirely left her mind. Aware that her job rested on a court's decision, that was months away was driving her insane with anticipation and was a crushing weight on her mind. What was she going to do? She couldn't apply for unemployment until after she was found guilty and terminated. And would she even be eligible for unemployment benefits if the cause of the termination was a felony charge? Janet panicked and in that panic hate began to grow and fester in her heart for Cleese, Dunning and Kahn. But hate could be a very exciting emotion, very exciting. There was a heat in the hate that she could feel and it warmed her as nothing ever had and she began to cherish it. She discovered that hate was real and merciless and she began again to contemplate striking back at Cleese and his cronies.

Janet initially entered the dark forest with revenge on her mind. She knowingly sought the path taken by many mistreated, bullied and unfairly treated employees with murder in her heart. She took steps toward planning retaliation against them in her mind. Continuous, mental pictures of their faces were a kaleidoscope in her mind and just wouldn't leave her alone. In her mind's eyes she could clearly see their faces and was amazed that she could hear the sound of their voices and she became lost to herself in the recollections until nothing mattered except revenge, retaliation and dare she contemplate it, murder. The anxiety over the upcoming court appearance vanished. She no longer feared or thought about it. She wondered if revenge was necessary. Did she really need the job? She had over half a million dollars in the bank, if she lost the job, so what. Used properly the money would last for years. So just why was she fighting? Janet concluded that it was the principle of the thing. Having the money, which so far she hadn't touched, was cool but it didn't make her world go round. There was only one thing of importance on her mind these days and that was revenge. She began to plan and discard all sorts of devious ways to kill them, one and all. Up close confrontation was out of the question. It wasn't in her to shoot, stab or mutilate a person. She'd long since forgotten the fight with Alfreda Whitehurst in high school where she'd broken bones, bit and clawed the bully into submission. Day after day, Janet spent obsessing on how to get them; how to make them pay for their deliberate sabotage and cruelty. Nothing existed in her world when she entered into the dark zoned corners of her mind except the three of them. She needed three different ways to avenge herself against three different individuals: Cleese, Dunning and Kahn. She'd sit for hours in front of the television not seeing or hearing it. Strangely enough it was the television that presented her with her first two concrete plans for revenge against Dick Kahn and Barton Cleese.

Five months passed before she finally met with her public defender. Janet explained what happened about the drugs not belonging to her, giving the names as well as the addresses of the guys who hid them in the back seat of her car. The public defender, Ms. Carson was a young woman dressed in a man's black suit. She had long blond hair, bright intelligent blue eyes and talked with quick hand movements, gestures and speech. Ms. Carson was unable to calm the agitated Janet down until she grasped Janet's hands and held them still. She informed Janet that she had the arrest report, the transcript from the initial hearing and the results of the drug test which revealed no presence of cocaine in her system. Ms. Carson informed Janet that due to police statement and volunteered drug test that things looked good but of course the decision rested on the court. Janet was sent away with a tentative court date for the following month feeling no better than she had when she came in.

Janet arrived in court visibly afraid and apprehensive. There was no way she could guess at the outcome. The courtroom was almost the size of a high school gym and just as noisy and still there was nowhere to sit. The benches were packed with defendants and the only available standing room was out in the hall. Janet's public defender was nowhere in sight in the chaotic arena of court staff, attorneys, police, reporters and defendants. The court clerk was calling out names which Janet could barely here as she continued to scour the room for Ms. Carson. She never saw her in the press of people but she did spot Dick Kahn from her job. This was as bad as it could get. Whatever the decision, her employer was there to personally hear it. Janet's stomach upchucked and coffee, donuts and bile suddenly filled her mouth so quickly she had to cover it and ran for the court room doors. The hot liquid mixture was squeezing between her fingers before she found the ladies room and plunged into an empty stall. She threw up with a force that left her trembling, dizzy and on her knees, her mouth feeling foul and slimy. Even as she vomited she was conscious of the fact that if her name was called she wouldn't be there to hear it. She felt as if she were going to pass out from the stress and had to grasp the edge of the sink as she rinsed her mouth. She splashed water on her face and after drying off with a paper towel she walked back out into the crowded, air-less corridor. As she neared the double court room doors she saw her public defender sitting on a bench against the wall. She would have missed her completely if the crowd hadn't taken that moment to part itself. Janet walked towards Ms. Carson. And with a trembling hand she tapped her on her shoulder. Ms. Carson looked up at Janet and said, "Hi Janet. You can go home." And she went back to shuffling the papers in her lap. Janet blinked, blinked again and then a third time. "Huh?" Janet said and began stammering, her heart in her throat. Ms. Carson smiled up at her and repeated, "Go home Janet. You have no business here today, charges dismissed, clean record and keep your back seats empty." And she returned to her papers and Janet stood there not believing the words she'd heard. Wrapped In a cloud of euphoria, she didn't feel the crush of people in the corridor or the elevator ride down stairs as she made her way, half running, out of the building. Outside it seemed as if she'd never seen the sky so blue, the sun so bright or felt a more caressing warm breeze on her skin as she had the moment she walked outside the doors of the superior court. Tears filled her eyes as she thought *This is what freedom feels like.* She couldn't believe it, dismissed! Dismissed? Dismissed!" she wanted to scream it out loud. Then she thought of Dick Kahn waiting in the court room for her case to be called and she did laugh out loud with hysterical relief and the irony of the fact that he might possibly be sitting there all day waiting for a case that would never be called.

At home the next morning, the phone rang. It was Dick Kahn instructing her to report to his office the following day. Janet smiled to herself wondering how long he'd sat in the court room. When she reported to his office he informed her (never looking up from his desk) that she could report back to duty the following day, as the drug charge had been dismissed. The new hateful Janet replied sarcastically, "Oh and when did you discover that Dic-Ka? And he winced at the foul usage of his name again. "I saw you in the court room yesterday. Who sent you there Dunning or Cleese? Never mind, it doesn't really matter now, does it? I hope you didn't have to wait long because I found out at 9:00 a.m. that the charge was dismissed. They hadn't even started calling cases when I was on my way home." She lied. Kahn had been more than pissed off, waiting hour after hour, through the lunch break and then back for more hours of waiting. At 4 p.m. he approached the court clerk only to learn that the case had been dismissed. He had stood there hot and tired hating not Janet, but Cleese and Dunning. When Dunning instructed him to inform Janet that she could return to work, he had squawked. It would make him look like the ass hole of the century. Three weeks after her return to work; she was summoned to Kahn's office where she was handed an envelope by Kahn and his request that she open it in his presence. "Are you suggesting that you don't know what's in this envelope? Come on, it's in an interoffice envelope and whatever is in here you placed it there. You want to see my face when I open it, don't you?" she asked quietly fingering the envelope. When he didn't respond she said, "If it's no problem for you, I'll open it later." She folded the envelope in half, pocketed it and left Kahn's office with the letter burning a hole in her pocket; as well as her mind, but she was determined not open it until she was at home. At the end of her shift, while sitting in her car, she opened the letter any way. It contained a State of New Jersey check for $16,213.00 with the explanation being that it was compensatory back pay for the time missed due to the unwarranted suspension. Attached to the check and held in place with a paper clip was a memo informing her of a second demotion; effectively immediately she was demoted from Cottage Training Supervisor to Cottage Training Technician. She couldn't believe it, back to her starting position of twenty years earlier? Janet was surprised and shocked by the memo. They were not going to allow her to get away with beating them again. This demotion was just another in the series of events intended to fire her or at least induce her resignation, but in her book they weren't going to get either one. As in the case of the first demotion; there were no disciplinary actions to support the demotion but it was done anyway. She was playing with the big boys who didn't like to lose. In the course of the demotions her salary had decreased from $53,500 down to $42,500 and in this new demotion her salary would stand at $38,400 a year. They weren't aware that money wasn't a contributing factor with her. They had no knowledge of the over half a million dollars currently retained in her bank account. Being demoted back to a direct care worker was no problem for Janet financially. She'd never been glamorized by power or titles and had always enjoyed working directly with the patients and she'd never let them see her sweat.

Dunning was the architect of Janet's second demotion and Cleese was pulling the strings. Demoting Janet back to her starting position was expected to embarrass her enough to resign. She would be placed in a unit where they were assured that she'd have problems because neither the Director Pamela McCoy nor the assistant Director Gloria Pitts liked her. McCoy disliked Janet without ever having met her curtesy of the constant string of negative comments from Gloria Pitts, Janet's former Head Supervisor. They had specific instructions from Dunning and Kahn to watch Janet judiciously for any infractions that could lead to disciplinary actions. With the administration firmly behind them, there was no attempt of sabotage they couldn't get away with or so they thought. Gloria never forgot Janet's calling her a bitch, threatening to kick her ass and bringing up seeing her having sex on Cleese's desk. Now Janet was under her power and she had carte blanche to proceed with immunity against Janet. Janet was placed in the worst building of the unit; where the clients were female, assaultive and hygienically disgusting. She would be supervised by a stoned brained supervisor in men's brogan boots who could barely read and write English and was a bully to the staff and clients.

Janet was considering resignation. She was ready to throw in the towel. She wasn't embarrassed at the demotions; it was the constant harassment that was wearing her down, making her depressed. She couldn't understand the viciousness of people who'd probably be in attendance at her grave side applauding and dancing a jig if she suddenly died. What was really at the root of her feelings was the fact that they were getting away with all the injustices against her. She was watching television or better yet, television was watching her, when the telephone rang. It was Sharon Nesbit, her union representative. "I heard about the demotion. It's all anyone is talking about. What are you going to do about it?" Sharon asked and Janet replied "What can I do?" "You can fight back!" Sharon encouraged. "How can I Sharon? What's the use?" Janet asked tiredly. "Oh come off it Janet. Get off your pity pot, wipe some dirt on their bull shit and go after them!" "There's so much bullshit and client abuse in that building there're sending you to its ridiculous. Keep your eyes open, you'll see a lot of illegal goings on in that building. Do what you did to Cleese, get proof and then blow the whistle. That will be the building blocks of your retaliation by reporting what you see to higher authorities. You know Dunning and Kahn are having you watched don't you? Don't give them anything. So you got demoted, so fucking what. You've worked for the State long enough that even the demotion won't cause severe money problems. You were pulling, what, about $50,000 a year? This demotion is going to knock a few thousand off your previous salary but that's manageable. It's your turn now Janet! Fight back, rough and dirty like them. You have the knowledge, intelligence and information to put them on the run again. Use it, dammit! "Sharon blasted Janet. Janet listened and thought that what Sharon was saying to her was exactly the same things Roger Wellington Lloyd had told her. Be prepared because they will come after you, observe and record, divide and conquer, report to higher persons, call bluffs and above all, take no prisoners. Janet was filling up with a new confidence, old hatred and unbelievable dark anger. There really was a silver lining in dark clouds. She thanked Sharon and hung up. The following day, after signing out on her last day as a Training Supervisor, Janet hadn't gone home she went to her bank to make a withdrawal from an account that held over $400,000 dollars plus fifteen years of interest.

SIXTEEN

Dick Kahn was weeks later, still smarting at his humiliating and embarrassing defeat at Janet's hands. Insult was added to injury when he'd sat for almost eight hours in court to learn that the charges against her were dismissed and he wasn't allowed to forget these things. The various people Dunning had invited to witness Janet's humiliation were still talking about the meeting and passing on hilarious episodes all around the grounds. Whenever he went to the administration building, where over sixty people worked, he'd endure respectful greetings to his face and smirking grins behind his back. He bristled inside trying to dismiss the whispered comments and laughter, carrying on as if nothing unusual had occurred. Sure he'd gotten his ass reamed and it was all Dunning and Cleese's fault. Dunning was fairing no better; he remained behind the closed doors of his office for days to avoid the humility. Dick's hatred for Dunning was passionate and all consuming. He harbored similar feelings against Cleese who just couldn't let the matter drop even after demoting Janet. They just had to keep after her with a second demotion and it all resulted in his public humiliation. Worst was that toxic list of probable drug users and distributors on grounds and Janet's threat to inform the police, the Commissioner of Human Services and the Governor if he didn't drug test each and every one of the people she named. He speculated on whether she'd act on her threat but deep in his soul Kahn felt she would without a blink of an eye if pushed and Dunning and Cleese were shoving her. She'd been very angry and yet brilliant at that meeting. Ripping up the check and tossing the pieces up into the air had been cunningly dramatic and had frightened him. She couldn't be bought. There was a high probability that she'd carry out her threat and it needed to be addressed immediately but how? That meeting had been months ago. Her threat had been that as soon as she received a date from him to take a drug test she would pass on the names to higher authorities. He didn't dare set a date for her drug test, that would just be suicide and yet she had not carried out her threat. Why, what was she waiting for? But if she passed on the names anyway, it would be very bad for them all for having those names and not following through on an investigation and subsequent drug testing. Years ago employees were notified that the institution would be conducting random drug test at their discretion but it had never been done. If they began conducting drug test it would have to start with the people on Janet's list. Talk was already going on about that list and the people Dunning had invited to that meeting would know the testing wasn't random, that they were testing specific people and they'd have another issue to contend with, stereotyping. It would be beyond obvious and still wouldn't explain why they waited so long to do the testing. They'd question why the so called random testing didn't begin in the administration building. It was all a mess with no way out and still Dunning and Cleese went after Janet with that damn second demotion! "Why couldn't they understand the repercussions of the meeting, the devastating reality of her threat and that the unveiling of their own conspiracies would come into play. She had them by the proverbial balls and he was literally the dick at the center of the maelstrom because of Dunning and Cleese.

After Janet and Sharon Nesbit left the boardroom no one moved, each afraid to be the first to leave. The copy of the tape that Janet had slid over to Dunning was still on the floor its contents silently screaming at him. Kahn's own astonishing, taped rested in front of him and looking at it hurt his eyes and he had a thumping headache. He strongly felt that if he put the slightest pressure on his stomach muscles that his bowels would squirt from between his tight ass into his pants in a steaming, hot, smelly puddle. Twenty minutes later, they still sat around the boardroom table that was littered with the pieces of the check that Janet had torn into pieces. It seemed to be what everyone was concentrating on as opposed to looking at each other. Dunning stood up, walked over to the windows with his back to the people sitting around the long table suddenly screamed, "Get out, everybody; get the hell out of here, now!" Chairs scraped the floor and some toppled over as the grateful twelve people, with their eyes on the floor, rushed to get out of the boardroom. When the last one was out the door Dunning slammed it shut and rounded angrily on Kahn, pointing his finger in his face, "You! You did this! You got me into this shit and you better find a way to get me out!" "What the fuck are you talking about?" Kahn yelled back, "I didn't get you into a damn thing. This whole idea, this entire meeting was yours and Cleese's, remember! It was you who put the meeting together and decided I should chair it! You who had me set up all the dummy locations to have her running from place to place looking for a meeting that didn't exist. Remember! You who thought it would be so hilarious to have me give her the check then threaten her with termination! You who decided I should tell her she was suspended until the court hearing on the drug charge! This is all your doing, you and that pompous ass Cleese just had to show her! Well, you showed her didn't you and now you want to put it all on me? Uh huh man, not me! How the hell you figure on making me responsible for your actions? I acted as I was instructed, by you! I did as I was told by superior, that's you! Jesus Christ, what are we going to do about those names? Instead of placing blame we need to figure out what to do about that list of names if you recall are recorded. Oh excuse me," Kahn interrupted himself sarcastically, "Your copy of the tape is still on the floor." He and Dunning both looked down at the tape, as myriads of emotions flitted across their faces. "Scared to pick it up?" Kahn said nastily. "You need to, no need for it to fall into more wrong hands! "What's this we shit? She's talking to you on that damn tape not me!" Dunning yelled at Kahn who looked at him unsympathetically. "I'm not going to justify that statement with a response." Kahn said. "You seem to think you're free of any responsibility!" Dunning yelled at him. "Yes, I am. I acted as I was instructed by my superior. Failing to do so would lead to disciplinary actions against me for failing to follow a direct order, remember? And please don't bother to tell me you wouldn't do such a thing!" Kahn said sarcastically. "So what, I gave you a direct order, so fucking what! It doesn't matter. What matters is that you're going to fix this shit." Dunning roared. "And just how am I supposed to do that?" Kahn asked equally angry. "Find a way!" Dunning screamed and walked out of the boardroom leaving Kahn alone. Seconds later he returned and retrieved his copy of Janet's tape from off the floor.

On the morning Janet was due to report for duty on her first day as a twice demoted employee, returned to her starting position of over twenty years ago; Dunning was sitting behind his desk in his spacious office looking at his copy of the disastrous taped meeting. The tape was never far from his eyes, mind or person. One of the hardest things to do he discovered was to wait on the outcome of events he had no control over. Events that could spew off into any of a dozen directions and he could only hope that the wheels of the future favored him. Only there was no way to predict the future outcome of something that was out of his sphere of control. He had left explicit instructions to be informed immediately if and when Janet showed up. If she did and was as much as a microsecond late he wanted a late slip. He hoped she wouldn't show; that she'd rather resign than face the humiliating demotion. This was the event he was waiting on. If she showed, he already had people and plans in place to make her assignment difficult and totally unbearable. He'd instructed Pitts and McCoy to pick a select group of patients designed to try the patience of Mother Teresa and St. Michael. All the buildings on grounds held 32 clients who were divided into four groups. No new employee to a building ever worked alone. Dunning wanted Janet to be a group leader with no one would be allowed to assist her. He wanted the worst behavioral clients in the building made them into a special group of eight just for her. The group selected included three habitual runaways, three that constantly moved their bowels and smeared the feces on themselves, the walls and floors. The last two wore mandatory full body restraints suits because of the violence they inflicted on themselves and others and these restraints had to be removed once every two hours. If she didn't show he still had to wait because she might have simply called out sick. Either way (ignoring Kahn's plea to leave Janet alone) he had to wait. It wasn't a long wait because a call came in from Janet's new Director Pamela McCoy that Janet had arrived for duty 45 minutes early and then left saying she was going to the store to get some coffee. "Did she sign in?" Dunning asked anxiously and when he was told, "No." he said, "Fine, let me know what time she signs in." He was looking like a cannibal hungrily eye balling a boiling fresh corpse (Janet) waiting for it to reach exactly the right stage of tenderness before beginning to feast on it.

Janet herself was feeling just fine. After leaving work and her supervisor's position for the last time the day before she'd gone directly to her bank. She arranged for a bank credit card and opened a checking account on her now released trust funds which totaled over $600.000 dollars. Her next stop was a car dealership and she made her first purchase from her trust fund account purchasing a spanking brand new hot, cherry red, convertible Trans Am. The following day proved to be a perfect summer morning; with a crisp clear blue sky, temperatures edging into the mid-eighties and minimum traffic on the highway as she headed to work and her newly demoted position. She cruised along the highway with the top down, the powerful engine humming smoothly and club music pumping from car's Bose stereo. She was in high spirits. There was no turmoil in her mind or anger in her heart at the demotion as the warm summer air flowed over her convertible. It was simply a turn of events that Roger Wellington Lloyd had told her to expect and she was ready to face it optimistically. She had no problem working directly with the clients again. She enjoyed the hands on contact with the patients. She was neither embarrassed nor ashamed at the demotion and didn't worry about what people would think about the unfortunate turn of events. She'd gained no enemies or animosity from her previous subordinates; they all liked and respected her. She encountered no problems coming down in position, in fact, no one even bought the subject up.

Returning from the store Janet turned onto the grounds of the institution. As she was rounding the road to her new building when who should she see approaching her walking on the side of the road way but Dunning. Janet slowed the beautiful car down and came to a full stop. She sat there with the powerful engine growling smoothly and waited as Dunning approached her from the side of the road. His eyes couldn't help but lock onto the hot red car. Janet opened her door, stepped out of her car, flipped her long dark hair over her shoulder and waved cheerfully to him. "Good Morning, Mr. Dunning lovely day isn't it?" and before he realized that he was doing it, he smiled and waved back. Janet laughed uproariously, got back in her car and drove off leaving him stunned with the knowledge of his returned greeting. He felt like a cartoon character that had been duped and the word 'sucker' magically appeared across its face. Dunning stared after her and the beautiful car seething. He was a pot of water just reaching its boiling point as simmering tiny air bubbles erupted into hot, angry, rumbling globules of trapped heat. If he could have, he would have erupted into a severe temper tantrum, falling out on the ground, pummeling the air with bunched impotent fist and intermittently holding his breath between indignant screams, but of course he couldn't. He did the only thing he could do after being made a fool by that bitch; he bowed his head, shoved his fisted hands deep into in his pockets and stomped off. She had just destroyed his entire day because he knew the image of him smiling and waving to her wouldn't leave his or her conscious mind and he was apoplectic with fury at the thorn in his ass that she represented. He imagined that she planned the entire episode (which was impossible) to run into him driving that car, waving and greeting him as if they were friends of old and haven't seen each other in days. Something had to be done with her but murder was against the law, but oh if it was only possible and he had the heart. He felt the thrumming of the tantrum rising inside him again and he did the most unexpected thing. It was too early in the morning for anyone at the institution to be out and about and so they all missed the most amazing sight of fat old Paul Dunning Assistant CEO sprinting, not jogging, but full out sprinting the almost quarter mile to the administration building. He had no idea why he felt the need to run other than to channel off the passionate ferocity of the sudden impulsive desire to turn around, follow Janet to her building, catch, maul, strangle, shoot, stab and/or bludgeon her to death. The strength of that sudden impulse terrified the shit out of him. In a moment of unchecked sanity he could have done it, killed her! His thoughts were alarming him. What the hell had he just contemplated, murder? And that's when Dunning's steps progressed from a walk to a jog, from a jog to a sprint and were those tears in his eyes as his humongous ass bounced and jiggled up and down from side to side all the way home or actually the administration building. His thoughts were coming to loud and frighteningly quick and he sought to get clear of his own mind. His heart was thumping hammer blows in his chest and his muscles were screaming indignantly. The only time he used them both together was when he made indifferent love to his wife and even then he had only two speeds, fast forward and stall. His slapping feet seemed to be chanting, "Janet" over and over carrying him to the quiet safety of his office where he locked himself in no longer concerned with what time Janet Nelson signed in for duty.

Janet entered the back door of her new building and proceeded to the supervisor's office. There she found two women supervisors. The one sitting at the desk was a rotund woman wearing a flowery smock, tiny gold framed spectacles covered a light skinned, pock marked face. The woman standing over her screamed bull dagger and had the body of middle weight boxer. She was tall with a dark shiny face and a too welcoming smile. She wore black brogan boots, black jeans and a black long sleeved shirt. Her hair was cut in a severe, screaming crew cut and she had a sneaky look about her face as she looked Janet up and down making her feel slightly uncomfortable. The woman at the desk introduced herself as Linda Mason and the other supervisor was Harriet Jenkins. "I know Janet." the big woman said smiling at Janet. Janet smiled back saying, "Then you have me at an advantage because I can't recall having met you before but good morning." There was no response from the woman as she reached over and took Janet's hand and said, "Come with me." Janet pulled her hand free from the woman's grip with a questionable look on her face and followed her out of the office and onto the dorm rooms. Harriet Jenkins pulled a piece of paper out of her shirt pocket and going into the first dorm room selected five female clients and in the next dorm room she selected three more. She handed Janet the list of the client's names informing her that this was her group. Janet's instincts went up as she asked, "You have five groups in your building and I'm to be a group leader?" "Yea, is that a problem?" Harriet turned on her. "Yes it is. Each building on these grounds has four groups of clients and this one has five? I'm new, made a group leader and I'm working alone?" Janet questioned. Harriet replied "Those are our instructions." All sorts of warnings flashed through Janet's mind as she repeated, "Your instructions?" She knew then that someone outside of this building was calling the shots surrounding her and she had a good guess who; Dunning! She was only partly right. The idea had been Dunning's but the client selections had been Gloria Pitts. Janet, of course, didn't know this and had no idea that she was about to be reacquainted with Gloria. Janet eyed the group of female clients and saw two in full body restraints, three smelling like holy hell and three were actively trying to escape out of the room. Janet suspected that there was a definite method for this madness and that the grouping of these particular clients was deliberate. She looked Harrier calmly in the eyes and asked,

"Can you show me where the client's charts are kept?" "Why?" Harriet responded, the welcoming smile now gone from her glistening face and Janet replied, "So I can acquaint myself with their behaviors. Seems to me that those three trying to get out are elopers, those two in restraints have to be watched as closely as the three elopers and I guess from the smell and look of those three that they are feces smearers. Isn't it unusual for one group to have three runaways, two severe behavior clients in full body restraints and three more clients who are feces smearers?" Janet questioned. "I heard you were a trouble maker and I see it's true!" Harriet replied sarcastically and continued, "The group will not be changed around to suit you!" "If that's the case, Ms. Jenkins, just who does this group arrangement suit, Dunning?" Janet came right back and Jenkins stared at her with open animosity. "I will do what I can. What time is my first break?" Janet asked and at her question Jenkins turned and walked away without responding.

Janet worked with the difficult, uncontrollable clients for two hours that felt more like ten and was totally exhausted. When they do something that you know is not right or fair, act on it immediately' Roger Wellington Lloyd's words rose in her mind and act on it she did. On her first break, she entered the supervisor's office where both supervisors were present and requested to use the phone. Janet called Sharon Nesbit, the union representative. "Hey Janet, how are things going there?" Sharon asked. Janet told Sharon about the group assigned to her and that she was working alone. Sharon exploded into the phone loud enough for the supervisors to hear and making it necessary for Janet to pull the phone away from her ear. "What? You got to be fucking kidding me!" "No, I'm not but I need help with this. I feel like just walking out." "No, don't do that, you'll be written up for leaving the clients unattended and that's what they want. I'm going to make a few calls and get right back to you. Who are the supervisors on duty, Jenkins and Mason? Put one of them on the phone. I'm sure they're listening." Janet handed the phone to Harriet who refused to accept it as did Mason and Janet said as much to Sharon. "Fine, I'll be there in about thirty minutes." she said and hung up. Janet returned to trying to control what couldn't be controlled.

About an hour later, Sharon was in a meeting with Janet's supervisors and the yelling could be heard throughout the dayrooms. Half an hour later, Janet learned that her old nemesis, Gloria Pitts was the assistant Director when she came to the building to join the meeting and then Janet was called into the office. When all was said and done the fifth group had been dissolved, the clients returned to their original groups and Janet was assigned to assist another employee with their group. With the help of Sharon things were set as they should be and Janet had firmly secured two new enemies. Sharon informed the supervisors that she'd be filing a grievance complaint for abuse of authority and employee sabotage against them. The charges were merely a smoke screen by Sharon to get to the real orchestrator of the sabotage attempt. Sharon knew it wasn't their game and hoped that one or both of them would give up the name of the person or persons responsible for their orders. Coming from the top it was bound to be Dunning then McCoy and Pitts. Unless Dunning could persuade one of them to accept the blame, he would be the person in trouble with the Union office. It would be interesting to see how things would play out, because they were all aware of how far Dunning's retaliation could reach against them and their positions.

Lack of intelligence will cause a person make stupid decisions. Add to that ego, vindictiveness and power and you have a volatile, unstable mixture whose forbidden combination will most likely explode, perhaps sparing a life but erasing forever a face. McCoy and Pitts were the architects of this lethal brew. When Sharon arrived with her unique form of temper reducing them to a fine, humiliating powder guilty of abuse of authority, employee sabotage and endangerment of patients and staff they backed off, temporarily. Using her own scruple-less form of manipulation, she offered them a reprieve. She intimated (Bluffed) that she knew that they had instructions from Dunning and Kahn to watch and sabotage Janet and that they were only following orders. She would be agreeable to dropping the charges against them if, and only if, they revealed exactly who gave them their orders. Sharon could read on their faces the effect of what she was saying. They were shocked and afraid but only for the moment. Sharon knew it wouldn't take them long to feel that since they were backed by the administration they had no reason to fear her. They couldn't be touched or so they would believe. Sharon had no scruples true but she wasn't cruel. She had no intention of filing the complaint; she just wanted them to back off Janet who didn't need any more on her plate. She had no idea that Janet was completely opposite of her and out for blood.

Pits and McCoy were shaken by Sharon's words but weren't too overly concerned; they had the strongest superiors on grounds backing them up. It never occurred to them that those same superiors would toss them to the lions if necessary. So they actually paid Sharon's threat no more attention than they felt it deserved. They were already plotting their next action against Janet. The following day was pay day and payroll checks were forwarded to Janet's building from McCoy's office. All checks were accounted for except Janet's; there was no check for her. Calling payroll she was informed that her check had been picked up by Pitts. Janet called over to McCoy's office and was told in a narcissistic, self-important manner by McCoy that yes, she had Janet's check and for her to come and get it. Janet asked why her check wasn't with the others and McCoy replied, "Because we took it. If you want it, come and get it!" and she hung up on her. In her anger, Janet snatched the phone cord out of the wall, threw the phone on the floor and stormed over to McCoy's office. Janet was breathing hard, her face a mask of anger as she rushed over to McCoy's office but just as she reached the building she stopped, thinking she shouldn't have thrown the phone. This was the reaction they expected after deliberately taking her check and she was speeding right into disciplinary actions by storming over to the office. Tears of anger and frustration welled in her eyes and then she had a thought that made her detour her course and she headed for the canteen building. There she used the public phone to call the local police and reported the theft of her paycheck and that she knew who had it and they refused to give it to her.

When outside police come onto the institutions grounds, they had to report their presence at the administration building, which they did and Dunning accompanied the police to McCoy's building where they found Janet sitting on the bench in front of the building. Janet stood up and followed by the police and Dunning entered the building. She requested that the police and Dunning remain outside but within hearing range.

Janet entered their office and looking directly at the both of them angrily said, "You stole my check and I want it, now!" McCoy, a light-skinned woman in her early fifties with close cropped, greying hair leaned back in her swivel chair smiling and said, "I'm not giving you shit, now get out of my office!" Pitts started laughing hilariously. Her laughter was suddenly choked off; as if someone had suddenly reached over and grabbed her around the throat. The police, followed by a furious Dunning entered the office. One of the officers asked, "Do you have this woman's check? If so give it up!" Pitts and McCoy were both stunned into paralysis and neither complied with the request. "You both stole my check and I want it, you bunch of thieves!" Janet yelled. McCoy looked to Pitts as she opened her desk draw and removed a check and handed it to the tall stern faced officer. The officer took the check, looked at the name on it and handed it to Janet. "Is this your check, Miss?" he asked. Janet looked at the check and replied, "Yes." "Will you be pressing charges or is this matter closed? You are aware that if that check is valued at over $400 the theft counts as felony theft and you are within your rights to press charges." the officer said. "If I do, what happens?" Janet asked. "They will be arrested." Janet handed the check back to the officer requesting that he open it. The check amount was $1,246.76! The officer looked at Janet and said, "This amount constitutes felony theft if you choose to press charges." "Janet asked the officers if they could step out of the office for a moment. After they left, she stared at Pitts, McCoy and Dunning. "Well, well, well, look what we have here. With no sorrow, remorse or mercy she said, "One: I can press felony charges, you both will be arrested and most likely terminated because I will be calling the Commissioner's office. You might even lose your pensions. Two: You can turn in your resignations and run as fast as you can to payroll and request your pensions before the charges are scheduled for court or three, you can write a statement outlining who gave you your instructions to steal my check!" The three of them, Dunning, Pitts and McCoy stared incredulously at her and she stared right back. Suddenly Janet turned and stomped out of the office and returned with the police and quietly stated without the slightest iota of mercy in her voice, "I wish to press charges." Pitts and McCoy were paralyzed with fear and Dunning just stared incredibly at Janet. McCoy began to cry when one officer came over to her desk, asked her to stand up and then cuffed her as he read her rights. The same was done to Pitts and they were escorted outside and into two separate police cars. Janet and Dunning stood a few feet apart glaring at each other with naked hate and then she simply smiled at him as the two police cars pulled off carrying Pitts and McCoy. As people will do when they see police cars they stopped to be nosey. When they saw Pitts and McCoy led hand cuffed and placed put in the police cars their eyes widened and their tongues were waggling as the cars drove off. They watched Dunning walk away from the building and then all eyes turned on Janet who answered their questioning looks with the following statement meant to get the word around "Pitts and McCoy were arrested for stealing my paycheck." And she turned and walked back to her building check in hand. It was another tremendous and embarrassing blow to the Sawyer administration at Janet Nelson's hands and as usual the employees were laughing their asses off. Dunning was beyond frustration knowing his course of action was already laid out before him. It would be his responsibility to report the incident to the Kahn in Employee Relations; whose responsibility it would be to prepare disciplinary actions against Pitts and McCoy with the only recommendation possible being termination; and technically, someone needed to call Janet in and apologize for the incident. Dunning had no time for Kahn; he had more jeopardizing matters on his mind consisting of what would happen when Pitts and McCoy started alleging that they were acting under instructions from him and Kahn to go after Janet Nelson anyway they could? God he hated that woman!" He would attach none of the blame where it belonged; with him and his good ole boys. He stopped at Kahn's office to relay what had happened (omitting Janet's terms to drop the matter) and Kahn was thunderstruck at the incident, the arrest and what might or might not be following for them. He wanted to repeat what he'd told Dunning over and over months ago, "Leave that damn woman alone. Let it go!" but it would serve no purpose, none at all. He lifted the phone and called Janet's building. He informed her that she needed to come to his office to make a statement. She responded that if he didn't mind could she do it tomorrow as she was so very upset at the entire ordeal and just wanted to go home. He complied, having no idea that Janet would be coming for him in the not too distant future. Needless to say no one else bothered Janet Nelson but unfortunately the die was cast, the damage was done and now it was her turn. Time was wasting and there were no guarantees.

Janet had been thinking for months how to get Cleese; he was the one she wanted to hit the hardest. She already knew what she was going to do to him and so she turned her attention to Kahn and her thoughts regarding him were simple, divide and conquer. Janet sat at home on her balcony watching two couples playing tennis and sipping a glass of ice tea. When she finished the tea she booted up her computer and began a letter to Dick Kahn Employee Relations Officer. The sun was already down by a couple of hours before she completed the carefully constructed letter and made three copies. She fixed herself a light dinner of fish and chips and then set about the destruction of Barton Cleese on paper. After outlining what she wanted to do she knew without a doubt that this was the way to go but couldn't figure out how or where to begin and decided to sleep on it.

When word of the arrest of Pitts and McCoy reached Cleese (through none other than Gertrude) he, having no sympathy for Pitts and McCoy burst out laughing fit to be tied. His eyes were streaming tears as he said to Gertrude, "I trained her well, didn't I? Damn, to come up with something like that was nothing short of phenomenal, simply phenomenal and hilarious. "I wish I could have seen their faces when they brought them out in handcuffs. I just bet that was priceless." Gertrude was laughing right along with him having no sympathies for her buddy Pitts and since her long ago secret against Janet was now null and void she brought it out saying, "Pitts should have taken Janet seriously when she called her a bitch and Janet called her a bitch right back and threatened to kick her ass." With his laughter tampering off Cleese looked curiously at Gertrude and asked when that had happened. Gertrude wanted to reply, "Just before you gave me the keys to the Head Supervisor position, took them back and gave them to Janet you bastard, but instead she replied, "The same day you put Janet on day shift." "Oh ho, you kept that one to yourself did you?" he said peering at Gertrude and she cleaned it up fast, "Yea, well, I didn't want Janet to get in any trouble. I wonder who she's going to go after next." Gertrude said swiftly and innocently changing the subject. "What?" Cleese whirled on her. "She's taken out Pitts and McCoy and if a hearing is ever scheduled she'll have Dunning. So whose next on her list?" "What makes you think she has a list?" Cleese asked but the thought was a seed planted and producing an unpleasant clinching of his testicles. "I know it's not me. If it was she'd have done something a long time ago." "Somethings take time." Gertrude responded suggestively. "Have you heard something Gertrude? Something someone might just be planning against me?" "If I did, I would have told you by now. You know we watch each other's back in this building." she lied with a smile. The Head Supervisor's position had not been filled since Janet was demoted well over a year ago and Gertrude wondered why. She had been unofficially performing the duties of the position, even receiving the pay, but had not been formerly given the title and this was pissing her off. If she was performing the duties with pay, why then didn't she not have the title? She had wanted to broach the subject with Cleese on several occasions but was afraid to ask. Somewhere in the recesses of her evilness she hoped Janet did have some really funky plan to get Cleese but she needn't have worried, there was something, but it was still in the planning stage.

It was about this time that the Human Resources Officer, Karen Stevens, decided to throw her own special brand of employee sabotage into the arena in search of the bounty for the termination of Janet Nelson. She was a straight up racist against all nationalities including her own and she was extremely fed up with the name Janet Nelson, sick of hearing it. For Christ sake it was only one fucking employee and none of those ass holes had been able to do what needed to be done, get the bitch off grounds and be done with it. She was acquainted with everything that revolved around Janet since the court hearing where she showed up with a white father and well known attorney, the first demotion (which after a year had still not been scheduled for a hearing) the lackadaisical attempts at sabotage by Cleese, Kahn and Dunning, the disastrous boardroom meeting, the dismissed drug charges and the huge back payment for lost wages, the second demotion which on the first day resulted in charges by Janet and that annoying union representative for abuse of authority and job sabotage and now the arrest of Pitts and McCoy for felony theft. She thought them all amateurs. They were so concerned with firing that damn nuisance that they were being caught up in their own schemes. Karen was the only one that realized that Janet was using the State's own rules, regulations and disciplinary actions against them. Dumb asses she thought of all of them. She announced to Dunning, a month or so later, after the arrest and latest charges against the institution that she'd need to show the butt heads how it's done. One might wonder how the Human Resource officer was able to refer to the Assistant CEO as a butt head in his face but she did; and for whatever reason he didn't put her or her mouth in check. Glad to get a little of the heat off his sweating ass, he opened the door and allowed the wicked witch of the institution to fly into the game and she didn't require a broom. Her own sad, empty, unfulfilling life was all she needed to carry her into the battle of the Sayer Developmental Center vs Janet Nelson. Unlike her predecessors, who she felt couldn't find their asses with two hands and a flashlight; she was very methodical, precise, disciplined, and logical in her manner. When she thought of a line of attack against someone, she examined all the areas in which it could backfire before putting it into action. Her methods when she settled on a plan were always full proof, binding and untouchable to retaliation and her plan was simple. Break her!

SEVENTEEN

Two months into her second demotion Janet wasn't actively bothered or embarrassed by it. Throughout the course of both of her managerial positions she had never abused her authority, treated everyone fairly and had made no enemies of her subordinates. Practically everyone on grounds knew who she was and about the battle going on between her and the institution's power people. Although she didn't know it and couldn't hear it, they were cheering for her. She was a minor hero on grounds, holding her own against the higher ups who they themselves detested. Those in power waited eagerly for her to resign and were baffled when she didn't. They had no idea that Janet was sitting on a half a million dollar trust fund and technically didn't need their job; yet she not only held onto it, she fought for it and fought well. She reported for duty every day with a smile on her face, ready for work. She had some strength in her and they couldn't break her and this both disturbed and perplexed them. The CEO and the CEO's assistant, the Employee Relations Officer, Human Resources Officer and numerous Hearing Officers and several Unit Directors had been stunned that she'd shown up for duty. It was these very mysteries that caused them to make stupid and costly errors. It was no secret on grounds that there was an invisible 'Wanted for Termination' poster hanging over her head; like the ten most wanted criminals faces hung in post offices around the country. She had no knowledge of how many people, including her peers had signed up to win the bounty prize. If she did, she might have run for cover but the operative word here was 'might'

Karen Stevens was the Human Resources Officer at the institution and she hated everyone indiscriminately, including herself. She was a merciless, contemptable, harpy that had no compassion for anyone at the institution. As her husband was a superior court judge, so she set herself up as judge and jury over the institutions employees and not surprisingly her superiors. She even set her will against the CEO by bringing not only her infant baby to work with her; she had a crib, bassinet and bottle warmer set up in her office. No one challenged her or the nursery in the Human Resources Office. Such a thing would never have been tolerated of any other employee. People lost their jobs due to child care problems but Stevens solved her problem by bringing her infant to work with her every day. She manipulated or dismissed the State's rules, regulations and policies concerning hiring and firing at her will, they were non-existent to her. She did what she wanted to do and her actions were never questioned or challenged by anyone including the CEO, until, that is, she came up against Janet Nelson. Never addressed by her first name, she was a scrawny, sexless, unhappy woman with dirty, stringy blonde hair that had at best a minimum acquaintance with a comb and brush. Her pinched face and beady eyes never failed to produce anxiety when one was called into her office and forced, for whatever reason, to answer to her. Ms. Stevens was disgusted at the goings on surrounding this Janet Nelson and couldn't understand the difficulty in simply firing the bitch. She had never seen Janet in person but she made it her mission to handle this person, personally. In other words, she would show everyone how simple it would be to get rid of one troubling employee as she entered into the conspiracies to terminate Janet Nelson. She had no idea that Janet was a stick of dynamite with a short fuse and Karen unknowingly struck the match and the flame flared.

Built on 65 acres of land, all nineteen patient buildings ran on a mandatory amount of staff. If a building was short of staff, workers would be transferred (for the shift) to work in the understaffed building. Such was the case on this one particular day. Janet's car was in the shop for some warranty work and wouldn't be ready until that evening so she caught a ride with a friend to work. When Janet arrived for duty she was informed that she had to work in another building which was short of staff that day. All nineteen buildings were built in a huge circle that was a little over a mile around and building sixteen sat at the furthest curve of the huge ring of buildings. After arriving in building sixteen, she was instructed to report immediately to the Human Resources Office. It was about a 20 minute walk from her building to personnel and it was already smoking hot outside. By 9 a.m. the sun was high, blazing and unforgiving and there were no trees along the road down to the personnel building. Janet took her time walking in the relentless heat to the personnel building. She expected that whatever they wanted wouldn't be good after the arrest of Pitts and McCoy. When she arrived she was directed to the Human Resource Office. Before she could enter the office she was met by a scary, deranged looking woman with stringy, dirty, blonde hair and a flushed, pinched face. The woman looked Janet up and down and incredibly said, "I just wanted to see what you looked like." And she turned her back and slammed her office door in Janet's face. Janet stared wide eyed and open mouthed at the closed door. The two women sitting at their desk in the outer office lowered heads, attempting to be invisible. Janet thought it would be a safe bet that they'd be a witness to nothing. Even though she knew that she shouldn't, she responded to the insulting summons and slammed door. She knocked on the closed door. "Enter." Stevens said behind the closed door. Janet reached over, turned the door handle and still holding it she opened the door. Looking at Stevens sitting behind her desk Janet respectfully said, "You called me all the way down here to find out what I looked like. I just wanted to make sure you got a good look." Janet stood there in Stevens' office doorway for just a moment then quietly pulled the door closed on her startled face and left the office feeling just a bit satisfied. She walked back, muttering under her breath about the insanity of it all. When she reached her building and went inside she was met by the supervisor telling her she was wanted in the Human Resources Office. "I just left there." Janet said and was told, "I know but you have to go back." Janet shrugged saying "Whatever." But she went to get a drink of water first. Without knowing it Stevens had advanced the flame closer to the short fuse that was Janet Nelson.

For the second time Janet made the long hot walk to Steven's office and it was even hotter outside temperature going into the nineties. She suddenly stopped in her tracks as an unsettling thought occurred to her that this was the beginning of some sort of fucked up game! Calling her down there to see what she looked like made no sense and now she was completely sure that a new game had started and Stevens had made the opening move. She didn't know what to expect but she knew nothing good was coming and she was determined to not play into it. She believed

Stevens was going to attempt to force her fly off the handle, perhaps shouting, cursing and throwing in a few threats for good measure. All of these actions would give Stevens grounds to terminate her on the spot. It would definitely be in her best interest to hold her tongue; which had long ago acquired the habit of lashing out not caring who was cut, but she had no intention of allowing that spooky bitch to manipulate her. Before entering the office she stopped, took a deep breath and walked into the face of the scrawny looking demon seed standing in the outer office. Stevens immediately began screaming in Janet's face like a deranged banshee as if she was a misbehaving child, "I can have you fired right now! Do you know that, huh?" Janet merely stared at her looking bored and saying nothing. Then Stevens by name, Human Resources Officer by title, reached over for her secretary's phone while yelling, "Do you want that? I'll do it right now!" she screamed again, her hand hovering inches above the phone handle. Janet swiftly weighted the pros and cons of the threat with the words "Bitch, if you're going to do it shut the fuck up and do it!" trying to force their way through Janet's clenched teeth and tightly closed lips. If she said it, it would be just another battle but this time she'd be fighting not to keep her job but to get her job back. She looked at the two secretaries who both concentrated on their green desk blotters. They wouldn't be testifying to anything. With difficulty, Janet swallowed the vicious, straining retort and nonchalantly replied, "Nope." into Stevens' red, incensed face. Stevens was fuming as she shouted "Get out of my office! Get back to work!" and for the second time that morning she turned, walked into her office and slammed the door in Janet's face. It was then Janet realized, she had been bluffing about making the call to have her terminated. She had wanted her distressed, begging, maybe pleading not to be fired. "Ha-Ha, not in your wildest fantasies you cow!" Janet laughed to herself. She wouldn't be begging anything from that hag in drag. Janet returned to her building seething and sweating from the heat of the day. She was frustrated and furious inside but there was nothing she could do about it but suck it up and Stevens unknowingly advanced the flame closer to the fuse that would set Janet off.

When Janet finally reached her building she was exhausted, hot, sweaty, and feeling a little light headed from the intense heat outside.

When she entered the air conditioned building she breathed a sigh of relief for the cooling air enveloping her body. She was getting a drink from the water fountain when the supervisor appeared announcing that Stevens wanted to see her in her office right away. Janet was still leaning over the water fountain with cold water splashing across her lips as she heard the words. She straightened up, water dribbling from her lips and looked incredulously at the supervisor. Saying nothing, she turned around without question and began her third trip to Steven's office distractedly wondering; what were the signs of a heat stroke. When she arrived, she was made to stand outside in the outer office for almost twenty minutes while Stevens, who was within her eye sight, sat at her desk eating a sandwich. Janet's anger was straining in its harness and she was losing the battle to shove it down inside her. It was then she heard a sound that was out of place for the office setting, a baby crying. She looked further into Stevens' office and saw there was a crib in there and inside the crib a crying infant. You can't bring your children to work, everybody knew that but apparently this bitch could. Janet was forced to acknowledge the power this woman held at the institution. "What do you want?" Stevens snapped at Janet between bites of her sandwich and chewing sideways like a cow chewing its cud. Puzzled and with a restraining edge to her voice Janet replied, "You tell me, you sent for me." Hesitating and again restraining herself she continued, "Three times in a row in case anyone's counting." Janet watched disgusted as Stevens wiped bits of sandwich and mayo from her mouth with the back of her hand. "I did, but I changed my mind. Now get out of my office. Go back to your job!" Stevens said as she approached her office door to slam it again in Janet's face, but Janet beat her to it. Trembling, incensed and infuriated, Janet reached out, grabbed the door handle and slammed the door in Steven's face and walked out of the office. God only knew what it took for her not to go back, kick that door down and slam Stevens. Instead she walked away on trembling, exhausted legs leaving Stevens, who had drawn the match's flame less than an inch from the short dynamite fuse that was Janet Nelson.

Janet had barely entered her building when personnel called informing her to report immediately to Steven's office. Janet blinked hard to dispel the tears of frustration that welled in her eyes. A rising rage was filling her heaving chest. Turning away from her supervisor, she wiped the tears that threatened to fall, and for the fourth time in a row, headed to Steven's office. Janet had been walking for less than five minutes on the shade-less road, her steps heavy and robotic when a queasy, nauseating sensation was slushing around in her stomach making her feel as if she needed to vomit and as if that wasn't enough she had the beginnings of a thumping wild headache. She wasn't aware that she was experiencing the signs of heat exhaustion which could be extremely dangerous. When she finally arrived at Stevens' office she was physically done in; weak and tired from the heat. Stevens got up close and personal in Janet's face and in a deceptively sweet, calm voice blasted her with question after question. "Do you not know who I am? Are you stupid or something? Aren't you aware that I can take your job anytime I want? Do you not recognize me for who I am and what I represent?" Stevens knowing just by looking at Janet's drained continence that she was done in, ready to snap and this made her supremely happy inside thinking that she had pushed Janet's final buttons but before she could deliver the coup de grace Janet suddenly and quite un-expectantly pushed back. She straightened her back with effort, held up her head which was spinning with the heat and stepped up to Steven's, welcoming the confrontation. The hell with dignity and pride she was running on instincts which shouted to knock the shit out of Stevens. Stevens was only one of many conspirators who wanted her fired and in this case there were two witnesses but they belonged to Stevens. Out of fear for their jobs they'd lie to Jesus, Mary and Joseph that Mary never had a little lamb whose fleece was white as snow. Innocently looking directly into Stevens's beady eyes Janet released just the head of the beast inside of her. She just as calmly and deceptively as Stevens replied, "I think I recognize you and just who you are although it was a bit difficult to recognize you without your broomstick and flying monkey!" Janet said sweetly. Dietz blinked, then blinked again in shock and took a step back away from Janet. Janet's words were echoing around in her head. *Broom stick and flying monkey, broomstick and flying monkey?!* The flesh of her face began to pucker and squirm as if a mass of bugs were scuttling just under its surface. No one talked to her like that; she was so incensed she couldn't immediately reply as the words 'Broomstick and flying monkey' continue to echo throughout her mind. Spitting and sputtering so that Janet had to step back to avoid the spray Stevens whispered menacingly, "What? What did you say? Janet looking just as threating in her eyes calmly stated, "I'm not in the habit of repeating myself and I didn't stutter. You asked me if I was stupid, well I'm not, are you deaf as well as… "Janet stopped there allowing Stevens to fill in the blank and could tell she had by the way her eyes widened in an undisguised look of shock and insult. With those statements Janet had successfully turned Steven's game against her. Stevens was now the prey to be manipulated and Janet the predator; but she didn't push it. The baby in the crib began crying loudly and Janet looked into the crib and said, "Somebodies hungry. Do you breast feed?" Janet asked as her eyes wandered over to Steven's grape sized, practically nonexistent breast. Stevens became choleric with rage when Janet's gaze left her tiny breast and returned Steven's eyes and said, "I guess not. Is there anything else or should I get out and go back to work?" Stevens was entirely speechless with embarrassment at Janet's innuendo about her breast, which were indeed flat as a board and that broomstick and flying monkey business. She turned and walked into her office and for the fourth time slammed the door in her face. "Get out of this office!" she screamed from behind the closed door. "OK" Janet yelled loud enough to be heard through the closed door. Smiling to herself she left, laughing at her statement of 'Broomstick and flying monkey' "Where did she ever get that from?" Beneath the laughter that queasy feeling was stronger and she found that she couldn't stop her body from heaving up its insides. Cupping her hand over her mouth she ran for the ladies room only to discover there was nothing to vomit up except nasty, stringy, slimy bile. Her body shuddered with the force of the convulsions and the room began to swim around her. She dropped to the floor breathing haggardly and knew she would have to remain there on the cool tiles before she could venture back into the sun. She hoped no one would come into the bathroom as her body slowly regained a normal semblance of breathing. She was suddenly extremely sleepy and fighting the urge to close her eyes but refused to be found passed out on a bathroom floor in the personnel building but as she lay there her dark anger was surfacing again. She felt as if she could no longer hold herself in check and this frightened her and she began to cry in frustration. She knew it was inevitable that she would strike first if this woman kept up this harassment; that had been proven before when she had been pushed over the edge by her stepfather and the school bully. What came out of her both times was not just anger; it was an undeniable desire to rip, tear and mutilate and Stevens had her sharpening three inch claws on stone. She had to get out of there before the unthinkable happened. She gathered her wobbly legs beneath her and holding onto the edge of the sink pulled herself up to her feet. The bathroom room continued to swirl and spin, but at a less alarming rate. She splashed cold water on her face and left the bathroom leaving water beads on her face to fight the heat. As she left the administration building she saw a co-worker driving by and called out for a ride. Janet collapsed against the car's seat thankful for the ride and glad the madness was over. She discovered how wrong she was when she entered her building and was given a message to report (for the fifth time) to the Human Resources office. She was reduced to an angry, trembling, terrified mess. She couldn't go back there. She was afraid to go back but she knew she had to or be fired. Karen Stevens had lit the match to the short fuse and it began to sizzle. In her blind, insane obsession to break Janet she had unknowingly placed herself in the belly of the beast.

Janet began her fifth trip to Steven's office taking heavy, wooden steps as sweat poured down her face, but this time she made a detour. She went to the union president's office and wonder of wonders, found Sharon Nesbit just leaving the office. Before Janet could speak she began crying profusely, unable to get a word out. Alarmed, Sharon drew her into the office, gave her a glass of water and some tissues and waited until she calmed down and the tears had been reduced to sniffles. She told Sharon everything that had been happening all morning and what was still happening. Sharon was livid, grabbing her pocketbook declaring that she'd be going with her to Stevens' office, but Janet told said, "No." There was something that she wanted Sharon to do for her. Sharon listened, agreed it was a good idea but a questionable thing to do but she would do it. Riding in Sharon's car, spared Janet a fifth walk in the heat to the personnel building. Sharon dropped Janet off at the personnel building, watched her go inside and then drove off grounds.

As Janet approached the outer office, Stevens met her at the door and stated in a nasty manner, "It's obvious that you have mental problems and are a danger to yourself, the patients and others. It's been decided that you are to sign yourself into a mental health behavioral program no later than tomorrow for not less than six weeks; with pay of course. Failure to do so will result in immediate termination. That's all." she said as she turned and went into her office but before she could slam the door Janet said, "For what we want most there is a price to be paid." Stevens puzzled over Janet's words but dismissed them and that wasn't a very smart thing to do when it involved Janet Nelson in her present dangerous state of mind. Stevens continued walking into her office and of course slammed the door. Janet was beyond shock and astonishment. She stood there immobilized by Steven's words and having severe problems understanding what had just happened. "Mental health problems; a danger to herself and others, mandatory, involuntary commitment to a mental health hospital?" she repeated incredulously aloud to herself. She had to get out of there as she felt heat enveloping her and she was going to vomit again. Turning abruptly, she ran into the revolving door, shoving it so hard that the door revolved around twice before she was allowed to exit. Standing on the edge of the personnel steps she looked around at nothing, still too bewildered to believe what had just been ordered. Her legs failed in their ability to walk down the outside steps of the personnel building and she couldn't recall how long she stood there or when she had walked back to her building. She was dazed and insulted at the suggestion of her being mentally imbalanced. When she went inside it was time for her lunch. She went to the lounge and just as she sat down the supervisor came in and informed her that she was to report Human Resources immediately. Janet shouted. "Leave me alone, just leave me alone!" The supervisor flinched at Janet's explosion and asked, "What's going on with you? What's happening?" Janet gave no response. She merely laid her head down across her folded arms with hot tears streaming down her face. This was the sixth request in a row and yet it couldn't be ignored. Leaving the building her eyes were dry and she no longer gave a fuck. What else could this woman possibly do to her? Actually, no longer caring made her extremely dangerous. As she began walking down to the Human Resources Office she no longer felt the heat of the sun beating down on her, her steps were strong and firm. She was essentially a dead man walking with a sense of purpose. Possibly it was God who intervened in the guise of Sharon who happened to drive up and motioned her into the car asking her where she was going. When Janet told her, Sharon said in no uncertain terms that she was going with her and she didn't want to hear any bull shit that she wasn't. She handed Janet a package which Janet opened and put in her top shirt pocket. "Are you sure you want to take that in there. You could get in trouble." Sharon said. "I haven't been given much a choice, now have I?" Janet replied just a little too calmly for Sharon. "You don't have to be a part of this, it's your choice but if you recall it was you who told me to fight back, hard and dirty you said!" Sharon replied "No, it's not my choice; it's my job as your Union President." Janet ignored her for a moment; then told her that if she chose to go she wanted her to remain outside the office but within hearing range. When they arrived Janet went in through the front door like a wild, wild, west sheriff entering the street for a show down, hands at her sides ready to shoot from the hip and Sharon entered through the rear door. They met at the outer office of Stevens' office and Janet indicated for Sharon to wait just outside of the door. As Janet went into the outer office she fingered the object in her breast pocket; while Sharon remained out of sight just outside the door.

Stevens came stomping out of her office, stepped up in Janet's face and made what was probably the worst statement ever of her six visits to personnel. "I just wanted to inform you for future reference that when you talk to me you are not to look me in my face; you are to look at my feet! When you talk to any white person in this institution you are to look at their feet, not their eyes. I don't care where you look at the black employees but you will remember your place in the presence of your betters. Am I making myself clear?" Stevens reprimanded. Janet didn't know what to expect on this trip to Steven's office but nowhere in her wildest dreams had she expected something like this and the beast came out. Just before Janet began to raise her fist she said, "By black employees in this administration building I assume you're referring to the CEO" Mrs. Klein. You know the black one." Stevens smiled and Janet's hand came up and at the instant before Janet could swing (which was just what she was about to do) smash that self-servicing, narcissistic bitch right in her face, Sharon stepped into the office and grabbed Janet's rising fist. "What did you say!? What the hell did you just say to her!? She asked stepping up to the side of Stevens' face. Steven's eyes snapped to Sharon but were not overly concerned, secure as she was in her dominance and position. She in fact smiled at Sharon and innocently asked, "What are you talking about and why are you here? I didn't say anything to her that's any of your business. " "You lying..." Sharon caught herself then exploded, "I was standing right the fuck here! Right here and I know what I heard and so did your two secretaries." "My secretaries didn't hear me say anything." Stevens said smugly. Sharon was so mad she snorted from her nose, "You told her to look at your feet and all white people's feet when she talks to them. Who the hell do you think you are saying something like that? You are way out of line!" Sharon breathed. "I'm way out of line about what?" Stevens smiled, unintimidated, "If you have something to say, spit it out. Say it. Don't be shy!" Stevens gloated, thinking, *I can get rid of two for the price of one.* This seemed to righteously incense Sharon and she went ballistic. "Alright I will" Sharon yelled getting in Stevens' face. "You are the most detestable, corrupt, masochistic despicable self-centered, soulless, racist bitch I've ever met!" Sharon was building up a righteous head of steamed rage, doing ninety-five on a highway with no exit ramps. Stevens' jaw dropped open and she stepped toward Sharon who said "Come on bitch – Let's see you tell me to talk to your feet. Come on, let's see what you got! Perhaps it was the look in Sharon's eyes that slowed Stevens' forward motion but Sharon didn't want her to stop. "Come on, just a little closer bitch, step to me!" she challenged. "Please, please tell me the same thing you told Janet. I'm granting you full god dammed opportunity to tell me to look at your feet when I speak to you!" "I never said such thing" Stevens lied. Then all eyes turned towards Janet at the sound of a very audible 'click'. Janet had removed a small tape recorder from her front pocket and pushed 'rewind' and then 'play' and held the tape recorder up to Stevens' stunned face.

Steven's voice rang out loud and clear, from the tiny tape recorder Janet held in front of her. The recorder played back Stevens' instructions regarding Janet's conduct when speaking with white people, to look at their feet when talking with them and so on. Everyone's eyes bulged and their jaws dropped open as if they were on invisible hinges whose screws had come undone. Stevens couldn't believe what she was hearing but it couldn't be denied or unrecorded and she fully recognized the consequences that tape represented and she did the dumbest thing ever. She swung a hay maker punch at the recorder in Janet's hand meaning to smash it to the floor. Janet, who if she had been a second slower, would have seen the recorder punched from her hand into the wall. Seeing the oncoming fist, Janet immediately dropped the recorder from her left hand and caught it smoothly with her right hand. Stevens didn't complicate her thoughts with her actions. Solely concentrating on the tape recorder she had no chance to pull back her blow and instead of smashing the recorder her hand smashed Janet on the side of her face. Janet's head slammed into the wall with a sickening thud and white lights exploded in her head. Somewhere within the mist of those flashing lights she was transported back in time to that same crippling blow rendered to her from her stepfather years ago. Before her thoughts could clear, she was back in the hallway of her old home and the image of Stevens had somehow in her mind transformed into the image of her stepfather and she did as she had done on that long ago day when her stepfather had smashed her head into the stone wall of their hallway. Janet leaped onto Stevens with a crippling blow to her head before the illusion could drift apart. There was pandemonium in the office even before Sharon, the secretaries and especially Stevens knew what was happening and all Janet knew was that she was again fighting her stepfather with all she had. Stevens never stood a chance after the first blow which knocked her across the secretary's desk; scattering pens, papers, desk lamp, telephone and computer keyboard to the floor. Janet was atop of Stevens, the fuse was lit, the dynamite exploded and the beast was loose. Stevens wanted the tape recorder and Janet gave it to her, right in her mouth shattering three of Stevens's front teeth. By the time Sharon pulled her off Stevens's security, the CEO and Assistant CEO and administrative staff had arrived from all around the building. Steven's face was a bloody twisted mask with both eyes swollen shut, busted lip, shattered teeth and in all probability a broken nose and still Janet didn't stop. She was delivering devastating blow after blow to Stevens' face and body. Triple blows for each trip, every step she'd taken in the hot sun that morning. Somewhere in the distance a siren's whoop whoop could be heard getting closer and closer. The security guard forcefully grabbed Janet off Steven's and Sharon shanked her free yelling, "Not her stupid!" She pointed at Stevens yelling "You've got the wrong person. She was assaulted by Stevens! The security guard, a black man, less than a year from retirement, looked from Janet to Stevens. He released his hold on Janet but made no attempt to restrain the Human Resource Manager. He was well aware of Steven's power at the institution and wanted no truck with her. He'd already decided he wasn't about to touch her. "Well I'll be damned!" Sharon said breathing like an exhausted runner. "You aren't going to do your job here are you? Why the hell not?! She assaulted this employee. I witnessed it along with those two secretaries and you aren't going to do anything!" He merely stood there, hands at his sides looking scared and confused and no one could have been more relieved than him when the State Police arrived. After ascertaining what had happened, Janet played the tape for all to hear including the CEO whose face clouded over when she heard what Stevens had said about her. The police asked Janet if she wanted to press charges and Sharon responded "Hell yea!" but was told Janet was the victim, it was her call. Janet said yes and the as the police attempted to cuff Stevens, she fought them like the mad, deranged woman she was and in the process she struck both police officers in the face, kicked and clawed at them leaving long scratches down the faces of both officers. The shit was crazy. Stevens was carried handcuffed, kicking and screaming between the two officers; both bleeding profusely from the face. Before they reached the revolving doors they were stopped by the CEO, Mrs. Klein who stated to Stevens, "Ms. Stevens you are hereby notified, effective immediately that you are terminated for assault on an employee, torment of the employee and racially incensed comments. This order will not be pending on a hearing. You are fired!" She turned to Janet and told her to take a week off with pay. Perhaps as an afterthought, noticing the egg sized lump on the side of Janet's head and told her she would call for an ambulance.

Stevens was charged with assault and battery on Janet Nelson, assault on two police officers, resisting arrest and her job was history. "One down, three to go" Janet was thinking as she began to feel a delayed throbbing in her head where it had struck the wall. "Another dammed tape!" Dunning was thinking, eyeing the bloody recorder on the desk that looked as if a piece of a tooth was imbedded inside its outer cover. Sharon followed his eyes as he reached for the recorder and his hand was batted violently away by Sharon. "Oh know, you're not getting your hands on that!" Sharon said picking up and pocketing the recorder just before stopping herself from saying 'Motherfucker!" She saw Dunning wince as she put the recorder in her pocket. The CEO's offer to go to the hospital was declined by Janet, Sharon would take her. For what we want most there is a price to be paid. Stevens wanted Janet's termination and the price she paid was her own termination with the added bonus of incarceration and a lawsuit against the institution. Stevens didn't get what she wanted but still paid the price.

EIGHTEEN

During the week off Janet she received a letter from Paul Dunning Assistant CEO informing her that prior to returning to work that it was still mandatory that she attend a six week mental health program. From this Janet knew that Stevens and Dunning had been working together and that he knew all about Stevens' actions against her. Sharon wanted Janet to fight it but Janet chose not to because the time away would be a good thing. It would give her the much needed time she'd need for her plans and for resting away from all the drama. She enrolled in a mental health program at the local hospital. The hours were from 8:30 a.m. to 4:30 Monday thru Friday. Janet attended the program but balked at the anti-depressant drugs they pressed on her. Informed that if she didn't take the medications she'd be released from the program Janet complied but palmed the pills whenever she could. She discovered that the program was actually beneficial to her. She talked about the things happening on her job and how they were affecting her. She received good and sound advice on how to deal with the stress, harassment and her fears. One night after a particularly instructive session Janet came home in a very positive mood. Taking the psychologist advice she put her mind to how to make things at the job more tolerable. It was suggested that she sleep on her troubles and a little prayer wouldn't hurt. Asking God for advice and guidance sometimes resulted in answers and that was just what Janet did, she said a prayer before she went to sleep. When she opened her eyes the next morning her dilemma for revenge against Cleese and the others was laid out in her mind as neatly and definitive as a White House dinner party table for visiting dignitaries. It would represent a tremendously, costly and unpleasant challenge to her but in their favor they, at least, would be left with their lives, well sort of anyway. It was strange that she had dreamed the entire plan. It was right there in her head, as dreams go, where everything is viewed from your eyes and the only thing you can't see is yourself. Although it was a simple plan in her mind she realized there

241

would be a lot of work involved, with some bound to be unpleasant. She would need the assistance of another person but not just any person. A person who could be trusted without question and that would be dicey. It would need to be a special person who desperately needed money and who would be willing to literally sleep with the enemy. Yes, that part would be extremely dicey. She had someone in mind but would she do it? It would also involve her doctor with whom she had a good relationship of mutual respect due to her knowledge of medical terminology. He would have to be convinced, unknowingly, to provide her with drugs she couldn't buy over the counter. She'd need a professional designer and lastly, she'd need information and wasn't it just great the things one could learn on the internet. That was where she had to begin and with six weeks off, time was on her side and she was anxious and impatient to get started.

Janet was in the middle of her second week of her mandatory mental health program and had just returned home for the day. Fixing herself a sandwich, she settled down to eat and afterwards promptly fell asleep. She awoke with one thing on her mind and that was to get started on her plans. She booted up her computer and went to Google typing the question 'What injectable drug could be used to render a person unconscious?' She briefly wondered about the security of the internet. Like millions of other people, she believed that somewhere, in some dark underground bunker, there were government workers whose job was to monitor what web sites people contacted. If this wasn't true, why then did all computers have to be registered with FCC (Federal Communications Commission) numbers? With that in mind she had to frame her question delicately. She didn't want to raise any red flags from the FCC. She had toyed with the idea of poison dipped darts after watching a documentary about South American tribes living in the jungles who used poison dipped darts for hunting and against their enemies. The idea fascinated her as she thought about how it could be done, what drugs could be used, where would she get these drugs and how much would be needed. She didn't want to kill anyone, just knock them out for a few hours. She tossed the poison dart idea out as being too complicated. She entered a different question to Google regarding sedations.

Google came back with not only a drug, but its uses, affects, side effects, methods of introduction to the body, length of time a person could possibly remain unconscious and a list of names the drug was prescribed under. That drug was Benzodiazepine and of most interest to Janet was that this drug was most commonly used as a 'Date Rape Drug' and was extremely popular in the United States to facilitate crimes associated with sex or rape. It was mostly used in bars and night clubs where it is slipped into an unsuspecting persons drink. In Europe it was known as 'Liquid Ecstasy' and illegal. If a person accuses another of date rape by use of this drug, in most cases the charge is unsubstantiated because the body eliminates it from the blood in about 8 hours and 12 hours in urine. Benzodiaziazepine came under a variety of names and lengths of time it kept a person unconscious. It's generally used for treatment of anxiety, seizures, panic attacks, and as a sedative and is also used as a general anesthesia before surgeries. Janet read on. The drug differs in how quickly it starts working and how it continued to work in the body. Janet looked through the list of drugs and settled on two particular ones she was familiar with, Halcion and Xanax both of which were short acting with duration of 3 -8 hours, and there were no lasting side effects. She smiled to herself. Her patient would sleep for not less than 3 hours and would awake just fine, physically. After gaining this information she placed a call to her personal physician, Doctor Edmar Lacay and made an appointment. The reason for the appointment she gave as anxiety, panic attacks and insomnia.

Janet had to restrain herself from devoting all her available time to what she was planning. She needed to have patience, to take her time; because many things were involved and she wanted to tackle them as they fit into her plans. She had her victims, her drug of choice and had made arrangements for a doctor visit to get the drug prescribed for her. She didn't think she'd have much of a problem getting him to write a prescription but she'd have to be careful because it was a government controlled drug and any dispensing by a doctor had to be reported to the government. When she met with Dr. Lacay the following week, she told him of the problems she was having on her job and the amount of stress, panic and anxiety she was experiencing and how she couldn't sleep. Dr. Lacay had been Janet's physician for years. She was one of favorite patients. He found her to be humorous, intelligent and he was impressed with her knowledge of medical terminology. She was diagnosed, as expected, with anxiety, stress and insomnia and subject to panic attacks. They discussed several drugs but he felt drugs weren't needed, although there were several over the counter drugs she could take to help her sleep. He recommended two good psychiatrists who could do much more for her issues. She needed professional counselling not drugs. Out the door went her drug of choice and her plan. Prior to the appointment, Janet had given thought to the possibility of not being given a prescription for the drug she needed for her revenge. Just in case she had come up with an alternative to the use of that drug and she broached the subject of her new interest with Dr. Lacay and asked him about Viagra. She wanted to know how it worked, its side effects and who could use it. Dr. Lacay found no problem with her change of subject. She always asked him numerous questions about diseases, treatments and causes. He explained that Viagra works for men with erectile dysfunction by increasing the blood flow to the penis so a man can get and keep an erection hard enough for sex, although results may vary. It usually starts to work within 30-60 minutes after digestion but it should only be taken when needed. It only works when a man is already sexually stimulated and should be taken at least 4 hours before sexual activity. There's no need to rush. After sex the erection should go away. There have been rare occasions of erections lasting 4 hours called Priapism but if this happens get medical help to avoid long-term injury to the penis. Viagra can cause side effects but are rarely reported such as sudden vision loss in one or both eyes, decreased or total hearing loss. "Basically it is a safe narcotic if not abused and we both know you're not going to abuse anyone, right?" he laughed and she laughed with him, "Of course not." "Why are you interested in Viagra?" he asked. Janet responded that she was writing a book where a woman was being sexually harassed by her boss. When the woman rejected the boss's advances he had her demoted and was trying to fire her. The woman out for revenge planned to get back at him through the use of Viagra. She continued asking, "If you gave someone too many pills would it kill them?" Dr. Lacay looked at her with new interest and shock saying none too kindly, "I'm not going to tell you how to kill someone!" Janet laughed saying she needed the information for her book. In truth she did want to write a book and would in the distant future write about these things and months later she would show Dr. Lacay her completed manuscript. He'd find himself a character in her book along with their conversation included in its pages and that he was listed on the dedication page. Janet thanked him for the information and as she prepared to leave the examination room she noticed he was looking at her strangely and eased his mind saying, "When I finish the manuscript I promise you'll be the first to see it. They shook hands as they usually did when they parted and Janet left for home laughing to herself at Dr. Lacay's imaginings that she was going to kill someone but was he imagining?

Janet next turned her attention to her twin sister of which she, of course, did not have and clones were currently scientifically out of the question. She questioned 'Google' "Where can a person get a mask that is a true replica of a person?" Google produced a page on a company called 'Doppelganger Face Mask' Terrifyingly Real. Japanese firm (surprise, surprise) will create an Ultra Realistic copy of your face in mask form. Exact replicas of faces down to the minute pores on the face and veins on their eyes lids can be produced for $4,920 and an entire head replica for $6,875 U.S. dollars with an option for additional face and head copies priced between $780 to $1,960 dollars. Janet emailed 'Doppelganger Face Mask' requesting additional information informing them that she wished to have an exact replication of made of a person and one produced from a photograph. She was informed that both were possible and that the company had two studios, one in Japan and another in Washington D.C. She chose the latter and booked a round trip train reservation to Washington for Friday evening after her counselling session. Arriving in Washington that evening she secured a hotel room and settled down. Her appointment with Doppelganger was scheduled for 10:00 a.m. Saturday morning. When she arrived at the studio for the appointment she wasn't disappointed. Frankly she was amazed. They showed her around the studio and the process used to create mask. She saw mask of the employees that were so terrifyingly real in their detail that they were creepy. She sat down with the artist and discussed what she wanted done. It would be no problem other than cash of front, no checks or credit cards were accepted and when did she want to begin. Her total cost for two full masks would be approximately $15,000 dollars. Her trust fund money would absorb that easily. On herself she wanted to start in three weeks but she'd be leaving photos of Dick Kahn, Employee Relations Officer for immediate production. She had special plans for him that would take Dunning out at the same time. She already had an idea of what she planned to put in motion and Kahn would be her star player with Dunning as best supporting actor. But one thing at a time, "Take it one step at a time!" she admonished herself.

Janet would need a discrete listening device that would allow for two-way transmissions and she was stumped, until one night while watching television she was startled and ecstatic when what she needed presented itself. She was watching a show with three female investigators who were at a party and were able to listen and communicate with each other through a device they called a 'Molar Mike'. Janet leaped up, went to her computer and Google. She typed the question, 'Is there such a thing as a molar microphone?' And bingo; the Molar Microphone with two-way transmission did exist! Bluetooth and the military had developed such a device that was installed over the back molar of the teeth acting as a transmitter and a discreet ear piece that was the receiver. The device could be purchased at most electronic stores for less than $100. All the chickens were coming home to roost. She now had everything she needed for her plan of revenge. Everything that is except a willing assistant and there was only one kind of assistant who would do - a prostitute!

Prostitutes strolling alone or in groups were as common and expected as the local bus coming every 20 minutes on Howard Street. The street was a monument to destitution. Its tall brick buildings were dark and intimidating and their outside steps were always inhabited with drunks, cigarette smoking teenagers, pregnant mothers and drug addicts and somewhere inside the buildings jive music played on and on. Its sidewalks were littered with overflowing garbage cans, broken glass and strolling prostitutes. If you didn't see one or more of them walking back and forth, up and down you wondered, in a distracted sort of way, where they were that day. They didn't have or celebrate holidays and like the mailman they came through in the rain, sleet, snow, hail and especially dark of night. On days of inclement weather they weren't allow to wear weather protective gear, it hid the merchandise. Only an umbrella was acceptable to their pimps and on really cold evenings they could wear coats as long as they weren't closed or buttoned. The surprise of seeing girls Janet had gone to high school with on the stroll with had long since worn off. The women were a rag tag bunch, some of whom whose beauty was marred by old fading bruises and others with fresh glowing splotches on their faces to match their black eyes and busted lips. Sometimes, Janet wondered what had happened to bring them to this sad and sorry state of affairs and then the question dismissed itself from her mind as insignificantly as a tree in the park. She was on a mission, had been for almost two weeks now, night after night, sitting in her car watching the woman walking pass. Some of them bending into the car to see if she was a prospective customer and then moving on. There was no shame in their game. Despite their lot in life, they were basically a cheerful group, laughing, catcalling greetings to their peers, regular and prospective customers. Janet was looking for one particular woman, Bonnie Adelson. Bonnie had been among the popular crowd in high school. A cheerleader, in fact, with blemish free golden skin, long, dark, straight hair (like hers) a tiny lithe dancer's body (like hers) and was practically engaged to the captain of the football team. Bonnie Adelson was one of the girls plain girls wished to be; who wore leather coats, leather loafer shoes, all the best outfits, had their hair done weekly at the beauty parlor and wouldn't be caught dead in a pair of sneakers unless they were in gym class or cheering. Janet didn't see Bonnie in the passing groups but she knew she would show eventually. She was again, sitting in her car one night when she happened to glance across the street and saw Bonnie on the ground getting repeatedly slapped by her pimp, who in another life had been her high school boyfriend, James Canter, captain of the football team. She felt bad for Bonnie but pushed those feelings aside. She had business to do and her business was with Bonnie. She needed Bonnie to want her as badly as she needed Bonnie. It was for that very reason that she chose her. She wanted her help; as much as wanting to help her.

Over fifteen years ago, $473.740.00 (the result of the law suit against the Board of Education) had been placed in a trust fund for Janet which was untouchable for fifteen years. The trust matured, and with fifteen years of interest behind it; it gave her a very hefty bank account and give or take a few $100.000 she was just shy of being a millionaire. The money was released to her four months ago and as of yet she hadn't touched a dime of the money accept to purchase her red sports car. Earlier she had made many withdrawals and the majority would be for Bonnie Adelson, if, and only if, she could persuade her to accept the terms. The night was warm and the street lit only by two street lamps and the lighted apartments on the block. The area of the block where Bonnie was being beaten for some imagined rule breaking was lit only from a partial light from an apartment in the building. Bonnie and the pimp were on the edge of the shadows, barely visible from the street. The boyfriend/pimp left Bonnie after a final kick in her thigh to pick herself up and stagger up the street to her corner. Janet had never seen a sadder sight as Bonnie limped up the street, her long hair surrounding and hiding her face. She was oblivious to all around her. Janet waited until the boyfriend/pimp pulled off in his car before she made a U-Turn and pulled up along the side of the woman bleeding from her nose and mouth. Bonnie never looked at the driver of the car, just opened the passenger side door and got in and the car pulled away from the curb.

Bonnie sat quietly in the passenger seat with her head hung low and her long hair covering her face. Blood was dripping onto the short, dingy, yellow mini-skirt that she wore. Janet drove on up Springfield Avenue to the shopping Center. Parking the car she said, "Wait here." and got out. It was Bonnie's first realization that the driver was a woman but from force of habit and beatings, she remained seated in the car. A woman's money was just as spendable as a man's. Janet went into a clothing store and purchased a sweat suit, under garments, socks and guessing at her shoe size a pair of sneakers. She returned, started up the car and after a few blocks turned onto the New Jersey Garden State Parkway. Seeing this, Bonnie rose a little from her stupor and became a little alarmed. She was being kidnapped! Ordinarily panic would ensue but Bonnie was so beaten down and worn out she said nothing. After about 30 minutes on the Parkway, headed south, Janet spoke, "Bonnie, you may not remember me but I'm Janet, Janet Nelson. We went to Grant High School together. You were a cheerleader and that person back there was your boyfriend James Canter. Bonnie's head slowly lifted and she turned puffy eyes toward Janet. It was all Janet could do to hold back her own tears at the look of hopelessness and despair in Bonnie's eyes. Bonnie didn't recognize Janet right away but was curious, "Where are we going?" she asked noticing they were leaving the Parkway and entering the NJ Turnpike. "For you," Janet replied, "A place away from this life and a new beginning in the state of Delaware." Bonnie began to cry bullet hard tears and Janet didn't interrupt but was thinking, *Go on and cry. Cry until your tears are done. No more harm will come to you and on that you can trust and believe.* Janet thought fiercely to herself as they drove south under the setting sun.

After exit four, Janet pulled over into a rest stop to get something to eat and for Bonnie to change out of the hooker clothes. After changing, they ordered meals and took them outside to the picnic area to eat. Bonnie said, "I do remember you, kind of. You were that little girl in our gym class that everyone picked on weren't you?" and then she admitted ashamedly, that she too had bullied Janet but only once. "Yea, that was me." "What's this all about?" Bonnie asked again stuffing fries in her mouth. The meal was a banquet to her. Janet replied, "Eat now, I'll tell you in the car." Finishing up, they got back on the road. As they approached the toll booth for the Delaware Memorial Bridge Bonnie was quiet and thoughtful. Looking out over the expanse of the Delaware River, under the glow of the setting sun, Bonnie was entranced at the beauty of the dark, slow moving river. "Beautiful isn't it?" Janet asked and Bonnie agreed. As she watched the lazy river waters flowing by she was assimilating all that Janet was telling her about herself, the entire story of what was happening to her on her job, her plan for fighting back, where and how she, Bonnie, factored into the picture, what would be expected of her and the compensation she would receive. Bonnie was speechless but willing to be on board. She'd agree to almost anything to be free from her past. She hoped deep inside that Janet would keep her promise and as if reading her mind Janet said, "Don't worry all will be as I said; if you agree." They drove on in silence.

After crossing the Delaware Memorial Bridge, Janet took the exit for Newark, Delaware. They drove on for about 20 minutes when she turned into a gated community. Inserting a card into the slot, the gates opened and they drove through. There were arrows pointing to three separate sections of apartments. Janet headed to section B. They exited the car and

Bonnie followed Janet, half limping, up the walk way to an apartment. She entered a series of numbers on the alarm pad, the light turned green and she inserted a key into the door's lock. As they entered the apartment, Janet turned on the light and Bonnie, looking around at the beautifully decorated room asked, "Is this your apartment?" After closing and locking the door, Janet reached into her purse, pulled out a thick envelope marked Bonnie Adelson on it and said, "No. It's yours." Janet replied handing her the envelope and a small box and she walked into the kitchen turning on the lights. Bonnie stood stunned as she looked after Janet and with trembling fingers she opened the envelope. She pulled out a sheaf of folded papers which indeed named her as the owner of apartment B-12 with the rent paid in advance for one year. Attached to the lease were confirmation letters from the electric, gas, phone and cable companies each had been credited with $1000 in Bonnie's name. There was a contract from T-Mobile for a Smart phone; also paid in advance for one year and another envelope that contained many $100 dollar bills. Dropping down on the plush brown sofa, Bonnie read the astonishing documents twice and then laid them down on a beautiful, smoked glass living room table and opened the box. It contained a top of the line T Mobile Smart phone. Janet called from the kitchen asking if she knew how to operate that thing because she sure didn't. She preferred her little old fashioned cell phone that did nothing but make and accept calls. She hadn't bothered to figure out how to send texts or go on line with the thing. "If you find your phone number in that thing, remember to give it to me before I leave." Janet said from the kitchen.

Janet returned from the kitchen with two glasses of white wine and tuna fish sandwiches while Bonnie was again re-reading the incredible documents. She handed a glass to Bonnie and as they sat down Janet picked up the remote control box and turned on the 65' inch Smart television. Neither one of them watched the television. They simply talked for almost two hours. Finally, Janet stood up, picked up her purse and headed for the door. "You're leaving?" Bonnie asked softly. She was still swooning over what was happening to her. It was all so incredible. Janet told Bonnie yes because she wanted her to be alone for a few days and feel what could become her new life, to explore the apartment, absorb the freedom and wonder at the possibilities this new life afforded her. Bonnie had mentioned during their talk that she'd like to return to college. Janet looked closely at Bonnie, "You need to decide if this is what you'd want to have, a new beginning, a fresh start. Bear in mind that a new beginning would mean that you could have absolutely no contact with anyone from your old life. You can't blend the old with the new. Ask yourself these things while soaking in a nice hot bubble bath if you can completely cut that life loose." She told Bonnie it was also for her protection. If no one from your past knew where you were your future couldn't be threatened. You have no children, your parents moved to the Deep South years ago. You have no ties back there. Janet didn't say but the price of it all was kind of – no it was shitty; but it was a onetime deal that involved nothing illegal or anything she wasn't familiar with and nothing she'd ever have to do again. Janet left, saying she'd return in two days. Once in her car and heading for home; she'd already decided that if Bonnie didn't want to pay the price she would let her keep what was already given to her anyway.

Bonnie stood in the doorway watching Janet drive off in the red sports car and then went back inside. She stood stunned and speechless looking around the living room with its plush, flowered sofa and love seat, the three matching smoke glassed tables, table lamps, the huge television, the computer desk (computer and printer included) book shelves and paintings on the walls and plush carpeting beneath her feet. She wandered into the bedroom and gasped at the large cannonball bedroom set with its dressers, night tables, tall wardrobe and floor length mirror. The walls were painted light lavender and the floor was plush with thick purple carpeting. Going into the bathroom she found a large, deep round tub, floor length mirror and shower. She found the linen closet stacked with sheets, blankets, thick towels, wash cloths and all sorts of body powders, soaps, shampoos and lotions. Bonnie felt like Alice in Wonderland as she returned to the living room and entered the kitchen. There was an island in the center of the floor and overhead a set of three globed lights. The cabinets were packed with food as well as the refrigerator and freezer. Cabinets were full of dishes, bowels and food containers. The lower cabinets contained every sort of pot and pan that she could imagine. The stove and refrigerator were a matched ivory set and as she opened the door off from the kitchen she discovered a washer and dryer. Another door opened onto a garage where there sat a blue convertible car and attached to the windshield was an envelope. Bonnie opened the envelope which contained registration and insurance papers made out to Bonnie Adelson and two sets of keys. Bonnie dropped the papers and keys and stumbled backwards out of the garage, through the laundry room, kitchen and living room and ran into the bathroom as her stomach heaved and she vomited into the toilet. Afterwards, looking in the mirror at herself she could see that her puffy eyes would be swollen soon. Her cracked dry lips still bore several small scabs. Her complexion looked dark and bruised; her eyes ghostly and her long hair which was dingy with dirt. Tears began in her eyes which she quickly wiped. Was this real? She simply couldn't believe it. She turned on the tubs faucets making the water steaming hot. Having several choices of bath salts, she chose a lavender scented container and poured almost half of it in the tub. This she followed with two bottles Aloe Vera mineral water. She stripped off the clothes and stood naked before the floor length mirror. Her shock was profound. Her body was a caricature of her over nine years on the street as a prostitute. Her body wasn't emancipated but looked well on its way. That last kick to her leg from her pimp was blossoming and would be black and blue by tomorrow. There were other bruises and scratches about her arms, stomach and legs and when she turned around looking over her shoulder she saw the same signs of abuse and neglect over her back. Bonnie closed her eyes to the sight, walked over to the tub with its mounds of perfumed bubbles and steam and stepped into the hot water. She continue to let the water run until she was submerged up to her shoulders and then turned it off. Her skin was stinging from the bruises and scratches as she submerged her entire body; head included, under the hot bubbly water. Six hours ago, after being beaten, she had been limping into a night of nameless sex for money and now she was here; in another State, in her own apartment, soaking in a scented, soothing tub of water. It was unbelievable but true. She cupped a hand full of bubbles, squashing their light foamy texture through her fingers still not believing. It was then that the tears came, hot, scalding bullets that wouldn't stop. They came in torrents and she let them come. She remained soaking in the tub for over an hour and when she emerged her hair was as squeaky clean as her body. The dirt, grime and tears leaving a telltale ring around the tub. She cleaned the tub and then turned on the shower full blast with cold water and stepped into it. When she finished she dried herself with a thick terry clothed towel, blow dried her long hair and nude she climbed exhausted and amazed into the huge bed beneath its cool sheets and fell instantly asleep having no thoughts or dreams, only thanks to God for sending Janet Nelson.

When Janet returned five days later, she was greeted by a grateful, cleaned up Bonnie Adelson wearing the same sweat suit Janet had purchased for her the night she picked her up off the street. Aside from the darkness around her eyes and fading bruises on her arms and legs, she was still a strikingly beautiful young woman. Bonnie hugged Janet with no intentions of letting her go until Janet laughing pried herself from her embrace. Bonnie cooked breakfast for them in her first ever apartment and they talked about nothing of importance. Afterwards, Janet took Bonnie clothes shopping at the Mall. At one of the stores Janet pointed out a sign that read 'Hiring for sales person' "Why don't you apply for the job." she said to Bonnie who was way ahead of her asking for the manager. The manger fit the cliché of "Tall, dark and handsome" to a tee and it seemed to be love at first sight for both of them. He took Bonnie into his office and although he found himself attracted to her, he was impressed with her knowledge of accounting and he hired her on the spot for his accounting office instead of sales clerk asking when she could start. Bonnie explained that she'd just moved to Delaware two days ago from out of state and still had a few loose ends to tie up and another trip back to her old home. Would starting in two weeks be a problem she had asked hopefully? Although the manager was drowning in her grey eyes he managed to tell her that would be fine. He was alarmed when tears welled up in her eyes. He jumped up, offering her some tissues which she accepted from a box on his desk. Wiping her eyes she apologized saying she was just overwhelmed with the move and the need to find a job and now she had one. It seemed a miracle to her. Everything that was happening to her was a miracle sent from heaven. The manager gave her all the necessary forms to fill out. It was the first W-2 form she'd ever filled out. She was embarrassed when she asked if she could go out and speak with her friend because she couldn't remember her new address. He laughed and sent her off. Bonnie ran into Janet's arms telling her she had a job but didn't know her address. Janet laughed and gave her the address of her new home. After completing the job application they continued shopping for clothes for Bonnie. Bonnie was on cloud nine and Janet was circling even higher because all the pieces were now in place. She was ready to act. All that was left was for her to do was to make arrangements for the mask to be made, pick up the listening device and a few other things including two packs of printing paper.

Janet went to the Washington based Doppleganger Masks Company for the making of the mask; the sitting took almost four hours. She sat in a large chair with neck and back supports wearing an off shoulder hospital gown and her face had been scrubbed squeaky clean and air dried. Just off the side of her vision was a large white screen, several computers with their own screens, some sort of tripod holding what looked like a laser camera was aimed at her face and when the camera thing was turned on her face appeared on the white screen. A thin, red line that stretched from her tip of her hair line to down to the hollow of her throat appeared. The red line traced its way maddeningly slow across her face and the image of her face was being etched onto the two computer screens and the large white screen. This process was done twice and then twice more only this time with her eyes closed and her mouth open. Images were also taken of both sides of her face and again with her eyes closed and her mouth open. The same process was completed twice on the back and top of Janet's head. In one, her head was held erect and then with her head bowed. The technician explained that the additional pictures of her mouth open and eyes closed was because the mask's eyes and mouth must be able to accommodate eye and mouth movements in a realistic manner. He explained that a caster mold would be made from the laser pictures on the screen and finally the mask would be made from the cast. The entire process took almost four hours and barring any difficulties, the mask would be ready in 2-3 weeks. Janet returned to her hotel room, packed and took the train home. The next day she went to Best Buy to purchase the Molar Microphone listening device and was told it would have to be ordered and would take a week. While in there she purchased two packs of printing paper (equally one thousand sheets) a flash drive and a digital camera. She went home and began to sketch an outline of a script for Bonnie. There were only twelve words on the script. The rest were all actions. She drew a pretty good representation of her victim's office. She outlined the placement of the desks, the file cabinets, the waist high counters that lined two of the four office walls. She diagramed where the coffee machine, printers and even the coat racks were in the office. She paid special attention to the four large curtained windows that looked out as well as into the office. On a separate paper she drew a representation of the outer office lobby with special note of the bathroom door that was directly next to the office door and the two lockable doors, one that led to the outside and the other that led to the work area. She looked at her work and saw that it was good. Two months had gone by before she contacted Bonnie Adelson again.

When Janet rang Bonnie up at the security gate of her apartment complex, Bonnie answered and heard Janet's voice and immediately buzzed her through the mechanical gate and was standing outside on her steps impatiently waiting for Janet. As Janet's car pulled up Bonnie ran over to it and before Janet could get out of the car good she was wrapped in Bonnie's arms and dragged into the apartment. Before Janet could say anything Bonnie was off and running chattering a mile a minute. "Slow down girl." Janet laughed, "I can't keep up. So what's going on girl?" Bonnie didn't know where to begin so she started by holding up her new driver's license and college identification card. She was working at the store in the accounting department and she'd enrolled in the university pursuing a master's in accounting at night and best of all she'd had a marriage proposal from her boss. Janet was genuinely thrilled for her and proud that she had helped take Bonnie off the streets and into this new life that she could have only imagined until she'd met Janet. The knowledge of a marriage proposal had however surprised her. It had never occurred to her that something like that would come into play. After small talk over a glass of wine, Bonnie ventured on the reason for Janet's visit. "Is it time?" she asked and Janet nodded yes.

"When do we start?" Bonnie asked excitedly. Janet responded that she didn't know what Bonnie's schedule was but a tentative date would be next Thursday evening. Bonnie replied that was no problem and if it was, and if she had to, she'd rearrange the world's orbit around the sun for Janet. Janet laughed saying that wouldn't be necessary but we must talk about what I need you to do. "Nothing you ask of me would be too much Janet."

Bonnie said taking Janet's hands with tears in her eyes causing Janet to tear up too. Janet began to feel just a tiny bit unclean about the deal that she'd made with Bonnie. Could she, with a clear conscience, insist that Bonnie keep up her end of the bargain when there was a wedding in Bonnie's future? For Bonnie, it would be an awful thing to insist that she carry out the terms of their arrangement. What would it do to Bonnie's conscience, going through with this thing and afterwards to her new husband? The very thought was causing Janet to feel a little disgusted with herself? She tried to reason with herself that a bargain was a bargain, but... She looked over at Bonnie's beautiful, happy face and she saw the new woman that she had created in her desire for revenge. She'd taken a dirty, bruised and abused prostitute off the street and transformed her into this beautiful young woman sitting across from her. Bonnie's long hair was a shiny raven's black and hung in thick tresses about her face and cascaded down her back. The haunted look was gone from her grey eyes; as well as the harsh lines of a face that had faced too much reality filled with nameless sex, abuse and defeat. Her copper colored skin was blemish free and glowing. All signs of physical and mental abuse were gone from her face and body. She had made a metamorphic rebirthing into the beautiful woman sitting next to her and now Janet would be re-tarnishing this new butterfly, returning it to its cocoon of defilement, corruption and ruination. A slow panoramic moving picture of what her plans for Bonnie entailed began playing in her mind and she shuddered, dropped her head in shame and a tear rolled down her cheek and splashed onto Bonnie's hands which were holding hers. Looking dry eyed at Janet, Bonnie got up, went into the bathroom and came back with a beautiful green terry cloth washcloth (curtesy of Janet). She gently cupped Janet's face in one hand and wiped the traces of the tears from her face. "Janet, for what we want most, there is a cost to be paid and I will pay, no matter what the cost is; I will pay it. You must not feel bad that the time has come, that I must do my part and you must on no account feel bad about what I must do. We made a deal and a deal it shall remain." She hugged Janet to her and let her cry on her shoulder. Thinking about the changes in her life over the last months, looking around with pride at her beautiful apartment and the stack of college books on her desk next to the brand new computer Bonnie hugged Janet even closer and whispered, "Thank you." in her ear and began crying herself.

When they parted, their tears reduced to sniffles, Bonnie wiped both their faces with the washcloth, got up, walked into the kitchen and threw the washcloth in the garbage and said in a determined voice, "There's an end to your conscience and mine! Now down to business. When you originally made this offer to me you said that there would be one thing I would have to do in exchange for what you've done for me. You said that the one thing was nothing that I wasn't familiar with and that I would only have to do it once. I've thought about your words often and have concluded that the one thing you needed me to do that I was already familiar with was sex. I wondered what type of sexual situation it would fall under, you know. Would I have to participate in a threesome or an orgy or would I be a gift to someone or perhaps perform in a movie? The possibilities are almost quite endless. So which is it?" Bonnie asked and Janet told her. Bonnie's eyes stretched wider and wider as Janet went on unveiling her plan and when she finished Bonnie fell back screaming with laughter that was contagious and Janet found herself caught up in the hilarity and they both sat there seeming as if someone was beating them over the head with a goofy stick. It was a while before their laughter tapered off into cramped stomachs. After settling down and over a glass of wine, Janet went into the details surrounding her plan. It was not only unbelievable but it was a work of genius and Bonnie understood why it would take time to put it all together and she was down with the get down. If she wasn't an actual participant, she would have paid to just be there and watch. However, that particular part was already taken.

Barton Cleese, Director of Unit Five, was alone locked in his office with orders not to be disturbed. It was 8 p.m. and he was working late due to State inspections. Once a year, the State Department of Human Services unleashed a team of plank faced inspectors to converge on its institution across the State and spend as many days as necessary to find anything wrong with anything. They inspected everything from the maintenance of the grounds up to the safety of the buildings. Their ultimate goal was to find anything that would make it possible for the State to reduce its funding to the institution. Every building had to pass these inspections or funding and high positions would be lost. Directors were (if the inspectors were in a good mood and seldom were) sometimes allowed to make corrections before the inspection team left. Everybody knew which buildings didn't pass inspection because the inspection team called a huge meeting called an 'Exit Summary' where they called by name the Director's name and buildings that didn't pass. It was a time of high anxiety at the institution and it wasn't unusual for Directors to work late into the night checking and rechecking their buildings, documentations, spending, medical charts, living arrangements, diets, medications, client personal items, the list was endless and Barton Cleese, Janet's former Director was not only responsible for four buildings he was wishing he had Janet Nelson. She had been gone well over a year and he needed her expertise while still longing for her sex. Just the thought of her caused unwanted throbbing in his groin. After that disastrous hearing years ago; he had released his full fury against her and nothing would satisfy him other than her termination at his hands, yet he still longed for her sexually, stilled dreamed lustful fantasies about her. Professionally, he couldn't deny her lost was a liability for she was fantastic at her job. If he hadn't had her demoted (twice) it wouldn't have been necessary for him to be pulling this overtime. With her he was assured and confident that everything would be spotless, correct and in order, but....

The knock at his door broke his concentration and increased his migraine headache, "Who is it?" He growled. After having specifically left instructions not to be disturbed he got angrily up from his desk when there was no answer. He stomped angrily to the door, unlocked it and when he opened it he was stunned to see Janet standing there. Her hair was loose and draped down her back. She was wearing a black lace choker around her neck that had little bells suspended from its edges. Her caramel colored shoulders were bare and she wore a tight black tank top which was hard put to hide her erect nipples and her torso was bare all the way down to the beginning curve of her hips which were encased in a short black, matching spandex micro mini skirt. He noted (and he didn't know why) that the zipper of the skirt zipped upwards from her thighs instead of down from her torso. He just stood there staring at her as she stepped pass him into his office wearing screaming, black, three inch stiletto heels, leaving a thick scent of the sweetest smelling ambrosia widening his nose. She closed the door behind her.

Janet stood facing him as he turned around. She was a fantasy real, standing there before him and he couldn't think but the long denied demon in his pants was making its thoughts known. Then she walked into to him, up close and personal, placed one sweet smelling arm about the back of his neck, pulled his head down and kissed him softly parting his lips with her tongue as her other hand slid down the front of his pants and cupped the growing bulge between his legs. He was lost in the scent of her perfume, the touch of her hand on the back of his head and her soft lips. The softness of her scented lips and the tantalizingly caressing of her hand down there had him teetering on his tippy toes and his brain fogged over. The kiss was long and deep, lasting perhaps over two minutes, he didn't know. She pulled back from him and led him over to the counter below the windows with her back to him. The drapes were closed and she parted them a little and looking up at the moon said, "It's a beautiful night isn't?" He could only mutter, "Huh?" He was standing behind her at the counter and she reached behind her taking both of his hands and brought them around to the front of her body pressed back against him. She placed one of his hands around her bare waist and the other beneath her skirt and he discovered there was nothing between his fingers and her moist sex and he exploded in his pants as she wiggled seductively against him making slow firm circles, dipping up and down against him. Cleese became filled with animal lust for her and was unplugging himself from the reality of the world around him one incoherent thought at a time. His face held the expression of a man careening out of control out of the blue and into the black velvet realm of mindless lust and there were no stop signs! His heart was no longer in his chest but was in his throat making it difficult to breathe as the force of his first organism nearly drove him to his knees. Janet barely let him catch his breath before she placed her hands over his hand under her skirt, felt for his long finger and pushed it up inside of her and began moving slowly up and down on the deeply buried appendage. Squeezing her muscles around his finger she leaned her head back against his shoulder and he crushed her mouth with his in a long wet sloppy kiss. Janet pulled back from his mouth a little and just before she sucked his tongue deep into her throat she tilted her head to the side and whispered, "I want my job back Barton." "Job, Job?" he stammered into her mouth. "I want my job back." she panted as she turned around freeing an upset finger from deep inside her moist heat and in one motion had his pants unzipped, his throbbing member out and firmly, tightly, sucked deep into her mouth. Cleese, struck with paralysis rose up on his toes. When he regained some semblance of movement he found he was back peddling away from Janet's insistent lips wrapped securely to the hilt around his penis; while simultaneously gripping the back of her head and shoving himself as hard and deep as he could deep into her wet velvety mouth. To stop him from both falling and moving backwards out of her control, Janet suddenly snatched his boxers down and securely gripped both sides of his hairy buttocks and pressed him ever more tightly into the unrelenting grip of her mouth, sucking him in deeper and deeper until she herself couldn't breathe. She placed her hands between his upper thighs and pulled his legs apart giving him a firm ground to stand on. Janet stood up, turned around, bent over and guided him inside of her from behind and he didn't need any encouragement, his hips knew what to do. He began slamming so hard up into her she was lifted up at each thrust and in response made it her business to come down hard and brutal against his thighs. He gripped her on both sides of her waist and was lost and didn't feel her pulling him across the office between thrust. Janet placed her hands on the top of the counter in front of the coffee machine. She arched her back and over her shoulder asked him if he wanted a hot cup of coffee or her. He chooses both and he closed his eyes and allowed himself to drown in her heat and moisture while she made two cups of coffee while he continued to thrust inside of her. He never saw her remove a small packet from under her breast and pour blue powder (crushed Viagra pills) into his cup and if he had it wouldn't have mattered. Only the heat mattered, only the squeezing pressure on his penis was important and both the heat and the pressure was increasing, becoming unendurable and he ejaculated for the second time deep inside her. He was gasping for breath but this didn't matter to Janet for she intended to get her job back through his penis. While he was shuddering deep inside of her, Janet back walked them both across the office and still inside of her they collapsed into his chair. He was still inside her as she handed him the Viagra laced cup of coffee. As he sipped the volatile mix she took his other hand and placed it over her sex and slipped in one of his fingers next to his softening penis and pressed it up inside of her. He gasped and sucked down the remainder of the coffee. Janet stood up, feeling the thickness of him sliding out of her and sat facing him, legs slightly parted, on his desk. She opened his desk drawer where she knew he kept packets of wet wash sheets. She pulled out several sheets of the moist tissues and began to slowly clean him off with slow erotic tenderness. He'd never felt anything like it. Sitting on top of his desk, Janet spread her legs and began to slowly clean herself. Combining the Viagra with the hot coffee speeded up the transmission into his body; as she noticed his semi deflated penis began to make small jerking motions back into readiness and she smiled to herself. Now was the time to see if she really had him by the balls. She took the longest finger of his hand and began sucking and caressing it with her tongue while his head fell back and he moaned in ecstasy, his penis jerking more firmly. Janet took his finger out of her mouth and opening her legs wide as she could she slid the finger inside of her and began masturbating on it. There had been lights flashing all around him since being led over to the coffee machine but he paid them no mind feeling it was all part of the amazing thing that was happening to him here and now. As she touched herself with his finger she leaned over, kissed him and asked him if we wanted to kiss her there? "Where?" he breathed with his eyes closed. "Here." Janet whispered and indicating the spot with his wet finger and he needed no more questions or instructions. He spread her legs even wider, pulled his chair up to the edge of the desk, lowered his head and stuck his tongue inside of her. Perhaps it was a special scent down there, Janet didn't know but once he started he was like a mad man, sucking, kissing and probing her with his tongue. Janet who had so far remained aloof from these proceedings found herself becoming aroused as she felt his thick tongue caressing up one side of her clitoris and then down the other. She lifted her hips and began a smooth gyration of her slender hips to the motions of his mouth and tongue and found that it felt good. He was so soft and tender with her that for a moment her resolve weakened she began responding to his touch; then caught herself. *Uh huh that's not the way things are supposed to be.* she said to herself and she turned her feelings off with a single thought. To regain control of the situation and her own growing lustiness Janet pulled his head away from between her legs. She looked at his face and felt a creepy shudder go through her. His face shined and glistened with the juices from her body and it seemed she couldn't take her eyes away from the drops of moisture clinging to his mustache. They made her shudder in disgust. She pushed everything off his desk and indicated she wanted him on top of her. Cleese stepped out of his pants which up to that point had been crumpled around his ankles. He climbed up onto the desk and inside Janet and was lost again in the heat of her. It seemed to him that the more he thrust inside of her the more sensitive, hotter and harder his penis seemed to be getting. He felt himself on the verge of his third organism, something that was only a fond memory of his teenage years. His muscles bulged with strength, his heart was thrumming along at an easy but increased rate and he felt like a bull elephant in musk. He could go on forever. His thinking now was that he didn't want to come. He grabbed Janet off the desk and pushed her back up against the closed door. Lifting one of her legs up to his shoulder he was momentarily distracted and turned on even more by the black stiletto heels of her shoes as he slipped inside of her again and again until it felt like his knees were about to buckle and his third orgasm burst from him in a teeth chattering explosion and still his penis was rock hard. He backed out of her and laid coats on the floor. He laid Janet gently down, lifted both of her legs over each side of his shoulders and all he could think between the flashing lights was that she was wide open to him and fell into her and darkness. Their erotic actions were performed all over his office in positions he'd only dreamed of and he came for the fourth, fifth and sixth time. During all the over the top lust of Cleese's fantasies come to life, he began repeatedly telling Janet that she had her job back. Later he amended this with the inclusion of a clause that they agreed that they could do it again. Janet replied that she had no intention of being his mistress, that was out but she did agreed that they could get together exactly six and only more times and then it was over. Cleese not only agreed, he gave Janet the keys to the Head Supervisor's office and told her she could start the following morning. "When will you notify personnel of my reinstatement?" Janet asked again tilting her head to the side. "In the morning," Cleese breathlessly stammered, "Personnel is closed now but first thing in the morning when you come in come straight to my office." After a few moments Janet inquired, "Is that a promise or a lie?" Janet asked sucking his penis deep into her mouth. "A promise, I promise; yes, yes, yes!" Cleese exclaimed as he climaxed for the seventh time.

When all was said and done the office, Cleese and Janet were set to rights. He walked her on unsteady legs to the door with a final squeeze of her ass. "I'll see you in the morning." he smiled wearily, "Bright and early there's a lot of work to be done for the inspections." "I'll be here." Janet said and stood there momentarily, her head slightly tilted as if she was listening for something. Then she turned and left the office. She opened the front door and walked out into the night. Cleese, supporting himself on the outside door, watched her walk away greedily eyeing her behind and her long legs ending in the shiny, black, stiletto heels. Once she was out of sight he returned to his desk and sat down as if there wasn't an ounce of energy let in his body and it was the truth. Looking at his watched he noted it had been over an hour and a half since Janet first appeared at his door deliciously interrupting his work. He didn't bother trying to go back to the work; he just slumped down in his chair reliving all that had impossibly happened. His mind darted from episode to episode, never completely viewing each act before moving on to the next. Finally he got his belongings together, locked his office door and walked out into the night still tingling from his encounter and the happy thought that there'd be much more than the six more meetings agreed upon between them; that is, if she wanted to keep her reinstated position. *He was such a bastard!* He chuckled to himself.

Janet's rental car was parked a few cars over from Cleese's car and she sat in it and watched Cleese stumble towards his car, walking as if he were completely drained of energy. He didn't start up right away; he just sat there for a few minutes. Then the engine started and he drove off passing right in front of her car. Inside of her car Janet snapped off the choker around her neck. Anyone watching would have been horrified to see the outlines of her fingers sliding up under the surface skin of her neck, under her chin and then across her cheeks. They would have watched with shock and surprise as Janet pulled her face off revealing a totally different woman. Bonnie Adelson pulled off the $6,000 dollar replicated mask of Janet's face and shook out her long dark hair. Reaching delicately into the back of her mouth she removed the molar microphone and lastly she took the microphone receiver from her ear. She placed these items in tissue paper and in a box on the back seat, started the car and drove to the mall where she met Janet sitting at a table in a restaurant reading a book. Janet looked up at Bonnie when she sat down but could think of nothing to say to her. Before she could say anything Bonnie said, "Janet we threw all conscience in the garbage at my house. You got what you needed and I got what I never dreamed possible. This ex-prostitute has a new life, a beautiful home, a job, a car, college classes and a fiancé. All debts paid and well worth the price. The matter is closed." Janet drove Bonnie back to Delaware were they hugged, kissed and said their respected thanks, good byes and parted. There was no reason for them to see each other again or so Janet thought; but two years later she'd receive an invitation to Bonnie's wedding. She was to marry the owner of the store where she worked and would be moving off to a much bigger home as a millionaire's wife. She'd had a little boy named Jan (after Janet) Three years later, she'd receive an invitation to Bonnie's graduation with honors with a Masters in Accounting and looking forward to opening her own accounting firm. They were both extremely, unabashedly happy.

Working along an appointed time schedule, it was time for Janet to mail her letter Dick Kahn, Employee Relations Officer at the Sawyer Developmental Center.

NINETEEN

TO: Mr. Dick Kahn, Employee Relations Office, Sawyer Developmental Center

FR: Janet Nelson, Ex-Head Training Supervisor, Ex- Cottage Training Supervisor, Ex- Cottage Training Technician, Human Services Assistant

Dear Mr. Kahn:

It's sad that things have reached this state of affairs and I humbly apologize that you have been forced to involve yourself in these matters surrounding me. When I look at the above titles, they represent for me what I have achieved and what I've lost at the institution and it hurts me deeply that these things have happened. I have no words for the loss of my mentors Ms. Mead and Mr. Cleese, I miss them severely but there's nothing to be done to repair what has happened and I cannot be consoled. As I sit here thinking about you and your involvement, I feel really bad. Before all this madness, you and I had a great relationship and now I've even lost you too. My sadness is profound. Now the reason for this letter to you, which I wish to remain private, for knowledge of its existence may bring you further grief from the powers that be. I say grief because I know you are not the orchestrator of the events that have fallen upon me. It is my sincere wish for you, especially you, to know that my responses to the hostility around me have not been pre-planned but were forced on me. I had no choice but to respond such as I have in order to save my job as well as my sanity. Actually, I've lost three positions as a result of the hatred surrounding me and I find myself back in the position I started in over twenty four years ago. It's amazing isn't it? My mentors, my positions and you are all lost to me and yet I don't understand why these things have happened to me. It all became totally clear and devastating to me when Pitts and McCoy stole my paycheck and Mr. Dunning announced that he had no idea that they'd done such a thing. I realized now just how toxic he is to me and my employment. I'm fully aware that it was his instructions to Pitts and McCoy to keep an eye on me because Pitts told me; as well as the fact that he arranged for the assignment I was given after my third demotion. I learned last year from Cleese that you were bucking the demotions; that you didn't want to have anything to do with these things but you received direct orders from Mr. Dunning. Mr. Cleese said that you requested that I be left alone and that your request was met with abstinence and refusal. I have also discovered that at that meeting, it was Mr. Dunning's idea to give me the $2000 dollar check, the recommendation for disciplinary action for sleeping on duty; to be followed by the suspension for possession of drugs. He also arranged for all those people to be in the boardroom. None of it worked because God doesn't like ugly and isn't too fond of pretty. I now know the entire affair was Dunning's including having me go from place to place looking for a meeting that was never meant to happen. I have a friend in the administrative building who told me that Mr. Dunning had you do those things to me so that his name would not be attached to the incidents and that if anything happened my fight would be against you. I heard about the argument the two of you had in the personnel building too where he blamed everything on you and told you to find a way to fix it. He made you responsible for fixing his madness. You were given the responsibility to fix what couldn't be fixed. As he well knows, when these attacks against me go before an Administrative Law judge in the Superior Court the charges I present will bear your name, not his, as the instigator (EEOC and Civil Rights complaints) I wish to let you know that I know who my enemies are and that you are not one of them. I want you to know that your name will have to be brought out in court as the instigator; but I fully intend to inform the courts that you were forced to act under the threat of termination from the Assistant CEO Mr. Dunning. He told Mr. Cleese that you'd comply or be out of a job. Didn't know that did you? Ms. Mead was there and she told me. Well, I believe her because a note was left in my mailbox and it was her hand writing. You are not my enemy but you must assure me of one thing, that this letter will remain private between you and I. It will be mailed to the institution certified and marked private. In closing, you must not worry about me. You have to worry about Cleese and Dunning. Keep your eyes and ears open on them. If you question the validity of what I've written then consider this: Ask yourself how would I know that you, Cleese and Dunning met in Cleese's office where you argued with them calling Cleese's plans juvenile, lacking morals, structure and character, in fact, you called his plan as lacking aristocratic training. I don't know what that means but I do know the argument happened. I wouldn't know these things unless I learned them from Cleese now would I? Actually, it was both, from Cleese through Gertrude Fleming and from Dunning through Karen Stevens. I'm stopping now but you must watch your back. Signed "I'm sincerely sorry" Janet Nelson.

The completed letter mailed certified and private to Kick Kahn was a scam, a con, a ruse, a sham, a deception. Pick any number of definitions to describe something that has no other purpose than to trick someone with false information and feelings and you'd have Janet's simple plan to divide Kahn from Cleese and Dunning. She wanted Kahn to be suspicious of Dunning and Cleese if they were simply waving good morning to him. She knew it wouldn't fail to invoke suspicion and mistrust because she included information that only Dunning and Cleese would have been privy to. It would cause anger because the bulk of the letter's content was true and Kahn would know it. She indicated that she knew Dunning was calling the shots but forcing Kahn to pull the trigger. The letter would serve a dual purpose. It would also cause Kahn to begin withholding what might be valuable information from Dunning in the hope that when the music stopped (like in the child's game of musical chairs) Kahn wouldn't be the only one left without a chair. Janet's plan to take them all down began on Wednesday and if all went according to plan it would be finished Monday afternoon. The letter was posted for one day delivery; Kahn would receive it on Thursday and Dunning on Friday. It was time for all the chickens to come home to roost. They had knocked on the devils door long enough and it was time for someone to answer.

When Bonnie had parted the curtains in Cleese's office it was to give Janet a full view of the entire office and she, with her digital camera, was snapping picture after picture of Bonnie and Cleese engaged in wild sex. She made sure that each picture showed no part of Bonnie's face so that no one could identify her as Janet Nelson. Janet's next move was to get the pictures of Cleese with the woman he thought was Janet developed and copied onto individual sheets of 8/11 high gloss paper. She had over 200 copies made in there various jaw dropping and erotic positions during that evening of drug induced sex. There were photos of Cleese sitting at his desk with his head between the wide open legs of a woman who was perched on the edge of his desk. Cleese's face was clearly visible as the photo captured his tongue entering the woman's sex. There was a photo of Cleese, eyes closed and tongue lolling on top of the woman on his desk with his pants crumbled around his ankles. Another showed him and the woman on the office floor with both her legs thrown over his shoulders. There was a side shot of him pinning the woman's back against the office door where with one hand he was holding up the woman's slender leg and the fingers of his other hand were buried between her legs. One of him against the office wall, his eyes closed in captured ecstasy as his hands held the back of the woman's head and his penis was buried almost to the hilt in her mouth. There was another shot of the woman's hands gripping the edge of the counter of front of the coffee machine that was labelled with his name and he was grasping both sides of the woman's hips was entering her from behind, doggy style. Looking at the blown up pictures it was unmistakably, undeniably Cleese and Cleese's office. Janet left the print shop with a bag heavy with humiliation, shame, disgrace and revenge. Out of a total of the twenty photographs, Janet chose twelve of the most seductive and raunchy, erotic acts and threw the rest away. Long before that lusty, drug induced night ended; Cleese had verbally reinstated the woman he thought to be Janet back into the position of Head Training Supervisor. He'd gladly given over the keys to the building; as well as her office. The following day, Thursday, when the real Janet reported to his office, he was tripping and stumbling all over himself as he personally escorted Janet to personnel and all necessary forms were filled reinstating Janet Nelson to her former position of Head Training Supervisor. Afterwards she left returning to the building while Cleese was with Dunning and was totally ignoring the angry tirade of the assistant CEO screaming after him, "What the hell are you doing?!" In the end it was Cleese's call and he wanted her back. Dunning was seething with rage and wanted to beat the shit out of Cleese's retreating back; while Cleese was fantasizing about the six upcoming meetings between him and Janet that would never happen. If there was a choice between what Dunning wanted from Cleese and what Cleese wanted between Janet's legs it was no contest, hands down or in his mind, legs up. As Cleese continued walking away Dunning yelled, "Cleese!" When Cleese turned around Dunning said, "Perhaps you should zip up your pants!" and as he walked away Cleese said, "What I want I take and no one cuts in on what I want."

When the staff discovered that Janet was back they were ecstatic; Gertrude however was stunned and puzzled but smiling like everyone else while inwardly she was seething. Would she never be rid of her? She had been passed over for the position of Head Training Supervisor five times; she couldn't get it through her head that she wasn't ever going to get the position while in Cleese's unit. When she arrived for duty and found Janet reading the log book and gathering up the attendance sheets she had been speechless, stupefied. Janet ignored her and taking the forms left the office. Gertrude had no idea what was going on until a staff member came into the office after Janet had left and said with a huge Kool-Aide grin on his face, "Have you heard? Janet's back! Isn't that just great?" Gertrude understood the words but had great difficulty in accepting it. *She's back, but how? When? What's going on?* Her shocked mind wondered. She waited a few minutes than followed Janet's steps to Cleese's office where she found him all smiles and full of good humor. "Gertrude have you heard our very own Janet is back in the fold. Wonderful, wonderful!" he grinned thinking of his not long ago evening between Janet's thighs. "Yes, I heard." Gertrude replied drily and walked back out of the office without making their coffee amid Cleese's laughter. When Janet returned to the work floor she went directly to the nurse's station where all the clients chart books were kept. She chose five specific chart books belonging to five specific clients and took them to her office. Closing her door, she opened each individual chart book and copied down the contact information for all five client's families and made copies of specific injury reports and treatments associated with the clients. Having done so, she walked outside and put everything in the glove compartment of her car. She returned to the building, returned the chart books to the nurse's station and then went about her duties.

Thursday night when Janet arrived home with the pilfered information she'd copied from the chart books she picked up the phone and while eating a Chinese shrimp roll, she contacted the five families on the list. Slightly deepening her voice she introduced herself as Mr. Dick Kahn Employee Relations Officer from the Sawyer Developmental Center. She Informed the families of a Class Action Civil Suit that was being instigated by the assistant CEO Paul Dunning for serious, unreported assaults to their family members at the institution by an inappropriately, possibly homicidal patient. Under the direction of Mr. Dunning he was notifying the families to ascertain their support for the lawsuit and a meeting with State officials was being scheduled for the upcoming Monday at the institution. He would like to visit them at their homes on the upcoming Saturday to discuss the matter in full and to gain their much needed support for the lawsuit. All five families agreed to meet with Mr. Kahn on Saturday at a pre-arranged timed. Janet hung up, finished her shrimp rolls looking at the five different addresses. They were quite a few miles apart from each other and in cities she'd never visited but this presented no problem. She booted up her computer and keyed in 'Map Quest' and had the computer setup the best possible routes between the five cities and the time needed to reach one place to the next. She saved and printed out her trip itinerary for Saturday morning which would begin at 6:00 a.m.

By Friday morning, Dunning had absolutely no use for Cleese. His intestines were still in a bunch at the blatant betrayal by Cleese in reinstating Janet to the position that they together, had fought and schemed so hard to take from her but there was nothing he could do to Cleese without implicating himself. *What had they done it all for if it ended where it began?* He raged impotently. This coupled with the arrest and termination of the Human Resources Officer Karen Stevens for assault against Janet and the police, taped racial comments, the arrest of a Director and Assistant Director, Pitts and McCoy for felony theft and that infamous list of drug distributers and users dropped by Janet at the board meeting was giving him a monstrous headache that wouldn't dissipate. All these incidents had short circuited his entire capacity for normal trouble shooting. There was nothing to be done about Stevens but Pitts and McCoy had acted on his instructions and if they talked. He didn't want to think about it but had no choice. If they talked and he felt certain they would (because in their position he would spill his guts) he would be found to be the orchestrator of a conspiracy of his own making. He was bone tired and feeling like a swimmer who'd been stroking for thirty minutes but was still no closer to the shore. And for Cleese to reinstate that bitch was all too much. Locked into all these situations at the same time had reduced him to mindless, idiot chattering sitting behind his desk and he began for some unknown reason (which no one, including himself could explain) began humming than actually singing in a low voice. "Camp town racers sing this song, doo dah, doo da. Camp town race track five miles long, oh doo dah day. Gonna run all night, gonna run all day. I bet my money on the bobbed tail nag, somebody bet on the bay. Doo dah…Doo dah…. He was oblivious to everything else. Doo dah.

Kahn too was sitting in his office that Friday morning again reading the letter he'd received from Janet Nelson and he believed (just as she planned) every word. He returned the letter to its envelope. A letter filled with confessions, sorrow and betrayal. He knew in his heart he was guilty of being a 'Yes man' but He had no idea that Dunning's plan would end with him being left out to dry on a cold wintry day but the truth was all in the letter. There was no conceivable way Janet could have known the things she spoke about in her letter. No way at all, yet she did! Kahn booted up his computer and began a fifteen page confessional letter of his own against Dunning and Cleese and all that he had done to sabotage Janet Nelson. He typed all morning and half of the afternoon and the finished product proved to be much too hot to handle.

Janet Nelson was that same Friday morning, going about business as usual in the sixth day of her reinstated positon as Head Training Supervisor but her concentration was centered on the following day, Saturday, and all she had to do in preparation. When her shift ended, she left the institution and drove to the shopping mall. Locating an upscale men's store where she tried on and purchased an expensive men's business suit, white silk shirt and tie. The salesman was a bit curious about the woman who preferred the cut of a man's suit as opposed to that of a woman's but his curiosities dissipated out of his mind when Janet left him a $100 tip. She proceeded to a jewelry store where she purchased an expensive men's watch, cuff links and tie clasp. Next she went to a men's shoe store and purchased a pair of men's dress shoes and as an added inducement a bottle of men's cologne and before leaving she stopped at an optical store and brought a pair of gold-wire framed reading glasses and left for home with her purchases. Janet got no sleep, she didn't need any; she was deep in the forest of revenge and had no intentions of turning back. Friday evening, as she prepared for her meetings with the five families on Saturday she found she wasn't nervous, anxious or remorseful as she removed a large box from beneath her bed. Lifting the lid off the box, she uncovered the Doppelganger Mask of her face that Bonnie had worn in Cleese's office when she (not Janet) had seduced him and next to it wrapped in soft silk was another mask. It was a mask of Dick Kahn's face; which the technicians from Doppelganger had re-produced from the secret pictures she'd taken of Kahn months ago. Janet carefully laid the mask beside the man's suit and accessories and then picking up the phone she called each of the five families informing them of what time he (Dick Kahn) would arrive for their meeting the following day. Afterwards, she sat down to watch her favorite cartoon, The Flintstones.

At six a.m. Saturday morning, Janet stood in front of her full length bedroom mirror and Dick Kahn was looking back out at her. He was a slightly tall, thinly built man (but so was Janet) with thick greying hair, a pleasant thin face with tension lines across his forehead and deep set brown eyes covered with gold framed wire glasses. His suit was immaculate, expensive and professional. Starring through her eyes, Janet felt a little frightened at the face staring back at her. It was so real, it was so Dick Kahn. Satisfied, she picked up a briefcase and left her home as Dick Kahn headed for Princeton NJ, the home of the Andersons. Janet arrived close to 8 a.m., knocked and the door was opened and he/she was invited in by a middle aged woman who accepted the offered business card of which Janet had made copies. The card read 'New Jersey Department of Human Services – Employee Relations Officer Dick Kahn –The Sawyer Developmental Center and a telephone number. Kahn/Janet was frankly surprised but pleased to see about nine individuals assembled in the living room of the home. Kahn/Janet introduced himself and got right down to business. He was there at the instructions of the Assistant CEO Paul Dunning who was instigating a lawsuit against the State for the family members of patients at his institution who were severely assaulted by an inappropriately placed child at the institution. The institution was not informed that this child possessed extreme homicidal tendencies and that their son's leg had been broken by this child and it was the law that the injury be reported and the family compensated. The family said they were never informed of the broken leg. Kahn/Janet informed them that that was the exactly the reason why he was there. Mr. Dunning was extremely upset about the incident but was held back from reporting it to you by the State. During this child's, Daryl Campton by name, four week placement at the institution he was found to be responsible for several assaults including the breaking of your son's leg. He also perpetrated broken arms, fingers, toes, black eyes and horrendous bruising of helpless patients. Kahn/Janet asked (knowing they didn't) if the family had been notified of their son's injury and when he/she was again told no, he/she continued. Mr. Dunning's hands were tied by the State's decision not to notify the families of the injured patients unless they were regular visitors to the institution. According to our records you do not visit often due to lack of transportation. Well, Mr. Dunning wants no part of the State's decision to keep the families in the dark about the status of their loved ones at the institution. He has chosen to act on his own by instigating this law suit and he needs your help. This matter will of course (for added inducement) involve a huge amount of money in compensation for the families of the injured patients by this inappropriately placed individual. The awarded monies will be divided among the five families but Mr. Dunning needs your support to get justice for you and your family member. Opening his brief case, Mr. Kahn/Janet removed copies of the incident report, findings and treatment of their son's injuries and gave it to the family, included was a letter informing them of the meeting scheduled for Monday next at 1 p.m. at the institution. In the meantime you are asked to contact this number for the Commissioner of Human Services. You will inform them that you met with me, at Mr. Paul Dunning's request, regarding unreported assaults against your family member at the Sawyer Developmental Center and will be attending the Monday meeting. Please make the call after nine a.m. and before 11 a.m. on Monday morning. Mr. Kahn/Janet concluded asking them if they could count on their support; which of course was given. Kahn/ Janet asked if they had any questions and when there were none, he/she shook hands all around, left a business card for each of them and hoped they would attend the meeting for their son's sake. Kahn/Janet left their home headed for Long Branch, NJ, Little Falls NJ, Lakewood, NJ and Wayne, NJ carrying the same message, documents and sporting the same false identity. Thy will be done. She arrived back at her home around 6 p.m. Saturday night. She removed the Doppelganger Mask, the suit and accessories and changed into a pair of shorts and sweat shirt. She sat down knowing she had nothing to do until 3 a.m. Sunday morning and she'd need her rest for this one.

"The idle mind is the playground of the devil. Janet was thinking as she cruised along the highway doing 60 mph at 2 a.m. early Sunday morning and her mind wasn't idle. She was headed for her place of employment, the Sawyer Developmental Center. Across from her on the passenger seat were four bulging nondescript book bags. Janet arrived at the institution and turned up the driveway heading for the administration building at the top of the curved road. Reaching the front of the building she put the car in park, pulled on a set of rubber gloves and reached into one of the book bags and pulled out several sheets of papers. She climbed the seven steps to the two tall, glass doors of the administration building and removing a roll of adhesive tape from her pocket she proceeded to tape twelve of the sexually explicit photos of Cleese and the woman on each of the twin glass doors. Returning to her car and pulled away from the building. Coming to a 3-way intersection she turned right and the road led to the rear doors of the administration building where she taped twelve more pictures across its doors. Back in her car, she followed the curving road down to the food service, maintenance and laundry buildings and she taped copies of the pictures to all the front and back doors of each building. In the parking lot, where the midnight shift workers parked their cars, she placed 6 photos apiece under each wind shield wiper. She returned to her car, made a U-turn and followed the road up to the hospital building whose three entrance doors were always open and she taped photographs of Cleese and the woman over all three doors. Entering the building she proceeded to tape copies of the pictures on every door on the hospital's first floor and second floors, on the mirrors and bathroom stalls inside of the men's and women's rooms and every office door in the building.. Returning to her car she drove up to the first of the 19 patient buildings. At this time of the morning, Janet knew there'd be no one walking about and she took her time at each building 1-19 taping the photos of Cleese and the unknown woman on the front and back doors of each building and slipped copies under all of the wind shield wipers of the employee's parked cars in the parking lot of each building. After she had successfully covered every building on grounds with the over the top, eye popping pictures of a naked Cleese performing sexually in his office with some woman, she returned to her car. She drove around the institution's grounds twice throwing the left over photos indiscriminately from her book bags out the window of her car until the bags were empty. Only then did she leave the grounds. Still wearing her gloves, she stopped at a post office mail box in that township and dropped six large, First Class, overnight delivery envelopes each with specific addresses: The Commissioner of Human Services, The Governor's office, Personnel, Paul Dunning, Dick Kahn and Barton Cleese. Each contained a full set of all the nineteen pictures of Cleese and the unknown woman that she had photographed. Each identified Barton Cleese, Unit Director and the institution where he was employed. With a simple caption 'Is this how our tax dollars are spent?' It was only then that she turned her car and headed for home where she undressed, made a cup of tea, toasted the night and slept the sleep of the just.

Janet awoke around 10 a.m. Sunday morning with a clear conscience, which was a good thing as far as consciousness was concerned, nothing should leave her open to suspicion. She had breakfast in bed and went back to a safe and restful sleep. She had no idea of the conflagration she had put into motion when she entered the dark forest seeking revenge beginning with the mailing of the letter to Kahn on Wednesday. She hoped deep in her heart of hearts that the seeds she'd planted would break through the surface bearing rotten, smelly, bug infested fruit. As it has been written, so shall it be done!

Between 6:30 and 7:00 a.m. Sunday morning, while Janet lay sleeping in her bed, day shift employees were turning onto the grounds of the Sawyer

Developmental Center. Over a hundred cars drove past the administration building without actually seeing it or the photographs taped to its front doors. The cars carrying anywhere between 2 and 6 employees viewed the building as a part of the scenery like a tree in a park; they knew it was there but it carried no significance. At the intersection, a right turn would take them to the rear entrances of buildings 1-10; a left turn to the food service, maintenance and laundry buildings and if they continued straight they came to the hospital and the rear of buildings 19 down to 11. Most of the drivers (there passengers usually asleep) noticed the scattered sheets of papers all over the grounds but they weren't grounds keepers and wouldn't be stopping to pick them up. They weren't after all interested in keeping America beautiful. Over a hundred employees parked, exited their cars and approached the doors of their perspective buildings but didn't enter. They stood silent and speechless staring at pictures of a man some of them knew and others didn't having sex with a woman. The pictures were of high quality, color and definition and they couldn't tear their eyes (which were darting from one photo to the next) away from the scenes of copulation. So they just stood there until the midnight shift supervisors from some of the buildings came to the doors perhaps wondering why the day shift wasn't coming in for duty. When their eyes fell on the photographs of Cleese and the woman they too were stunned into speechlessness. Some people felt they should take the pictures down. The pictures were after all (some admitted to themselves and no one else, erotic) dirty, obscene, awful and were of a person they knew but no one dared to as much as touch the photos much less remove them. That was until Gertrude Fleming joined the group of huddled employees at her building and seeing the astonishing photos of Cleese she burst out in uncontrollable laughter. Holding her ample stomach, her body shuddering with hilarity and her eyes streaming with tears she began to carefully remove each picture from the door and took them inside with her. Gertrude went straight up to the front office where she knew no one would be; Cleese and Mead didn't work on the weekends. Following her intuition she opened and stepped outside the front door of her building. There taped all over the front doors were the same photos of Cleese doing the 'Wild thang' in his office. There was no mistaking his identity or his office. It was Barton Cleese. The front of each building was built in a huge circle so she could see the front entrances of six other buildings as she looked around. There were groups of people standing in front of each of the other buildings all staring at the front doors of their buildings and Gertrude's laughter resumed knowing that who so ever had done this had taped the photos on every building on grounds and she loved it. She loved it so much that she didn't remove the photos from the front door of her building and hoped in her dark, vindictive heart that no one else would. She maliciously wanted Cleese to come to work on Monday and see them. She began laughing again as she went back inside leaving the pictures on the door. Between laughter she was chanting "Lions and tigers and bears, oh my!" Her laughter continued throughout the day as much as the office phone which wouldn't stop ringing. She was getting calls from all over grounds about the pictures of her boss and she loved it.

Gertrude's wish for the photos to smack Cleese in the face on Monday morning would never materialize. Someone had taken some of the pictures to Mead's, Cleese's assistant, whose little house was directly across the street from the institution and early Sunday morning she contacted Cleese hysterically yelling at him to come to her house, it was an emergency. When he arrived an hour later, without speaking she thrust the pictures into his hands and declared to him that they were on every building on grounds. Cleese's eyes grew wider and wider looking at the pictures. His face went completely pale and he was beyond shock and speech. The photos slipped from his trembling hands and fluttered to the floor. Some landed face up and he could see himself on top of Janet on his desk. In another, his head was buried between her legs. His head began to swivel back and forth negatively refusing to see what his eyes couldn't negate. His breathing began coming in short alarming gasp as he stumbled backwards his hands across his heart into Mead's arms and his brain did the only merciful thing it could do considering the circumstances, it shut down and like a delicate, gentile young lady seeing a horrendous act, his eyes closed and he fainted dead away. No one could know what was said or done after he was brought around to consciousness and reality; but there was one thing for sure that everyone on grounds eventually discovered and that was that that great, magnificent, bastard Barton Cleese, the untouchable Barton Cleese, the master of Cleese's Plantation was never seen at the institution again, Monday or any other day. Official status, retired.

On Monday morning, the families that Janet (disguised as Mr. Kahn in the Doppelganger mask) visited did as he requested. They contacted the State Commissioners Office of Human Services to inform them that they'd be attending the meeting later that afternoon to discuss the Class Action lawsuit regarding the unreported injuries of their family members housed at the Sawyer Developmental Center. Of course, no one at the Commissioner's office knew what they were talking about. The family members went into a little more detail regarding Mr. Kahn's visit to their homes and the assistant CEO Mr. Dunning's request for their support in the lawsuit. Still no one knew anything about a meeting or law suit. They would look into it and call the families back. The families all agreed that would be just fine but they would still be at the institution at 1 p.m. that day. The Commissioner's receptionist relayed the information from the five families to Commissioner Wojohorwitz who also knew nothing about any lawsuit instigated at the Sawyer Institution. It would be insane and employment suicide if any representative of the State Department of Human Services did such a thing. Whatever was going on at the institution the Commissioner couldn't make heads or tails of it. Over all he was sick of the institution and its issues. He'd been against the appointment of Paul Dunning in the beginning. Talks were already in progress concerning the closing of the Sawyer Institution, had been for years. He hoped it would be closed. He decided to handle the matter himself. Getting his hat, he left his office informing the receptionist that he was going to the Sawyer institution to find out what this meeting and lawsuit was all about. As he left his office he walked pass the mailroom employee delivering his mail, so he didn't receive the large envelope containing the photographs of Cleese until re returned back from the institution.

Dick Kahn was sitting at his desk Monday morning looking at the photographs of Cleese and the woman spread across his desk. They were all over his office door when he arrived and a second set was delivered to him in the mail. He felt no shock, sympathy or disgust at the pictures. In fact, he felt nothing for the photos, Cleese, Dunning or the institution. Over the weekend he'd made up his mind that he was through with all of them. He'd worked over forty years, earned his pension and he was taking it. He placed the pictures in an envelope and threw it into the waste basket. He didn't have any feelings one way or the other about what Cleese did or who he did it with, he, himself, was through. He left his office and went up to Cleese's office determined to have it out with him but when he arrived he wasn't surprised to learn from Ms. Mead that Cleese had put in for retirement and wouldn't be returning to the institution. Kahn said nothing just turned and left the office.

That same Monday morning, the administration building of the Sawyer Institution was silent, silent and silent. It was absent of its normal hustle and bustle of staff going about their duties. It seemed no one wanted to leave their offices. All of them were aware of the photographs of Cleese that had been taped to the front and back doors and they were shamed for him but no one was discussing the pictures. In fact, no one in the entire building was having any form of conversation with anyone in the building. The door to Dunning's office was closed as was the door of the CEO Ms. Klein. No one talked and no one looked another employee in the eyes. All was silent, silent and silent in the huge building.

On the same Monday morning, Paul Dunning assistant CEO, was sitting at his desk. At first he had spread the entire set of pictures of Cleese and the woman across his desk and was mesmerized staring at them. Finally he gathered all the pictures together and placed them in a large envelope. But it seemed to him that he could see right through the envelope and the pictures were glaring right back at him. It was insane! All this shit that was fucking happening was insane! The arrest and firing of the Human Resources Officer, the felony theft arrest of a Director and assistant Director, that list of drug distributors and users, a copy of a letter sent to Kahn by Janet Nelson and anonymously sent to him, now this; these totally insane pictures of Cleese having sex in his office. It was all too overwhelming and if he had thought about it, he might have taken the same route as Cleese and fainted dead away. Out of everyone on grounds, Dunning was the only one to closely study the woman in the photos. She looked down right familiar to him but it was just like a person trying to remember something whose answer danced right on the edge of their memory but they couldn't grasp it. What he did deduce was that Janet Nelson was knee deep involved in every last one of the incidents except the pictures. He removed the photos from the envelope again and began to take in all the details of the woman and indeed there was something familiar but he just couldn't put his fingers on it. What he did noticed was that in every photo the woman's face was either totally hidden by her hair (that hair, he thought) or was only partially visible. There were no clear shots of her total face. *On purpose?* He wondered. It was obvious to him that the woman didn't want to be seen. Only Cleese was to be identifiable. He studied the woman's body which was small, lithe and light brown skinned. So familiar but again the connection eluded him. He was dangerously close to total recognition but couldn't, shall we say, connect the dots because too many other matters were echoing around his mind. He stared at the woman and something was coming to him. Something that was interrupted by the ringing of his office phone and out of frustration he made the mistake of letting the machine take the call. If he had answered it he would have known that the Commissioner of Human Services was on his way to the institution and his office, to discuss a Class Action Civil lawsuit that he, Dunning was instigating against the State. He dropped his head to his desk over his folded arms. Out of all the issues swirling around in his mind he settled on the letter that Janet Nelson had sent to Kahn and what was probably going through that scrawny little mother fuckers mind when he'd read that letter. If nothing else the contents of letter were true, he was indeed setting up Kahn to be left holding the bag when all the shit hit the fan but how did Janet know? Where was she getting her information? It was a flat out lie where the letter indicated that she got her information from him. That was the stupidest supplication but would Kahn believe it? He thought that he would. He was a weakling, having no backbone or heart for the game and a weak link had to be removed. Dunning remained locked behind the doors of his office all morning thinking about how he could terminate Kahn.

Meanwhile, Kahn looked at his watch; it was 11:30 a.m. Monday morning. Since arriving on grounds he had waited rather patiently for the payroll office to open its doors at 8:30 a.m. When it did Kahn went there and submitted an application applying for his pension, he would be giving his retirement notice to personnel after completing his business with payroll. Which was a smart move because his application for his pension would already be in the system before all the really good shit hit the fan. Everyone in the payroll office had of course seen the sex photos of Cleese. The head of payroll knew and was right in her estimation that Kahn was retiring because of the photos. With all the disastrous happenings going on at the institution it was a good time to get the hell out of Dodge because he would be the first person in the chain responsible for enacting disciplinary actions against Cleese, Stevens, Pitts, McCoy and Dunning. It was a good time to take a powder. She didn't envy him his responsibility nor were they aware that Cleese's application for his pension would soon arrive in the hands of Ms. Mead. Kahn knew Dunning went to lunch from 12-1 p.m. and at 12:30 he was taking his last walk down to the administration building with his application for retirement snug in his inner suit jacket right next to his fifteen page confessional of all the acts Dunning had given him direct orders to enforce. He planned to say nothing to Dunning but would simply hand him the explosive letter and then leave his office and the building for the last time. He was through with everything.

At 12:30 p.m. Monday afternoon, a string of cars began pulling into and parking around the curved perimeter of the administration building of the Sawyer Developmental Center. There were so many cars that the line extended half way back to the entrance of the institution's grounds. A little over two dozen people exited the cars and proceeded to the entrance of the administration building whose revolving doors kept revolving and revolving until all of its passengers were clustered inside of the building's lobby. The receptionist hadn't been notified that a large group of people were expected at the institution therefore there was no reception for them. One well-dressed woman detached herself from the group and approached the receptionist and informed her that she was there for the 1:00 meeting with Mr. Paul Dunning and Mr. Dick Kahn regarding the civil suit. The receptionist had no knowledge of any meeting or lawsuit. If she had she would have had the board room prepped. At any rate, there wouldn't have been sufficient space to seat all those people. She phoned Mr. Dunning's personal receptionist informing her that the group was here for the 1:00 meeting with Mr. Dunning and Mr. Kahn. Dunning's receptionist informed her that she had no such meeting scheduled. She transferred the call directly to Mr. Dunning who hadn't left his office all morning.

After taking the call from his receptionist, Dunning exhaled deeply thinking, *Now what? What meeting with him and Kahn. What lawsuit?* He tiredly lifted his portly frame from his chair and shuffled more than walked towards the lobby with his headache thumping blindly. When he arrived there he found he could only take approximately eight steps before his path was blocked by a huge group of people and he was at a total lost as to what this was all about. He excused and pardoned his way up to the receptionist desk and asked what this was all about, who were all these people? A woman stepped forward, introduced herself as an attorney and extending her hand and Dunning obliviously shook it. "Good afternoon, we're here for the meeting." "What meeting?" Dunning responded with as much courtesy as he could behind the rip roaring headache that was making his eyes bounce around in their sockets. The attorney filled him. They were here at his request to discuss the civil lawsuit regarding unreported assaults on their family members. According to Mr. Kahn, who visited the homes of all the families involved (She waved her arm to indicate all the families) were to meet with you and Mr. Kahn today. Dunning felt a hood of suffocating confusion slipping over his head was thinking disjointedly, trying to make heads or tails of what this woman was talking about. He had no idea what the woman was talking about and when he attempted to explain as much the lobby erupted in chaotic, angry voices and was fast becoming unruly, as people's comments and questions suddenly lashed out; colliding with Dunning's stalled senses and pounding headache. "What are you trying to pull!?" "I want to know what happened to my child!" "Why are you trying to hide the truth from us?" "Why wasn't I told my son's leg was broken!? "Or my son's broken foot!" "What are you hiding!?" "You're trying to get out of the lawsuit!?" "You're not getting away with this!" "Mr. Kahn came to my home Saturday and told us what was happening!" "My son's eye needed surgery. No one told me!" "What kind of place is this?" "Yes, what kind of place is this?" a new voice came from a man just stepping out of the revolving doors and facing the angry crowd which turned towards the deep booming voice of Commissioner Wojohorwitz, a tall imposing man, almost a full head taller than everyone in the lobby. His iron grey haired was neatly trimmed in a manner that suggested business and authority and was backed up by cold dark eyes beneath thick brows that were wrinkled with sternness. He was built like a tree, thick of body, barrel-chested with long arms. His appearance belied the real man. For all his size and looks Wojohorwitz was a kind, understanding, Christian man. As the Commissioner of Human Service he had many detractors because it was well known that he was an honest man who lived his life by the scriptures. He'd never tell lies, cover-up indiscretions or tolerate conspiracies with anyone within his jurisdiction and he was not well liked for these reasons. Everyone in the lobby including Dunning turned at the sound of his voice and presence and then all of them began unharmoniously talking and asking, "Who are you!?" The voice responded, "I'm John Wojohorwitz, Commissioner of the Department of Human Services". The crowd began to settle down. "My office received several calls this morning from concerned families regarding this meeting and pending lawsuit. I thought I should attend. Perhaps we should adjourn to a place where we can all be seated and discuss your concerns." he said with his cold, unblinking eyes settling on Dunning who was feeling both hot and cold with goosebumps shooting up his entire body when the man stated his name and title. Dunning's testicles took cover, receding up into themselves and he felt like he was under water, all the sounds muffled and the press of bodies around him was claustrophobic. He was suffocating. Until he noticed the revolving door spinning around yet again and his heart became filled with fear and his eyes grew wide as he felt sure that the next person to step out of the traitorous revolving door would be The Hangman, dark, hooded, cloaked and carrying a rope attached to a very huge, thick branch. He felt as if he was going to pass out until he watched Dick Kahn step out of the revolving door. All Dunning's feelings of fear and panic evaporated into overwhelming feelings of rage. If it had been at all possible he would have snatched Kahn up and throttled him to a lifeless pulp as he remembered the crowd of people all stating that Kahn had been sent by him. Kahn stood questionably next to the revolving door taking in the crowd of people in the lobby. Dunning, thankfully only in his mind, saw himself thrashing through the crowd, knocking down and trampling over screaming people in his maniacal desire to reach Kahn, to get his hands around his scrawny neck and snap it in two pieces. The fantasy was quickly dissolved and replaced by the crowd and the Commissioner all turning to face the newest member to the throng, Dick Kahn. "That's him, that's Mr. Kahn. Now what do you have to say?" "Mr. Kahn, Mr.

Kahn" voices called out to him. "Mr. Dunning is trying to say he doesn't know anything about the meeting. Tell him! Tell him that you came to our homes and told us about the lawsuit he was planning! Tell him; tell him!' was close becoming a chant. Mr. Kahn looked around at the mass of shouting, definitely confused crowd and stated, "I'm sorry." he shouted over the crowd in apology, "but I've never met any of you in my life" There was a moment of silence and then the crowd erupted in angry disbelief. They were yelling, pushing and shoving and the frightened receptionist picked up the phone and dialed 911 to report a riot at the institution.

The 911 call was received at the police station. Riot in progress in the administration building of the Sawyer Developmental Center, officers dispatched. The meeting/riot was now going to hit print in the papers. With the approaching whoop, whoop of sirens in the background growing louder and closer, the atmosphere inside of the building reached epic, out of control proportions as the incensed families all rushed at Mr. Kahn shouting, "What do you mean you never met us?!" "You were at my home Saturday morning!" "And mine! And mine!" several voices shouted at him. Some of them produced Kahn's business cards, frantically waving them in the air shouting, "See, you left me your business card!" "Wait a minute!" another voice rang out, "I've got a copy of the letter from Mr. Dunning you gave to me about the lawsuit and the meeting!" "May I see that?" the commissioner yelled out over the crowd. He was handed several letters as Dick Kahn's business cards were waved in his face. The Commissioner read the letter which was not very long and it indeed spoke of a lawsuit instigated by Dunning, a request for their support and if necessary an attorney would be provided for them. He lifted his eyebrows at Dunning when he read that part. He continued reading about an appointed time for a meeting at which he was to reside to be held on Monday at 1 p.m. at the Sawyer Developmental Center in the office of Paul Dunning. The Commissioner was livid and it showed in his face. "Exactly, what is going on here, Dunning, Kahn!?" the Commissioner shouted over the crowd more to himself but his question was directed at Dunning and Kahn. While off to the side of him, one person was requesting to have their letter back as it was proof of the meeting and lawsuit. At this time the Commissioner noticed four police cars pulling up to the building discharging officers who were rushing up to the building and shouted, "Ladies and gentlemen, please, please may I have your attention. Would you all please settle down and follow the receptionist into the boardroom where we can discuss this matter." The crowd reluctantly began to quiet down and followed the nervous receptionist into the boardroom which was soon packed and more chairs had to be brought in to accommodate everyone. The Commissioner spoke with the officers informing them that everything was under control and their services wouldn't be needed. He successfully avoided police intervention but not the headlines in Tuesday's newspaper that would scream 'Riot avoided at State Institution'

The boardroom was over crowded. The fourteen chairs around the table were filled with the Commissioner, Dunning and Kahn taking up three of the seats and every available space along the four walls was taken by family members. Commissioner Wojohorwitz opened the meeting by re-introducing himself and explaining that his presence there was due to several calls received in his office from families attesting that they would be at a meeting that he knew nothing about. The family members again began to become ruffled at this speech but Wojohorwitz held up his hands to keep things in order saying, "What I want is for one representative from each family here to identify themselves, their family member housed at this institution and how they came to be here." One family member raised her hand. Commissioner Wojohorwitz listened as the woman, a Ms. Kingston explained, "On Friday, I received a phone call from Mr. Kahn (she looked at Dick Kahn as she continued) He informed me that he worked at the institution and that he was calling me at the instruction of someone named Paul Dunning. He told me about my son's arm being broken by some homicidal child who wasn't supposed to be at the institution and asked me if I had been told about the injury. When I told him no, he said that the reason he was calling was that it was against the law for me not to have been told about the injury. He said the people from the State offices wouldn't allow me to be told and this made Mr. Dunning angry because he knew we should have been told and that he needed my help to push a Class Action Civil lawsuit against the State Commissioner's Office. Then he asked me if he could come to my home on Saturday to talk about this stuff and the lawsuit that Mr. Dunning wanted me to sign up for and

I said yes. Mr. Kahn," here she paused and again pointed at Dick Khan and continued, "Came to my home on Saturday at 11:OO clock and he told me about what happened to my son and how Mr. Dunning needed my help and would I come to this meeting." Mr. Kahn stood up and yelled, "That's a lie. I've never seen you before in my life!" "Sit down Mr. Kahn." Wojohorwitz admonished Kahn calmly. "But she's lying!" Kahn yelled again. "No, you're lying. I'm looking right at you and it was you. You even gave me your card and these papers and the Commissioner's phone number and told me to call him to let him know I'd be at the meeting. I don't know why you're lying but you are!" "This is insane!" Kahn yelled gawking at the woman. "Perhaps it is." Wojohorwits said taking the papers from Ms. Kingston, "But this is your business card is it not?" Kahn took the card from Wojohorwitz with trembling hands and had no choice but to admit it was his card. "How could she have your card if she's lying on you, Mr. Kahn?" Wojohorwitz asked staring unblinkingly at Kahn. "I don't know but she didn't get it from me!" Mr. Wojohorwitz then asked all the families if there experience with Mr. Kahn was similar and they all said yes. He then asked for all the papers given to all the families. What he held were copies of incident reports, description of the injuries and treatment received. He asked everyone to remain seated until he returned. Wojohorwitz went to the receptionist and had her call each building where the patients were housed and requested that the patient's chart books be brought down to him in the boardroom. He returned to the boardroom and addressed Dunning and wanted to know what he knew about these matters. Dunning was as lost and faltering in the water, as dumbfounded as Kahn was at what was happening. For a few moments he was speechless then his mouth began moving but nothing was coming out. When he found his voice he mimicked Kahn in saying that he never instructed Kahn to contact anyone. He knew nothing about any lawsuit or meetings or client incidents. At this Wojohorwitz knew he was lying. The Assistant CEO was always made aware of client incidents, major or minor. Heated denials began flying back and forth across the boardroom between the families, Kahn and Dunning and Wojohorwitz was hard put to maintain any order until the door opened and the head nurse entered. She carried the medical chart books for all five clients between the screaming people. Wojohorwitz asked the nurse to look up each individual client for the injuries listed on the letters that Kahn denied giving to the families. The nurse did as instructed and handed each book to Wojohorwitz and he saw that the reports given to the families were accurate. He then looked for proof of the letters that should have been issued to the families of the injured clients. He was shocked to see that there was not one notification of the injuries sent to any of the families and he wanted to know why; but this was not a question to ask in this setting. What he said was, "Ladies and gentlemen it appears that you all have valid issues here. I would like for you all to leave me your names, addresses and a number where you can be reached. Rest assured that this is not the end of this matter. I would also suggest that if you have attorneys that they be contacted regarding this situation because it will definitely see the inside of a court of law. I cannot explain to you what has happened as I don't work at this institution. I work in the State office and I assure you that my office had no knowledge of these matters until your calls were received in my office this morning. It is however, true that by law you should have been notified of any injuries to your family members, an investigation held and some compensation made. As I've stated, my office too was not notified. It is not true that patients who have infrequent visitors are treated differently than any other patient or at least they shouldn't be. He passed out his business card to all the families and told them if they had any questions to feel free to call or have their attorneys contact his office. On that note, Wojohorwitz adjourned the meeting and all the families left the boardroom leaving Wojohorwitz, Dunning and Kahn. The discussion between them was heated, long and loud but produced nothing other than the facts. No matter how much Kahn and Dunning denied knowledge and involvement the facts remained binding and irrefutable. The home visits, business cards, the letters of the scheduled meeting, incidents reports, staff statements, hospitalizations and treatments were noted with nothing to indicate that the families had been notified and it all spoke for itself, bummer. As a bewildered Paul Dunning stumbled out of the boardroom on shaky legs headed for his office Commissioner Wojohorwitz voice halted him in his tracks. With cold fingers of dread crawling up his body; Dunning slowly turned around to face the Commissioner. They were about ten feet apart, two western cowboys facing each other in the street, preparing for the shootout at the O.K. Coral. The Commissioner shot first, Mr. Dunning didn't return the fire. "Mr.

Dunning, if you're returning to your office I assume it's clean out your desk, pick up your hat, coat and coffee mug, you're fired, effective immediately!" He yelled turning to Kahn but before he could speak Kahn spoke softly saying, "I've already turned in my resignation long before this, whatever it was, took place. I'd just come down to drop off the necessary paper work for my retirement and this letter which I intended to give to Dunning. It's my confession of all the things Dunning manipulated including me. I had no choice but to comply because he gave me direct orders and I feared losing my job. I wanted no more of his schemes especially when he was forcing me to do his dirty work. I reached a limit but was too much of a coward to stand up to him. Well, I took and made my stand. I'm done with him, my job and this institution" Kahn turned and walked away but not before Mr. Wojohorwitz informed him that it would be prudent to leave a forwarding address. Dunning heard Kahn's entire speech and later would be able to make an extremely good guess at what was written between the pages of that letter he'd given to the Commissioner. Kahn would have been stretched out dead on the floor waiting for his coffin from the stare Dunning was giving him. Dunning turned away from them and lurched drunkenly towards his now defunct office, past his wide eyed secretary realizing that he had been set up; and set up well. Whoever did this made sure there wouldn't be a hole to hide in. He vowed to find the person responsible and they would pay big time and he'd start with Kahn. When the enormity of what had happened he lost control and wet his pants as he staggered stupefied to his office and position of Assistant Chief Executive Officer for the last time.

By the time Janet signed out from duty in her reinstated (courtesy of the retired Barton Cleese) position of Head Training Supervisor that Monday afternoon, the word was all over grounds about the riot in personnel, the police, the lawsuit, the retirement of Cleese and Kahn and the termination of the assistant CEO Dunning. Everyone was staggered by the news but no one knew exactly what had happened. Questions and rumors were flying around like a mass of angry hornets with no destination. It was unbelievable but true; Paul Dunning had been fired, Kahn and Cleese suddenly retired. That is no one except Janet Nelson and she had no comment on these things and left the job as soon as her shift ended. Driving home Janet had no feelings of remorse or for that matter happiness. She had done what she had wanted to do, get revenge. She had entered the forest of revenge and like so few others; she came out the other side unscathed. She felt no sorrow or guilt at the things she'd set in motion or their outcome; other than the fact that justice had been served and she was satisfied. Some people needed to die and she had killed them all without spilling their blood. Her conscious was clear.

When Janet returned to work on Tuesday morning she found Ms. Mead sitting behind Cleese's desk as the new Unit Director. Mead stared at Janet as she entered the office but her thoughts were her own. She asked Janet to sit down a moment and informed her that Cleese had retired and that she was currently the Unit Director. Janet sat looking innocently at Ms. Mead saying nothing. Ms. Mead went on to say that she was appointing Janet as the Assistant Unit Director effective immediately. Janet was speechless but she continued staring at Ms. Mead. Ms. Mead asked Janet if she had any problem accepting the position and like before when she was promoted by Ms. Mead into the position that started all the hoopla, she hesitated. This would represent her second promotion without her knowledge or consent and that first promotion had resulted in three demotions and devastating fights to keep her job and now she was being pushed into a position higher than the first one she'd been demoted from.

On Wednesday Janet reported for duty in the new position of Assistant Unit Director, she found Gertrude Fleming and Ms. Mead in the office. Janet sat down at the Assistant Director's desk under the questioning gazes of Mead and Gertrude who had obviously been discussing her prior to her arrival because they became quiet when she entered the office. Ms. Mead stood up and walked over to Janet and informed her that she was retiring on Friday and that according to regulations the Assistant Director immediately assumed the position of Unit Director. Janet and Gertrude were both stunned by this news. Ms. Mead handed Janet the keys to the entire unit saying that although her retirement wouldn't be official until Friday she was officially retired as of that day and the position of Unit Director now belonged to Janet. She gathered some personal items and without saying good bye she left the office and building without looking back for the start of her retirement. Janet Nelson, the three times demoted employee was now Unit Director. Janet and Gertrude stared after the retreating Ms. Mead and then looked at each other. Gertrude noticed that Janet was taking this sudden, unbelievable occurrence of reinstatement to her former position of Head Training Supervisor, then promotion to Assistant Unit Director and now promoted to Unit Director in less than a week as calmly as she had taken the demotions and Gertrude was extremely uneasy as to where this would leave her in the overall scheme of things. She knew Janet knew her for what she was; as well as being an integral instrument in some of Janet's previous situations. She was thinking of all the things she'd done against Janet and she saw herself as perilously dangling from the edge of a sliding precipice. She watched with a cold dread in her heart as Janet walked over and stood behind the recently vacated desk of the retired Barton Cleese and the just vacated desk of the two day Unit Director, Ms. Mead. It was now Janet's desk and Janet's power and Gertrude was, in her heart afraid. Janet Nelson somehow became the Unit Director replacing the Director who demoted and attempted to fire her. Gertrude watched Janet as she opened the top drawer of her new desk and dropped the huge bundle of unit keys inside. She then picked up something inside of the drawer and casually tossed that something across the office to Gertrude. Gertrude opened her hands out of reflex and caught what Janet had thrown at her. What she caught in her hand were the keys to the Head Supervisors office. Gertrude was speechless with astonishment as she looked down at the heavy key ring in her hands and recognition what they represented; the Head Training Supervisor office and position. Her first thought was to quickly close her fingers protectively around the keys but she didn't and Janet noticed this as a good thing. Janet looked Gertrude in the eyes and softly said, "Don't fuck up the job and don't fuck with my staff. That's all." Gertrude was speechless but not quite tearful at this turn of events. When she left Janet's office she wasn't in high spirits or any type of euphoria. Janet's simple act of trust had broken something inside of Gertrude evil heart, something that freed her to be a good person, a dedicated employee to her position and her new Unit Director, Janet Nelson. This woman whom she hated passionately and had actively worked against to bring about her ruination had given her not only the position she coveted but she also gave her her trust and she had no intention of making Janet regret her decision.

Janet was alone in the office where it had all began, sitting in the chair and position of the person who had started it all. She was just thinking about these things when the union representative Sharon Nesbit walked into the office. She stood in the doorway just looking curiously and questionably at Janet and then she pulled up a chair to Janet's desk. Sharon spoke first. "You know when the pictures of Cleese doing the wild thang popped up all over the place I wondered not who'd do such a thing but who would benefit from posting those photos and I came up with you. Only I couldn't imagine you actually having sex with that asshole but the woman somehow reminded me of you." She was looking deep into Janet's eyes. "Only that didn't make sense either nor the probability of you having or finding a double. And now all this madness about Kahn and the families that identified him and Dunning instigating a lawsuit against the State is all too much. Again I thought about how many fingers did you have in that pie? But that was hardly probable since there aren't too many people who look like Kahn and where the hell would you get someone to impersonate him anyway? Besides, I didn't know house elves could leave of their own accord she said referencing the elf Dobby in the Harry Potter books who wasn't allowed to leave without permission. It's all too confusing as well as impossible." Still looking Janet in the face she continued, "Every bone in my body says that you set up all this shit! I know you fucking did it! I don't know how but it was you; wasn't it?" Janet laughed and Sharon said, "That doesn't sound like a denial." Janet continued laughing and Sharon having no choice began laughing along with her and Janet raised one hand laughingly simply said, "I plead the fifth."

THE END

Printed in the United States
By Bookmasters